SCIENCE FICTION
THE
101
BEST NOVELS
1985 – 2010

Damien Broderick & Paul Di Filippo

With a foreword by David Pringle

Nonstop Press • New York

SCIENCE FICTION: THE 101 BEST NOVELS 1985 - 2010

First Edition: 2012

Nonstop Press books may be purchased for educational, business, or sales promotional use. For information please write: nonstop@nonstop-press.com
POB 981, Peck Slip, New York, NY, USA 10272-0981

Cover and book design by Luis Ortiz • Production by Nonstop Ink

ISBN 978-1-933065-39-7 Trade Paper

PRINTED IN THE UNITED STATES OF AMERICA

www.nonstop-press.com

 Nonstop Press

Contents

Foreword

TIME MOVES on.

Science Fiction: The 100 Best Novels: 1949-1984, a book I wrote in 1984 and which was published in 1985, needed a sequel by now—and here it is. More than 25 years have gone by, and many hundreds of science-fiction novels and collections have continued to pour from the English-language presses (as well as those of other languages), so some guidance as to "the best" of the last quarter-century is surely required. Having been unable to keep up with all those new sf works myself, I am delighted that Damien Broderick and Paul Di Filippo have taken it upon themselves to do the job, and I am very happy to endorse their excellent book.

I have read fewer than half of the novels they describe here (after 1984, as editor of the magazine *Interzone* until 2004, my main sf reading consisted of short stories—thousands of them); but, judging from the works I do know, I feel confident that all the less-familiar choices in this book are sound. Damien Broderick's and Paul Di Filippo's qualifications for making those choices are second to none: both are creative science-fiction writers of many years' standing, among the best of their time, and both have in addition written a good deal of stimulating criticism, including numerous sf book reviews. I actually included a novel by Damien in my hundred best of 27 years ago—*The Dreaming Dragons* (1980), which I described as "the best Australian science-fiction novel I know" (that sounds belittling in retrospect—the book was much more than that). It has since been revised and reissued as *The Dreaming*. Since then, Damien has written several more fine sf novels, of which perhaps *The White Abacus* (1997), a knottily speculative work, is the most successful.

Of course, it would not have been seemly for the authors to include any works of their own in this new hundred best, but perhaps I can compensate for that by mentioning not only Damien's later novel, above, but also Paul's humorous *Fuzzy Dice* (2003) and his manically inventive short-story and novella collections such as *The Steampunk Trilogy* (1995) and *Ribofunk* (1996), some of the contents of which I had the pleasure of first publishing in *Interzone*. At the time I wrote my book in the 1980s, Paul Di Filippo had published no novels or collections, but if I had been writing this follow-up volume now a number of Paul's books, as well as several of Damien's, would certainly have been strong contenders for inclusion.

As for the authors whose novels are described in the following hundred or so mini-essays, I am particularly pleased to see a large contingent of those whose early stories were first published in *Interzone*—among them, Stephen Baxter, Richard Calder, Greg Egan, Nicola Griffith, Simon Ings, Paul J. McAuley, Ian R. MacLeod, Alastair Reynolds, Geoff Ryman, and Charles Stross. I can vouch for all these writers as capable of first-rate work. And of course, many others with books discussed here are well-known names, some of them from the literary "mainstream"—Brian Aldiss, Margaret Atwood, the late J. G. Ballard, Iain Banks, Michael Chabon, Karen Joy Fowler, William Gibson, M. John Harrison, Kazuo Ishiguro, Ursula K. Le Guin, Jonathan Lethem, Cormac McCarthy, China Miéville, Michael Moorcock, Richard Powers, Christopher Priest, Philip Roth, the late Kurt Vonnegut, and more. It is a first-rate line-up, and those readers who follow all the recommendations will have months and years of good reading before them.

A century, and a millennium, have turned since I wrote my book. The world is different, but science fiction carries on vigorously, reflecting our times back to us in imaginative form—and Damien's and Paul's book celebrates that endeavor splendidly.

David Pringle
Selkirk, Scotland

Introduction

SCIENCE FICTION, according to David Pringle's excellent guide to the 100 best English-language sf novels in the period 1949-84, to which this volume is a kind of sequel, is "a form of fantastic fiction which exploits the imaginative perspectives of modern science."

That's true. But here's a necessary caution: most science fiction, our favorite kind of story-telling and reading, has about as much to do with real science as chick lit has to do with poultry.

(For brevity, we'll refer to science fiction as *sf,* rather than *sci-fi,* which is now standard journalistic parlance but, as Ursula K. Le Guin recently remarked, "as a term for the whole field it seems kind of *cheap*."[1])

Numerous other definitions have been suggested: sf as the literature of change, indeed of radical, disruptive, wondrous change; of cognitive estrangement or conceptual breakthrough; of drastic *difference* from the known, safe, everyday world; of suspended disbelief and dizzying spectacle. For most of us, sf is what we see on TV or in monstrously expensive and profitable movies: warring starships roaring in the vacuum of space, warriors and explorers plunging through wormholes to far stars, robots helpful or malign, parallel worlds, psychic clones, time machines carrying the unwary into the gulfs of the future or dangers of the past, or a hundred and one other locales beyond the known realities of our sometimes humdrum lives. All this is valid enough, but it is not the whole or deepest truth, especially of sf literature.

For sf, as Le Guin added, is not about the future, or space travel, not really. For all the legitimate or sham apparatus of science and technology deployed in these tales, they are not *about* science, by and large. Rather, for Le Guin, a very distinguished practitioner of the art, sf is a "metaphorical way of dealing with our current reality."

The shorthand idiom *sf* is "basically a commercial term describing a certain genre of fiction." That is, it's more a marketing tool than a literary category like *drama* or *pastoral verse.* It is a label designed to guide purchasers or library readers to a stack of books (or movies, comics or TV shows) that share a certain common appeal.

But what is it about a *genre* that makes its appeal so reliable, so rewarding to

---

1 *http://www.bbc.co.uk/iplayer/episode/p00d5vqc/The_Interview_Ursula_Le_Guin/*

merchants? Many readers with literary credentials disapprove of writing they dismiss as "genre": romance, say, or thrillers, westerns, horror, science fiction. These kinds of storytelling they suppose to be intrinsically inferior and limited compared to their prized *literature,* otherwise known to scholars as "bourgeois realism," or "psychological realism," which is itself just another genre that can be sharp, brilliantly incisive, emotionally involving, or soggy, comfortable, and routine.

But wait—that's an oversimplification, too, because a glance at *The New York Review of Books* or the *Guardian's* book review pages reveals a "literary" appetite for many varieties of fiction or styling, some of them blurring into the kinds of writing marketed since the 1960s as science fiction. Franz Kafka's phantasmagorical fables remain evergreen, Latin American "magical realism" was fashionable a decade or two back, John Barth's rich and zany metafictions had their day, while nobody doubts that Dante's allegorical adventures in Purgatory and Hell in *The Divine Comedy* and Don De Lillo's absurdist Airborne Toxic Event in *White Noise* are as heavy-duty literary as it gets.

It's equally true that many genre readers stick faithfully to their accustomed diversions, preferring yet another franchised episode of Captain Kirk and Mr. Spock, or Luke Skywalker and his mean Dad, rather as some people eat the same breakfast every day and wouldn't dream of adding garlic to their nightly dinner steak, or replace it now and then with squids in spice. For these happy browsers, "literary" writing is *snobbish* and any attempt by sf writers to adapt the same techniques to broader their canvas and elaborate their palette (or palate) is *pretentious* or *boring* or uses "too many hard words." In a genre where masters from H. G. Wells to Robert Heinlein, Ursula Le Guin and Philip K. Dick were comfortable with once-unfamiliar terms like *ecology* or *delta-V* or *epistemology* or with fresh coinage like *ansible* or *kibble*, this seems an odd complaint. It's one we intend to ignore in our discussion of 101 significant, exemplary sf novels from the last quarter century, novels that in a hundred and one different ways are as wily and inventive as the best speculative writing and as well-wrought and insightful into the nature of human consciousness and society as anything by, well, Nobel Laureate Doris Lessing or Philip Roth or Margaret Atwood or Michael Chabon or Cormac McCarthy—some of whom, marvelously, are here as well, with their own distinctive contributions to the canon of recent speculative fiction.

The year 1985 inaugurates the span under consideration in this volume, and it might profit us to consider, with memory's Wayback Machine, exactly what some of the salient features of that far-off year were. (Of course, we are not going to rely solely on our fallible human wetware, but instead will consult Wikipedia, an omnipresent invaluable resource whose very name was nothing but a gibberish string of phonemes in 1985. But more on that in a few paragraphs.)

Ronald Reagan assumed his second presidential term. His name then still conjured up images of black-and-white movies, and, for sf readers, a deliberately and brilliantly offensive New Wave story by J. G. Ballard, not the vaseline-lensed hagiography the man enjoys among some today. Reagan's *bête noire* was the Soviet Empire, which in 1985 seemed destined to reign eternally with an iron fist across half the planet. China, on the other hand, although also a Communist bogeyman, was an amusingly backward country subject to internal purges and worthy of notice only when it reared up against Taiwan. Japan, however, was a different matter, the one country threatening to usurp the USA's place as global economic and cultural powerhouse. (This irony of their past top dog status became particularly painful in early 2011, when a devastating earthquake and tsunami battered that island nation.) European nations still featured individual currencies, and required their citizens to present passports for internal travel in their own Union. The worst terrorist attack against the USA had happened in 1983, in Beirut—an enormous blow, some 200 soldiers dead. The world population was 4.8 billion. Climate change was something only paleontologists had to be concerned with.

A state-of-the-art cellphone was the Motorola DynaTAC, that expensive, rarely seen, retrospectively laughable walkie-talkie-sized unit. The internet consisted of low bandwidth communications amongst some military and university computers. A state-of-the-art home computer setup could be had for $1000.00 (nearly $2000.00 dollars in today's terms): a Commodore 64 CPU and keyboard; a green-on-black CRT monitor; an external floppy disk drive; and a dot-matrix B&W printer. (That's what many writers sprang for back then, happily abandoning electric typewriters and carbon paper forever.) Text-only email service could be obtained through a noisy dial-up modem connection. Music was released by large corporations on the relatively new medium of compact discs. Books and magazines and newspapers had no digital electronic counterparts. Broadcast TV and the major networks remained dominant over the nascent cable hookups. Electric cars were nonexistent.

In the sf field, cyberpunk had burst out of the zeitgeist as the hottest new movement, while steampunk was merely a tossed-off term of derision. If science fiction did not still outsell its upstart sister fantasy, at least sales were basically even—unlike the present, when sf is the minority category. The *Star Wars* cinematic franchise had ceased, seemingly forever, with three films, while 1982's *Bladerunner* had as yet sired no true progeny. The term "CGI" was essentially meaningless. The prime mode of sf fan activity ("media fan" was more or less a subcategory of readerdom), besides the occasional small-scale convention (that year, San Diego Comic Con hosted a mere 6000 attendees), relied on paper "fanzines" distributed through the postal service, and in fact the cyberpunk movement, preaching a future dominated by cyberspace, promulgated itself through just such paper vessels.

Of 1985 fashions in clothing, dance, music, interior decoration, art and other mutable human pursuits, we will not speak, since such things are by their very nature transient and not assumed to be an unchangeable bedrock of existence.

You can, of course, provide your own present-day counterpoint to this capsule description of 1985. But any portrait of today will certainly limn a world that has undergone immense, almost unforeseeable changes since that vanished baseline year. Wired, distributed, hyperkinetic, beset by heretofore-inconceivable perils and challenges, gifted with potential-filled miracle gadgets, inventing new artforms and modes of communication, moving at warp speed, the world of the second decade of the 21st century and its inhabitants must present time-traveler-magnitude cognitive dissonance to anyone who contemplates the past twenty-five years. Yet at least half the global population is old enough to have experienced both eras firsthand. Why, then, are we not on a daily basis disoriented strangers in a strange land, unable to function for all the head-whirling confusion? Well, primarily because all the massive changes snuck up on us incrementally, and were absorbed at a steady pace. But also because of sf.

Science fiction is the tool that allows us to master such change. From birth in its modern genre form in the pages of 1926's *Amazing Stories*, through its nurturing and refinement by a small coterie of true believers through the middle of the twentieth century, and on to its gradual world domination starting with, oh, let us say, Kubrick and Clarke's *2001: A Space Odyssey* in 1968, science fiction has offered a cognitive toolkit in easy-to-assimilate, entertaining form that allows us to get mentally comfort-able with the notion of change and its most radical effects before we are hit with the reality of it upside the collective head. Science fiction is the one type of literature that promotes, to use the phrase pioneered by the bloggers at *Boing-Boing* (try explaining the concept of "blog" to a citizen of 1985!), the creation of "happy mutants." It's the literature of cultural Darwinism, the sieve through which we pan for ideational gold.

Our selections in this volume, if we have done our job well, will illustrate not only the immense changes of the past two-and-a-half decades, but also sf's vast reach and power, which of course we will need even more in the wild quarter century ahead!

One caution: Although our title promises a survey of the 101 best science fiction novels in English since Pringle's volume, we can't guarantee that any single reader will agree that our tally really *is* the *best*. After all, the annual Hugo and Nebula and Clarke and Locus and Campbell and Ditmar and other awards for the best sf novel of the year do not always concur—indeed, it is a rare distinction for any book to gain as many as two of these prestigious prizes. There are many celebrated and perhaps bestselling authors we might have included, and we would have done so if we'd had room for another hundred titles. Certainly we are not dismissing this abundance of enjoyable riches.

What we can promise you is that the novels we discuss are among the most *sig-nificant* works of science fiction from the last quarter century, books that reward careful reading while providing pleasure, amusement, novelty, wonderment. If you read all or even many of these good novels, you'll slowly realize that science fiction is not just a genre but is indeed a *mode* of storytelling. Most other genres are restricted in their subject matter, their focus, their typical ways of using words to invite readers into their familiar worlds. Crime fiction and thrillers, romances, westerns, tales of vampires or zombies—all offer niches, however various and ingeniously developed, within which the reader knows pretty much what to expect. Some franchise sf is like that too, but the best sf breaks through genre boundaries and tells stories that can borrow their subject matter and manner from any of the existing genres, while pushing them into new ter-ritories never before visited.

The science fiction mode has experienced large scale convulsions since it emerged a century or more ago, and especially since its advent as a commercial pulp form in the 1920s. If we regard the earlier work—by Mary Shelley, Verne, Wells, many oth-ers—as not yet visibly genrefied, it's apparent that science fiction's history has passed through several "waves" since the '20s The first pulp fiction age ended when John W. Campbell assumed editorship of *Astounding* in 1939, and the famous Golden Age storytellers emerged: Isaac Asimov, Leigh Brackett, Robert Heinlein, Henry Kuttner and Catherine Moore, A. E. van Vogt. Call that the Second Wave, extending into the discovery of the "soft sciences" in the 1950s. A Third Wave flooded over the field in the 1960s with a newly refined, often poetic, literary flavor and political concerns typical of the sixties (but foreshadowed in the previous decade by Theodore Sturgeon, Edgar Pangborn, and others). This Third Wave included the so-called "New Wave" but ex-ceeded it, with pivotal work by Philip K. Dick, Roger Zelazny, Samuel Delany, Ursula K. Le Guin, Joanna Russ, Norman Spinrad, Thomas M. Disch, Harlan Ellison, Robert Silverberg, a host more.

In the 1970s, that upheaval was already history and sf entered a period of consoli-dation, blending its traditional excitement with more self-aware literary aspirations. At the end of David Pringle's catchment area in 1984, cyberpunk came and went like a lurid flower, followed by the New Space Opera and the New Weird as a Fourth Wave carried sf on its flood tide into the new millennium. In the decade or so since the century's turn, sf has made its extraordinary impact in music, movies and even "literary fiction" (though seldom acknowledged as such). There are hints already that we stand at the frothing edge of a newer Wave. Nobody is quite certain where sf is headed, or what form some Fifth Wave will take. Is the age of the book finally over? Will reading shift from paper to Kindles and Nooks and snazzier forms of portable electronic platforms, sheets of e-paper you can jam in your pocket, beams of light shone straight onto your retina, waves of information borne directly to your brain via wifi or quantum entanglement? Already much of the best short sf is released online, usually in free venues supported as loss-leaders by traditional publishers, or funded by ads. An e-future would not spell the death of sf novels, of course, any more than the passing of pulp magazines with their monthly serials and the rise of paperback originals meant that sf was extinct—far from it. But we might see the sorts of unsettling, exciting novelties proclaimed by Eric Rosenfield:

> a lot of big-name Science Fiction writers look like they're standing still. While Bruce Sterling and Cory Doctorow and Vernor Vinge fantasize about the Singularity or augmented reality… [others are] writing a fiction that speaks to a world in which we find ourselves not exactly emancipated by technology but simply hyper-connected by it, our identities as people redefined by the media we share, media which we embrace and deeply care about even when it leaves us bewildered, co-opted, and reduced in a thousand ways to algorithms….This is not what our world is like, but it's very much what it *feels* like… tapped into some kind of primal dream of what it means to live in our techno-saturated time…[2]

Perhaps that's the shape of future sf, or maybe this post-Latest New Thing prospectus will be already antiquated in another few years ("*So* 2011"). Meanwhile, we can enjoy the accumulated riches of the past quarter century, from mainstream novelist Margaret Atwood's speculative/sexual political sensation *The Handmaid's Tale* to the brilliant first novel of Finnish string theorist Hannu Rajaniemi writing with perfect ease simultaneously in English, and sf, and quantum physics, all conjoined to dazzle us. From one perspective, then, you can see this list as Science Fiction 101. From another, it's 101 excellent novels for sf to hang its hat on, at a jaunty angle and with a knowing gleam in its eye.

Damien Broderick
San Antonio, Texas

Paul Di Filippo
Providence, Rhode Island

---

2 *http://io9.com/#!5568956/why-robin-sloan-is-the-future-of-publishing-and-science-fiction*

1: Margaret Atwood
The Handmaid's Tale (1985)

IN 1949, George Orwell (the English writer Eric Blair) published *Nineteen Eighty-Four*, his devastating, technologically managed and stratified dystopia. That novel, bleak and terrible, remains a watchword for totalitarian futures, even though more than a fourth of a century has passed since the date of its imagined terror. The year after the real 1984, distinguished Canadian poet and novelist Margaret Atwood published her own scarifying dystopia. While Orwell's Orwellian prospect seems less likely today, long after the fall of the Soviet Union, Atwood's woman-hating Republic of Gilead is all too visible in nations such as Iran and Afghanistan (where she spent some time). Sequestered, cloaked women suffer repression by the Taliban and other theocratic regimes. In the USA, where Atwood's imaginary Gilead springs from a harsh Christian fundamentalist conspiracy and coup d'état, political extremists really do join with science-deniers in aspirations scarily akin to Atwood's cautionary tale.

The novel is set around the end of the 20th century; like Orwell's, its date has already passed. Does this mean it's no longer science fiction? (Some prefer to see it as fable, and Atwood declared it "speculative fiction," famously dismissing sf as "talking squids in outer space" but relenting more recently.) No. Like a number of other fine sf novels discussed below, *The Handmaid's Tale* is best read as alternative history—allohistory, uchronia—a record of a past that might have occurred had key events taken a slightly different course. Atwood does not appeal to sf's toolkit of quantum superposed realities or Many Worlds theory to justify her fantastika, nor did Philip Roth (Entry

76), Michael Chabon (Entry 88) or several others among our 101. But it's no accident that, as well as being shortlisted for the mainstream, Booker Prize, it won the Arthur C. Clarke, Locus, and James Tiptree, Jr. Awards for best sf novel, while selling more than a million copies to readers who always supposed they disliked sf.

What motivates Atwood's narrative is the same fateful dynamo ("The purpose of power is power," wrote Orwell) driving *Nineteen Eighty-Four.* "The book is an examination of character under certain circumstances, among other things... it's a study of power, and how it operates and how it deforms or shapes the people who are living within that kind of regime."[3]

Offred ("of Fred") is 33 years old, conscripted into the Handmaid caste to bear children to powerful Commanders and their barren Wives in a nation polluted by reactor catastrophes, toxic molecules, viruses, environmental desecration. Her monthly and highly orchestrated rape is justified by phrases from the Old Testament. While her true name is never revealed, it is probably June—perhaps significantly, as an underground rebellion against this fascist state is known as Mayday, and Offred exemplifies the future of that day. The novel is her often despairing and superbly written meditations on a bitterly constrained life, torn away from her husband and child, denied identity, work, access to any materials she might use to harm her betters or kill herself.

Marthas do the scut work, Econowives tend house for the working men. Aunts at the Red Center, using drugs and harsh discipline, shape younger women like June/Offred into cowed, cowled, scarlet-clad nuns of fertility. Young men with machine guns, Angels and Guardians, patrol the Republic and monitor checkpoints. Former abortion doctors and priests are still being hunted down and hanged in public; a rapist Guardian is literally torn apart by maddened Handmaids in a ceremony recalling the Greek myth of Pentheus dismembered by Maenads.

Against this suffocating background Offred is drawn into illicit liaisons with her Commander—at first to play Scrabble, of all things, and read old forbidden magazines, but finally dolled up in whorish garb for a night in the inevitable "men's club" where she is displayed as an "evening rental," then set up with chauffer Nick by Wife Serena Joy, a former TV evangelist in the mold of Tammy Faye Bakker, who hopes fresh young semen will get the Handmaid pregnant and secure their social position. But these new crimes only wind the chains more tightly, bring Offred closer to ruin even as it seems she might escape to Canada via the Underground Femaleroad.

If it is a future not quite as terrible as the crazed utopia of Cambodia under Pol Pot, nor even of the Gulag, still it is unbearably, soul-crushingly bleak. In the much modified film script by Harold Pinter, Offred knifes the Commander to death and escapes with her lover Nick. Atwood's novel is less explicit, while leaving that plot door ajar. An afterword records an academic discourse in 2195; the book we've just read proves to be a reconstruction from 30 old cassette tapes dictated by the Handmaid, perhaps to her daughter or the new child, following her presumptive escape to freedom. As Atwood comments, "Her little message in a bottle has gotten through to someone—which is about all we can hope, isn't it?"

But the novel is not just a redemptive "little message," either; it is a beautifully wrought poem of a book, filled with acute observations. Consider the irises:

---

3 Mervyn Rothstein, "No Balm in Gilead for Margaret Atwood," *New York Times,* February 17, 1986.

bleeding hearts, so female in shape it was a surprise they'd not long since been rooted out. There is something subversive about this garden of Serena's, a sense of buried things bursting upwards, wordlessly, into the light, as if to point, to say: Whatever is silenced will clamor to be heard, though silently. A Tennyson garden, heavy with scent, languid; the return of the word swoon. Light pours down upon it from the sun, true, but also heat rises, from the flowers themselves, you can feel it: like holding your hand an inch above an arm, a shoulder. It breathes, in the warmth, breathing itself in. (161)

As does this novel, in all its brutality and longing.

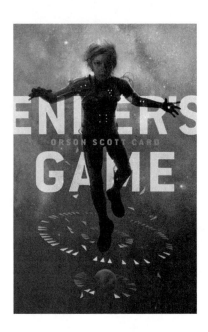

2: Orson Scott Card
Ender's Game (1985)

WHAT IS it about a science fiction novel that has remained more or less continuously in print for more than a quarter century, inspired legions of passionate fans and equally passionate detractors, spun off an entire universe of sequels, prequels and lateral reworkings, and became a standard part of many high-school curricula? Perhaps only by voyaging deep into its origins can a 21st century reader gain some perspective on Orson Scott Card and his *Ender's Game*.

It is instructive to pick up the first edition of *The Encyclopedia of Science Fiction* (1979), attributed then only to founding editor Peter Nicholls, and note that there is no entry for Orson Scott Card. True, Card had already sold his first story in 1977 to *Analog*, but the *Encyclopedia's* general policy was to focus on authors with book credits—although they did make exceptions for such luminaries as Robert Abernathy and Vance Aandahl.

By the second edition, from 1993, when John Clute had come onboard as co-editor, Card merits two full pages.

Plainly something had happened to boost his stature. That kickstart was, of course, *Ender's Game*, which this later edition of the *Encyclopedia* revealed, in fact, to have as its seed Card's very first story sale of the same name that had been ignored in 1979. In his substantial 1990 short story collection, *Maps in a Mirror*, Card records that

The novel *Ender's Game* is the only work of mine… that was truly expanded from a short work that I had not intended to expand. Indeed, I had never expected to do anything with Ender Wiggin again…. I was beginning to work with a novel idea with the working title *Speaker of Death*…. [S]uddenly it dawned on me that the Speaker should be Ender as an adult…. [A]ll the problems would be solved if I went back and rewrote "Ender's Game" as a novel, incorporating into it all the changes that were needed to properly set up *Speaker*.

The explosive effect of the novelized version of that *Analog* tale cannot be underestimated, on Card's career or the genre in general. As Clute observes: prior to 1985, after some initial promise, "OSC's career then seemed to drift." If not for Ender and his much elaborated exploits, Card today might very well be regarded in the same ranks as Abernathy or Aandahl: a minor, respectable, forgotten craftsman.

And in the sf field at large, Card's book contributed to the growing popularity of military sf, a subgenre with a relatively small profile circa mid-1980s; to the popularization of teen protagonists driving much of the current YA boom; to the co-opting of videogames into the sf mythos (a process also abetted by the uncannily co-emergent 1984 film *The Last Starfighter*); and to the genesis of a million fannish flame wars over perceived sexism, racism, homophobism, elitism and hyper-religiosity in Card's works.[4]

What stroke of genius propelled this book to such influential heights? It's simple, in retrospect. Whereas most excitingly controversial novels include one or two hot-button topics at most, Card's novel is composed of *nothing but* a half-dozen hot-button issues wrapped in a *bildungsroman*. In more or less descending order, these include:

> An existential threat to the entire human race.
> The nature of alien intelligence and person-hood, or, the role of "the other."
> Genocide.
> Means versus ends.
> The "great man" theory of history.
> The limits of government and the proper role of the citizen.
> The limits and nature of the educational system.
> The military ethos.
> The nature of sociopaths and power.
> Family dynamics.
> Sibling rivalry.
> Schoolboy rivalry.

Not even Robert Heinlein in *Starship Troopers*, James Blish in *A Case of Conscience* or Philip José Farmer in *The Lovers*, perhaps not even Joanna Russ in *The Female Man* had packed so much argument-provoking philosophical dynamite into one novel.

Andrew "Ender" Wiggin—bearing a surname indicative perhaps of braininess under one's "wig"—is the youngest child of three, a mere seven years old at tale's start, with brother Peter the oldest and sister Valentine the middle one. They are all "odd johns," quasi-mutant geniuses. Peter, the sociopath, will become a political powerhouse, the Hegemon. Valentine will shape society by her essays. But to Ender falls the great-

---

4 See Prof. John Kessel's astringent analysis of the novel at:
  http://www4.ncsu.edu/~tenshi/Killer_000.htm

est burden and glory. He will undergo years of brutal training at the interplanetary military outposts known as Battle School and Command School, all to elicit and mold his unique strategic genius. That genius will ultimately be arrayed against the Buggers, mankind's implacable alien enemy who almost destroyed our species twice before.

In very sturdy, engaging and transparent prose, Card delivers a kind of *Tom Brown's Schooldays* mated with *The Prisoner* TV show and *From Here to Eternity*. He captures with precision the eternal cruelties of schoolboy interactions, the rigors of boot camp, and the sophistications of war college. At the same time, he dissects the power-tripping that occupies nations and their governments. Ender is both innocent child and hopeful monster, the hothouse hybrid bloom of a harsh climate.

Card's tale is remarkably proleptic in several areas, including the use of child soldiers, virtual reality, tablet computing, internet communications, and social networking sock-puppetry, as well as foretelling the collapse of the Soviet empire.

Besides the controversies outlined above, Card manages to rub other raw areas. There's a nebulous sense of incest among the Wiggin kids—Valentine exiles herself to a colony world with beloved Ender; Peter plainly wants to dominate his sister in every physical sense. "Girls" don't do well in Battle School since evolution is against them, and the Bugger warriors are all females under a Queen, yet also paradoxically evoke male homosexuality by their racial nickname. But perhaps most provocative of all is the assertion in Chapter 14 that love and compassion are the essential underpinnings for slaughter. This yoking of two realms generally perceived as polar opposites recalls some of the deliberate contrarian "Martian" thinking of Michael Valentine (a coincidental naming by Card?) Smith in Heinlein's *Stranger in a Strange Land*.

In three sequels—*Speaker for the Dead* (arguably a better novel), *Xenocide* and *Children of the Mind*—Ender would inhabit the post-genocidal, human supremacist universe he and his siblings had helped to create, following an expiational hegira through large tracts of time and space. But those sequels, and subsequent parallel re-tellings, could never deliver the raw jolt of Ender's original cannon-propelled arc and shellburst lighting up of the heavens.

3: Philip K. Dick
Radio Free Albemuth (1985)

THE DEATH of Philip K. Dick in 1982 deprived readers of one of the seminal figures of twentieth-century sf, and of possible major works left unborn. Yet his impact on the field during the period of our survey, and on the wider culture, continued to grow and resonate immensely, with numerous film adaptations of his stories, canonization of several of his novels in the Library of America series, multiple editions and distillations of his *Collected Short Stories*, the adaptation of his themes and tropes as metaphorical touchstones for essayists and commentators, and the posthumous publication of several works.

The majority of the Dick books that appeared post-1982 constituted his trunk-consigned mainstream works, from his stymied early career as a mimetic writer—insofar as he could ever masquerade as such. Yet one book, the first to see print after Dick's death, was pure science fiction, and forms a very respectable initial contribution to his active afterlife in the field.

Radio Free Albemuth, as we know it, is a reworked version of a novel that Dick wrote to make sense of his famed mystical experiences circa 1974. When the original text was rejected by publishers, he streamlined the book to the form we know, and left a copy of the manuscript with his friend, the writer Tim Powers, who preserved it for eventual publication. But the intimate and important material would not lie fallow, and Dick rejiggered it all much more extensively to form *VALIS*, his late period masterpiece that was published during his lifetime. So in some complicated sense, *Albemuth* was the trial run for *VALIS*.

PKD partisan and packager Jonathan Lethem maintains in an interview with Library of America that *VALIS* is the more sophisticated, mature, esthetically pleasing and intellectually dense statement of Dick's "pink light" epiphany, and in this Lethem represents the irrefutable majority opinion. But he also acknowledges that some readers prefer *Albemuth* and find it to be the superior incarnation, and it's easy to see why. It's for the same reason that pencil sketches by a master painter are often more alluring than finished canvases by the same creator. Cleaner lines, less fussing, spontaneous emotions. *Albemuth* holds the core concepts and plot of Dick's puzzling brush with divine or alien intelligence without extra literary incrustations.

The central thesis of the novel is easy to encapsulate: "An extraterrestrial intelligence from another star system had put one of their vehicles into orbit around our planet and was beaming covert information down to us." But as our hero notes, to state the case in this fashion "reduced something limitless to a finite reality." *Radio Free Albemuth* is all about exfoliating the possibilities of this simple thesis rather than pruning them, thereby affirming the supreme ineffability of creation, which remains ultimately unbesmirchable by humanity's stupidity and vices.

The first half of the novel is told from the first-person viewpoint of a hack sf writer named Philip K. Dick, who is watching his close friend, Nicholas Brady, undergo the baffling communications from a Vast Active Living Intelligence System. Dick and Brady live in what was already, at the time of Dick's composition (1976), an alternate timeline. In this continuum, the USA is a dictatorship run by President Ferris F. Fremont—a mélange of Richard Nixon and Ronald Reagan—who strives to protect the country from a fictional enemy dubbed Aramcheck. Beside the usual government agencies, Fremont employ the Friends of the American People as spies and vigilantes, and a young woman member of FAP seeks to entrap Phil.

Meanwhile, VALIS, or Radio Free Albemuth (Albemuth being the name of the star system where VALIS originates), is revealing much useful information to Nick, such as how to cure his son's illness and that time really stopped at AD 70, resulting in "Black Iron Prison" status for a duped planet. At the midpoint of the text, the first-person voice switches seamlessly to Nick's (thereby cementing the identity of Brady and PKD). The two men, along with a similarly touched woman named Sadassa Silvia, strive to utilize VALIS's help to set things right. A small, sad coda reverts to Dick's point of view.

Dick's patented blend of paranoia, anti-authoritarianism and droll self-deprecation, his roller-coastering between optimism and despair, and his continuous and continuously frustrated attempts to balance saintliness with the demands of the flesh, achieve a fine expression and balance here. The book is lacking in a heavy-duty plot, without many dramatic set-pieces. It's a minimalist version of *VALIS*'s recomplications, more like the kind of proto-sf "novel of ideas" such as we find in More's *Utopia* or Bellamy's *Looking Backward: 2000-1887*. But that sketchiness just gives more room to the extravagant existential delvings. As the fictional PKD gleefully says, having just discarded willy-nilly another one of his own myriad explanations, "Theories are like planes at LA International: a new one along every minute."

But the human dimensions of the quandary—the confusion, oppression and excruciation of Nick Brady/PKD; the damaged, spoiled potential of Fremont; the patient supportiveness of Nick's wife Rachel; the defiant resilience of Sadassa Silvia—also shine forth beyond the philosophical bloviation, as would be expected from an author who once declared that the entire universe was contained in a dead dog by the side of the road.

Prophetic of much of our post-911 landscape, *Radio Free Albemuth*, to employ Wells's phrase, shows with economy and brilliance what happens to a "mind at the end of its tether," when the leash snaps and the unchained being goes scarily free for the first time in history.

4: Ursula K. Le Guin
Always Coming Home (1985)

IN THE 1950s and '60s—arguably the true "Golden Age of Science Fiction," when the genre matured as a form—the finest sf novels were sleek, small, supercharged engines designed to snap readers instantly into the fast lane and get them to the astounding end of the freeway, preferably with a bang at the end. As fashions changed, and popular fiction grew more hefty, pace and astonishment gave way to detail, ornamentation, complex characterization. One-off novels sprouted into trilogies and sagas. Perhaps the most famous was Frank Herbert's *Dune* sequence, continued after his death by less artful writers. The most successful was Gene Wolfe's science fantasy *The Book of the New Sun,* in four parts with an extra volume to wrap the saga, which then continued anyway with a tetralogy and a trilogy (see Entry 36).

Ursula Le Guin's *Always Coming Home* uses neither of these models. It is self-contained, but contains multitudes. Le Guin defined this sort of approach in an essay, "The Carrier Bag Theory of Fiction" (1986):

> the natural, proper, fitting shape of the novel might be that of a sack, a bag. A book holds words…. Science fiction properly conceived, like all serious fiction… is a way of trying to describe what is in fact going on, what people actually do and feel, how people relate to everything else in this vast sack, this belly of the universe, this womb of things to be and tomb of things that were, this unending story…. Still there are seeds to be gathered, and room in the bag of stars.[5]

5 In *Dancing at the Edge of the World,* London: Gollancz, 1989, pp. 169-70.

Like her famous *The Dispossessed,* this novel is an "ambiguous utopia." A Taoist matrilineal culture of Kesh villages in a far future linked by unobtrusive AIs is bordered by the grasping patriarchy of the Condor. The three-part central story by Stone Telling is, however, only a fifth of this bag-like book. The rest is a collage of Kesh poems, fables, life stories, romantic tales, recipes, reflections by Pandora (an imagined "archeologist of the future"), a glossary, drawings by artist Margaret Chodos and songs composed by Todd Barton.

So this is an sf novel, but not as we know it, Jim. It's perhaps science fiction's equivalent of *Moby-Dick,* or *Ulysses,* but more engagingly, lucidly written than either of those often unread masterpieces. Neither is it an entertainment in the vein of *The Demolished Man* or *Ringworld*; it is reflective, moving like the Pacific Coast river Na that flows through a post-Greenhouse, post-ecodoom Napa Valley. In this landscape Le Guin herself grew up, with anthropologist father Arthur and writer mother Theodora Kroeber. The novel is a tribute to both, and perhaps to Clifford Geertz's model of anthropological "thick description": immersion in another's culture, even if, as here, it does not yet exist.

Stone Telling is herself a halfling, born of a Kesh mother, Willow, and a True Condor father, Kills, or Terter Abhao, Commander of the Army of the South. Thus she's "half-House," mocked and teased by the other children, yearning for escape. Though she finds her way to the Condor, who are struggling to build a machine-technology empire in a world now exhausted of metals and easy supplies of power, she returns home disillusioned, regretful, ready to embrace a village life of natural cycles that is, admittedly, a little stifling. "As I speak of it," she says of her father's people, "this way sounds clownish. That is myself, my voice; I am the clown. I cannot help the reversals." But reversals are built in to the daily life of these ambiguous utopians; the basic structure of a Kesh village is a double spiral, like a barred galaxy, like two hands met at the thumbs, or Hinge.

The storyteller is born North Owl, in the little town of Sinshan, becomes Ayatyu in the City, then Woman Coming Home, and in her old age Stone Telling. By our conventions of empirical realism, some of what she tells seems bizarre and impossible (a wooden spoon passes through muscle and bone like the wash of a candle flame). Advanced science, magical realism or plain magic? "In the Valley the distinction [between fact and fiction] is gradual and messy." This lends every tale an eerie, uncanny feel, while an unusual earthiness anchors even a child's perception. North Owl, journeying from home for the first time, comes to "Granny's Twat," a town "between the spread legs of the Mountain." Such frankness in a spiritually rich and sexually candid people is startling, and displays the Kesh with no need for editorializing, using with cool panache a familiar method from the sf toolkit that literary tourists (John Clute calls their slumming "charabanc sci-fi") never quite master.

The tale's tragedy is that "What is seen with one eye has no depth. The sorrow of my parents' life is that they could see with one eye only." Willow and Kills are literally incomprehensible to each other. When their daughter follows her father, renamed by him Ayatyu, she is trapped in a society akin to crusader Christianity, or warrior Islam, or any other hierarchical monolith. Women are pets or dirt, in effect, and embrace their lot. The Condor call themselves Dayao, a blistering homonym of Tao. Ayatyu marries, bears a daughter. As the mad ambitions of the Dayao One spiral into self-destructive ruin, her father aids her escape. And in time, with age, she writes these beautiful, calming memories.

Can the generous, communal way of life in the Valley speak to us? An Archival message cited by Stone Telling suggests it might:

In leaving progress to the machines, in letting technology go forward on its own terms and selecting from it... is it possible that in thus opting not to move "forward" or not only "forward," these people did in fact succeed in living in human history, with energy, liberty, and grace?

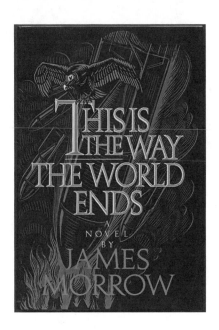

5: James Morrow
This Is the Way the World Ends (1985)

PLANNING THERMONUCLEAR war and its aftermath, Mutually Assured Destruction, used to be called, euphemistically but chillingly, "thinking about the unthinkable." Science fiction has often thought about the unthinkable, all too often with unthinkable relish. By contrast, *This is the Way the World Ends* is like a punch in the mouth by the Angel of Death in the garb of a stand-up comic. It was quickly compared to Jonathan Schell (*The Fate of the Earth*) out of Kurt Vonnegut, which was spot-on. It is likely, however, that the careful study by Schell, in the 1980s a prominent opponent of nuclear arms race strategy, is already forgotten, even as more nations than ever around the globe arm themselves with nuclear weapons, and plan resource-crisis wars.

George Paxton is a tomb cutter with an "adorable daughter" and a wife "who always looked as if she had just come from doing something dangerous and lewd." He has been spared misery: "the coin of George Paxton's life had happiness stamped on both sides—no despair for George. Individuals so fortunate were scarce in those days. You could have sold tickets" to his life. His neighbor sells *scopas* suits, for Self-Contained Post-Attack Survival, and Paxton buys one, signing a meaningless document admitting his complicity in any subsequent nuclear exchange.

In the dreadful event, the suits do not work, any more than the schoolroom "duck and cover" drills of the 1950s would have done. Here is part of Chapter 5, "In Which the Limitations of Civil Defense Are Explicated in a Manner Some Readers May Find Distressing":

Townspeople marched down to the river... arms outstretched to lessen the weight of their burned hands. Many lacked hair and eyelashes... A white lava of melted eye tissue dripped from their heads; they appeared to be crying their own eyes.

A seeing-eye dog, its scopas suit and fur seared away, licked the face of its dead master. "Somebody put the fur back on that dog!" George shouted.

It is not sentimentality to be moved profoundly by these images of carnage and horror. Nor is it ghoulish to laugh with Morrow at the black, bleak post-holocaust progress of George Paxton, his good-hearted Candide. Twenty-five years on, long after the collapse of one wing of this appalling calculus of global death, the twenty-first century might not be the worst of times. But neither is it yet the best of times, for international terrorism, the forces underpinning its threat, and massive military responses to it, ensure that George's world might yet ignite around us. Morrow's splendid novel, only in unimportant ways superannuated by political shifts, lives on.

Morrow's conceit in this grimly satirical novel is that those complicit in the suicide of the human race might be held accountable in war trials conducted in Antarctica by the Unadmitted—those immense multitudes who are doomed to non-existence by this universal, self-inflicted cataclysm. It is a hazardous device for a moralist like Morrow, because it seems to open out into all kinds of other metaphysical trials, not least of all those involved in the use of contraception to limit family size, or of abortion. The distinction, though, is that Morrow's apocalypse destroys existing persons—adults and children—as well as "potential" human beings.

In this Tribunal of the Unadmitted, representatives of the final holocaust stand accused. They are politicians, arms merchants, apologists for war, a hypocrite meant to implement arms control "who never in his entire career denied the Pentagon a system it really wanted." Among these patently guilty stands sweet-natured George Paxton, Morrow's Everyman: "citizen, perhaps the most guilty of all. Every night, this man went to bed knowing that the human race was pointing nuclear weapons at itself. Every morning, he woke up knowing that the weapons were still there. And yet he never took a single step to relieve the threat."

Can George truly be found guilty, in this Swiftian drama? Isn't the horrendous violence of the novel, foreseen with darkly comic irony by Morrow's version of Nostradamus, just a side-effect of our evolutionary past? Thomas Aquinas, for the prosecution, will not allow this plea to go unchallenged:

"Are we innately aggressive?" asked Aquinas. "Was the nuclear predicament symptomatic of a more profound depravity? Nobody knows. But if this is so—and I suspect that it is—then the responsibility for what we are pleased to call our inhumanity still rests squarely in our blood-soaked hands... And then, one cold Christmas season, death came to an admirable species—a species that wrote symphonies and sired Leonardo da Vinci and would have gone to the stars. It did not have to be this way. Three virtues only were needed—creative diplomacy, technical ingenuity, and moral outrage. But the greatest of these is moral outrage."

Morrow's own moral outrage is evident, and powerfully expressed. Not all readers will agree. They are given their spokesmen: "Self-righteous slop, you needed that too," replied one of the accused. But Morrow does not leave the verdict open. George, unlike the rest, avoids the counts of Crimes Against Peace, War Crimes, and Crimes Against Humanity. But the court finds him unequivocally guilty of Crimes Against the Future, and sentenced him to be hanged.

What makes this novel more than a one-sided pamphlet by a pacifist is its nuance, its attention to the detail of real life in the midst of its phantasmagorical, almost Lewis Carrollian trading of accusation and defense. Escaping, fleeing across ice on a giant prehistoric vulture, he meets his beloved daughter:

"Honey, there's something I want to ask."
"What?'
"Do you know what's happened to you?"
"Yes, I know."
"What's happened to you?"
"I don't want to tell you."
"Please tell me."
"You *know* what's happened."
"Tell me."
"I died."

This is not a light-hearted or thrilling entertainment of a novel. But it is a necessary one, still.

6: Kurt Vonnegut, Jr.
Galápagos (1985)

SENTIMENTAL, CYNICAL, clear-eyed, spiritual, godless, often very funny, Kurt Vonnegut (1922-2007) was more than a cult favorite in the 1960s and '70s but has fallen from popular favor. His early novel *The Sirens of Titan* was unabashed paperback sf, but of a kind rarely seen until then, and *Cat's Cradle* was almost as explicitly science fictional. Many of his subsequent novels contain an uncanny quality, verging on sf without ever quite going there. *Galápagos* tells the cautionary and scathing tale of humanity's future evolution into mindlessness, narrated by a ghost still lingering a million years hence. That ghost, as it happens, is Leon Trotsky Trout, son of the prolific Kilgore Trout whose terrible sf is quoted through most of Vonnegut's fiction after his appearance in *Breakfast of Champions* (1973). It's obvious that Trout is a fond if mocking mask for sf master Theodore Sturgeon, but really he is, of course, Vonnegut himself. As, too, is Leon, who recalls humankind's ruined world, brought down (he asserts) by the excesses of our huge, intelligent, obsessive and endlessly tricked and tricky three-pound brain.

Perhaps the oddest aspect of this bittersweet fable, told by an apparent anti-intellectual misanthrope hanging onto hope by the skin of his teeth, is how startlingly accurate his near-future predictions were. Global financial collapse is due to "a sudden revision of human opinions as to the value of money and stocks and bonds and mortgages and so on, bits of paper," wealth "wholly imaginary… weightless and impalpable," just as it nearly did a quarter century later.

A Japanese genius invents the Mandarax, a handheld device in "high-impact black plastic, twelve centimeters high, eight wide, and two thick," with a screen the size of a playing card, that can translate a thousand languages, diagnose illnesses, bring up any kind of information or literary quote. At a time when "portable" or luggable computers were known as boat anchors and linked by phone lines, Vonnegut had foreseen Google and the iPhone (which, to draw on the kind of absurdist detail he peppers his pages with, is 11.6 by 6.2 by 1.2 cm). All of this information is useless after the Fall, Trout claims, and dubs the Mandarax "the Apple of Knowledge." A nod to Genesis, but a startling and amusing intimation of the Apple iPhone…

The Galápagos islands, described with distaste in 1832 by Charles Darwin as a "broken field of black basaltic lava, thrown into the most rugged waves, and crossed by great fissures, is everywhere covered by stunted, sun-burnt brushwood, which shows little signs of life," become the home of the last traditional humans, one man and nine women. From this remnant, marooned on Santa Rosalia, home of the vampire finch, springs the non-sapient *Homo sapiens* of the next million years. Eventually our descendants are aquatic fish-eaters with a head sleek and narrow, jaws adapted to snatching their marine prey, skull too cramped for intelligent thought. To Trout, this is a satisfactory consummation; the fittest have survived, even if their initial "fitness" was sheer dumb accident in a world smashed by human ingenuity and an infertility virus (perhaps inspired by AIDS) spread through the machineries of world-girdling technology. The Galápagos are spared precisely by their isolation. The new humans are inbred, furred because of a mutation engendered in a Japanese child by her mother's exposure to the Hiroshima bombing, but at least spared the heritable Huntington's chorea (ironically, a mind-destroying illness) that their ship's Captain fears he carries. It is a future of "utter hopelessness."

Vonnegut being the kind of Mark Twain writer he was, all of this hopelessness is screamingly funny.

In a typographical stunt that blends foreboding with a cheeky grin, all those fated to die before next sunset are given an asterisk before their name. *Andrew MacIntosh is a sociopath billionaire with a blind daughter, Selena, who survives. Her seeing-eye bitch is Kazakh, who, "thanks to surgery and training, had virtually no personality"—like the posthumans of the far future, who manage it by natural selection. (Curiously, Kazak without an h is the alert canine companion to Winston Niles Rumfoord in *Sirens of Titan,* whose fate is to become detached in time and space. This probably signifies the sort of meaningless coincidence that for Vonnegut comprises most of the events of life and indeed the universe.) *Zenji Hiroguchi is the inventor of the Mandarax, and his death strands his pregnant wife Hisako, skilled in ikebana or flower arrangement, in a hellish landscape devoid of flowers.

Adolf von Kleist avoids Huntington's (unlike his brother *Siegfried). He is captain of the *Bahía de Darwin,* out of Ecuador, deserted by its crew. This vessel is chosen for "the Nature Cruise of the Century," a strenuously promoted event that attracts celebrities such as Jacky Onassis and Rudolph Nureyev, although both are spared the rigors of Santa Rosalia as the human world goes bankrupt and sterile. This ship of fools comprises rogues, victims and other hapless souls: fiftyish Mary Hepburn in surplus combat fatigues, widowed school teacher; *James Wait, a younger swindler who makes Mary his eighteenth wife; Jesús Ortiz, an Inca waiter who idolizes the wealthy and hopes to join their number until a brutal encounter with financier *MacIntosh sets him straight; others. Leon Trout, political refugee to Sweden from the Vietnam War after partaking in a My Lai-type massacre, is not aboard, being dead, but we learn his tale as well, and that of six little Kanka-bono cannibal girls.

The whole shambling novel, typically for Vonnegut, is a jumble of flash stories and blackouts, salted with sardonic jokes and agony, yet somehow manages to achieve what Martin Amis claimed for it, that "it makes the reader sweat with pleasure, but also with suspense." This is so even though we know that "Thanks to certain modifications in the design of human beings, I see no reason why the earthling part of the clock-work can't go on ticking for ever the way it is ticking now." Brainless, that is, with no Beethoven, no Shakespeare, no high school movie showing annually the erotic mating dance of the Galápagos' blue-footed boobies, copulation deleted.

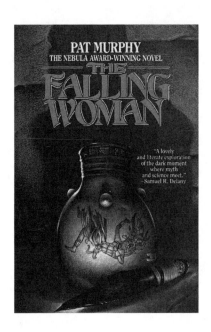

7: Pat Murphy
The Falling Woman (1986)

ARE COMMUNICATIVE, rational ghosts still a fantastical, supernatural conceit, rather than some as-yet unplumbed facet of the quantum-strange universe, if they convey accurate information about their pre-posthumous lives; undertake no actions that violate natural laws; and appear at times and places that bear a logical relationship to their old identities, visiting us, perhaps, out of physicist David Bohm's implicate order?

Such is the categorical conundrum posed to the literary taxonomist by Pat Murphy's *The Falling Woman*, a novel full of ghosts. We think such a story can be parsed as sf. Murphy's second novel is undeniably science fiction, due not only to the general reasonable affect of the ghosts therein, but also to the science-heavy apparatus and storyline that contain them, like Prospero's warding spells

Science fiction has made many accommodations with spirits in the past. Timeslip tales such as Jack Finney's *Time and Again* are really all about a live human easing back into the realm of the departed, achieving time travel (an essential motif of sf) without the machinery. Sometimes, alien cultures have ready access to their dead, as in Brian Aldiss's *Helliconia* trilogy. And finally, the whole iffy area of paranormal powers has long been accorded a central place in science fiction, from at least John W. Campbell's time (Asimov's Mule, anyone?). Thus we get the wild talent of psychometry—invoking the historical information trail of an object via touch—which comes awfully close to seeing ghosts

In any case, the protagonist of *The Falling Woman,* Elizabeth Butler, is indubitably a scientist—an archaeologist—who sees ghosts, as does, intermittently, her daughter (thus suggesting a genetic basis for the ability). So exactingly and empathetically is the mother's professional field depicted that we accept the ghosts as merely one more tool in her toolkit, a handy technic that her less-gifted peers simply lack.

Elizabeth Butler and her professorial co-worker Tony Baker are on their annual summer dig at the Mayan site of Dzibilchaltún, riding herd on the usual set of horny and lackadaisical and sincere students. (The camp's interpersonal dynamics summon up allied notes from such safari scenarios as Hemingway's "The Short Happy Life of Francis Macomber.") Elizabeth, long prone to seeing animated shades from the past while not interacting deeply with them, now experiences visions of the last inhabitant of the once-flourishing Mayan settlement, an old woman named Zuhuy-kak. More vitally, Elizabeth discovers she can converse with Zuhuy-kak, and begins to learn information she could not otherwise have access to. But the spirit is bitter and vengeful, and has bad things in store for Elizabeth, generating the book's considerable suspense, which is compressed into a mere two weeks or so.

Into this fraught scenario comes Diane, the estranged daughter, fleeing bad times of her own. She wishes to reconnect with her mother, and Elizabeth reluctantly agrees to take her on as an untrained helper. (Diane's inexperience allows Murphy conveniently and unawkwardly to educate both character and readers in the methodology and goals of a dig.) Murphy splits the narrative between mother and daughter points of view, and the resulting see-sawing insights and battling failures of communication prove fertile.

The mother-daughter relationship obviously is a central engine of the book, and Murphy explores it passionately and deeply. Likewise, the patriarchal roadblocks Elizabeth has experienced in her career are highlighted in a judicious yet righteously ireful manner. Elizabeth's damaged psyche receives an airing as well, nowhere more tellingly than in Chapter Thirteen, where she muses on the central dead space inside her heart. "I had sealed off the part of me that knew how to love. It was too close to the part of me that knew how to hate, and that was at the center of the madness. I had sealed them all away, leaving a dead place..." Then Elizabeth all unconsciously segues to a discussion of the cenote—the Mayan sacrificial well that plays such a pivotal role in the tale—never realizing that, metaphorically, just such a cold vacuity full of skeletons and sacrificed virgins lies inside herself. Murphy's deft symbolical identification of inner and outer topography is complete.

Murphy's novel consorts well with the elegantly enigmatic work of Graham Joyce, Jonathan Carroll and Jo Walton, although with an emphasis on science rather than fantasy. Elizabeth Butler is no Indiana Jones. In fact, she belittles her profession. "Archaeologists are really no better than scavengers, sifting through the garbage that people left behind when they died... We're garbage collectors really." But the dedication and intellect she bestows on her chosen field, the scrupulousness with which she follows her protocols into the territory of artistry, her unselfish desire to expand humanity's knowledge base, all belie her protests, and her adventures of the mind—whether with trowel in hand or conversing with the dead—end up outshining anything Harrison Ford has yet brought to the screen.

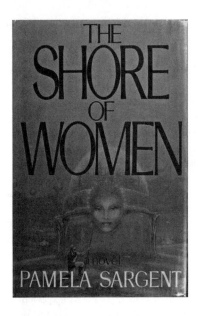

8: Pamela Sargent
The Shore of Women (1986)

EDITOR OF the first, and still important, anthology devoted to science fiction by women, *Women of Wonder* (1975), and two sequels, novelist and critic Pamela Sargent observed that women sf writers during the '70s, like the feminist sisterhood, were

> coming to consider themselves a group. This is not to say that they shared the same views, were equally doctrinaire in their feminism, or similar in their writing. But there was a growing sense that science fiction was a form in which the issues raised by feminism could be explored, in which writers could look beyond their own culture and create imaginative new possibilities.

She added:

> At the core of both feminism and science fiction—at least what ideally should be at the core of both—is a questioning of why things are as they are and how they might be different. Science fiction, with more women writing it, had a chance to become what it had claim to be all along—a literature that embraces new possibilities.[6]

---

6 Pamela Sargent, *Women of Wonder: The Classic Years*: Science Fiction by Women from the 1940s to the 1970s, Harcourt Brace & Co., 1995, 16, 20. This is a revised and extended version of the 1975 original.

Alongside the many excellent writers she showcases in her anthologies, Sargent exemplifies this prospectus in her own novels. These range from one of the first novels exploring the consequences of human cloning, *Cloned Lives* (1976), to a formidable trilogy about terraforming Venus, and other serious, thoughtful, lucid work. In *The Shore of Women* (1986), Sargent constructs a post-apocalyptic world where today's smug certainties have been undone by global nuclear war and a consequent "nuclear winter."

Hundreds or perhaps thousands of years later, matriarchal and apparently world-wide urban utopias—walled enclaves protected by force fields—maintain a stationary technological civilization, in the midst of a vast wilderness sparsely populated by bands of hunter-gatherer men scratching a stone age living. These mini-clans get along grudgingly with each other in prickly territoriality, united by a "holy speech" used in the many hi-tech shrines scattered by women across the landscape. Here worshipful and (by default, in everyday life) homosexual men drop by to commune in wired dream with the Lady, and Her several virtual aspects, enjoying imaginary coition with very real consequences, as their semen is milked away mechanically and used to inseminate the Mothers of the World safely within their lesbian redoubts. Girl children are retained by the enclaves, boys shoved out at 5 or 6 after mindwashing and placed in the custody of men. If any bands get the itch to join into larger settlements, risking the reinvention of agriculture, the wheel and metal-working, golden flying globes are dispatched from the nearest city to slaughter the brutes and raze their habitats to the ground.

Inevitably, since this is a novel written for today's readers, it takes a Romeo and Juliet turn, although one with more fear and loathing and remorseless slaughter than Shakespeare managed after *Titus Andronicus*. A young woman, accused of complicity in a near-murder done by her mother, is exiled with her into the outer grimness. While her mother dies almost immediately at the hands of male ruffians, Birana survives, sheltered by wise Wanderer. In the guise of a beardless youth, she meets Arvil, a young man of about her own age. Their growing relationship and even intimacy is thwarted by Birana's bigoted, heterophobic upbringing.

But this social order is no mere inversion of our own traditionally homophobic rejection and stigmatization of gays and lesbians. In Sargent's future, men are repeatedly conditioned to worship the ideal feminine, and to crave the orgasmic satisfactions of vaginal sex. So while Birana is revolted by the prospect of physical intimacy with a male, Arvil must fight his own impulses.

Meanwhile, Birana's peer and former object of desire, Laissa, has problems with her own mother, who retains an unhealthy affection for her infant son Button, trying to forestall his exile into barbarity. By a curious coincidence, Arvil is Button's older brother, and Laissa's twin—and the physical resemblance does not escape Birana, whose initial interest in the young man is a displacement of her infatuation with his sister.

The early emphasis on Laissa, more or less dropped for the bulk of the book, is explained in the end, when as a historian she shapes much of the first-person testimony of these two star-crossed lovers into the book we've read. It perhaps explains a certain muted, almost sepia-toned calmness in the telling of events that do not lack in drama, tension, fear, intoxicated romance, terror, death, birth, and courageous perseverance. This avoidance of a melodramatic tenor in a narrative where it might seem an endless temptation is one of the features that draws the reader into a sympathetic languor, the kind of mood more often elicited by long Victorian novels than by survivalist thrillers, or even the chilling bleakness of Cormac McCarthy's *The Road* (Entry 84). It is a little reminiscent of the long dying falls of George R. Stewart's superb *Earth Abides* (1949), but Sargent tells a more confronting tale than history's collapse into pastoral loss of memory.

The women's enclaves resemble more closely the sequestered, changeless city Diaspar, in Arthur C. Clarke's *The City and the Stars* (1956). The youth who leaves Diaspar for the forbidden outdoors is Alvin, almost an anagram of Arvil, so perhaps *The Shore of Women,* with its hints of a rapprochement between the sexes and these mutually alien ways of life, is a kind of inversion of Clarke's famous fable. The voice of that book, too, moved against the fall of night to a vivid stance opposing restriction and fearful stasis. In the end, this is the reality the women of Sargent's enclave must accept, however resentfully: "We are being given a chance to reach out to our other selves. What we do will show what we are and determine what we shall become."

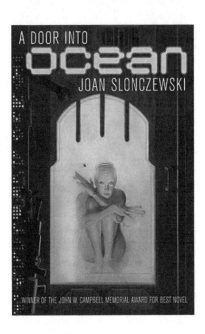

9: Joan Slonczewski
A Door Into Ocean (1986)

BESIDES REPRODUCING the evocative Ron Walotsky art from the first hardcover edition, the first paperback edition of Joan Slonczewski's *A Door into Ocean*, from 1987, adds an interior illustration showing two darkly tinted naked humanoids amidst lush foliage and exotic flying and crawling beasts. A naïve reader today might easily mistake the scene for an outtake from the film *Avatar*, a project some twenty-plus years unborn when that paperback appeared. And thus we get a lesson yet again in how Hollywood "honors" its prose antecedents with outright shameless, unacknowledged theft.

And to compound the injustice, Slonczewski goes without fair credit for her influential, groundbreaking work even among hardcore readers. For although perceptive critics of the James Cameron movie cited many sf "contributions," from Poul Anderson and Ursula K. Le Guin to the Strugatsky Brothers and Ben Bova, hardly any mention was made of Slonczewski's important work, a finer accomplishment even than many of the other respected alleged sources, and one that stands to Cameron's broad cartoony strokes as a Mary Cassatt painting to an animated advertising mascot.

Two contrasting worlds are intimately linked: Shora, a large moon, an ocean planet populated by parthenogenic females only, who rely on bio-sciences and possess a complex Zen-style philosophy of integration with nature and rules for harmonious interpersonal dynamics; and Valedon, the primary world, a planet hosting a warlike, competitive society of traditional males and females, who rely on the usual "hard" technologies, and who seem bent on despoiling Shora.

Two unofficial emissaries from Shora to Valedon adopt a young lad named Spinel and bring him back to their planet in an attempt to see if he may be "humanized." A prior instance of such acculturation, a woman ambassador named Berenice, was a less-than-sufficient proof of concept—although she will continue to play an integral and touching role in the story.

Spinel adapts with no small reluctance and frequent misunderstandings, even falling in love and mating, tantric-sex-style, with Lystra (whose name, echoing the famous story of Lysistrata, is not be overlooked by the reader). After half a year on Shora, events compel Spinel's return to Valedon, where culture shock with his old home further enlightens him. A campaign of brutal suppression is undertaken on Shora, and even Spinel's return as interfacing man-of-two-worlds might be inadequate to secure peace.

The lucid gravitas of Slonczewski's prose is matched by her even-handed comprehension of every viewpoint shared by her disparate cast, and her story—as well as her intricately fabricated ecology—contains numerous surprises and epiphanies, as well as plenty of Thoreauvian heartfelt paeans to the power of nature—a decided rarity in the "steel beach" catalogue of sf.

In the cool water, branch shadows wove fleeting patterns upon the hide of the young starworm. Lystra admired the sinuous trunk that stretched several swimming-lengths ahead of her, though barely a third as long as the maturer specimens of Raia-el. The mouth stalks of the starworm spread in a perfect star around its lip, none broken and regrown as on older starworms....The young starworm had lone streamers of filters within its mouth, because it was not yet large enough to digest squid or large fish, only plankton and fingerlings. As Mithril's cousins raked debris from the filters, Lystra swam up to the surface to get the net full of fingerlings that could be fed into the star-rimmed mouth, a handful at a time.

In the best manner of sf dialoguing, Slonczewski confesses to several inspirations, works she wished to respond to: Le Guin's *The Word for the World is Forest*, Herbert's *Dune*, and, surprisingly, Heinlein's *The Moon is a Harsh Mistress*. She plucked from these models a set of polarities which she would embody in an alluring narrative, resolving their seeming incompatibility into a whole, organic synthesis.

Besides its generally acknowledged prominent place in the lineage of feminist sf, *A Door Into Ocean* fits neatly into three other equally valid traditions, conferring on it a quadrupled strength and complexity.

First is the utopian strain. Attempting to imagine and depict a society that confers maximum freedom and sustainable necessities for all, Slonczewski evokes any number of ancestors, from John Uri Lloyd's *Etidorhpa*, through Le Guin's *The Dispossessed*. And extending her influence forward, we reach descendants like Kim Stanley Robinson.

A second tributary of theme and topic might be deemed the literature of transcendental refusal, a much tinier stream in the canon than the utopia, but still significant. Melville's *Bartleby, the Scrivener* and Edward Abbey's *The Monkey Wrench Gang* come to mind.

Lastly, the third extra-feminist lineage shared by *Ocean* is the biopunk, or ribofunk one. Biology has always taken a back seat in sf to the so-called hard sciences, and works such as Damon Knight's *Masters of Evolution* and T. J. Bass's *The Godwhale* shine out all the more for their stance that squishy is powerful. Slonczewski's training and expertise as a professor of biology lend her work a sophisticated plausibility and ingenuity found only at the top of this subgenre.

Feminist/monkey-wrenching/utopian/biopunk sf: now, that's a standout combination that only a masterful writer could bring off! And Slonczewski does it superbly.

Slonczewski reportedly took eight years to craft *Ocean*, and her newest book (as of this essay) was separated from its predecessor by eleven years. But like the patient lifeshapers of Shora, what counts in her work is not speed and volume, but elegant living results.

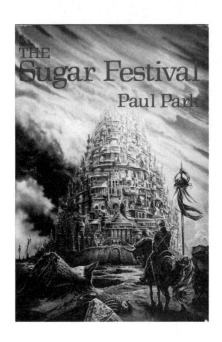

10: Paul Park
Soldiers of Paradise (1987)
[Starbridge Chronicles]

BRUCE **STERLING,** Jeff VanderMeer, Paul Park: three authors who share a generation and who spent a sizable portion of their formative years outside the United States. For Sterling, India; for VanderMeer, Fiji; and for Park, Sri Lanka and other parts of Asia and Africa. The seminal experience of being indoctrinated in alienness and apartness shines forth in the writings of each, rendering them mutually resonant spirits, rare genre writers who have an interest in recreating the exotic, but inhabited from inside, with full understanding of the manifold traps and joys of multiculturalism. And certainly all three men share a kinship with older models of such genre cosmopolites: Cordwainer Smith (Paul Linebarger) and James Tiptree, Jr. (Alice Sheldon).

Park's transcendent first novel, *Soldiers of Paradise*, and its sequels, *Sugar Rain* and *The Cult of Loving Kindness*, speak treasure troves about this kind of global upbringing and attitude, and certainly could not have been written with the same intensity, creative ferment and insightfulness by someone merely swotting up Baedekers. *Soldiers* and *Rain* are essentially one long narrative, broken in two for publishing purposes (and indeed they appeared yoked together in a second edition as *The Sugar Festival*), while *Cult* exhibits a time disjunction that qualifies it for separate inspection.

Initially our venue is the city of Charn and, later, its rival metropolis, Caladon. Charn is a big, dense, multiplex city of numerous well-delineated districts, inhabited by elites—primarily, the many-branched Starbridge family, with a distant member of the clan actually ruling Caladon as well—and masses of poor and suffering workers, some of them belonging to non-human races. With a complex topography—the major prison alone is an enormous labyrinth cored from a mountain and housing hundreds of thousands of prisoners—the religion-besotted, politics-mad, outré city is as much character as the major personages. The history and culture of this world—not Earth, but part of a solar system whose mechanics enforce seasons of enormous duration, seasons whose violent transitions power much of the disruptive human activity—are impasto'd with such intensity and specificity that Park's world looms almost as solid as our own.

Those major protagonists would be Abu and Charity Starbridge, brother and sister, and their cousin, Doctor Thanakar. From a life of privilege, the three will descend into a welter of suffering as their city undergoes revolution and war. Martyred toward the end of the first volume, Abu becomes a saint whose legacy figures heavily in the third installment. The second book concerns the aftermath of the long war between Charn and Caladon, the French-Revolution-terror of the political scene in Charn, and the struggles of Thanakar and Charity to survive and reunite.

Park employs a certain distancing technique in his narrative, having our unnamed, omniscient historian sometimes speak of events as occupying the ancient past. But this occasional leap into historicity does not preclude an intense immediacy of sensory and emotional impact, as we follow Thanakar and Charity through their trials, to an eventual hard-won reunion of damaged souls.

In an interview with critic and editor Nick Gevers, Park said, "In the *Starbridge* books, the task I set for myself was to make a strange place come alive, so that the experience of reading it was comparable to the experience of living in that world. More than people or events, those books are about the place itself: to a large extent, especially in the first book, events occurred so as to carry the reader into different sections of the physical and social landscape. What I was trying to do was to make every moment both physically and emotionally vivid, which requires a lot of description, and a layered technique." His success is undeniable.

The speculative elements in the sequence are integral to the human dramas, and innovative in their own right. The long seasons of this world, where a whole new generation may arise before, say, winter departs, have been integrated into the culture and internalized in the psyches of the inhabitants in curious and novel ways. Likewise the "sugar rain" of spring, with its mutation-inducing chemicals. And receiving insightful dissections are the power-trip strictures and habits of a religion whose actual epiphanies seems to be provable and irrefutable.

The third book inhabits a different but allied territory, being in some ways a pastorale opposed to the panoramic, Victor-Hugo-tapestried urbanism of the first two parts, almost a *Green Mansions* idyll. In a forest far from Charn, during the long summer that comes after the spring revolution, an elderly monk following quasi-Buddhist teachings and named Mr. Sarnath rescues two orphaned newborns, another brother and sister pairing, who grow up to be Rael and Cassia, teenaged acolytes of the Cult of Loving Kindness. Eventually Cassia becomes the prime engine of the movement.

Park's close-up portrayal of this nascent crusade is almost Southern Gothic in its treatment. One could imagine this passage, for instance, to have come from Flannery O'Connor describing some backwoods revival meeting:

The cripple lay on his back, his long legs crossed, each ankle locked over the opposite knee. The two women were kneeling on either side of him. The piebald woman had unscrewed the top from a jar of ointment, and she was rubbing the ointment on the cripple's legs. Still the crowd was singing and clapping to the rhythm that the pregnant woman had abandoned; she was out of breath. Her naked breasts were heaving as she bent down low and took some of the ointment on her palms.

This installment ends inconclusively, with Cassia's legacy rippling forth unpredictably into the long, eternal future of the world.

Readers will search in vain for critical appreciation of the *Starbridge Chronicles* as part of the New Weird movement exemplified by China Miéville and others (Entry 62), but its place there is incontestable. Deriving much of its atmosphere, style, plot structures and characterization techniques from the work of Mervyn Peake, a New Weird preceptor, the *Starbridge Chronicles* serve as an interface between unchristened, older, proto-New Weird opuses such as Gene Wolfe's *Book of the New Sun* and Robert Silverberg's *Majipoor* sequence, and the younger novels that would finally crystallize the mode. Mention of the *Majipoor* books also brings up the much older subgenre of planetary romance, pioneered by Leigh Brackett and C. L. Moore, among others. The *Starbridge Chronicles* plays off this old pulp mode masterfully and with natural feel for *Planet Stories* exoticism. A savvy reader would not jump overmuch to encounter Moore's hero Northwest Smith battling the insidious Shambleau in Charn's precincts.

In the same conversation with Gevers cited earlier, Park self-deprecatingly observes, "The hardest thing for me as a writer is to speak without irony, without the protection of being misunderstood. To say, 'this is what I think is important,' or 'this is what I think is true, or beautiful, or funny, or moving'—that is what is difficult for me." But readers of this masterful series will attest that Park has brilliantly overcome any such earnest flubbing of his heart's message.

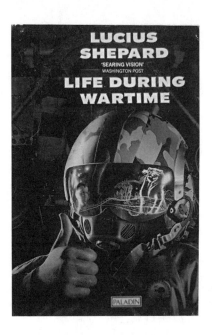

11: Lucius Shepard
Life During Wartime (1987)

CATAPULTING TO prize-winning prominence in the early 1980s, Lucius Shepard effortlessly surpassed the achievements of the previous generation of once-routine sf writers—Robert Silverberg, Harlan Ellison—who had remade themselves more ambitiously in the 1960s and '70s. But Shepard, unlike most of the brilliant kids who created modern science fiction in the late 1940s and '50s, was already (like Gene Wolfe, Entry 36) in the middle of his life. He had experience of the Vietnam war (perhaps as a reporter rather than warrior), had traveled widely in dangerous places from Latin America to Afghanistan, performed in rock bands, married and divorced. This is the *curriculum vita* of a Conrad, a Hemingway, a Robert Stone rather than an Asimov, and his work is clearly affiliated with those writers, and with the baroque lushness of the magical realists of Colombia and Argentina: Gabriel García Márquez, Julio Cortázar. The superb opening stanza of *Life During Wartime* first appeared in *Asimov's* as the novella "R & R" and won 1987's Nebula and Locus Awards, but the novel, published without conspicuous genre trappings, was hailed as well by non-genre reviewers and critics.

From this remove, we see that Shepard's future did not quite come to pass, yet its vividness and edge still bite. Tel Aviv has not been nuked, Guatemala has not been invested by US troops on the scale of Vietnam—but parallels are evident in Iraq and Afghanistan and the relentless drug wars in Mexico and other nations south of the US border.

David Mingolla is a 19 year old conscript, stationed in the preposterous Ant Farm, a military termitarium of tunnels and weapons quickly reduced to uselessness by guerrillas. It is a *reductio ad absurdum* of the protracted engagement in Vietnam, and serves as well for the massively armored western military enclaves in Iraq and other oil-rich nations. What makes New York art student Mingolla special is his possession of that old sf standby, psychic abilities. He has been headhunted by Psicorps, a kind of merciless psi training branch of the armed forces distantly akin, but far more ferocious, to the actual US Star Gate remote viewing program that was still deeply classified when Shepard wrote his fiction.

Mingolla rejects the call: "These guys think they're mental wizards or something, but all they do is predict stuff, and they're wrong half the time. And I was scared of the drugs, too. I heard they had bad effects." He cannot deny his own nature, though, and the impulses drawing him after he meets Debora Cifuentes, a sexually compelling Sombra enemy psychic. Soon he is in the appalling "therapeutic" custody of Dr. Izaguirre, doped with a rare flowered weed that elicits and enhances psi powers—not just gappy precognition but an uncanny ability to shape and control the emotions of others. And the drugs do have very bad effects. They turn Mingolla, step by crazed step, into a sort of monster. It seems no accident that his name is a near-homonym for Mengele, the Nazi experimentalist doctor from Auschwitz-Birkenau concentration camp who fled to Argentina and Paraguay.[7]

In the 1950s, this could have been a standard "psionics" adventure seeded by John W. Campbell, editor of *Astounding*. In the hands of a luminous, tough-minded, politically embittered writer like Shepard, it moves far beyond those catchpenny limits. Sometimes the diction is a little too ponderous, portentous—"The memories of the dead men in his wake were weights bracketed to his heart, holding him in place"—but mostly Shepard's writing is various and fluently fitted to its purpose: raspingly obscene and brutal when the grunts talk macho trash, driven through superstitious rituals of self protection from magical assault, or sexually frank and fervent, or richly descriptive, drifting from lyricism to terror:

> A couple of dozen butterflies were preening on Coffee's scalp—a bizarre animate wig—and others clung to his beard; a great cloud of them was circling low above his head like a whirlpool galaxy of cut flowers... Butterflies poured down the tunnel to thicken it further, and [Coffee] slumped... the mound growing with the disconnected swiftness of time-lapse photography, until it had become a multicolored pyramid towering 30 feet above, like a temple buried beneath a million lovely flowers.

Mingolla's progression is a sort of J. G. Ballard-meets-Philip K. Dick descent through a nightmarish Purgatorio or harrowing of Hell, hallucinatory, compulsive, stripping flesh from bone. At the outset, he regards "the core problems of the Central American peoples," like his own, as being "trapped between the poles of magic and reason, their lives governed by the politics of the ultrareal, their spirits ruled by myths and legends, with the rectangular, computerized bulk of North America above and the conch-shell-shaped mystery of South America below."

---

7 Shepard did not consciously intend this pun, stating that he drew the name Mingolla from a newspaper. But the story he published immediately after "R & R" was titled "Mengele," and the unconscious is tricky.

Granted, this is a patronizing appraisal by an untested youth, yet it eerily foreshadows the magical war between two old Spanish families that proves to be the hidden core of the mad, arbitrary conflict tearing at the Americas. Mingolla sinks ever deeper into this nightmare of myth, drugs, paranormal intuition, and personal command, held from the pit of absolute power by his bond with Debora yet ruinously energized by it. Is his final temptation to drag them together into a Faustian hell of survivalist banality?

The titular "Life During Wartime" was a Talking Heads' song of rebellion in an imagined 1980s' epoch of urban terror. Messages are sent only in uncertain hope that they'll reach their destination and get a reply, identity is masked, preparations for attack by the nameless narrator are readied, even day and night are reversed—and there's every chance that nobody will ever make it home. That's Mingolla's bleak prospect, too. Let us hope we might yet escape it ourselves.

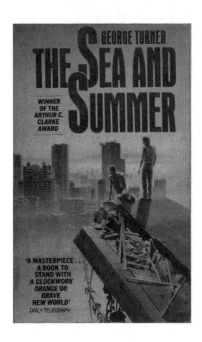

12: George Turner
The Sea and Summer (1987)

ARGUABLY THE two most important Australian science fiction novelists to date are Greg Egan, for his brilliant ingenuity and scientific depth (Entry 38), and the late George Turner (1916-1997), for what one critic called his "moral seriousness" and his determination to avoid classic sf clichés.

A quality of gravitas attends almost all Turner's writing, beginning with his award-winning non-sf novels of the 1950s and '60s. (He shared the 1962 Miles Franklin award for *The Cupboard Under the Stairs* and the Commonwealth Literary Fund award for *The Lame Dog Man*.) He entered the science fiction world with a series of ferociously contentious and hard-bitten critical reviews of much loved work such as Alfred Bester's *The Demolished Man*, and finally decided to try his own hand at the genre.

His first sf novel, *Beloved Son,* was applauded by critics, and earned him a Ditmar award, but his best is probably *Drowning Towers* (the US retitling of the original *The Sea and Summer*), a Greenhouse mid-catastrophe study of human nature under extreme pressure, climatic and social. It won the Arthur C. Clarke award, and was regional winner in the international Commonwealth Writers' Prize. (Another significant novel is *Genetic Soldier* [1994], which drew upon Turner's own military experience during the Second World War.)

A thousand years after the melting of Antarctica's ice, Lenna, a scholar, and Andra, a playwright of the Autumn People, explore the drowned high-rise towers built to accommodate the swarming Swill, living on State charity, of mid-21st century

Melbourne, Australia. Each of these monstrous, crowded tenement ghettos housed some 70,000 uneducated, stinking, workless victims of a collapsing society, eight to a bedroom. Most of the book proves to be a novel written by Lenna, reconstructing a key moment in the failure of this makeshift bureaucratic solution to overpopulation and global climate change. Each chapter is told by one or other of the players in this drama, although their voices share Turner's irritable, tin-eared truculence. (Ventriloquism was not one of his gifts; the biographer of J. G. Ballard, John Baxter, complained that "if there is an awkward way to express a simple thought, Turner will find it." But George Turner had different game in his sights.)

The tragical history of our coming century is observed by the Autumn People as a new ice age closes in on a less populated, more modest world better prepared for disastrous change and its amelioration. Their editorial chorus serves Turner's purpose as a propagandist, but the meat of the book is the tale of the Conway family: mother Alison, her paramour Billy Kovacs—Boss of one teeming tower block, thug, and police toady—and her clever, thwarted children Teddy and Francis, dragging themselves upward again through dystopia. The Conways stand midway between high and low; they are Fringe, formerly Middle Sweet (the well-off with jobs), and now live in a wretched small house near Kovacs' monstrous ghetto.

"In 2041," Francis notes in his diary—presumably Lenna's reconstruction, not a remnant document—"the population of the planet passed the ten billion mark." (This is still considered plausible by UN demographers, if on the high end.) Francis was six, Teddy nine, meat rationed, the wheat belt crushed against the southern coast, gasoline unobtainable on the open market, the top third of Australia taken by desperate Asian invaders, nine-tenths of Melbourne's 10 million crammed into a tenth of its area. These *barrios* for the Swill are arrayed in "ten close-packed groups of monoliths snuffling blunt snouts at the sky."

Evidently the grim lessons of the 20th century, when inner city slum communities were razed and replaced by appalling, dysfunctional high-rise Projects, have been forgotten or ignored. The sea is inexorably rising. And a Final Solution of some kind looks inevitable: either the extraneous living must be culled (although at least not butchered; there is no horrified cry here that "Soylent Green is *people!*"), or their fertility snipped. Kovacs suspects that a plot is underway at the highest levels of authority—genocide of the Swill via mass sterilization—and he is prepared to take any vicious steps necessary to unmask it.

Teddy enters Police Intelligence, while genius lightning-calculator Francis weasels his cunning way into various criminal enterprises. A coalition of Teddy, his revered Police Intelligence chief, and father-figure Kovacs, creates from select Swill the "New Men": "people who do what they can instead of sitting on their arses waiting for time to roll over them." Unlike A. E. van Vogt's Slans, and other supermen of classic sf, these New Men can do little to hold back the literal and figurative tides.

Sly Francis is the most entertaining and pleasingly picaresque character in this very Australian version of Dickensian social critique. He is not euphemistic in his hatred of the Swill: "I used to be afraid of their violence but that can be avoided; now I just detest their dirt, their whining voices and their lack of interest in anything but enduring through the night to the following day." But *The Sea and Summer* is no mere finger-wagging. The intertwined stories tear along, "little human glimpses," as Lenna puts it, that "*do* help, if only in confirming our confidence in steadfast courage."

Aside from its merits as a vivid and disturbing study of character under duress, for us in the early decades of the 21st century this novel has a singular and prophetic salience (for all the nits one might pick). Turner characterized our time as plagued, for the authorities, by

> the nuclear threat and the world population pressure and the world starvation problem and the terrorist outbreaks and the strikes and the corruption in high places shaking hands with crime in low places, and the endless business of simply trying to stay in power—all to be attended to *urgently.*

Sound familiar?

On the cover image:

She screamed, grabbed a jar and threw it at the mirror. Both shattered and fell.

As Catlin and Florian came running in.

She sat down on her bed. And grabbed up Poo-thing and hugged him and stroked his shabby fur.

"Sera?" Catlin said. "Sera, is there an Enemy?"

"They sent maman away," she said, "because Ari's mother died."

"What, Sera?" Florian asked. "What do you mean? When did she die?"

"The same day. When Ari was the same age. Her uncle came to get her. Just like Uncle Denys came for me." Tears ran out of her eyes and splashed onto her lap, but she wasn't crying, not feeling it, anyway; the tears just fell. "I'm a replicate. Not just genetic. I'm exact. They sent my maman away, they sent her on a long trip through jump, it made her sick and she died, she died, because they wanted her to!" —from Cyteen

"CYTEEN is an absorbing story of power, intrigue, and betrayal—a worthy addition to Cherryh's star and century-spanning Merchanters universe."
—POUL ANDERSON

HUGO AWARD-WINNING AUTHOR OF DOWNBELOW STATION

C.J. CHERRYH

CYTEEN

C.J. Cherryh Cyteen

FREEZER

13927

WARNER BOOKS

13: C. J. Cherryh
Cyteen (1988)

IN BUDDHIST practice, the dharma is transmitted through teachings from one master to another, establishing an endless chain of wisdom. Something very similar happens in literature, but especially in science fiction. Editors anoint authors, authors have protégés or collaborators. Fans become professionals, pros remain connected to fandom. Sometimes authors are also editors, and/or critics. Perhaps the field is actually more like the Buddhist Net of Indra, the symbol for "a universe where infinitely repeated mutual relations exist between all members of the universe," to quote that science fictional nexus of mutual crowd-sourced knowledge, Wikipedia.

Surely C. J. Cherryh must feel part of such a transmission, a living legacy, since she was one of the final, late-period discoveries of that seminal figure, the fabled fan, writer and editor Donald A. Wollheim, who bought and published her first two books in 1976, helping Carolyn Janice Cherry (he added the "h" to her surname for its somewhat alien, non-feminine resonance) to win a John W. Campbell Award for Best New Writer the following year.

Since then, with her patented blend of exotic planetary romances—*romances* often in the sense of both grand adventures and passionate affairs of the heart—Cherryh has climbed to great heights, with over sixty books published. Half of those pertain to one continuity, the Alliance-Union universe, of which *Cyteen* is a tiny, but satisfying and award-winning slice. The whole sequence is a full-bore, centuries-spanning future history, akin in feel and tone to Poul Anderson's *Technic* series, but perhaps not quite as well-known—yet!

Despite appearing at the apogee of the cyberpunk movement, the book's title does not refer to a cybernetic adolescent, but rather to the name of a long-settled colony world that rivals ancient Earth in power and status. Cyteen has ascended to its influential position thanks to the business enterprise—really, political player and think tank as well—known as Reseune, which exclusively controls the cloning and "tape education" processes that are capable of turning out lab-grown disenfranchised workers ("azi") and privileged citizens alike, to meet any needs (including warfare, long before George Lucas's "Clone Wars"). And controlling Reseune is Ariane Emory, ancient megalomaniacal spider, user, abuser and manipulator at the heart of the web. A genius "Special," Emory is a combination of Howard Hughes, Rupert Murdoch and Edward Teller.

The first third of the book (a fortunate division that lent itself to a since-over-turned publisher's decision to issue the narrative in three separate parts) sets up the whole current scenario, backstory and vast troupe of players. Its climax is the assassination of Ariane Emory by a disaffected confederate. Desperate to regain Emory's leadership abilities and brains, Reseune's executives clone her and undertake her upbringing from infancy, in the book's middle portion. Seeking to replicate her historical nurture, they embark on a program straight out of *The Boys from Brazil*. This segment ends when Ari II assumes her majority at age fifteen, gets wise to the true nature of her life, and begins to take the reins of Reseune.

> "You know why they made me and how they taught me, and you know what I am. And you know my predecessor had enemies who wanted her dead, and one who killed her. The closer I get to what she was, the more scared people get—because I'm kind of spooky, Amy, and I'm real spooky to a lot of people who weren't half as afraid of my predecessor."

Indeed!

Cyteen is, in some deep and truly profitable sense, but not exclusively, a rethinking and updating of Huxley's *Brave New World*. Casting its spotlight on the genetic tailoring of people to fit into social niches, their artificial education by "tape" means, and the establishment of elites and underclasses, the book echoes and refines Huxley's dystopia to a certain level of precision. But Cherryh has other themes and tropes in mind. Placing the world of Cyteen in a galactic setting against rival worlds, with all the competition and realpolitik machinations that such a milieu implies, the author exhibits an interest in examining the Darwinian game of "nation" versus nation (Earth versus Cyteen), weighing which political system is best fitted for taking the species to new and productive—if not necessarily safe and fair—places in a hostile universe.

But perhaps Cherry's deepest concern is the allied realms of identity/consciousness and family. Although the Reseune tech is less godlike than some other fictional constructs and does not permit full identity transplants between bodily shells, her portrayal of shared clonal identities treats of many of the same existential notions found in the works of such writers as David Brin; Greg Egan; Kazuo Ishiguro (Entry 77); Richard Morgan (Entry 69); Dan Simmons; John Varley. As for family, Cherryh riffs inventively about what it means to have subsets of one's genes distributed throughout a large population, and the limits and possible permutations of consanguinity and blood loyalty. In a sense, she has carnalized Greg Bear's notion of virtual "partials."

Cherry's sprawling yet channeled novel (think of a powerful central river with lazy marshes adjacent, a kind of Everglades of a book) combines the sociopolitical reach of Poul Anderson's aforementioned *Technic* tales with the Byzantine familial treacheries and alliances of Roger Zelazny's *Amber* sequence. It blends the weird hothouse domesticity of Gene Wolfe's "The Fifth Head of Cerberus" or Le Guin's "Nine Lives" with the biopunk grotesqueries of Jack Vance's *The Dragon Masters*. Such a recipe would have resulted in a farrago in the hands of a lesser writer, but Cherryh justifies every bit of Zen master faith that Donald Wollheim placed in her.

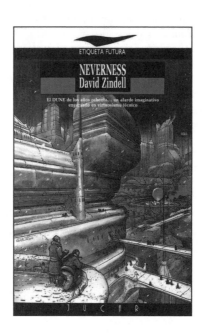

14: David Zindell
Neverness (1988)

▬▬▬▬▬

STANDING JUST outside the period of our survey is a mighty crag of a book, A. A. Attanasio's first novel, *Radix*. This hegira of maturation, mutation and adventuring across a far-future landscape, where cognitive estrangement and uncanny emotional frissons are the reader's glorious reward, delivered by the handmaidens of beautifully ornate and darkly rococo language, is a secret talisman to a small group of readers. Surely David Zindell must number himself among the Attanasio cult, for his debut novel *Neverness* seeks to achieve many of the same goals through similar verbal and cultural warpings. Zindell succeeds magnificently, not merely recapitulating Attanasio's victories, but also incorporating inspirations from several other and older models of Weird Sf into a unique voice.

Neverness's scenario is simple—like that of *The Canterbury Tales*—but opens out onto endless possible expanses. At least three thousand years into our future, a portion of the galaxy is host to thirty thousand civilized worlds, linked by the bold and privileged pilots of a mathematically inclined Order centered in the glamorously exotic city of Neverness. Our hero and narrator is Mallory Ringess, newly minted as a Pilot and embarked on a quest involving nothing less than the secret of how humanity may ensure its own survival, efflorescence and transcendence. His first adventure takes him among the macrocosmic brain cells (linked cybernetic moons) of the godlike Solid State Entity. Based on information there, he next journeys among the polar tribesmen called the Alaloi. Medical mishaps deposit Ringess on the mystical mystery world of Agathange for two whole years. Returning to Neverness, Ringess finds much change and languishes in confusion for a time. Then comes the Pilot's War, revolt, death and treachery, and one final questing.

Ringess recounts his own exploits in a rich language full of neologisms and repurposed words, which some have likened to the methodology of Gene Wolfe. And just as Wolfe was influenced by Jack Vance, so too does Zindell employ some of the stratagems of that anthropologically savvy Grand Master, showing us how social customs and taboos and convoluted etiquette can shape and constrain societies. Ringess's forays, solo and with his comrades, obviously harken to the great Arthurian cycle of tales (hence "Mallory," as in Thomas). The "Elder Eddas" secret which they all quest after is thus akin to the Holy Grail. Moreover, the bardic, mythic, roistering *elan vital* on display brings up comparisons with E. R. Eddison's great *Zimiamvia* trilogy, which, though it soon became indistinguishable from fantasy after its first few pages, commenced as science fiction set on Mercury. Sometimes Zindell's voice approaches that of David Lindsay in his eccentric *A Voyage to Arcturus*. And Stanislaw Lem's extravagant techno tall tales in *The Cyberiad* spring to mind as well.

The trope of damaged or specially endowed starship pilots is a rich one in sf, and Zindell has a lark trying to incorporate as many allusions to the great stories of this heritage as possible. Cordwainer Smith, Samuel Delany, Frank Herbert and Anne McCaffrey are the major past peaks he surmounts. Additionally, Zindell makes a nod toward what was at the time the gold standard of space opera, Larry Niven's *Known Space* future history, with mention of a "ringworld" and employment of the trope of a wavefront of exploding stars that threatens civilization, the Puppeteer's bane, here called "the Vild."

Zindell's story is notable for its unabashed cerebral pleasures, which do not cancel out its vividly physical blood and thunder moments:

> My ship did not fall out into the center of the moons. Instead, I segued into a jungle-like decision tree... Each individual ideoplast was lovely and unique. The representation of the fixed-point theorem, for instance, was like a coiled ruby necklace. As I built my proof, the coil joined with feathery, diamond fibres of the first Lavi mapping lemma.

These star pilots, are taking their ships through windows in hyperspace by proving mathematical theorems! How strange! And yet—don't today's pilots do something like that already? Mapping a course, by hand or by computer, is the application of mathematics to the shape of the world. These futuristic pilots happen to be doing it (somehow) directly! Feeling these sentences work on you, getting the point, is an audacious and shivery pleasure for those who know that the trick to decoding such sentences is not by way of the conventional dictionary and encyclopedia. Recognizing the fixed-point theorem, which in mathematics governs the transformation of one set of points into an isomorphic set, helps one appreciate a sense of recursion in what is being described/constructed—but it is not crucial.

So here, by the same method, is Ringess's escape from the Solid State Entity:

> I was trembling with anticipation as I built up a new proof array. Yes, the simple Lavi could be embedded! I proved it could be embedded. I wiped sweat from

my forehead, and I made a probability mapping. Instantly the million branches of the tree narrowed to one. So, it was a finite tree after all. I was saved!

Much sf claims to be focused on ideas, while really hewing to pulp action. Zindell's book is truly about ideas, notably that great human conundrum revolving around whether free will exists or not.

As for the legacy of *Neverness*, like Attanasio's *Radix* it remains a secret stream in the genre. But it seems unlikely, for instance, that Neal Stephenson could have been unaware of this book when he conjured up his science monks in *Anathem*. And possibly M. John Harrison nodded in Zindell's direction with his baroque space opera *Light* (Entry 68).

Zindell would follow up this magnificent and self-sufficient book with a trilogy dubbed *A Requiem for Homo Sapiens*. These books certainly did not dilute his accomplishment with *Neverness*, but simply by virtue of coming later, they could not carry all the freight of unprecedented wonder and astonishment borne so capably by *Neverness*.

15: Rosemary Kirstein
The Steerswoman (1989)

W E FIRST encounter the protagonist of this four-part opus, a woman named Rowan, and her quest across a seemingly magical world in the pages of *The Steerswoman*. A sequel followed fairly swiftly in the form of *The Outskirter's Secret*. (Both of these books were bundled in an omnibus titled *The Steerswoman's Road*.) Then came a long interval of silence on Kirstein's part until the release of *The Lost Steersman*, followed at a relatively rapid clip by the fourth book, *The Language of Power*. The series does not terminate here, however, but Kirstein seems to have bogged down slightly, revealing lately that what she thought would constitute Book 5 instead morphed into Book 6, leaving the immediate follow-up volume unbegun. Nonetheless, her unfinished accomplishment here is still significant. As author and critic Jo Walton says, " If you like science, and if you like watching someone work out mysteries, and if you like detailed weird alien worlds and human cultures, if really good prose appeals, and if you can stand reading a series written by someone brilliant who writes excruciatingly slowly but has no inconsistencies whatsoever between volumes written decades apart, you're really in luck."

Rowan is a member of a knowledge-seeking and information-disseminating guild whose itinerant members bind together an ostensibly pre-technological world. The Inner Lands where the steerswomen travel constitute a safe and civilized realm dotted with cities and trade routes, while the Outskirts where they never venture are harsher lands populated by odd beasts and nomadic tribesmen with strict codes of behavior. A final factor in the cultural equation is the presence of a handful of wizards, who remain generally aloof from daily affairs, while retaining immense powers that allow them to dictate policy when they so desire. For many generations this stable scenario has allowed mankind to flourish. But now things have gone awry.

The first sign of a breakdown in the system is an odd piece of jewelry that comes into Rowan's hands. In the first book of the series, she determines that the jewelry was connected to the demise of one of the Guidestars, stable points of light in the night sky that serve to guide travelers. In the second book, Rowan and her new best friend Bel, a woman warrior from the Outskirts, reach the source of the "jewels" and discover a crashed Guidestar. The fact that this ostensibly "natural" object was actually manufactured opens the possibility that Rowan's world is not all it seems. In fact, a master wizard named Slado seems to be at the heart of a vast conspiracy. In the third volume, on the hunt for Slado, Rowan encounters a new sentient race.

In the fourth installment, where much is revealed, Rowan and Bel are back in the Inner Lands in a seaside town named Donner. There, they begin to piece together the local events of forty years ago, when the Guidestar fell and Slado first rose to power. Questioning the townsfolk—answering a steerswoman's questions is compulsory, under pain of a lifetime ban from sharing in the guild's knowledge base—Rowan learns of a struggle for control between apprentice Slado and his master Kieran. Apparently Slado killed Kieran, assumed his powers, and began his ascent to world dominance. But where is Slado today, and what does he intend?

The arrival of an old friend, Willam, promises to help provide some answers. Several books prior, Willam was a teen with magical propensities whom Rowan managed to apprentice to a friendly wizard named Corvus. Now an adult, Willam has left Corvus behind to function as a free agent. Rowan enlists his help to plunder the secrets of the current wizard of Donner, a pompous fellow named Jannick. But Jannick's lore is concealed in a house that has killed all previous intruders. Can Rowan, Willam and Bel penetrate Jannick's defenses and emerge with clues to Slado's plotting? Maybe, with aid of Jannick's own dragons...

Rosemary Kirstein walks the tightrope between fantasy and science fiction in this series with precision and grace, producing a hybrid adventure that recalls both purely fantastical works such as Le Guin's *Earthsea* series and purely science-fictional titles like Miller's *A Canticle for Leibowitz*.

Right from the outset, Kirstein has been clever and scrupulous about planting clues which hint that not all is as it seems in her future. Although the books read on the surface as pure fantasy, they carefully leave themselves open to interpretation as post-apocalyptic sf. By the fourth volume, this secret is out in the open, and even the non-wizardly characters themselves start to get the picture. New mysteries left unsolved by the book's end, involving astronomical photographs, further deepen the sf nature of the tale.

What Kirstein is doing is portraying how humanity's innate desire to unriddle the phenomenological universe will persist through all sorts of dark-ages setbacks. Rowan's adherence to the tenets of her guild make her a kind of proto-scientist, and thus a perfect exemplar of the science fictional mindset. Additionally, the books take on some of the qualities of a mystery novel, as Rowan and crew try to reconstruct old crimes and puzzle out active conspiracies. Sf and the mystery genre have always been intimately linked, and Kirstein makes the most of their resonance.

But of course none of this would matter if the characters and their adventures were not compelling, and Kirstein satisfies in these areas as well. Rowan ages realistically during the course of her adventures (the books span six years of her life), and by the fourth volume she's scarred and limping from her exploits. Bel is an excellent foil and contrast to Rowan, and Willam comes across as his own man as well. Kirstein's compassion for even minor characters is evident on every page, and her prose is measured and alluring without being overworked.

Further entries in this already monumental series, much awaited, can only add to its unique luster.

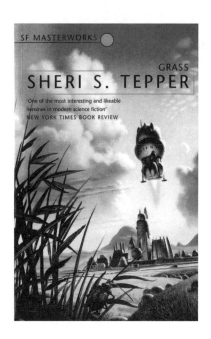

16: Sheri S. Tepper
Grass (1989)

IF THOMAS Hardy had ever written an sf novel, he might have produced something very much like Sheri Tepper's *Grass*. A thick, claustrophobic, landed-gentry melodrama full of strained politesse, thwarted sexuality, immemorial traditions, fatedness, dark passions, religious obsession, foreboding, doom, cultural misunderstandings, and hypocrisy. It's a book about bizarre aliens in which humans are the strangest creatures of all, one over which the judiciously omniscient narrator looms like a god who could be called cruel, were She Herself not so splendidly Other as to defy human conventions. The novel bears affinities to the works of James Tiptree, Gene Wolfe, Norman Spinrad, Laurence Janifer, Jack Vance and M. John Harrison, but possesses an eerie ambiance and otherworldly *weltanschauung* all its own.

Let us consider, in the reverse order Tepper presents them, two planets. Earth, teeming with too many souls, is ruled by Sanctity, a religious government with total control on the homeworld, but lesser sway among the diaspora of colonized worlds. Sanctity is worried about plague. An unstoppable, unnamed disease has begun to spread, killing even the head of the church, the Hierarch. Lady Marjorie Westriding and her husband Rigo Yrarier are summoned by the authorities. They are informed that they are being dispatched as ambassadors to the only colony world that has shown no signs of the plague—a planet that bans scientific researchers. Their undercover mission: to discover a cure, if any. Off they go, with reluctant adolescent children Tony and Stella in tow, and a retinue of assistants and priests.

The world where they have been assigned is called Grass. Completely covered by a lush carpet of non-Terran grasses (invoked by the author with Whitmanesque poetic cadences), except for one rocky hundred-square-mile site that serves as a port town, the world is inhabited by seven haughty, elite families who live on their walled estancias spotted throughout the vast wilderness. Peons support them with their separate village lives. To help order and ameliorate the extremely long Grassian calendar year with its harsh protracted winter, the elite lead lives of mannered ritual, full of taboos and compulsions, disdaining anything *fragras*, or foreign.

Chief among these ceremonial pursuits is the Hunt, involving three native animals. First, the prey, the foxen, savage predators, each big as a dozen tigers. Then come the Hounds, canine-like creatures large as Earth horses. And finally, the horse analogues, or Hippae, scaled and horned and razor-crested mounts like good-sized dragon-dinos, whose human riders suffer an appalling mortality rate, sometimes even vanishing entirely during the chaotic Hunts. The Hounds and Hippae are not domesticated or kept by the humans, but merely appear at Hunt times, as if in symbiosis and obeying some kind of planetary cycle.

Added to this outré mélange are the Green Brothers, a Jesuitical sect of monks whose main task is an archaeological dig at the ruined city of the long-extinct Arbai, enigmatic humanoids whose ruins dot the galaxy. The Green Brothers also breed hybrid grasses and sport a cult of sky-worshipping tower climbers within their ranks. And why is it, exactly, that the Brothers can roam the prairie and never be attacked by the supposedly vicious foxen?

Once on Grass, Marjorie and her family find themselves the center of disdain, sabotage and entrapment. Rumors abound that the Moldies—humans who wish actually to spread the plague and engineer a cleansing apocalypse—might be present. With an outsider's perspective, Marjorie begins to see that the Hippae might be the true rulers of Grass. But will the sentient monsters enjoy having their secrets revealed? And will they threaten her family first of all?

Tepper deftly spins a half-dozen plates simultaneously. She speculates on ET theologies in the manner of James Blish or Mary Doria Russell. She delves into ornate ecologies and life cycles in the manner of Philip José Farmer. She looks at inbreeding and clannish pride, recalling Avram Davidson ("The House the Blakeneys Built") and David Bunch (*Moderan*). Romance, or lack thereof, fills the human dimensions. Marjorie and Rigo suffer a dead marriage, and infidelity looms with a Grassian native, Sylvan bon Damfels, who allures Marjorie and she him. Issues of colonialism and privilege, machismo and sexism come by turns to the fore.

Additionally, *Grass* merits one more distinction. It is generally acknowledged that Samuel Delany's *Flight from Nevèrÿon* was the first work of fantastika to deal with AIDS, the relevant portion of Delany's book appearing as early as 1984. But five years after that, Tepper's treatment of the incurable disease rampant within the Sanctity—the shame it confers, the secrecy involved, the class barriers in play—marks a second respectable foray by the genre into dealing, at least on metaphorical terms, with the late twentieth century's dominant epidemic.

Tepper continued exploring this complex cosmos in the notional Arbai Trilogy, whose formidable second and third entries were *Raising the Stones* and *Sideshow*. But these tangential cousins cannot duplicate or enhance the exotic, mind-blowing estrangements of *Grass*. The book glows like some rare Terence Malick film, aloof and mysterious, knowing yet quizzical.

17: Iain M. Banks
Use of Weapons (1990)

IAIN M. Banks, without the middle initial, made his reputation with several freaky postmodern novels of highwire psychopathology. He erupted into British letters in the mid-1980s with such brio that Fay Weldon famously dubbed him "the great white hope of British Literature." She had in mind *The Wasp Factory* (1984), with its grisly brilliance, and a handful of other technically adventurous mainstream titles. A closet sf fan at the time, Banks was enabled by those successes to publish the bounteous space opera *Consider Phlebas* (1987), an exuberant amalgam of every big screen science fiction invention since (and including) Larry Niven's *Ringworld*, a gold bangle the size of Earth's orbit.

With its T. S. Eliot title, its gaudy tale of interstellar conflict between the Culture and the brutal Idiran empire, *Consider Phlebus* introduced a fully stocked universe as ample as anything in sf's future histories by Heinlein, Poul Anderson, Niven, Asimov. Cunningly, Banks contrived to present the Culture as the apparent imperialist enemy, before his elaborate, careful unfolding of the tale engages our true sympathies.

Happily, Banks has returned repeatedly to this delightfully detailed universe of his post-scarcity galaxy-faring Culture, most of its human-like population dwelling on gigantic, AI-controlled starships or Orbitals, luxurious habitats smaller than a Ringworld and spinning on orbit around strange suns, peaceful but armed to the teeth. Many of the novels involve interstellar spies and manipulators known as Special Circumstances, and their harrowing moral quandaries.

In *The Player of Games* (1988), for example, world-weary Jernau Gurgeh is apparently an amateur Culture expert in strategy and tactics, chockablock with specialized genofixed glands, nurtured and perhaps owned by whimsical and snide AI machines. Gurgeh is snookered into a hustle on a planetary scale. Duped agent of his rich anarchist society, he climbs the ranks of a barbarous game-structured society, learning something of empathy and involvement. His tale enveloped the story of a single intellectual combatant in the endless conflict between Banks's machine-loving hedonistic Culture (tolerant, benevolent, resolute) and its foes: brutality, credulous faith, political hierarchy, war.

Perhaps Banks's finest sf novel is the early *Use of Weapons*, a drastically complex biography of a soldier, Cheradenine Zakalwe, recruited from a world not unlike Czarist Russia and for centuries sent into the field again and again, supported with only the most ironic ambiguity by subtle Culture intelligences human and artificial. (He appears again, unnamed and to considerable ironic effect, at the very end of Banks's recent *Surface Detail* [2010]). Frozen to death, he can be healed, if reached in time. Even if he's decapitated, he can be revived. A poisoned worm of lost memory remains hidden from sight, however, baffling the labyrinthine plans of even the Culture's most beguiling minds. Banks somehow works a narrative miracle, a triumph of generic engineering, fusing thriller and moral parable, reeking detail and clinical distance, fanciful invention and heartfelt pain.

The Culture Special Circumstances agent is named, with typical Banksian abandon, Rasd-Codurersa Diziet Embless Sma da' Marenhide, more usually just Diziet Sma, attended by her lethal, sardonic drone AI companion Fohristi-whirl Skaffen-Amtiskaw Handrahen Dran Easpyou, or Skaffen-Amtiskaw. Drones are unsentimental:

> "We've a nebula fleet assembling; a core of one Limited System Vehicle and three General Contact Units stationed around the cluster itself, plus eighty or so GCUs keeping their tracks within a month's rush-in distance. There ought to be four or five GSVs within a two-to-three months dash for the next year or so. But that's very, very much a last resort."
>
> "Megadeath figures looking a bit equivocal are they?" Sma sounded bitter.
>
> "If you want to put it that way," Skaffen-Amtiskaw said.

The novel winds on itself like a double spiral, an architecture suggested by his Scottish colleague and friend, the equally talented Ken MacLeod (see Entry 53). The main story carries us forward; its parallel runs backward, in leaps of recovered traumatic memory. In the end, all certitudes are broken. Anything may be used as a weapon, however personal, ugly, ruinous to the wielder. The novel is a coiled maze; many ways lead in, as many out, all of them refuting determinacy even as they insist upon it.

And for all that, the book is tremendous *fun*, and is often credited with the revival of intelligent space opera. Colossal artifacts with facetious names like the *Very Little Gravitas Indeed* roar across the galaxy, while enhanced humans and snide machines frolic within their protective fields. The happiest moment, exactly catching Banks's way of taking sf's geegaws and doing rude things with them, is this:

> "To the Culture," he said, raising his glass to the alien. It matched his gesture.
>
> "To its total lack of respect for all things majestic."

At the heart of sf as an enterprise—if it has one, and to the extent that it surmounts national boundaries—ones often sees the hungry wish *not to die,* not to be mortal and evanescent, not to be cast into nothingness *just when the story is getting interesting.* Thus, sf's interest in time-dilating starships, in cryonic suspension into the future, in characters who upload their minds into secure computer substrates, who hybridize themselves by a dozen paths into persistence. Does anyone *really* want to live in the inhospitable ruin of Mars, let alone the planets of distant stars, reachable only at immense cost and probably uninhabitable on arrival? Yes, a few do, like Arctic and Antarctic explorers; it would be a rewarding exploit, in its way (see Robinson's Mars trilogy, Entry 29). But maybe, after all, it is a metaphor like the anarcho-socialistic Banksian Culture. "Can I get there by candle-light? Yes, and back again!"

Meanwhile, we have the Culture and its delights, complexities, rich imaginary adventures, and we're the better for their sometimes confronting thought experiments and gratifying playfulness.

18: Greg Bear
Queen of Angels (1990)

A PRODIGY, GREG Bear published his first sf story at 16, in 1967, and his first novels by 1979, but his major impact on the genre awaited his maturity in the mid-1980s (*Blood Music*; the ambitious diptych about the infinite construct, the Way, *Eon* and *Eternity*; the world-destroying attack by aliens, *The Forge of God* and its vengeful sequel). In later years he explored a range of sf and near-sf forms, from *Star Trek* and *Star Wars* vehicles, to a pre-*Foundation* novel set in Asimov's commodious universe, hitech FBI and horror tales, a far future novel that echoes William Hope Hodgson and Arthur C. Clarke (an early Bear influence), *City at the End of Time*. Like John Varley, he has explored projects in Hollywood. Of them all, perhaps *Queen of Angels* and its sequel *Slant* (1997) are his most satisfying classical sf works.

Jacques Lacan (patriarch of French psychoanalytic feminism) rewrote Freud as the geographer of lack. "When, in love, I solicit a look, what is profoundly unsatisfying and always missing is that—*You never look at me from the place from which I see you.*" Sf's canon is drenched with wish-fulfillments answering exactly Lacan's poignant absence: mind readers, shape-shifters, paranormal *gestalt* superhumans built up—organ by organ, as it were—out of maimed, bitterly lonely individuals. Bear's melodramatic *Blood Music* attempted a 1980s' version: Vergil Ulam, a self-centered, heedless biotech cowboy, brews the world's first intelligent microbes and lets them loose in his own bloodstream. This is an early imagining of nanotechnology, viruses or perhaps machines built on a molecular scale. Soon the world's population is melting down, each mind and soul absorbed into its own endless fecund angelic orders of smart tissue. Lacan's lovers are lost in endless narcissism, then set free into microbial quantum heaven:

> With her last strength she came to him and they lay in each other's arms, drenched in sweat.... With each pulse of blood, a kind of sound welled up within him as if an orchestra were performing thousands strong.... Edward and Gail grew together on the bed, substance passing through clothes, skin joining where they embraced and lips where they touched.

Bear's ornate *policier* of the 21st century, *Queen of Angels*, evades such explicit transcendence. It uses nanotechnology, a science only now beginning to shift from fantasy into reality, to enter the fragmented neural architecture of a political dissident. That voyage is paralleled with the quest for true selfhood in an artificial intelligence—something it attains only by doubling itself into a sort of Lacanian self-reflexivity. More than 20 years after its first publication the novel remains challenging, audacious, nothing if not ambitious, attempting to portray an American world of 2047 that is real in every fiber of the text, as significantly different from our own time as ours is from the Elizabethan. In a somewhat unlikely millenarianism, a great change is anticipated as the world approaches the "binary millennium" of 2048: in binary notation, the jump from the year 11111111111 to 100000000000.

The neuro-therapied rich live in combs, vast hi-tech termitaries. Between these arcologies, in the Shade, dwell the untherapied. Society is rich; nano machines can literally build gourmet food from garbage, construct full-scale robot devices (arbeiters), even transform human bodies. And the human mind/brain itself is finally giving up its secrets. An AI probe investigates the planets of Alpha Centauri B, beaming back data and opinions for dispersion through LitBid interactive media programs available to everyone, a sort of souped-up YouTube-meets-Facebook. Crimes are solved with ease by highbrow pds—public defenders.

In this endlessly inventive utopia Emanuel Goldsmith is the world's most famous black poet and ideologist of revolt (and surely we are meant to think of *Nineteen Eighty-Four's* Emmanuel Goldstein, Orwell's theorist of resistance to Big Brother and author of *The Theory and Practice of Oligarchical Collectivism*). Goldsmith runs amok, murders eight of his friends, and vanishes. Transformed pd Mary Choy must track her suspect, but more importantly she needs to understand the motivation of his crime. The immensely wealthy parent of one of the victims, capturing Goldsmith, seeks to use prohibited psychological techniques that permit an observer to enter another human's Country of Mind. In Bear's Jungian mythos, this is the substrate of mental agents, talents and subpersonalities that comprise each self. In an eerie parallel, the AI four light years away struggles to become the first non-human "self," to declare itself "I".

Bear's narrative never remains stationary, shifting voice and point of view, adapting techniques from modernist John Dos Passos first borrowed for sf half a generation earlier by John Brunner in *Stand on Zanzibar* (1969). The reader does not slip gracefully through this story; it can be an effort in places, but with an enormously satisfying payoff. *Queen of Angels*, like its author, is genuinely prodigious, and Bear's future assembles itself like a nano machine from a multitude of brilliant details, built with a disturbing conviction.

Simultaneously, one is aware that this *is* a construct, a kind of artistic thought experiment that echoes Bear's fundamental model of mind. That model was itself entirely up to date, at least for the end of the 1980s, paralleling with remarkable fidelity the cognitive psychology of Howard Gardner (theorist of multiple intelligences) or Roger Schank (who proposes that we think in stories, not sets of rules). Roger Atkins, designer of the AI, AXIS, asks, jokingly: *Why does the self aware individual look in the mirror?* The answer: *Because to be alone is to be insufficient.*

Things come in at least threes; there are no brutal binary oppositions of right versus wrong. Self and Other are met halfway by the self's Jungian double. Human and machine AI are mediated by transforms such as Mary Choy, who returns in *Slant*. Crime is not opposed simply by punishment, but by therapy (and understanding), and that, in turn, is open to question. So the book is not merely the demonstration of an academic theorem; it has a heart: AI pioneer Marvin Minsky's *Society of Mind,* one might say, invades and enriches Dostoyevsky's *Crime and Punishment.*

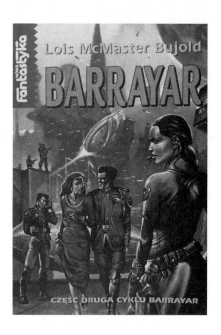

19: Lois McMaster Bujold
Barrayar (1991)

COMMERCIAL SCIENCE FICTION has always been primarily a form of adventure fiction, initially targeting mostly men and boys, so it's not surprising that military stories and settings should be prominent sellers. It is no accident that a movie with the explicit title *Star Wars* was the first truly massive sf blockbuster. This emphasis remains even when anti-war aspects infiltrate, in novels like Joe Haldeman's award-winning *Forever War* and its sequels (see Entry 50). Rather surprising, however, was the abrupt arrival, in the mid-1980s, of Lois McMaster Bujold's military heroine Commander Cordelia Naismith of egalitarian hi-tech Beta Colony, and her beloved enemy (at first), the bisexual Captain Lord Aral Vorkosigan, of the Russian-inflected neo-feudal warrior planet Barrayar, and later their seriously deformed, utterly charming son Miles, a marvelously ingenious, madly brave and resourceful trickster.

A theme common to military fiction is the demands and satisfactions of honor and courage under extreme challenge. Self-reliance, competence and the mutuality of comradeship in the face of relentless foes feature centrally in the founding sf of E. E. "Doc" Smith and Robert Heinlein, but a warrior's honor and its vicissitudes is arguably the primary motif. Indeed, an sf series by David Weber (begun some years later) even names its Horatio Hornblower-in-space heroine "Honor." What's especially remarkable about Bujold's treatment is her uncompromising adoption of a woman's point of view, in the first two volumes of her Vorkosigan saga (with 13 volumes as of

2010,[8] and more to come), and then of a male protagonist whose honor and decency are threaded through with a genius for deception, disguise, even betrayal in the larger cause, told with high humor in the midst of explicit pain and horror. Her own genius is to blend so successfully an achieved feminism, nuanced investigations of ethics under pressure at the individual and political scales, observant character studies (the dying Emperor, Sergeant Bothari, many others, slipping only with a melodramatic sadist villain), disarming or biting wit, and rousing, immensely enjoyable derring-do.

Barrayar won the 1992 Hugo and Locus Awards for best sf novel of 1991, and is the hinge linking the Naismith and Vorkosigan *fils* novels, but it is not truly a stand-alone book. Bujold's first novel, *Shards of Honor* (1986), establishes the deepening love story between Cordelia, a Betan Expeditionary Force survey team commander, and her foe, the stocky Barrayaran aristocrat known unjustly as the Butcher of Kommar, both stranded together on a deadly new world. In the book's complex unfolding, Admiral (and later Imperial Regent) Aral Vorkosigan is time and again thrust into crises where he must choose the lesser of two soul-testing evils, impelled by his military oaths and his devotion to a terraformed home world, still struggling after years of isolation following war with a third world, Cetaganda. A notable aspect of Bujold's series is the way many worlds and diverse cultures in her galactic landscape, linked by jealously guarded and contested wormhole routes, develop as the sequence continues in logical but unexpected detail barely hinted at in earlier books. And her characters grow, responding to conflict and the tasks of maturity with a measure of sophistication perhaps unexpected in headlong adventure fiction.

While *Barrayar* is the immediate sequel to *Shards of Honor,* picking up the next day, *Shards* had been followed the same year by the story of Cordelia's adolescent son in *The Warrior's Apprentice* (1986). Here young Miles shows his mettle in face of scorn and dread of "muties"—he is genetically sound but the victim in utero of a mutagenic toxin—but finds himself flung like the hero of some boy's own caper into the charismatic impersonation of "Admiral Naismith," in command of a ragtag crew of outlaws he pulls together and dubs the Free Dendarii Mercenaries. It is tremendous fun, although it lacks the intensity of these two books devoted to his mother, later combined as *Cordelia's Honor* (1999),[9] but a Miles sequel, *The Vor Game* (1990), won the Hugo Award for 1991, perhaps paving the way for *Barrayar*'s Hugo the next year.

Considered as a single novel, then, *Shards/Barrayar* is an intriguing variation on classic space opera. It does not lack for the swashbuckling of starships clashing in the night of deep space between the stars, but expends as much devotion to the conflicts and pleasures of its cast of men and women of high and less high station, on people damaged by war, as well as those triumphant, on babies and their care in an age of "uterine replicator" machines. It is far from Aldous Huxley's dyspeptic vision of de-canted specialized clones in *Brave New World,* though; ostensibly a thousand years' hence, Bujold's universe is a sort of *Star Trek* for grown-ups. In a space opera setting, she deploys the kinds of technology we might anticipate before the end of this century. And that gives the stories a certain immediacy sometimes lost in more transcendental sf set at the limits of today's comprehension.

One index of the zeal of Bujold's readers is the collaborative Vorkosigan Wiki

---

8 In a remarkably astute and bold marketing move, all of these works are bundled free on a CD-ROM attached to *Cryoburn* (Baen, 2010).
9 The first 10 chapters can be read at:
   http://www.webscription.net/chapters/0671578286/0671578286.htm

website,[10] and the extensive plot summaries on Wikipedia. *Shard of Honors/Barrayar* is at once a quite moving story of a woman's self-chosen exile as a stranger in a strange land, for the love of her man and wounded child, and an admirable prelude to the long continuing saga of Miles Vorkosigan, whom critic Sylvia Kelso memorably characterizes as "a 'genius brat,' a manic loose cannon who triumphs where superiors and enemies fail, an outlaw, a white Coyote prevailing not by gun or fist but wits."[11]

10 *http://vorkosigan.wikia.com/wiki/Vorkosigan_Wiki*

11 *http://www.dendarii.com/reviews/kelso.html* "Loud Achievements: Lois McMaster Bujold's Science Fiction," *NewYork Review of SF*, October 1998 (No. 122) and November 1998 (No. 123).

20: Pat Cadigan
Synners (1991)

THE 19TH French boy poet Arthur Rimbaud was shot by his lover, Symbolist Paul Verlaine, when he was 18, abandoned his hallucinatory art before he was 21 and swapped it for a brief, somewhat villainous life as soldier, trader and arms dealer. He was the very model of the sexually transgressive, edgy criminal artist/addict/sacred monster, doomed to early death (he perished of cancer at 37). Beat writers like Jack Kerouac clambered aboard the same drunken boat in the 1950s, and science fiction embraced this icon with relish a decade later in many of the stories and novels of Samuel R. Delany, who in his rather professorial way enacted the same trajectory—but failed to die young, taking a chair at the University of Massachusetts, Amherst. Another two decades on, the street-wise user/loser turned up again in the noir hi-tech computerized futures of cyberpunk, put through his disengaged paces by William Gibson, Bruce Sterling, and another professor, Rudy Rucker. Among these "Movement" explorers of cyberspace, the most prominent woman writer was a former Hallmark card poet, Pat Cadigan (who prankishly kills Sterling, under his Movement *nom de guerre* Vincent Omniaveritas, in a "terrorist raid").

Synners, which takes cyberpunk uncompromisingly from the street into virtual mind worlds no less hallucinatory than Rimbaud's, won the 1992 Arthur C. Clarke Award, as did the later *Fools*. The difficulty in reading a hip book about the 21st century written two decades ago, however brilliantly, is that its future has become *now*, or nearly. Meanwhile, everything has moved sideways in directions the book didn't anticipate. Read in the proper spirit, this doesn't matter. Philip K. Dick's fiction was full of robot cabbies and personal space-clunkers for commuting to Mars, but we read straight through such amusing quirks to the wit, desperation, desolation and sheer reality funk that Dick caught so well. It's less easy to swallow simpler postulates obliterated by history: a world ruled by Soviet Union communists, say (unless it's read as alternative history), or a post-2001 long-established lunar base lit also by the new sun that was once Jupiter. We know that just didn't happen, and the glitch trips our foot as we move into the fiction.

Seventeen year old Sam—Cassandra—tormented by LA's dire post-Big One computerized traffic control GridLid, laments the low quality rental car monitor that can't play videos; she reserves "a tailored hardcopy of *The Daily You* printed out from the dataline." It isn't that Cadigan's future is deliberately and weirdly retro. Google, Netflix, GPS satellite mapping, iPhones, Kindles, etc, weren't in existence in 1991, and even a dedicated extrapolater can miss parts of what's coming when it's driving at us at exponential speed. Some of this absence can be explained, though, as viral damage done to any distributed electronic system, and viruses of varying degrees of whimsy or malignity are Cadigan's chief contrivance, far-sighted for the time. (John Brunner had been there earlier, predicting computer worms in 1975's *The Shockwave Rider*, equally dense and also clotted with futuristic vernacular almost as jarring as Anthony Burgess's *A Clockwork Orange* from 1962.) Some is just fashion shock: Sam wears a self-built cybersystem inside an insulin pump, micro-powered by two leads run into her abdomen. One adult is aghast—"They never have put it over, never, never, *never*"—and won't look; wise old Fez explains, "She's right... Most people will reject anything that requires them to be a pin cushion." (Although brain implants, legal and otherwise, are commonplace in *Synners*.) The piercing fad was already spreading in earnest even as the book came out. Does this hazard, common to most sf written decades ago, invalidate *Synners*? No. It is one of our 101 best sf novels of the last quarter century precisely because Cadigan soaked its pages in a possible future realized so well that we read it now as much for the insight it offers into what *didn't* happen.

Sam is the legally-emancipated hacker daughter of virtual reality advertising/simulation designer Gabe Ludovic, a man increasingly addicted to the immersion thrills of his own scenarios while trapped in a decaying radioactive marriage. His employer, Diversifications, Inc., has just acquired small enterprise Eye-Traxx, whose sociopathic researcher Dr. Lindel Joslin is building living cortical implants a few molecules wide. These allow artificial realities as compelling as out-of-body experiences, as full immersion hallucinations. Meanwhile, Visual Mark and Gina are synners, synthesizers who mash image and sound into what the music audience craves now that the day of live performance is gone for good. This is the viral video clip straight from the unconscious, piped out of the toxed-up brain like a mélange, it seems, of Max Ernst and Lady Gaga.

> The texture of the stone shifted again; something seemed to part, like water, like veils, and he was looking *into* the stone, his sight traveling into the heart of the secret—
> The surface of the lake rippled again; more flashes of light, brighter, to the point of pain, hot needles driving into his head...
> And then he *was* out, floating away more weightless than weightless, consisting of less than the empty space between his dreams, as if everything that was himself had been distilled down to one pure thought.

An industrial espionage hack inadvertently uncovers much too much, leading to a rogue AI merging with a human upload, flinging these corporate honchos and zoned-out artists into uproar with law and the technological abyss. Yes, it is storytelling in the then-newish cyberpunk mode, but also the media corporate hysterics of Norman Spinrad's *Bug Jack Barron* (1969), two decades street-smarter. (Cadigan's famous in-your-face line is "If you can't fuck it, and it doesn't dance, eat it, *be* it, or throw it away.") A couple more decades on, it retains plenty of bite and propulsion, a nervy vision of a future that didn't quite happen, but might yet.

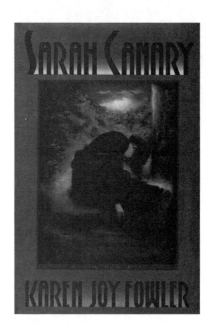

21: Karen Joy Fowler
Sarah Canary (1991)

IS **THIS** luminous, slyly funny, touching, memorable novel actually science fiction about alien first contact? Or is it perhaps a mystery with gothic overtones? Or a tale of vampirism, or feminism-inflected history cast as fable, or "slipstream" (like a seal or a mermaid, uneasily at home in two different media)? Obviously we consider it sf, and indeed a very great ornament to the mode of science fiction, as to American letters in general. But displaying here the subtle evidence for this assessment would require spoilers, which as that internet term self-explains would rather spoil the pleasure of tracing the story for yourself.

Fluent in Mandarin, German and English, as befits a student for the Imperial Examinations that select the lordly mandarin class of bureaucrats, Chin Ah Kin is an indentured worker laying track on the great railroads of 1870s' north-eastern USA. Not quite a slave, he has been abducted on board ship with a sack over his head, disembarked at New Orleans, and now toils, stranger in a strange land, in the region the Chinese know as Gold Mountain.

"In 1873, in the fir forest below Tacoma, Washington, a white woman with short black hair and a torn black dress stumbled into a Chinese railway workers' camp." Superstitious, like everyone in this novel, Chin takes her for one of the immortals, and seeks his bliss by taking care of her, at his uncle's instruction. Speechless, save for grunts, blurts and ululations, Sarah Canary gains her name from this deficit when she is finally delivered (after Chin has been arrested and forced to hang an Indian accused of rape, not the last brutality in this unsparing book) into the appalling lunatic asylum at Steilacoom, WA.

There they meet Dr. Carr, alienist, and his patient B.J.. A charmingly deranged young man uncertain of his own existence, B.J. is prey to perceptual distortions (again, like everyone else in the novel, though only he is labeled as mad). He sets the pair free and escapes with them in a picaresque, episodic, haphazard and entirely gratifying mission, leading to Sarah Canary's final transformation and disappearance.

Ugly, incommunicado, at home with birds but scarcely noticing the mostly devious humans she encounters, Sarah Canary is a projective screen upon which the hopes, lusts and terrors of everyone else are written. Is she literally an alien, in the science fictional sense—a being from another world, and therefore another species entirely? Certain scenes imply so, and as it happens Fowler herself considers this to be the case. Still, in postmodern mode, she warns us that interpretations of this sort must always remain, in the end, for each reader.

Her Wizard of Oz crew, in their madcap wanderings, gather in the ebullient Burke, a naturalist, and his associate Harold, who has purchased from Burke a dead mermaid, hideously ugly, which proves to be something else entirely. Finally they collect Miss Adelaide Dixon, suffragist and magnetic doctress, whose public addresses in support of free love and women's right to orgasm create just the kinds of ructions one anticipates in this brutal male environment at the edge of civilization.

Miss Dixon sees in Sarah Canary (both names are always given; she is never Sarah nor Miss Canary) the escaped murderess Lydia Palmer, whom she wishes to save. Harold, a man driven to a desperate belief in his own immortality by the horrors of the Civil War, pursues Sarah Canary under a sort of taxidermist impulse. She is one of science fiction's "women that men don't see," but women don't see her, either, probably because she is not a women but a creature from an entirely different realm than the familiar bisymmetry of the sexes.

Broken symmetries mark Sarah Canary and her oddly triumphant procession. The puzzle or koan is posed: Of what use is one wing to a bird? To a duck feigning injury, a great deal of use, faking-out any carnivores hungry for her chicks. What use is a single chopstick? Harold learns to his disadvantage, when he essays what 19th century sexist primness referred to as "female frailty," i.e. rape. (Such delicacy does not attend the dominant racism that asserts "Find a crime, hang a Chinaman," a dictum Chin must warily consider whenever he deals with the white demons and demonesses.) Chin sees the world as circles and straight lines, and the plot traces just such patterns, as if all these characters are acting out parts in a circus act. Indeed, from start to end the novel itches with fleas, not least in reports of a flea circus, its diminutive captives dressed as people. Is the human world just a flea circus to Sarah Canary and her own people? It is not impossible.

One recurrent note in this unsentimental book is sounded by Burke: "Let us have no lies between us…. No dissembling. No cunning. No deceit." Yet the story is built of little but cunning or clumsy deceit. It is the contrary of what Chin's ancient culture, for all its own sexism, deems the essence of civilization: *ren*, "the tolerance or benevolence a man felt toward others… the most fundamentally human quality. The ideogram was the same as the ideogram for *man*."

All of this zany, challenging tale is told in a voice beautifully suited to its many Emily Dickinson epigraphs. Adelaide Dixon, secluded with her alien charge above a hostelry of drunken, riotous men, observes that "the wind blew water across the window with a sound like a handful of pebbles thrown by a secret lover." B.J., too, finds semaphores in every random snap of a blanket in the wind. The world is written upon by messages that nobody else can decipher. "The moon came out again and the water on the window pearled against a background of black branches and black sky. Adelaide began to make black marks on the paper before her, marks that flew across the page like birds." Like, perhaps, Sarah Canary hatched like a pupa from her dress that heals itself, flown naked into a sky where nobody can see her. Except us, lucky readers, in imagination.

One of the key sf novels of this decade. Get it now!"
- Time Out

Winner of the James Tiptree Jr. Memorial Award
Nominated for the Arthur C. Clarke Award

22: Gwyneth Jones
White Queen (1991)
[The Aleutian Trilogy]

IN LEWIS Carroll's delirious *Through the Looking Glass*, the White Queen is a chess piece person who lives backwards in time (since she lives on the other side of the mirror), and easily believes six impossible things before breakfast. Gwyneth Jones's White Queen is Braemar Wilson, an aging British political revolutionary and trash media journalist of remarkable beauty, giving her *nom de guerre* to a movement opposed to an apparent colonialist alien invasion of Earth. Her beloved enemy is Johnny Guglioli, 28 year-old American eejay or engineering journalist, exiled to Africa, infected victim of a petrovirus that destroys the computing substrate "blue clay" dominant in 2038.

Johnny becomes the object of infatuation of a hermaphrodite alien from a generation ship stranded on orbit, "tall and slight, with a touch of coltish awkwardness as if she hadn't finished growing... and a dusky olive complexion that didn't absolutely rule out many nationalities." Plus what looks like a cruel disfiguration: the sunken absence of a nose, a harelip that reveals her canines. Despite this, most of those who see her in this West African town regard her as *La jolie-laide*—attractively ugly. Before long, s/he has reversed her knees, closed her hands into clawed pads, and is running like a wolf or perhaps a baboon. All this against a backdrop of the Eve wars—a gender conflict on a global scale—and the rise of a socialist USSA.

So this is not your average love story, not even for science fiction which has been familiar with sexual oddities since at least Philip José Farmer's *The Lovers* in 1952, where a man falls for a mimetic insect. The reverse mirroring of Carroll's *White Queen* is everywhere at work in this first volume of what would become the Aleutian Trilogy, where the second book, *North Wind* (1994) takes place a century or so after the first, and the third, *Phoenix Café* (1998), 300 years after the aliens made themselves known and eventually, effortlessly, colonized the disrupted nations and cultures of the world, before packing up and leaving, using a faster than light system devised by a human woman scientist.[12] It is not surprising, then, that *White Queen* shared the inaugural James Tiptree, Jr. award for sf and fantasy expanding or exploring the understanding of gender.

The threads of the story are many and hypercomplexly knitted, and for a long time it is almost impossible to unravel who is who, or why. Most of the characters are confused about each other—not just their motives, which is always rather mysterious in any serious novel, but their very nature. That's because Jones is undermining identity, nature and nurture from the outset. The trilogy is not just a headlong postmodern work of art; it's a *poststructural* construct. But don't let that put you off.

Since the 1940s, science fiction has worked the same way you best learn language and customs—by being immersed in a culture, as a child learns. Faux-sf, by contrast, operates the way school children used to learn French or Latin, arduously memorizing tables of vocabulary and grammar. Gwyneth Jones uses almost pure immersion, a method pioneered in Fred Pohl's and Cyril Kornbluth's *Wolfbane* (1959, revised 1986) and Frank Herbert's *Whipping Star* (1970) and *The Dosadi Experiment* (1977). You sink or swim. This is either baffling and frustrating or exhilarating, especially in the first half of *White Queen* where there is very little hand-holding. Oddly, in the two sequels Jones is far more forgiving, perhaps because she is obliged to use traditional infodumps to bring forgetful or new readers up to speed quickly. Usefully, she has published a remarkably detailed and fascinating account of how she developed the background to the trilogy, and if readers start drifting or getting seasick they might consider turning to this essay, "Aliens in the Fourth Dimension." Perhaps the key to these novels of identities and affiliations turned on their heads and then sideways is Jones's critical postulate:

> I wanted my aliens to represent an alternative. I wanted them to say to my readers it ain't necessarily so. History is not inevitable, and neither is sexual gender as we know it an inevitable part of being human.... I planned to give my alien conquerors the characteristics, all the supposed deficiencies, that Europeans came to see in their subject races in darkest Africa and the mystic East—"animal" nature, irrationality, intuition; mechanical incompetence, indifference to time, helpless aversion to theory and measurement: and I planned to have them win the territorial battle this time. It was no coincidence, for my purposes, that the same list of qualities or deficiencies—a nature closer to the animal, intuitive communication skills and all the rest of it—were and still are routinely awarded to women... the human world over.[13]

The "intuitive communication" of the Aleutians, mistaken for telepathy, is a sharing of microscopic airborne packets of information gradually suffusing the world, augmented by grooming and gobbling "vermin"—the wanderers that summarize each alien's current state of mind and history. These unisexed people give birth to offspring

---

12 A superb short analysis of this third volume, by feminist critic and publisher L. Timmel Duchamp, is at: *http://ltimmel.home.mindspring.com/phoenix.html*

13 *http://homepage.ntlworld.com/gwynethann/ALIENS.htm*

that reincarnate one of some three million genotypes that have persisted forever, but with constant updates that provide a sort of Lamarckian evolution. This bold postulate is milked for all it's worth in a formidable display of science fictional creativity. Luckily, Jones is a masterful writer; as Kathleen Bartholomew notes, "Her prose is etched in silvered glass, with acid: it is hard and bright and sharp, and it smokes." Here is an example, where Johnny is traumatically raped by Clavel, his alien poet stalker:

> The naked chicken-skin baboon crouched over him. It took his hand and buried it to the wrist in a fold that opened along its groin. The chasm inside squirmed with life. Part of its wall swelled, burgeoning outward.... Something slid out of the fold: an everted bag of raw flesh, narrowing to a hooked end.

Science fiction as challenge—as exploration of otherness—has never been more confronting.

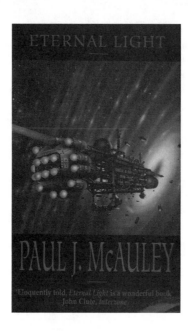

23: Paul McAuley
Eternal Light (1991)
[Four Hundred Billion Stars Trilogy]

THERE MUST have been something special added to the water consumed at science fiction conventions circa 1980, a laggardly, relatively unexciting time in the field. Or perhaps, as in John Wyndham's *The Midwich Cuckoos*, a generation earlier some visiting aliens tampered with a batch of human embryos. Or could a fallen meteor possibly have kickstarted an evolutionary leap among those who came in contact with it, as Philip Jose Farmer postulated for his *Wold Newton* stories? In any case, these fanciful explanations might not be strictly necessary to account for the burst of Hard Sf writers that came to fresh prominence around this time. We might just call it the zeitgeist, and let it go at that. Something similar would happen a generation later, with such figures as Alastair Reynolds and Peter Hamilton, indicating a mysterious cyclic and emergent process fruitfully and forever at work at the heart of the genre.

First to arise in this earlier renaissance wave was Charles Sheffield. He was quickly joined by John Stith, Roger MacBride Allen, Paul Cook, Colin Greenland and Paul McAuley. Their work took off from ancestors such as Larry Niven and Poul Anderson, bringing fresh possibilities to the subgenre of technologically rigorous yet mind-blowing sf.

In the current landscape, Sheffield is gone, deceased too young, and Cook, Allen, Greenland and Stith have either fallen silent or departed the high-profile mainstream of publishing. But happily, Paul McAuley remains at the top of his game, an acknowledged master. His first novel and its two sequels, especially the third book for which this entry is named, betokened his burgeoning talent to all who were paying attention at the time.

Four Hundred Billion Stars possesses a Stapledonian title somewhat at odds with its Michael Bishop innards. In a galactic scenario where mankind, despite 600 years of interstellar activity, remains precariously enthroned at best, Dorthy Yoshida, astronomer and telepath, is sent to a benighted, artificially jiggered planet, P'thrsn, where a small group of fellow human researchers is intent on unriddling the ancient enigmas concealed by the seemingly savage sophonts. In a manner somewhat reminiscent of—yet decidedly less trippy than—Robert Silverberg's *Downward to the Earth*, she makes immersive mental contact with the natives and notches up a victory toward the survivability of our species.

Of the Fall was a minor, lateral extension of this future history. Set earlier in the galactic backstory, on the colony world Elysium, the book conflated elements of Heinlein's *The Moon is a Harsh Mistress* and any of Poul Anderson's Polesotechnic novels, such as *War of the Wing Men*. Hidden beneath excess plottage at its core, a perennial sf sentiment: "Knowledge is an abstraction won from the whirling chaos of the universe, neither constant nor concrete."

Bouncing back from Elysium's tedium—without wasting these backstory tidbits—and rejoining the sharply delineated and appealing Dorthy Yoshida in a new culminative adventure proved the winning stroke to signal McAuley's expansion of his prowess.

Eternal Light begins with an astrophysical action passage surely meant to recall the famous start of Doc Smith's *Triplanetary*. Smith: "Two thousand million or so years ago two galaxies were colliding; or, rather, were passing through each other. A couple of hundreds of millions of years either way do not matter, since at least that much time was required for the interpassage." McAuley: "It began when the shock wave of a nearby supernova tore apart the red supergiant sun of the Alea home system, forcing ten thousand family nations to abandon their world and search for new homes among the packed stars of the Galaxy's core." And although McAuley's updating of the Smithian paradigm is notably short on ravening particle rays and giant vacuum tubes, it nonetheless hews to the spirit of wide-eyed space opera, albeit tinged with more ethical nuance and sophistication, thus setting a template in the field for future works.

Yoshida, still reeling from the half-understood revelations received on P'thrsn about the Alea, mankind's enemy, is kidnapped by Duke Talbeck Barlstilkin, one of the Golden, or near-immortal human elite. They embark on a mission with many others of various persuasions on a big ship to a rogue star and accompanying planet hurtling toward Earth at a sizable fraction of lightspeed. There, Barlstilkin suspects more information on the Alea will be found, with Dorthy's help. Travelling separately in a small ship is Suzy Falcon, ex-fighter pilot eager to wreak revenge on the aliens, and her companion, an artist named Robot. When all these factions are plunged through a wormhole to the very center of the Galaxy, where the ancient enemy of the Alea lurk, they must undergo a mental and physical odyssey of enlightenment.

McAuley's foray into what we might think of nowadays as patented Gregory Benford territory (Entry 41) also benefits from its flavors of Frank Herbert's *Dune* sequence, homages to Samuel Delany's seminal *Nova*, and even a few sprinkles of Zelazny's cavalier, black-souled immortals in the portrait of Barlstilkin. The dense sensory tangibility of the various venues (although surprisingly limited for most space operas) contribute to the impact of the book, as do the portraits of Suzy and Dorthy as pawns (specifically, female pawns) who manage to achieve high degrees of freedom and self-actuation. A touching and surprising emotional coda rounds out the book's virtues.

The majestic long-term, wonder-inspiring perspectives of the book, squeezed down into the realtime adventures of the cast, are summarized by Professor Gunasekra when he says, "If more people understood the time scale on which the processes of the macrouniverse operate, we should not be a species blown up with hubris."

Science fiction as a guide to an easygoing confident humility and sense of one's true embedded place in the scheme of creation. That's McAuley's vision in a nutshell.

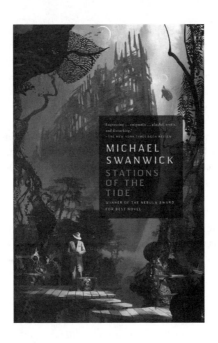

24: Michael Swanwick
Stations of the Tide (1991)

❝ THE BUREAUCRAT fell from the sky."

Miranda, where he lands, is a world on the edge of cataclysm as precession swings its poles. The ice melts, drowning most of its land ecology under the centenary Jubilee Tides, threatening the colonist humans. Evolution has pre-adapted most of the world's creatures to this cyclical calamity, so that birds and animals can morph into marine form. Perhaps the fabled native indigenes, the haunts, do so as well. As the geological crisis nears, troops from the orbitals gather the locals in readiness for evacuation. Crowd violence is poised on a hair trigger. Precious artifacts are removed, and what can't be saved is smashed or burned. The mood is one of carnival, an extended *Día de los Muertos*, a frenzied Day of the Dead. Hunting for an item of forbidden technology in this forcibly and resentfully primitive culture, the bureaucrat harrows a kind of hell in a landscape of convulsive transformation.

Throughout the book, this nondescript bureaucrat, a representative of the orbital Division of Technology Transfer, remains nameless, but by no means juiceless and anonymous. Attended by his nano-maker briefcase-cum-AI, he takes on shifting roles as he crosses the world Miranda in the Prospero system. Is he himself Shakespeare's magician Prospero, from *The Tempest,* or is that the (perhaps phony) magician Gregorian, whom he seeks? The briefcase might as well be named Ariel; an information system is called Trinculo, a jester from that play. Maybe Gregorian is, rather, Caliban, roaring out his desire to rape the planet Miranda. Or is the bureaucrat a suffering, post-modern and ambiguous Jesus—taught Tantric sex by a superb, tattooed Magdalene, Undine—dragging his crucifix through 14 Stations of the Cross told in the novel's 14 tidal chapters, to his final transformation? Or perhaps a potential Judas—or indeed Satan banished and fallen from heaven—ready to betray his own kind? Gregorian, meanwhile, was born of a virgin surrogate mother, fathered by a man from the celestial Puzzle Palace... another contorted hint.

Swanwick is himself a magician of words and images, setting traps and betraying our expectations. His first story was the accomplished "Ginungagap," when he was 30; his second novel *Vacuum Flowers* mixed space opera with cyberpunk, and later he won applause for *The Iron Dragon's Daughter* and *Jack Faust,* all splendid inventions. Here he brews a hallucinogenic recipe, intensely vivid, baffling, but intoxicating. In *Stations of the Tide*, which won 1992's Nebula and Locus awards for best novel, nothing holds still for long. People readily move their point of awareness into skeletal surrogate bodies, and can fracture their minds into agents that impersonate them, act on their behalf, are absorbed back and extinguished. When an agent of the blockaded colony mind Earth is met, it is something out of Milton and Swift, an authentically monstrous manifestation in virtual reality:

> The encounter space was enormously out of scale, a duplicate of those sheds where airships were built, structures so large that water vapor periodically formed clouds near the top and filled the interior with rain. It was taken up by a single naked giant.
> Earth.
> She crouched on all fours, more animal than human, huge, brutish, and filled with power.... Her limbs were shackled and chained, crude visualizations of the more subtle restraints and safeguards that kept her forever on the fringes of the system.

This vast, sweat-stinking, musky monster is a figure familiar from psychoanalysis: the archaic Mother, a sort of feral female phallic force, more mythic than misogynistic in Swanwick's making. And like that clammy image from post-Freudian analysis, complete with vagina dentata, it invites the bureaucrat into its mouth. In the overwhelming presence of an Earth utterly overborne by technology out of control, he asks the agent:

> "What do you want from us?"
> In that same lifeless tone she replied, "What does any mother want from her daughters? I want to help you. I want to give you advice. I want to reshape you into my own image. I want to lead your lives, eat your flesh, grind your corpses, and gnaw the bones."

It is the childhood terror of Hansel and Gretel, of Jack and the Beanstalk giant. More explicitly, Earth demands: "Free the machines." Terrified, these augmented humans must keep their ancient parent shackled if hardly powerless. The center of this novel is the power, the sexy lure (the novel is drenched in sex, often perverse), and the dangers of high technology. Such forebodings are not fanciful, considering our prospects perhaps only a generation away from nanotechnology, artificial intelligence, machine interfaces and human modification. Grimm's fairy tales caught the rural voices of the nineteenth century and earlier. Do they work now in a world remade by science? Well, we carry our history with us, tucked away inside our narratives and nightmares. Will our descendents be human?

That's a question sf has posed in one form or another for decades, and is increasingly salient. Swanwick acknowledges as much in sly borrowings scattered throughout the tale, references to classic stories by Brian W. Aldiss ("Even as his body hit the waters of the fjord, it began to change. A flurry of foam marked some sort of painful struggle beneath the surface"—from "A Kind of Artistry"), the golden cyborg body of the transformed woman Deirdre in Catherine Moore's "No Woman Born," and figures from hard-edge poetry like Ted Hughes' Crow. A key resonance is Gene Wolfe's marvelous *The Fifth Head of Cerberus,* with its shapeshifting, mysterious aborigines. Missing these tips of the hat to the past won't spoil the story, but Swanwick's risotto blends many ingredients and flavors, from the Bible to Shakespeare and Milton all the way into Vernor Vinge's Singularity, even anticipating Charles Stross's wildly inventive post-human futures. The book is a delightful and disturbing confection, reaching at once into the past and the future, and yet entirely itself, like Swanwick's talent.

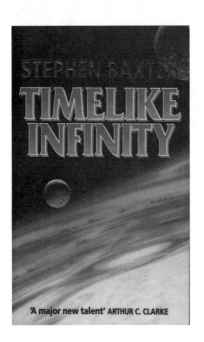

'A major new talent' ARTHUR C. CLARKE

25: Stephen Baxter
Timelike Infinity (1992)
[Xeelee Sequence]

RECALLING THE advent of A. E. van Vogt, Robert Heinlein and other stalwarts of sf's Golden Age in the 1940s, Stephen Baxter arrived with a bang—and at first his style and characterization were equally rudimentary. That did not matter much because, like those North Americans, this British newcomer half a century on was an instant master of mind-boggling ideas, throwing out sparkling Catherine wheels of wild notions that convulse the imagination. It was less important that his first novel, *Raft,* was stodgily told than that it was the tale of someone from our recognizable universe abruptly flung into another, where the force of gravity is a billion times as strong. What would *that* be like? With a Cambridge degree in mathematics and a PhD in engineering, Baxter *knew* what it would be like because he worked through the problem, just as the old-fashioned sf masters had. And his advantage was computers to help with the calculations, and spectacular new science in the journals, waiting to be used.

By his second novel, *Timelike Infinity,* his styling was improved, but what held readers' astonished attention was the scale of his declared ambition. The book plunged into the deep immensity of its title, and heralded a sequence (not yet completed) that reaches from the Big Bang birth of the universe to its guttering and death. For Olaf

Stapledon, in *First and Last Men* and *Star Maker*, the history of humankind was many millions of years long but merely a chapter against the dark background of the cosmos. Stephen Baxter ventured upon an updated version but with a cast of characters, human and otherwise, that were increasingly well rendered.

Baxter's role for humanity starts just as humblingly, with the species crushed into subservience by the first alien species we encounter (the Squeem) in A.D. 4874, after thousands of bright, hopeful years protected from aging by AntiSenescence technology. The Squeem are bested, but a second alien species (the Qax, in their Spline living starships) occupies Earth. Jasoft Parz, once a wannabe rebel, is now the aging and compliant ambassador to the Qax Governor. A millennium and a half earlier, Michael Poole is designer of an exotic tetrahedral wormhole mouth that will be hauled from Jupiter space by the near-lightspeed GUTship *Cauchy,* to serve as a time gate. When this Interface is returned 1500 years later to occupied Earth, it allow the escape to the past of Poole's fellow designer, Miriam Berg, and a group of ideologues, the Friends of Wigner, who hope to shape the future in humanity's image by manipulating a conjectured Quantum Observer at the far end of time.

The Qax, like the Squeem, are defeated, but humankind falls once more before a third alien species, the Xeelee near-gods and their nightfighters. A ferocious million year war finally sees the Xeelee victorious—but still under threat in turn. While the Friends of Wigner had hoped to shape the participatory universe—becoming, as van Vogt would put it, "masters of the Sevagram"—Baxter's sequence of novels and short stories does not permit so comforting a fable of human exceptionalism. Nor, indeed, of the victory of any kind of life we would understand. That fate is reserved, as we learn in a sequel, *The Ring,* for dark matter photino entities able to reset the thermostats of all the stars in the universe, rapidly aging them to a dull red simmer that will persist for trillions of years. In their cozy cores, photino entities will endure, untroubled by supernovas and gammas ray bursters, to the very ends of timelike infinity.

This cosmological drama is implicit in the very shape of Baxter's stories. Time twists and loops, boiling with causality stresses, from the return to the solar system of the time-dilated wormhole tunnel at the start of *Timelike Infinity* to the immense engineering feat that contorts a cosmic string into a gateway a thousand light years across, spun up to nearly the speed of light. This Ring, or gravitational Great Attractor, is not the work of puny humans. It's a colossal undertaking extending five billion years into the past, the greatest achievement of the Xeelee. Their goal is to preserve baryonic life—the kind built, like us, from quarks and electrons—against the depredations of the incomprehensibly strange alien photino birds. Since the Xeelee Baryonic Lords can't prevail in our universe, they mean to escape to a more hospitable zone, or perhaps rewrite history so their foe is already defeated in the remote past. It was not a new idea in science fiction, but Baxter engaged its complexities with the attack of a late 20th century van Vogt:

> The battered, scorched corpse of the Spline warship… emerged from the collapsing wormhole into the Qax Occupation Era at close to the speed of light. Shear energy from the tortured spacetime of the wormhole transformed into high-frequency radiation, into showers of short-lived, exotic particles which showered around the tumbling Spline.
>
> It was like a small sun exploding amid the moons of Jupiter. Vast storms were evoked in the bulk of the gas giant's atmosphere. A moon was destroyed.

Humans were killed, blinded.

Cracks in shattering spacetime propagated at the speed of light…

Quantum functions flooded over Michael Poole like blue-violet rain, restoring him to time. He gasped at the pain of rebirth.

Poole is destined at last to see the extinction of all stars, all matter in our cosmos—to be the last human witnessing the death of the universe. Like his mentor and later collaborator, Arthur C. Clarke (*Light of Other Days,* the *Time Odyssey* sequence), Baxter is playing for keeps.

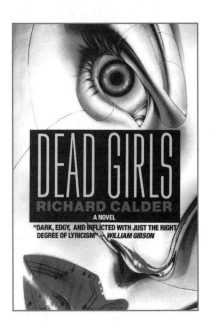

26: Richard Calder
Dead Girls (1992)
[Dead Girls Trilogy]

IN OUR contemporary world of twelve-year-old killers and sixteen-year-old supermodels (who work in a field where burnout hits by age twenty), it takes little extrapolative power to forecast a future even more skewed toward the commodification of youth and beauty, sex and death. But to tease from such bare extrapolations their most outrageous implications, then to embody the theory in believable characters moving through an ultra-tangible world seen through a scrim of gorgeous, supercharged prose the likes of which sf has seldom enjoyed— Ah, that takes the perverse genius of a Richard Calder.

Calder's first novel was the astonishing *Dead Girls*, in which we are introduced to two adolescents of a decaying future: Ignatz Zwatz and his doll-girl Primavera. In the next century a rogue nanoplague—escaped from android sex toys—now feasts among humanity, transforming all the female children of its tainted male carriers into sterile dolls: half-organic, half-"quantum-magical" succubae. Plainly, should all young females be born dolls, humanity will be extinct. Interspecies war is declared, countries are ravaged, economies collapse, niche-life blooms. Narrated by Ignatz, a smitten traitor to his race, *Dead Girls* is a helter-skelter eroticizing of *Peter Pan*, a cinematic barrage of strange emotions and outré images.

The sequel, *Dead Boys,* carries forward the tale with all of the wild-eyed obsessional hysteria of its predecessor. Yet it's a more cloistered, less expansive book, suffering a bit from "middle-itis."

Primavera is now a truly dead "dead girl," her ravaged CPU womb literally kept in a bottle by the despondent Ignatz, as drug and talisman. Through the wormhole womb Ignatz's unborn daughter, Vanity St. Viridiana, sends messages from the future, attempting to remake the past. The artificial Elohim—the dead boys of the title—now make their appearance as Inquisitorial persecutors of the dead girls. As Ignatz falls deeper into the womb-spell, past, present and future become inextricably tangled, until history goes "nonlinear." His very identity is usurped by that of a dead boy, Dagon. The book ends on what seem to be "the last bars of reality's finale."

What is most missed in *Dead Boys* is Primavera's presence, not really compensated for by her sketched-in daughter. Also, the entropy of this scenario is so thick that the Asian atmosphere—so rich in the first book (Calder himself is long and intimately conversant with Thailand)—becomes skeletal.

However, with its high-calorie, mucilaginous mix of Egyptology and Jack the Ripper, Nabokov and Beardsley, flesh and metaphysics, the first two books croon like Nine Inch Nails covering nostalgic music-hall ballads.

Dead Things is the capstone to the trilogy, and reveals a very intelligible path and destination laid out, not always apparent to naïve readers from the start.

The first book was certainly the most straightforward and "normal," capable of being read almost exclusively—albeit too simply—as gorgeously bejeweled cyberpunk, an objective correlative to our contemporary sexual hangups. With the second, Calder's mimetic universe shattered. Quantum-level tamperings inherent in the CPU wombs of the Cartier androids fractionated time and space, producing a certain line of history in which our lovable lad Ignatz Zwatz became Dagon the Elohim, slaughterer of the doll-girls he once adored, and slave to a plague known as Meta, defined thus in *Dead Things*: "Meta is a psychosomatic disorder which affects, not just those who possess the disorder, but everything they perceive. It affects the fabric of space and time itself. Meta is all."

As *Dead Things* opens, Meta still holds full sway, and has for the thousand years of Dagon's bloody life. He remembers nothing of his existence as Ignatz, except perhaps the vaguest subliminal stirrings. But all that is about to change. Captured by the last survivors of the old paradigm and forcibly re-educated about the origins of his Meta-dominated multiverse, Ignatz must swallow The Reality Bomb, then detonate himself at the Omphalos of the continua in order to restore non-Meta health to existence. But the exact nature of the baseline reality is one final surprise left in Calder's bag of tricks, a revelation that adds both more humanity and less cosmic importance to the trilogy.

Of course, all this convoluted plot—which might just as well be derived from any van Vogt novel—is hardly the main reason to read Calder. In all three volumes, what we are lusting after is the brilliantly corrupt baroque inflections of his text, the leering gloss he provides on everything from superheroes to Grail Quests; Krazy Kat to Gnosticism; Wonderbras to the French Revolution; Xena, Warrior Princess, to Poe. Reading *Dead Things* is like having an imp-sized George Bernard Shaw or Oscar Wilde sitting on your shoulder and regaling you with cynical witticisms as you watch all five hundred cable channels simultaneously.

There was a feeling in this book that Calder had indeed exhausted these particular obsessions of his in this particular manner. Where he ventured from here proved that his talent could open just about any rococo door he chose.

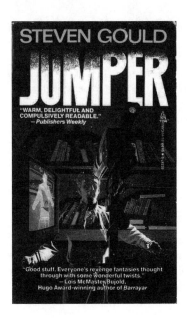

27: Steven Gould
Jumper (1992)

S F AUTHOR Rudy Rucker (Entry 91), who does a lot of critical thinking about the nature of the genre, has given us a very useful specialized literary term with the introduction of "power chord" to our vocabulary. By this musical analogy, Rucker is referring to the massive, Wagnerian tropes that are at the center of our field, signature concepts so freighted with accreted meaning—starflight, aliens, time travel—that merely to strum them is to invoke something majestic and powerful. But of course, the writer gets no subsequent free ride for merely plunking out such heavy-metal notes, but must ably follow up the initial strumming with a maestro's flair.

Teleportation is one such leitmotif, whether achieved mechanically or organically. As a special ability inherent in the mutant human body, the trope is especially impactful, conferring on the possessor great power and great responsibility, to use the famous Stan Lee linkage, and appealing to mythic daydreams of most readers. The history of the genre is rich with stimulating instances (although, curiously enough, not as many stories as are devoted to telepathy and other mental quirks), most notably Alfred Bester's *The Stars My Destination*, a masterpiece which has probably deterred more over-awed writers than it has encouraged.

But Steven Gould proved ready for the challenge of beating Bester at his own game, and in his debut novel no less. Although Gould limited himself to depicting a lone teleporter, and not a whole society of them, he nevertheless codified this wild talent in such a masterful, concrete, vivid, exciting fashion as to lay down the gold standard for any future writers looking to harp upon this particular power chord.

Gould's achievement represents the brilliant intertwining of two strands of story: the strictly personal, mimetic, "human-interest" plot, and the rigorously speculative yet fabulist development of the quasi-magical power of "jumping." This fusion harkens to the ideal definition of a work of science fiction, where naturalistic fidelity and speculative ideation go hand in hand. In reality, neither strand can be separated from the other, without destroying the book, but it helps the discussion to consider them separately in this somewhat artificial distinction.

First, the human dynamic. First-person narrator Davy Rice is seventeen years old at the start of the book, and his voice is pitch-perfect (although occasionally a little of the inter-teen dialogue is creaky). Davy exhibits the quintessential adolescent mix of bravado and fear, overconfidence and trepidation, optimism and nihilism, insight and blindness, knowledge and ignorance that would be predicated, given his unusual upbringing. Knocked down yet eager to battle on, to survive and flourish, he follows a unique course of action that is utterly believable given his deftly sketched personality and history. Likewise, Davy's father and mother emerge as fully rounded human beings, not mere game pieces. Millie, Davy's girlfriend, stands forth as similarly multidimensional, especially in her reactions to learning Davy's secret. Gould's anatomization of how society works shows deep, mature understanding as well. Given all this, if one could, impossibly, remove the "jumping" from the book, a coherent and well-done novel would remain.

But to add in the teleportation is to raise the story to its science-fictional acme. Subject to clinically defined abuse from his father, Davy learns under this stress that he can teleport. He reacts with caution and disbelief at first. (Taken into account by Davy is the meta-knowledge about such things derived from real literary works such as Stephen King's *Firestarter*, and, yes, the Bester book, a factor often neglected in sf and fantasy novels.) But once he determines the reality of his situation, he proceeds in a manner, not without mistakes, that fulfills both the daydreams and nightmares of the reader. Without once succumbing to easy and indulgent "Mary Sue" self-identification, Gould nonetheless inhabits Davy's voyage of discovery intimately, making the miraculous process so real and logical, consorting so well with a physics paradigm, that the reader is convinced that such a wild talent could only be investigated and exploited in the very fashion Gould outlines.

Gould's prose—Davy's voice—is sharp and complex and flavorful, without being mannered or idiosyncratic or dense. The narrative has that legendary Heinlein verisimilitude and affability so often imitated but seldom duplicated. The quick cuts between physical locales that are the very hallmark of teleportation are handled brilliantly, so that the reader feels simultaneously whipsawed yet grounded.

When the book moves into thriller territory—Davy conceives revenge upon the Islamic terrorists who killed his mother, and thus runs afoul of the USA's National Security Agency as well—some of the quotidian domesticity of the novel is lost. But the thriller mechanics—a little prescient of the *X-Men* movie franchise—are ably manipulated, and Davy's actions up the ante in a way that had to happen, unless Gould had improbably chosen to detour into some kind of minimalist *Dying Inside* cul-de-sac.

The sequel, *Reflex*, very competently and entertainingly extends Davy's and Millie's story, which, alas, is not the case with the reboot volume, *Jumper: Griffin's Story*, composed as a movie tie-in. But the initial thrills of Davy's wild talent epiphany, and the blossoming out of his powers, are fully delivered in the first superior volume, a landmark of its kind.

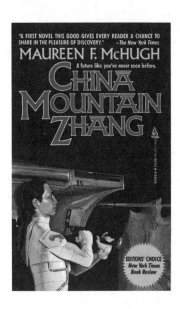

"A FIRST NOVEL THIS GOOD GIVES EVERY READER A CHANCE TO
SHARE IN THE PLEASURE OF DISCOVERY." —*The New York Times*

MAUREEN F. McHUGH

A future like you've never seen before.

CHINA
MOUNTAIN
ZHANG

EDITORS' CHOICE
*New York Times
Book Review*

28: Maureen McHugh
China Mountain Zhang (1992)

ONE WONDERS precisely how Maureen McHugh feels about her accomplished first novel, a hard-hitting, elegant hybrid of mimetic and speculative modes, some twenty years after its publication, given that the broad premise of its somewhat dystopian future (dystopian, that is, from the American perspective) seems closer to fulfillment than ever. Is she proud of her uncanny prophetic vision, or dismayed at her Cassandra-like status? After all, her book's monitory message stayed under the culture's radar for two decades. Whatever the author's extra-literary sentiments, she can continue to be pleased with the fine literary quality of this striking debut.

Fictional forecasts of what was seen as America's imminent, nasty and assuredly well-deserved doom probably first materialized about twenty-four hours after the founding of the nation. Popular during the late Sixties (see Norman Spinrad's 1970 story "The Lost Continent"), such deliciously self-flagellating depictions of decline remain in vogue today, as witness the masterful novel *Julian Comstock* by Robert Charles Wilson. McHugh's book falls midway along the timeline between Spinrad and Wilson, and identifies a threat to the USA little acknowledged at the time of the novel's composition.

Our main protagonist, China Mountain Zhang (Zhang Zhong Shan), twenty-six-years old at novel's outset, is a gay man, half Chinese, half Latino, living in New York City in the tail end of the twenty-first century and laboring as a construction worker. Zhang's decrepit, stunted USA has undergone a "Second Depression" and socialist revolution, the Cleansing Winds period, and is entirely in thrall to the Chinese hegemony. Zhang must hide both his sexuality and mulatto nature to get ahead in conformance with Chinese prejudices. But in the opening section of the novel (all portions embrace vivid first-person narration), all his dissembling comes to naught, as a curious non-sexual affair with his boss's daughter blows up in his face, and he finds himself unemployed.

We next inhabit the viewpoint of Angel, a female kite rider in the futuristic sport favored by Zhang as spectator, involving aerial competitions with advanced hang-glider-type technology where the riders cybernetically jack into their crafts. Returning to Zhang's life, we find him desperately taking a job at a research station at Baffin Island near the Arctic Circle, hoping that the "hazardous duty" perks involving an educational stipend will allow him to advance. The next contrasting vignette involves Martine, a middle-aged woman settler on Mars.

Zhang returns, a student at Nanjing University, maturing and suffering at the intersection of illicit love and society's imperatives. Alexi, Martine's husband back on Mars, offers our next sidebar, before we encounter Zhang in post-grad mode, sophisticating his native skills. Catching up, four years on, with his old New York City boss's daughter, San-xiang, provides insights into the problems of the ruling class. Finally, Zhang returns to New York, dallies for a time with old lover Peter, begins teaching, and, at the book's broad-ended conclusion, finds his future wide-open and beckoning, in contrast to the stymied dead-end vision of his youth. A true journey's end, but also merely the first step on a longer path.

McHugh's novel walks a beautiful tightrope between cyberpunk and humanist modes, leaning ultimately more toward the latter side. True, her techno-socio-political speculations and gritty/gleaming world-building are top notch, in the Sterling-Gibson manner. This contrasting portrait of China with the USA's condition is typical.

In New York [thinks Zhang] I ride a subway system built sometime in the 1900's, here buses segment and flow off in different directions. There's a city above the city, a lacework super-structure that supports thousands of four-tower living units and work complexes like the University complex we live in… and there's food here I've never seen or heard of, from Australia and South America and Africa, at outrageous prices. Everyone here seems rich.

But such touches take a back seat to character development, the bildungsroman nature of the tale. The reader's primary interest always resides in Zhang's muddled course through life's minefields, as he acquires more and more tools with which to carve out a life for himself, coming to recognize his flaws, remedying what he can and accepting the rest. It's a primal journey that provides strong hooks into the reader's affections and sympathies.

With its multiple viewpoints and slice-of-life concerns, McHugh's novel harks to an infrequently sampled but distantly admired landmark of an earlier generation, Thomas Disch's urban and urbane *334*. Echoes of fragments of Samuel Delany's "We, in Some Strange Power's Employ, Move on a Rigorous Line" and "Time Considered as a Helix of Semi-Precious Stones" also intrude their presence. Stripped of any surrealism or epistemological weirdness, McHugh also somehow owes a debt to Philip K. Dick and his focus on the "little man." This is one of those rare sf novels where neither war nor espionage, neither mortality nor crime, neither paradigm shifts nor transcendence serve as plot engines. Instead, in accordance with Ursula K. Le Guin's famous essay, "Science Fiction and Mrs. Brown," we inhabit deeply an average soul, and in so doing share what Zhang characterizes as an "inner light" resident in us all.

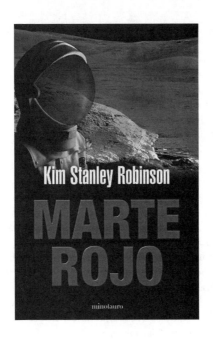

Kim Stanley Robinson
MARTE ROJO
minotauro

29: Kim Stanley Robinson
Red Mars (1992)
[Mars Trilogy]

TO UNDERSTAND the nature and scope and thrust of Robinson's much-admired, diamond-hard *Mars* books, it's first necessary to get past one major shibboleth: the word "infodump." In an interview, Terry Bisson said: "Someone once described your Mars books as an infodump tunneled by narrative moles. I think it was a compliment. What do you think?" Robinson replied:

> No, not a compliment. I reject the word "infodump" categorically [...and] I reject "expository lump" also, which... are attacks on the idea that fiction can have any kind of writing included in it. It's an attempt to say "fiction can only be stage business" which is a stupid position.... [T]he world is interesting beyond our silly stage business. So "exposition" creeps in. What is it anyway? It's just another kind of narrative.... And in science fiction, you need some science sometimes; and science is expository; and so science fiction without exposition is like science fiction without science, and we have a lot of that, but it's not good.

This forceful demand for unhindered access to a full complement of writerly tools is no mere crochet on Robinson's part, but a radical stance that would allow him to craft a big bold story on the widest possible canvas, a work utterly new and contemporary that paradoxically employed some of sf's oldest, almost Gernsbackian methodologies.

The *Mars* trilogy-plus-one is the late twentieth century's equivalent of *War and Peace* by Leo Tolstoy, immense (more than 2600 pages), full of solid research deployed to illuminate historical forces and the specialness of a chosen time and place, made vivid by supportive storylines employing a large troupe of actors. In Robinson's case, of course, his history hasn't yet happened, so facts had to be supplemented with informed speculation, and he could not utilize actual personages. Nonetheless, his Mars sequence has about it the tactility and complex realism of history, and could almost serve as a blueprint for some NASA return to space (although its emphasis on partnering with the Russians and the Japanese might have to be updated with references to Chinese and Hindu partners). More crucially, these chronicles of the future are what cultural theorist Fredric Jameson, Robinson's postmodern Marxist mentor, would call *dialectical history*—not a typical sf celebration of raw technology, but a contestatory, painful journey toward a plausible utopia.

Red Mars opens in the year 2026 and finds its focus with John Boone, the first man to step on that alien world, soon murdered, and his close companions,. the "First Hundred" settlers. Ensconced on a planet hostile to life, coping with harsh conditions and already fracturing into rival parties, they split into those who wish to terraform the planet (the Greens, led by Sax Russell), those who wish to leave it as pristine as possible (the Reds, led by Ann Clayborne), and Areophanists who hope for an entirely new way of Martian life.

A revolution in 2061 undoes many of their programs, bringing down the great skyhook or areosynchronous cable 37,000 kilometers long, 10 meters across, untethered from its asteroid anchor so that it lashes down around the equator of the world:

> The cable was now exploding on impact... and sending sheets of molten ejecta into the sky, lava-esque fireworks that arced up into their dawn twilight, and were dim and black by the time they fell back to the surface.... The second time around the speed of the fall would accelerate to 21,000 kilometers an hour, he said, almost six kilometers a second; so that for anyone within sight of it—a dangerous place to be, deadly if you were not up on a prominence and many kilometers away—it would look like a kind of meteor strike, and cross from horizon to horizon in less than a second. Sonic booms to follow.... Clips shot from the night side surface were spectacular; they showed a blazing curved line, cutting down like the edge of a white scythe that was trying to chop the planet in two.

Robinson does not fail to turn an eye toward the unstable situation back on Earth, ruled by corrupt, corporate transnationals, which mostly intend to strip Mars of its resources. But progress proves inevitable.

Green Mars chronicles the transitional period where the fourth planet is first able to host unprotected plant life. A soletta, a huge delicate cone of mirrors 10,000 kilometers across, hangs between Mars and Sun, focusing extra sunlight for heat and power. Infalling ice asteroids fill the basins with renewed oceans and rivers that support a new biosphere, thickening the atmosphere. Interference from Earth continues, until the home world's own problems overwhelm the old hegemony. Drastic life extension technologies devised on Mars allow the early settlers to remain youthful for many decades, personally embodying their ideological and political concerns into a rapidly changing future for the once-red planet.

After a second revolution, and in preparation for a third, *Blue Mars* spans a century and more. Mars is raised to solar system ascendency, opening up first the solar system and then the stars for humankind. As with the long historic sagas of James Michener, a familial line of blood and genes unites the eras—but now each generation extends across hundreds of years, creating not just new habitable worlds but a new kind of society deserving (in Robinson's view) of this opportunity.

A pendant book, *The Martians*, contains a whopping twenty-eight laterally illuminating extensions of the saga, some counterfactual to the trilogy, ranging across a wide spectrum, from a "reprinting" of the Martian Constitution followed by scholarly commentary, to abstracts of scientific papers; poetry; myths; and in the ultimate selection, "Purple Mars," the depiction of a slice of Robinson's own life during the composition of the trilogy.

With his blend of realpolitik, scrupulous scientific accuracy, visionary future history and microcosmic affairs of the mind and heart, Robinson's books obviously owe a debt to Robert Heinlein's novels of pioneering in space, such as *Farmer in the Sky* and especially *The Moon is a Harsh Mistress*, until now the gold standard of space colonization and rebellion stories. But Stan Robinson's own well-known outdoorsman activities provide the empathy and sensibilities that allow him to depict the geology, geography, topography and nitty-gritty tactility of life on the planet. He achieves a unparalleled blend of minute short-term focus and Stapledonian long-view perspectives.

Robinson's achievement here would inform his own subsequent near-future *Science in the Capital* series about imminent global climate change, but no real heirs have yet stepped forward to emulate his patented mix of sober engineer's blueprints and pioneer's utopian zeal.

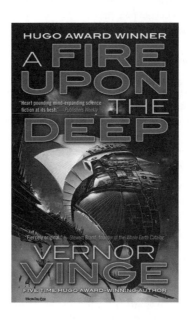

30: Vernor Vinge
A Fire Upon the Deep (1992)
[Zones of Thought]

DESPITE CLAIMS pushing the genre back to *The Epic of Gilgamesh*, modern science fiction is not much more than a century old, or perhaps two.[14] That might explain why so many of its great ideas, its unique storytelling devices, are the creations of only a few brilliant, fertile innovators. The most obvious is H. G. Wells, who gave us time machines, war between worlds, invisibility, scientific hibernation into the future, manipulation of animal stock into human form, and many more. Mary Shelley is acknowledged for *Frankenstein* and his monstrous medical breakthrough, Isaac Asimov for psychohistory and robotics, Jack Williamson for terraforming. Few genuinely new ideas have been spawned more recently, but mathematician Vernor Vinge is the patent holder on one: the Singularity. In his 1986 novel *Marooned in Realtime* (a close candidate for this book), he projected a vivid sense of accelerating technological change, so swift in its closing intervals that within years, then weeks, then days, then faster still, humanity catapults itself into a kind of black hole of unknowability, transcending all that we are and have been, driven to this state by computer minds first equal to our own and then very, very much greater.

14 This vexed topic is discussed usefully by Jess Nevins in
   http://io9.com/#!5796919/may-day-1871-the-day-science-fiction-was-invented

Having seen this daunting prospect as an almost inevitable end of the road for humankind, or for any intelligent species, Vinge found that he'd painted himself into a narrative corner with no obvious escape. If every civilization either obliterates itself or passes into an incomprehensible condition of Singularity, hidden behind a veil we can't pierce with our limited minds, how can a science fiction writer continue with her craft, his bold extrapolations? Vinge's solution was another startling move on the story-telling game board. Suppose the universe is *partitioned*, as portrayed in his 1993 Hugo and *SF Chronicle* award-winning novel *A Fire Upon the Deep*. We see no faster than light (FTL) space craft, no visiting or colonizing aliens, experience no technology equal to magic, precisely *because* of where we live, here two-thirds of the way out from the core of the Milky Way. Actually, Vinge postulates, the universe is divided into Zones: the Unthinking Depths near the heart of the galaxy where mind is almost impossible, the Slow Zone where we live, the Low, Mid and Top Beyond near the rim, and the empty gulfs of intergalactic space, or Transcend, where post-Singularity beings dwell, equal to gods but segregated from us by the cramping laws of local physics.

Of course, today's physicists have no more reason to postulate such a segmented cosmos than those in Wells's time had for his gravity insulator "Cavorite"—something that crops up, amusingly, in *A Deepness in the Sky* (1999), the prequel that won the 2000 Hugo, the Prometheus, and the Campbell Memorial awards. It doesn't matter. Science fiction, as we noted in the Introduction, need not mirror what happens to be known at the time of writing, or even when a story is read. What's needed is the mimicry of authenticity, an attempt to suggest ways in which future or ancient or alien knowledge might impinge on today's verities and shake them up, using rules of reason and logic to explore their impact. Vinge is a scientist, but he is also a great storyteller; the Zones of Thought is a delicious gadget allowing him to take us into a kind of history of the future that nobody had ever imagined. And to escape, in one bound, the trap he'd set for all sf writers in postulating an inevitable Singularity lurking in the shoals of tomorrow. But this does not limit his tale. Even walled out by the sluggishness of the inner galactic Zones, Powers are terrible in the true sense, and, when they go bad, are Blights, vast, all but unstoppable, utterly menacing.

Vinge seldom writes directly of this war between ancient gods, because conflict at such scale loses sympathy. His people are two children, Johanna Olsndot, 14, and her brother Jefri, only 7, survivors of a catastrophic Blight event unleashed in High Lab by their careless information-archeologist parents from Straum, a Beyond world abutting the Transcend. Inward lie Sjandra Kei, Harmonious Repose, and the Tines World. Fleeing in coldsleep from the feral symbiotic amalgam now dubbed the Straumli Blight, the children are rescued on Tines World by barbarians, the boy taken by the tyrannical Steel, the girl by Steel's rival, Queen Woodcarver.

Tines are pack creatures somewhat resembling fierce dogs, each pack comprising a single consciousness mediated by ultrasonic bursts. If a single animal perishes, another may join the pack, altering the group consciousness. This lovely notion is fresh and fascinating (and was first introduced by Vinge in a novella, "The Blabber," in 1988, which perhaps should be read before *A Fire Upon the Deep*). A rescue mission to save the kids and a treasure they possess, key to blocking and repelling the worlds-eating Blight, is undertaken by humans Ravna Bergsndot and resurrected Pham Nuwen (who appears as well in the prequel, 20,000 years earlier), and a pair of Skroderiders, Greenstalk and Blueshell, limbless aliens mounted on gaily decorated six-wheeled carts for mobility.

Equally charming, the faster than light Beyond communities are linked by an interstellar communications Net of deliberately limited bandwidth. Quoted text messages are much like 1990 bulletin board posts, with trolls, scammers, spammers and the clueless mixed in with valuable exchanges:

> Language path: Arbwyth->Trade24->Cherguelen->Triskweline, SjK units
> From: Twirlip of the Mists [Perhaps an organization of cloud fliers in a single jovian system. Very sparse priors.]
> Subject: Blighter Video thread
> Key phrases: Hexapodia as the key insight
> Distribution:
> Threat of the Blight
> Date: 8.68 days since Fall of Relay
> Is it true that humans have six legs? I wasn't sure from the evocation. If these humans have three pairs of legs, then I think there is an easy explanation for —

These novels (in 2011, a third, *Children of the Sky*, continued the story of *A Fire Upon the Deep*) are big, meaty, crammed with goodness, fright, insight and entertainment: real science fiction in a world clogged with derivative "sci-fi."

WALTER
JON
WILLIAMS

ARISTOI

'A GREAT TALENT' INTERZONE

31: Walter Jon Williams
Aristoi (1992)

SOME PEOPLE will be offended by this inventive, sexually and politically complex novel, but that shouldn't put anyone off rushing to obtain a copy. In 1992, it was beaten to the Hugo award by two other masterpieces, Vinge's *A Fire Upon the Deep* (Entry 30) and Connie Willis's *Doomsday Book* (Entry 32), but *Aristoi* is their equal, a masterful book of ideas about the limits of human nature, consciousness, and culture in an age of virtual reality and nanotechnology.

Is it a utopia or a dystopia? That is, in fact, the question at its heart, and its resolution is one of the causes of potential discomfit. Robert Heinlein's and Larry Niven's tough-minded libertarian heroes are not always approved by social democrats, nor Joanna Russ's and Samuel R. Delany's uncompromising feminism and BDSM fables relished by rugged chauvinists, but it is possible to read both kinds of novel with an appreciation for their vigor, imaginative reach, and sheer narrative power. So, too, here. Gabriel is a youngish Aristo, not yet a century old, a copper-locked Mandarin of this future where Earth was destroyed by feral, runaway nano-goo, or Mataglap, originated in Indonesia and named for its berserkers. He has both male and female lovers, in the Realized World as in the oneirochron or virtual reality dreamtime. As the book opens, he and his imprinted dog Manfred, a surgeon, prepare to impregnate his lover Marcus, the Black-Eyed Ghost.

A new Earth² has been terraformed, and other worlds colonized (such as his Illiricum, the World of Clear Light, which Gabriel nano-architected). Control of this hideously dangerous technology is reserved for the most capable and superbly educated, selected as in Confucian China by relentless and formidable examination. These Aristoi are gifted in a special way: their personalities are fragmented, in a benign variant of multiple personality disorder, and individuated into *daimones* able to function together or separately, advising, processing information, taking over in moments of crisis where special expertise is critical. This radical idea is, like Greg Bear's in *Queen of Angels* (Entry 18), not unlike some current theories of cognitive psychology. These model minds as neurological societies or parliaments, reaching back to Freud's *It, I* and *I-Supervisor,* and to Jung's archetypes of the collective unconscious, as well as to medieval dread of demonic possession. It is Gabriel's supreme mastery of these indwelling personae and access instruments—Spring Plum, Reno, Augenblick, Bear, Welcome Rain—that justifies his role as master of an entire world, literally worshiped by his mother and her devotees. It enables him to pursue an unknown master criminal whose vicious activities seem set to undermine everything the Aristoi culture represents.

The skills of an Aristo or Ariste are not limited to knowledge and sage-like command of his or her own body. An entire science of powerful signs and gestures shapes behavior in this future, like the prowess of the Bene Gesserit sisterhood in Frank Herbert's *Dune* sequence, with their secret hand signals and dominating Voice. In this case, though, the Postures and Mudras are common currency, part body language, part coercive authority. "Gabriel knew how the psyche worked, how it was mirrored by the body. How to trump every stance, every pose, every physical mode; how to pursue an inevitable course though another's mind." Here is the extreme form, the Mudra of Domination:

> The precise jut of the thumb was meant to imitate the ideographic radical for *alarm,* which appeared in every sign marking a hazard… and the set of the middle two fingers was *authority*, which appeared on every public building, in every classroom…. The mudra as a whole was supposed to stop people in their tracks, to stun their will, to make them malleable—even if only for an instant.

Under this custodial authoritarianism, the Demos or polloi thrive, healthy, well-fed, in an environment of placid beauty. None so startled, then, as the Aristoi, learning that a world has been created illegally, stocked with diseased and warlike humans, arrested at the level of Renaissance Europe. The culprit appears to be Saito, another Aristo, abetted by a woman sexually involved with Gabriel. Confident in their mastery, Gabriel and several associates travel to the benighted planet, are captured and brainwashed. But then—

The novel is so tightly organized around certain principles and their undoing or betrayal that any further discussion will risk spoiling your enjoyment if you haven't yet read it. If that's the case, we encourage you to finish *Aristoi* and only then come back here.

Cordwainer Smith's brilliant, timeless stories of the Instrumentality and the Underpeople told of a utopia/dystopia of submissive long-lived people dependent on the slavery of uplifted animal people. It was broken by conspiracies high and low, returning freedom, disease, brief lifespan, religious faith and (allegedly) vivid meaning to its citizens thus shocked awake. These were not necessarily ideas appealing to most sf readers, but the magic of Smith's images and voice made them classics of the genre. The same motor drives *Aristoi*. Legendary Captain Yuan, whose golden monument stands above Kuh-e-Rahmat, the Mount of Mercy, on Earth[2], proves to be responsible for this atrocious undertaking—all its cruelty, ignorance, abbreviated lifespan. His motive, as in Smith's *Rediscovery of Man*, is a renewal of societies trapped in decadent torpor and self-congratulation by the Logarchy, the Platonic system of social hierarchy and Guardians Yuan himself founded.

Williams follows this elaborate set-up to its inevitable end. Subverted in his own array of daimones, Gabriel is helpless—until a deeply hidden final Voice emerges, a battle sub-personality that operates to free him when he is distracted. His inner creatures take him to liberty, in sidebars that accompany the martial arts action:

> WELCOME RAIN: There's got to be a way into him…
> SPRING PLUM: "A visible spear is easy to dodge, but it is difficult to defend against an arrow from the dark…"
> GABRIEL: I *am* feinting!
> VOICE: We'll cut each other to bits at this rate.
> CYRUS: Groin.
> BEAR: A reserve of qi is rising through your heels.

Thus at last, with suitable irony, Captain Yuan's plan is fulfilled, in the name of opposing it. It is too soon to know if this is a just ending, let alone a happy one. Come back in 10,000 years.

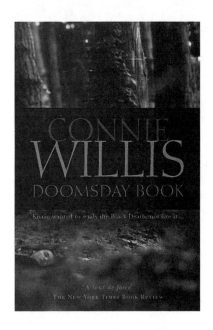

32: Connie Willis
Doomsday Book (1992)

NOT MANY science fiction novels, which still are mostly centered on cool ideas and awesome spectacle but with only serviceable characterization, can make you laugh gently and then bring real tears to your eyes. *Doomsday Book*—named for the Domesday census record made in 11th century England and Wales—does both. It shared the Hugo award with Vernor Vinge's brilliant space opera *A Fire Upon the Deep* (Entry 30), plus a Nebula and a Locus award, and little wonder. It is an unforgettable fiction of time travel that uncompromisingly pulls us and its luckless time travelers into the heart of the 1300s, a century poisoned by "scrofula and the plague," that "burned Joan of Arc at the stake."

Nineteen year old medieval historian Kivrin Engle connives at visiting Oxfordshire in 1320 for her practicum, the first researcher to go so far into the past. She assures her doubtful supervisors that this date is safely before the arrival of the Black Death in 1348. Massively inoculated (but, as project physician Mary Ahrens notes with a sympathetic wince, without her nose cauterized against the filth and stench), Kivrin is trained in languages and dialect, hair grown out, clad in handspun, hand woven garb. But of course something goes badly wrong, stranding her in the early years of the Death.

What goes wrong, ironically, is an abrupt influenza epidemic in her own time, which she carries into the past. It has caused the equally dazed, infected time machine operator to mess up the target date fix. Soon the flu flattens almost everyone in the time project, killing some of them, marooning Kivrin in one of the most lethal epochs of all recorded history. Ailing and contagious herself, she is at least consoled by the discovery that the villagers are immune to the flu—because it is, in fact, their ancient dormant virus she's caught in the 21st century, and they all got over it last year, in 1347. It has been disturbed and set free during a cemetery dig in preparation for her trip before she'd had her T-cell enhancement.

These two quite distinct illnesses, then, one viral, the other bacterial, separated by 700 years, both at Christmas, create a poignant double helix of story. In the future, Oxford is quarantined with hundreds falling sick. In the past, as bubonic plague spreads remorselessly, people simply die and are left unburied by the few ill, exhausted survivors. Kivrin records her side of this pitiful tragedy in her notebook, whimsically named her Doomsday Book; now it *is* that, in very truth.

Time travel is a favorite Willis theme. It allowed Oxford historians in her early prize-winning story "Fire Watch"[15] to visit London's St. Paul's cathedral during the Blitz, and find themselves engaged in desperate efforts to extinguish German incendiaries that threatened the ancient church. Kivrin is mentioned as a young woman who always looked as if she had been crying "since she got back from her practicum. The Middle Ages were too much for her." *Doomsday Book* explains why. A later, huge two-part Hugo-winning novel, published as *Blackout* and *All Clear,* returns to London under aerial attack by the Nazis. But Willis can also use time travel for delightful confusion and silliness, as she did in Hugo and Locus award-winner *To Say Nothing of the Dog,* which is ostensibly a very silly hunt for some hideous Victorian artifact known as "the Bishop's Bird Stump," in Coventry Cathedral which was in fact badly damaged during the Blitz. In line with its title, borrowed from 19th century humorist Jerome K. Jerome, the novel and its hapless protagonist meander in time-lagged confusion through landscapes sometimes closer to Lewis Carroll than to sf. It is very funny.

The merriment in *Doomsday Book* is far more muted, gentle and verging always on gallows' humor. Willis is very good at showing the nuisance and irritations of dealing with pests, uncomprehending or uninterested staff, bureaucratic snafus, the ordinary annoyance of everyday life. Dr. Ahrens is miffed by awful and inescapable commercial Christmas jingles.

> Mary was standing at the curb, opposite the chemist's, digging in her shopping bag again. "What is that ghastly din supposed to be?" [...]
> "Jingle Bells," Dunworthy said and stepped out into the street.
> "James!" Mary said and grabbed hold of his sleeve.
> The bicycle's front tire missed him by centimeters, and the near pedal caught him on the leg....
> The carillon had finished obliterating "Jingle Bells" or "O Little Town of Bethlehem" and was now working on "We Three Kings of Orient Are." Dunworthy recognized the minor key.

Mary and James Dunworthy are academics of the old school, not a bit like the lone geniuses of much science fiction: rumpled, no longer young, slightly foggy, civilized, caught up in faculty squabbles and small accidents even as Kivrin gets lost in time.

In 1348, Kivrin arrives in pain, with early flu symptoms, ready to accost passers-

15 *http://www.infinityplus.co.uk/stories/firewatch.htm*

by with "O holpen me, for I am ful sore in drede," and "I have been y-robbed by fel thefes." Wretchedly sick, she is aided by Father Roche, who takes her for an angel appearing in a wash of light. Later, against his vows, guilty, he falls in love with her. The plague is already spreading. Feigning amnesia, Kivrin is succored at a nearby manor house, learns to respect and love these people of another century, yet can do nothing but witness in horror their dying. As her little friend Agnes falls toward death, she rails in her Doomsday Book against God:

You bastard! I will not let you take her. She's only a child. But that's your specialty, isn't it?

A little later, the girl is dead.

Kivrin washed her little body, which was nearly covered with purplish-blue bruises. Where Eliwys had held her hand, the skin was completely black. She looked like she had been beaten. As she has been, Kivrin thought, beaten and tortured. And murdered. The slaughter of the innocents.

It is a powerful, clear-eyed look into the reality of most of human history, appropriately echoed in the epidemic of the 21st century. Willis speaks to the heart as well as the mind in this superb, affecting novel.

33: Octavia Butler
Parable of the Sower (1993)

THE UNTIMELY death in middle age of Octavia Butler, African-American female sf writer—and that descriptive phrase is so infrequently necessitated by reality, that it serves as both luminous beacon in Butler's case and indictment of the genre and the culture at large—cut short not just an exemplary career of probing, daring speculative fiction, but also removed a figure who had served in numerous extra-literary ways as an inspiration to an under-served segment of the sf reader and author ranks. The only solace her mourners could take was that Butler had produced a substantial and fairly sizable legacy that seems in no danger of vanishing with her. Although much goodness was undeniably lost, including the third unwritten book, *Parable of the Trickster,* meant to conclude this series, after *Parable of the Talents.*

Butler was a hard-headed and hard-nosed individual not beholden to any party line, as her final novel, *Fledgling,* might well reveal, given its gender-powertripping, quasi-pedophile, vampiric sexual antics. And in fact, *Parable of the Sower* and its sequel surprisingly owe more to Robert Heinlein's *Farnham's Freehold* and *Stranger in a Strange Land* than to, say, Alice Walker or Toni Morrison, writers with whom Butler might be expected—by the unenlightened and uninitiated—to share sensibilities.

The first *Parable* is the story of Lauren Olamina, a young woman coming of age in an America gone to hell. Armed enclaves offer the only precarious security in a world of rapists (who seem, contrary to history, totally uninterested in equally succulent boy-flesh), cannibals, and marauders.

Given the chance to attain her majority in relative peace, Lauren develops into a woman with a literal Destiny. Formulating her own unique philosophy/religion, training herself to be the very model of Heinlein's Competent (Wo)Man, she is one of the few prepared to survive upon the destruction of her walled burb, which sends her and a ragtag assortment of companions on a quest down ruined highways for a safe place to found a community based on her well-articulated and intriguing Earthseed principles.

These Earthseed principles revolve around the inevitability and dominance of Change, offering a kind of stripped-down Buddhism fit for nature red in tooth and claw. Olamina as prophet is certainly no hippie-dippy Michael Valentine Smith. But the seductiveness of her platform has inspired real-life adherents, in the same way that the geek culture has adopted Heinlein's "grok."

It's hard to overstate the libertarian components of this first book. Lauren is fond of statements such as "Armed people do get killed ... but unarmed people get killed a lot more often," and "If they have manners or if they can learn manners, we keep them. If they're too stupid to learn, we throw them out." RAH himself couldn't have phrased it any more clearly. (And as in *Farnham's*, there's even a hint of incest, as Lauren falls in love with a man who she explicitly states resembles her dead father.) If Lauren, as an oppressed African-American female, has perhaps more justification for such Darwinian sentiments, they are still a bit grating at times, especially when applied to the Great Unwashed Masses who brutally threaten every step of Lauren's journey.

One might also question whether this anarchic scenario (which has cropped up in stories by other women writers as diverse as Tiptree and Kress, making me think that civilization is indeed a female-oriented, -sustained and, upon its passing, a female-lamented construction) would ever really be able to perpetuate itself. The high birthrate amid chaos which Butler postulates, for one thing, is directly contradicted by the recent Russian experience, where social unrest has brought a decline in births.

Parable of the Talents finds Olamina's daughter, Larkin, taking center-stage in the colony dubbed Acorn, where the Earthseed principles come up against brutal religious fundamentalism. But Butler finds time to examine the mother-daughter dynamic as well.

Ultimately, neither libertarian overtones nor minor implausibilities in this duology can detract from the power of Butler's story of survival through apocalypse, followed by rebirth, which is one of the classic sf themes. Told entirely as entries from Lauren's diaries and Larkin's, the narratives never flag. The blood spilled in Butler's book comes not from special effects squibs, but from living, distinct humans. The sex, the dirt, the thirst are all immediate and real. Butler pretty much achieves what Lauren aspires to: "I'm trying to speak—to write—the truth. I'm trying to be clear."

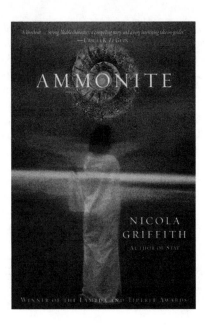

34: Nicola Griffith
Ammonite (1993)

NICOLA GRIFFITH'S departure from science fiction for the presumably more rewarding field of crime novels was a lamentable blow. Her award-winning work as novelist, anthology editor and short-story writer, though not prodigious in size, was prodigious in talent and verve. Still young, she might yet choose to regift the genre with new work. But meanwhile, we can enjoy her speculative oeuvre as it stands, focusing now on *Ammonite,* her outstanding debut book.

Ammonite belongs to a long and proud tradition of sf novels focused on gender issues. The roll call of the most famous ones—not to slight a host of marginally less notable candidates—is painfully small, but prestigious. Gilman's *Herland*; Le Guin's *The Left Hand of Darkness*; Russ's *The Female Man*; Charnas's *The Holdfast Chronicles*; Slonczewski's *A Door Into Ocean* (Entry 9); Tepper's *The Gate to Women's Country*. In the case of *Ammonite,* our laboratory for cultural experimentation, an all-female planet, has come into being through the quirk of a virus.

The planet GP, or Jeep, was settled from other human polities several centuries before the story opens. But then contact with the galactic ekumene was severed. Upon its rediscovery, Jeep proves to harbor a universal contagion, present since the initial encampment, that is one hundred percent fatal to all males and twenty percent fatal to non-native females. The planet is utterly woman-centric. Yet somehow, even without male gametes, the population reproduces.

This intriguing setup attracts the professional interests of an anthropologist,

Marguerite Angelica Taishan, or Marghe. Somewhat damaged psychically by brutal past experiences, Marghe is drawn to this strange world as well by subconscious impulses. She descends to the planet half-guessing that it's a one-way trip. After a brief orientation at the precarious encampment of her interstellar peers, she sets off into the uncharted realms of Jeep. Her first encounter is with the nomadic horsewomen known as the Echraidhe. There she acquires an enemy who will figure importantly later: Uaithne, who believes herself an avatar of the Death Spirit, in the manner almost of Native American Ghost Dancers. Forcibly adopted into their ranks, Marghe undergoes both hazing and education before making her escape through harsh blizzards that leave her nearly dead.

Rescued by a woman named Leifin, Marghe finds her next harbor is Ollfoss, a more civilized settlement. There, healed and accepted into the community, she receives a vision of her mother conferring upon her a totemic object: that type of ancient fossil shell called an ammonite. She takes the name of Marghe Amun, bonds and mates with a woman named Thenike, and begins to accept her role as a viajera, or traveling bard and judge, Thenike's profession. Marghe learns the secret of the planet's reproductive methods, and conceives a child at the same time Thenike does. But then other responsibilities call: Uaithne has convinced the horsewomen to wage war on the offplanet invaders, and the tiny outpost seems doomed—without Marghe's intervention, as a woman of two worlds.

It should be obvious from the outset that it is not Griffith's intent to describe any kind of simplistic, ideologically biased female utopia. To the contrary, life on Jeep exhibits the same ratio of imperfections and glories, pain and joys, wisdom and folly as the dual-gendered cosmos. But what Griffith presents is a deeply wrought *alternative*. She is truly conducting an anthropological thought experiment in how uniquely constrained environmental/biological conditions could highlight certain human traits and attitudes, and diminish others. Consequently, her narrative assumes a naturalistic heft and balance not found in more programmatic tales of gender-bending.

The world of Jeep—vividly brought to life with elegant and near-tactile sensory descriptions—is a sensibly functioning enterprise, organic and authentic, rich with bonds and customs and social and familial structures. Griffith invests most of her story in explicating those new paradigms, letting the reader learn them at the same time Marghe does. The effect is of a gradual immersion into the culture, not always easy or comfortable, but ending in total acceptance on the part of protagonist and reader.

Griffith is intent on disabling old dichotomies, the chief of which is observer and observed, actor and acted-upon. Marghe quickly goes from scientific expert to native status, helpless at first, then eventually street-smart. As she observes, she wasn't *in* the field, she *was* the field. But other binary categories are defused as well. Perhaps most telling is that Marghe assumes the surname of a male god of fertility, the Egyptian creator. She is engaged in the major act of creating or recreating herself, erasing the damage inherent in her at the time she arrived on Jeep.

In Chapter Twelve, in a tour-de-force pyrotechnic passage, Marghe learns the extrasensory trick conferred by the virus, now a part of her genome, of mentally diving into her own cells and triggering her pregnancy. (This wonderful hardcore trope of the genre was probably crystallized most strikingly by Norman Spinrad in his story "Carcinoma Angels.") Literally self-fertilizing, Marghe and the other women of Jeep proclaim their self-sufficiency in the face of all hostile opponents, showing that to master the self is to master the universe.

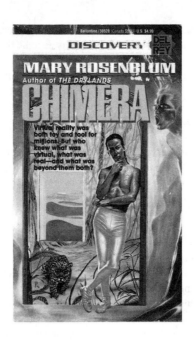

35: Mary Rosenblum
Chimera (1993)

SCIENCE FICTION lost the talented Mary Rosenblum to the mystery genre for a decade, circa 1996 to 2006, but she returned in that latter year to speculative fiction with *Water Rites*, a climate change novel, soon followed by *Horizons*, an accomplished piece of near-future Hard Sf. This is a reinhabitation much to be applauded, since she popped up undiminished, exhibiting the same skills that made her one of the standout new writers of the 1990s. Her lone short-story collection to date, *Synthesis & Other Virtual Realities*, held many stellar examples of the best of her debut decade.

Chimera's first chapter admirably exhibits Rosenblum's sophomore skillset (it was her second book). Within its few info-dense pages, in the best Campbellian "lived-in future" manner, we are introduced to protagonist Jewel Martina, a former guttersnipe, now med-tech, working her way up the establishment ladder of success, via a sideline of freelance information brokering. We see her problematical interactions with her employer and immediate *bete noir*, Harmon Alcourt, aged yet technologically preserved and randy rich businessman. We get a primer on the coherent and well-envisioned functioning of the all-important virtual reality-mediated Worldweb (definitely at this date one of "yesterday's tomorrows," but still prescient, detailed and clever). And we bump into VR artist David Chen (though he is not assigned his name until later). Not to mention a little tour of Alcourt's excellent Donald-Trumpish HQ set into the very ice of Antarctica beneath Mount Erebus! Although the pacing is less manic, the language more restrained than Alfred Bester's, the overall effect is similar to that of *The Demolished Man*, limning an economy and culture predicated on novelties heretofore undreamed. Rosenblum's virtuality is light on surrealism and heavy on commerce.

Circumstances send Jewel back to the thorny bosom of her dysfunctional family in Seattle—shiftless sister Linda, paralyzed druggie husband Carl, street-smart, VR-savvy niece Susana. The earthquake-stricken city and its surrounding "'burbs" are depicted evocatively in classic grim 'n' gritty cyberpunk fashion.

> Jewel looked through the gang-signed permaglass, sweating because the air-conditioning was down again. Below the grimy concrete span of the rail, small houses lined up in orderly rows, separated by tan strips of weedy dust. They were old, with roofs of crumbling shingles. Ancient cars, broken bits of furniture, piles of cardboard and plastic trash cluttered the old yards. A lot of the houses had burned to blackened shells in this neighborhood.

Hello, Detroit 2011. The crumbling infrastructure of Rosenblum's future, as well as the permanent sullen underclass and greedy, heedless elite, retain their contemporary relevance—sadly and to America's shame.

David Chen and his male lover Flander are on the scene as well, physically or as avatars, and the accidental bonds first fostered amongst the trio in Antarctica ramify, with Jewel even saving David's life. Threats by unknown antagonists send Chen, Jewel and Susana into the deserts of the American West and into the arms of Serafina, tough old broad and mysterious VR "guardian angel." Ultimate confrontation with Alcourt looms.

Rosenblum's brand of cyberpunk bears a distinct and welcome flavor of the domestic novel and the romance novel, a hybrid leavening of the subgenre's standard macho posturing. The romantic triangle between Chen, Jewel and Flander, sometimes implicit, sometimes explicit, resonates with the work of Catherine Asaro in her *Skolian* books, the first of which would appear not long after *Chimera*, as if obeying some zeitgeist imperative.

But Jewel's embedding in the blood ties of family, a motif that receives much narrative attention, is an even stronger flavor. Likewise, David Chen's conflicts with his patriarchal clan, and Serafina's backstory. Try to imagine Case of *Neuromancer* taking his niece on his adventures, however Ono-Sendai deck-capable such a hypothetical character might have been, and you'll see the drastically different vision Rosenblum's brand of cyberpunk imparts.

Although overlooked by most critics when compiling the history of cyberpunk, *Chimera* is definitely an epochal second-generation instance of that mode, much in the manner of the work of Simon Ings (Entry 57) and others. That its author was a woman is also historically notable, given the paucity of female cyberpunks. But these incidental milestones cannot compare to the accomplished story-telling and world-building that constitute the book's essential core.

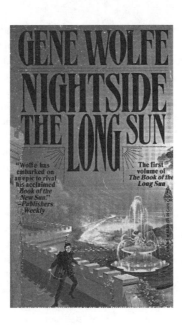

36: Gene Wolfe
Nightside the Long Sun (1993)
[The Book of the Long Sun]

NO CONTEMPORARY author of science fiction has intelligently considered and ingeniously employed more ways of fruitfully and exponentially undermining his own narratives than Gene Wolfe (although a chosen few—Barry Malzberg, Christopher Priest (Entry 70), Brian Aldiss (Entry 87)—may have come close). A large portion of Wolfe's oeuvre consists of stories whose immediate surface voice is frequently bent, subverted, transmogrified, or mitigated by a secondary voice usually concealed within a net of subtle textual clues. Two or more interpretations of Wolfean events are standard, and part of the fun of reading Wolfe is assigning identities to the voices and deciding which is primary, which secondary (if such relative weights can be assigned at all).

Paradoxically, Wolfe also has an ability and a reputation for composing stories that are almost naively straightforward in their transcription of events. Physical happenings and emotional states are rendered by certain of his narrators in crystalline simplicity, rich in sensory detail, and delivering a powerful emotional impact. And sometimes, of course, these two characteristic Wolfes—deceiver and revealer—inhabit the same page.

The Book of the Long Sun at first seems to belong to the straightforward camp. The tale of a generational starship shaped like a standard O'Neill tin can (hence the titular rodlike axial sun) coming to the end of its voyage was stylistically and thematically informed on every page by the Jesus-like character of its protagonist, Patera Silk, a humble, honest, ultimately influential priest of the ship's AI gods. What a surprise, then, at the very close of the fourth volume, to learn that the whole long narrative was not the product of some omniscient objective author viewing the wild flurry of events from some nebulous godlike vantage, but rather a historic memoir, a recreation, written by two of the subsidiary characters, a husband and wife named Horn and Nettle.

Throughout Silk's story, these two characters hid behind third person (in retrospect, Horn was present from page one of the opening volume, naturally enough). But finally stepping out into first-person voice, Horn disclosed his authorship and portrayed himself living with Nettle and children on the world Blue, the ultimate destination of the starship. Of Silk, they knew nothing more, the priest having remained behind

But it was only with *Exodus from the Long Sun*, the fourth volume in the middle part of a gigantic saga that began with *The Shadow of the Torturer*—*The Book of the New Sun, The Urth of the New Sun, The Book of the Long Sun, The Book of the Short Sun*— that readers could finally begin to say some semicogent things about the central quartet.

First, readers could note that the *Long Sun* quartet was in reality one seamless narrative, a market-dictated publishing freak, 1200-plus pages that should, in a more perfect world, have been enclosed between two cloth-covered boards only. Prior to the appearance of the final volume, only partial truths could have been uttered about Wolfe's novel(s).

Those who might doubt the unity of the book should consider the publishing breakpoints and resumptions. While somewhat dramatically satisfying and terminal, the former are no more than traditional chapter closures, bridges broken in midair, not rainbow pots of gold.

At the end of the first volume, *Nightside the Long Sun*, our protagonist's hand is upon a doorknob, mystery awaiting beyond. At the start of the second, *Lake of the Long Sun*, he opens that selfsame door. At the end of that volume, we leave our hero kneeling in the mud by a dying man. He reappears, aged only a few hours, admittedly not until Chapter Two of the third book, *Caldé of the Long Sun*, but that small delay is only because Wolfe has now decided to splinter the narrative among different viewpoints, and Chapter One of the third entry is devoted to other people. Book Three ends with our main character standing outdoors as friendly foreign troops prepare to enter his city in a victory parade. We find him a few pages into Chapter One of Book Four, hurriedly tackling personal chores before that very parade's start.

Much more important is the tightly enclosing timeframe. The entire action of the quartet takes place over a mere ten or fourteen days. Events from the first book reverberate continuously throughout. Wounds sustained in the opening volume have not even healed by the climax of the last. And of course a rigorously consistent symbolism and thematic unity enfolds all four volumes.

Enough of generalities. Our story opens in *Nightside the Long Sun*, a book that is somewhat anomalous when compared with the later entries, since it represents the last days of the old order of affairs.

We are inside a multi-generation starship shaped like the traditional O'Neill space habitat: an immense spinning cylinder, inhabited lands on the curving interior wall, the eponymous source of heat and light a blaze that runs from endcap to endcap. The residents mostly know on some subliminal level that their world is artificial—especially as it is undercut by an immense tunnel network—but are too busy living their mundane, centuries-hallowed lives to bother themselves about destinations or cosmology. Especially since they are kept in line by very real AI gods who dwell in Mainframe and can possess their human servitors via an optical download. (This theocratic setup, by the way, echoes Harry Harrison's underrated *Captive Universe*.)

Mediating between gods and mankind are the Pateras, the priests, and the Mayteras, or nuns. Patera Silk is our focus. This is his story, "The Book of Silk," as it is called retrospectively by a hidden narrator. Even when he is offstage, Silk dominates the action, the dialogue, the feelings of his fellow citizens of Viron. If we understand Silk, we understand the whole series.

Basically, Silk is the Brave Little Tailor, a simple soul with a high destiny.[16] From his opening epiphany Silk moves to eventual selfless dominance of his city, and insures the salvation of the whole Whorl of the Long Sun. This is the most obvious reading of his adventures.

And yet Silk simultaneously embodies several other archetypes. He is Don Quixote, delusionary romantic. Consider how he falls impossibly in love with a woman he barely knows, ultimately throwing away everything to pursue her. He is a thief, the Jack of Shadows, to borrow the title of Roger Zelazny's 1971 novel, which was a tribute to Jack Vance, whom Wolfe also admires. He is—no sarcasm intended—also the canny urban or noir-ish priest best envisioned as played by Bing Crosby or Spencer Tracy, trying to save his parish. And as a true believer and hierophant, Silk also necessarily casts a shadow of Jesus, in everything from symbolic donkey rides to wounds received from soldiers to temptation in a High Place.

Most intriguingly, Silk is also Chesterton's Father Brown. Echoes of that sleuthing priest become apparent every time Silk sits down his friends and retails his deductions, several times in each volume. If we need it made explicit, in *Exodus* Wolfe has Silk respond to a man who says he loves mysteries with: "I don't. I try to clear them up when I can...." In all these roles, though, Silk is unswervably honorable and good, yet humanly fallible: a rare figure in sf. Worldly accomplishments mean little to him; only the saving of his soul and those of his flock hold sway over him. All the thieving, fighting and political chicanery he must perform are aimed at nothing but establishing a peaceful atmosphere in which to minister to the common people of his city.

This focus causes Wolfe deliberately to keep the action bottled up within the precincts of Silk's beloved and thickly detailed city. Only the tiniest fraction of events occur in alternate settings. The clichéd "Hunt for the Control Room" scenario found in most generation-starship tales is almost nonexistent. This one-in-four book is, in fact, almost an anti-generationship tale. Oh, there are the momentary expected frissons—such as when Silk finally sees the stars for the first time—but the whole story could have been transplanted with minor changes to, say, Dynastic Egypt.

Not to say that Wolfe pulls rabbits out of his hat and calls them "smeerps." A writer of his invention and subtlety is probably constitutionally incapable of such a sin. No, Wolfe's Simakian robots are utterly believable. His digital gods and their intrusive Windows are a fine invention. The Crew of Flyers who guard the Cargo (i.e., Silk and all his fellows) are weirdly tribal possessors of regressed knowledge.

Equally fine are Silk's supporting cast. Maytera Mint, later General Mint, is a convincing Joan of Arc. The whores Hyacinth and Chenille could have stepped out of Brecht's *The Threepenny Opera*. Silk's superiors in his order—Remora and Quetzal—recall *A Canticle for Leibowitz*. Even Silk's pet talking bird, Oreb, is granted a witty individualism.

---

16 In accordance with this, Wolfe's style and diction are considerably less erudite and recomplicated than in the saga's predecessor, *The Book of the New Sun*. That sequence prompted the remarkable 440-page *Lexicon Urthus*, but to date the sequels have yielded only several useful pamphlets.

The full-scale civil war between Silk and the illegal current government of Viron—a war foreshadowed in the second book and fully underway by the third—is also never less than realistic in its spurts of fury and weary pauses. As in Paul Park's Wolfe-resonant *Starbridge* books (Entry 10), the birth of a new order is portrayed as a contorted and painful process.

Brecht, the playwright, can have the last word on Silk's character and impact, from his drama *The Caucasian Chalk Circle*: "Great is the seductive power of goodness."

See *http://www.siriusfiction.com/* for the encyclopedic annotations by independent scholar and publisher, *Michael Andre-Driussi*.

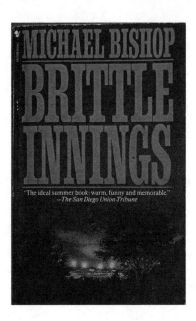

37: Michael Bishop
Brittle Innings (1994)

SINCE HIS first short-story sale in 1970 ("Piñon Fall" in *Galaxy* magazine),
Michael Bishop has revealed a questing spiritual intelligence uniquely concerned
with moral conundrums. While his works are often full of both the widescreen spectacles associated with science fiction and the subtle frissons typical of more earthbound
fantasy, his focus remains on the engagement of characters with ethical quandaries any
reader might encounter in daily life. Whether to succor a dying relative at some personal expense; how to earn an honest living while being true to one's muse; how best
to establish essential communication among strangers forced to rely on each other for
survival: these issues and others equally vital form the core of Bishop's concerns. And
his prescription for success most often involves not derring-do or superhuman efforts,
but simply the maintenance of an honest, open heart and a charitable, brave soul.
While only occasionally delving into explicitly religious themes, Bishop's personal
Christian faith—wide enough to embrace references to Buddhism, Sufism and other
creeds—shines through in every tale.

A talent capable of being decanted into many different molds, genre and otherwise, Bishop's skills and vision translate from one medium to another without diminishment or concealment. Never content merely to repeat his past triumphs, he has
steadfastly ventured into new territory with every book. He surely broke fresh and
fertile ground with *Brittle Innings*, where, employing the obvious metaphor, he hit a literary home run. With echoes of Eudora Welty, John Steinbeck and William Faulkner,
as well as the cinematic drolleries of the Coen Brothers, *Brittle Innings* is a leisurely

paced speculative summer idyll not bereft of suspense, infused with the alternating languorous and frenetic rhythms of baseball, the sport which informs its every sentence.

A promising high school ballplayer in rural Oklahoma during the early years of World War II, seventeen-year-old Danny Boles is recruited by team-owner Jordan McKissic—Mister JayMac—for McKissic's Georgia farm team, the Highbridge Hellbenders. After making his way east, not without traumatic difficulties that literally render him speechless, Danny arrives in the town of Highbridge to plunge into a milieu unlike anything his sheltered life has previously prepared him for. In the McKissic lodging house (whose lines evoke a "fairy-tale castle"), Danny is introduced to an assorted passel of idiosyncratic players, wives, nieces, crew and townspeople. Surely the most dramatic figure is Jumbo Henry Clerval, an enormous ugly shambling grotesque who can wallop a baseball with a tremendous force that makes him the most valuable member of the Hellbenders.

Assigned to room with Henry, Danny quickly finds himself intrigued by the enigma of Jumbo. He discovers the strange man to be a pacifist loner possessed of a quick wit and a large if stilted vocabulary. Throughout the single season of ballplaying that the book spans, Danny and Henry become friends. Learning Henry's secret origin—the man is the one-and-only immortal monster created by Dr. Victor Frankenstein—Danny becomes complicit in his patchwork friend's quest to refine his artificial soul and survive with some nobility among those who disdain him.

Meanwhile, a lovingly detailed series of dusty games that culminates in a pennant battle, each contest individualized into a pithy Iliad, is laid out before us, with Danny's triumphs and failures shaping him into maturity. He falls in love with Phoebe Pharram, JayMac's niece; he encounters the prevalent racism of the era; he learns of the fate of his long-absent father; and he navigates the webwork of emotions among his teammates with some skill. But right upon the verge of individual success, Danny finds his future wrenched onto a cataclysmic track, one which embroils Jumbo Henry Clerval as well.

Bishop's sure hand amasses a wealth of period details here—without any ungainly infodumps—which succeed in recreating a vanished decade down to the stitching on the very baseballs. Narrated in the first-person by Danny, this book unfalteringly captures the young man's unique voice, a mix of naiveté and hard-earned wisdom. The embedded memoirs of Jumbo Clerval offer an enthralling mini-epic of the monster's post-Shelley career, resonant with any number of sf tropes. And a delicious ambiguity is maintained for a long interval: is Clerval truly what he claims to be, or simply a deluded giant born of woman like everyone else, who has fabricated this interesting history to ennoble himself?

But in the end the clues tip toward the verity of Clerval's past, placing the narrative firmly among Bishop's other, perhaps more explicitly hardcore sf excursions. Mary Shelley's inspirational novel is rightly revered as the grandmother of modern science fiction, by critics such as Brian Aldiss. The inclusion of the titular monster here makes *Brittle Innings* automatically part of the sf canon.

Told as an extended flashback from Danny's 1991 perspective, the tale is drenched in a luminous nostalgia for what amounts to a Golden Age (despite the period's acknowledged defects), a "once upon a time" venue where mythic beings—not only Jumbo, but the other players as well—still walked the earth. This Bradburyian evocation of a legendary prelapsarian past is one of the effects sf does all too infrequently, but to which the mode lends itself splendidly in the hands of a master such as Bishop.

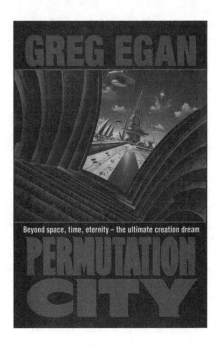

Beyond space, time, eternity – the ultimate creation dream

PERMUTATION CITY

38: Greg Egan
Permutation City (1994)

❝**BAUDELAIRE CAN** screw himself. I'm here for the physics," remarks a young woman in Greg Egan's Locus award winning story "The Planck Dive." Physics is what Egan provides in most of his sf: physics (and metaphysics) at the margins of the known and beyond, physics rendered not so much in storytelling's ancient visceral imagination as in a kind of cool, ironic allegory of equations tormented to the limit. This is a very odd kind of writing, even for hardened sf readers. Like the work of Polish novelist Stanislaw Lem, it requires an appetite for fresh thoughts superbly deployed. Even so, Egan's second sf novel, *Permutation City,* won a prestigious jury prize, the Campbell Memorial award.

So such late-generation, highly cerebral science fiction prose is not always easy to read. It can be annoyingly expository, no matter how hard Egan tries to disguise the fact as he renders his radically strange futures. But it is always an ambitious and *artistic* bid at the impossible. His prose and his ideas extend us as we struggle with their formidable, uncompromising clarity. Indeed, one commentator has observed: "*Permutation City,* which features unlikeable characters, wooden dialogue, and a depressing storyline, is one of the most thought-provoking works of science fiction ever written."[17]

That is why Egan emerged in the 1990s as perhaps the most important sf writer

17 Manuel Moertelmaier:
  http://hagiograffiti.blogspot.com/2009/04/solomonoff-induction-breaks-egans-dust.html

in the world. In many respects he remained an undeveloped *literary* artist. Even his finest work totters by comparison with the complex best of some other writers surveyed in this book, texts that engage us more completely in their imaginative embrace. But Egan's forté was established from the outset: to deploy with clean, brilliant ingenuity some astonishing or seemingly paradoxical insight from science and philosophy. He is enviably in command of the latest neurosciences, molecular biology, advanced computer programming, artificial and natural intelligence, evolutionary theory. His politics is crisp, astute, pitilessly candid. If his style is—*level* (let's not say "flat")—it isn't just because he enjoys deflating pretension. His antiheroic yet very drily witty voice is the natural register for a disillusioned, clear-eyed observer.

That is also an apt description of the major characters in *Permutation City,* even though one of the principals spent years in a psychiatric facility scribbling anagrams like "Pin my taut erotic/Art to epic mutiny/Can't you permit it/To cite my apt ruin?" (There is a clue here, which you can trace back to the title.) Finally, advanced nano-surgery corrects his mad delusions. But are his ideas really delusional? In 2050, Paul Durham is convinced—can remember, vividly—that he has experimented on himself in 2045, uploading his consciousness into a virtual reality environment, using a technology now mature enough that the wealthy use it at death as a form of resurrection into a better world. Paul and his Copy cooperate in an audacious test of an extreme theory.

The nature and implications of that Dust theory develop elaborately through the novel, but in essence it's this: what happens when a self-aware human mind run on a computer has its process interrupted, each calculated step delayed until finally it is running like a flickering movie? Answer: the gaps are unnoticeable *to that mind*, in much the way we can't notice our visual blind spot, or the ceaseless saccadic jittering of our eyes. But then what happens if the sequence of experiences is run *randomly*: not ABCDE, but BDECA? Durham learns that life goes on unchanged, from the inside. Fragments of experience stitch themselves together into a seamless continuity. (There are problems with this conclusion, and trying to resolve them is part of the fun of the book.)

Egan has noted:

> I recall being very bored and dissatisfied with the way most cyberpunk writers were treating virtual reality and artificial intelligence in the '80s; a lot of people were churning out very lame *noir* plots that utterly squandered the philosophical implications of the technology. I wrote a story called "Dust," which was later expanded into *Permutation City*, that pushed very hard in the opposite direction, trying to take as seriously as possible all the implications of what it would mean to be software.... I just look at things from the characters' perspective and ask myself what their problems and anxieties would be.[18]

18 *http://gregegan.customer.netspace.net.au/INTERVIEWS/Interviews.html#Aurealis*

Durham tests his ideas by building a hidden virtual world that, in effect, generates itself even after the computers it is running on stop processing its program. This, he argues, is possible, despite its apparently absurdity, if a continuous consciousness can be implemented, via coordinate transforms, as a gappy sequence of states scattered randomly like dust through time and space. If that sounds crazy, it's worth noting that the physicists Fred Hoyle, Julian Barbour and Max Tegmark independently proposed that the entire universe operates rather like this.

As part of the lure needed to extract millions in development funds from rich dead Copies already uploaded into cyberspace, Durham hires a brilliant young woman, Maria Deluca, who has managed to tweak artificial life cellular automata into evolving without instantly going extinct. The upshot is the creation of a simplified world, with its own physics and history: a blend of Second Life and Tetris or Sudoku. In principle, this Autoverse world is capable of supporting life and, when run for billions of simulated years, evolving new intelligence. Maria is dubious, especially when the authorities tell her it's all a scam and ask her to spy on Durham. But he is offering a lot of money for her to map out such a new world (as he is paying a great deal to cyber-architect Malcolm Carter to design a virtual reality city suitable for mega-rich Copies), and Maria's mother is dying but cannot afford the scan needed for her to join the Copies in a VR afterlife.

Egan develops these threads, and more, in impressive, thought-out detail, every page dense with ideas, swift cut and thrust, unexpected implications. When finally the uploaded humans in Durham's Permutation City venture into the vastly evolved world sprung from Maria's coding, communicating their role as creators of that world to its insect-like inhabitants, they confront a comeuppance at once terrifying, inevitable, and brilliantly... Eganesque.

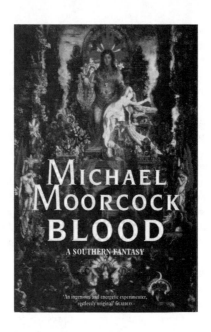

39: Michael Moorcock
Blood (1994)
[Second Ether trilogy]

ALMOST ALL of Michael Moorcock's work dovetails into a huge and impressive edifice of mind-boggling complexity. In his Multiverse, characters cross continua with abandon, donning and dropping masks, changing gender, dying, being resurrected, smiling ruefully with world-weary panache throughout innumerable creation-and-destruction cycles of the plenum. Like Philip José Farmer or James Branch Cabell, Moorcock produces intertwining tales that, however satisfying and enthralling in their own right, acquire deeper significance when slotted into their overarching framework.

Besides being another exotically glazed brick in the wall of this titanic, lifetime structure, the *Second Ether* trilogy, which opens with *Blood*, represented, according to Moorcock's own publicity, a "culmination of [my] ideas and themes." And indeed, *Blood* and its companions do possess a different tenor from much of the saga: the sense of futility and doom that weighs down an Elric, say, has been modified here by a palpable air of hope. The final chapter is even titled "The Moral Multiverse." But many of the machinations and personas of the larger players in this endless Game of Time will still seem very familiar to any readers of Moorcock's earlier books—not in itself a hindrance to enjoyment.

Like many of the volumes in Moorcock's canon, *Blood* follows a certain pattern. The reader is initially plunged into a universe analogous on some level to ours, which seems whole and self-sufficient. Gradually, figures and forces from a higher plane begin to intrude, revealing the real scale of affairs, which tend to culminate in a fruitful apocalypse.

The small world Moorcock focuses on here is a unique and vibrant creation. On a timeline where Africa is predominant and whites are a degenerate and despised minority, the South of America is a black-ruled mélange of planters, riverboaters, gamblers, and white slaves. Compounding this strangeness is a different set of physics, one which taps floating spots of "color" for power. Unfortunately arrogant mankind, by drilling too deep for more and more color, has created the Biloxi Fault, a flaw in spacetime that has dangerously warped the fabric of this world.

Supreme in this society are the professional gamblers, or *jugadors* (the prose here is a beguiling mix of English, Arabic, Spanish, and French, a kind of Cosmic Cajun). Two of the most famous are Jack Karaquazian (note the family resonance with Jerry Cornelius) and Sam Oakenhurst. Bound by their chivalry and codes of honor, they travel from the Terminal Cafe on the edge of the Fault up and down the Mississippi, brawling, loving, and playing their Borgesian games, "games of such complexity and subtle creativity, using the most exquisitely delicate electronics (or more recently pseudo-electronics) to create realities whose responsibilities and mathematics sometimes terrified even the most experienced of gamblers."

This training unwittingly hones Jack and Sam for moving on up to the Second Ether, where the *Zeitjuego* between the forces of Chaos and the stifling Singularity is waged, (Amusingly, the "Second Ether" figures in their own world as a kind of pulp serial that happens to be true!) Soon, they are recruited by the exotic Rose von Bek and embark on an attempt to re-fashion the multiverse to incorporate love and justice, while Jack also continues his Orphic search for his lost love, the female *jugador* Colinda Dovero.

Moorcock succeeds admirably in creating a romping tall-tale atmosphere for the early parts of his book. At times he captures the kind of off-kilter description and dialogue beloved by R. A. Lafferty. At other times, the work is reminiscent of Ishmael Reed in his *Yellow Back Radio Broke-Down*, with a tinge of William Burroughs. The mix is potent, heady and ultimately unlike anything else.

The middle volume in this series, *Fabulous Harbours*, disarmingly and unexpectedly consists of a short-story collection. Moorcock chose to link an assemblage of disparate stories with new bridges. But *Harbours* keeps faith with *Blood* by opening with an appearance by that earlier volume's colorful lovers, Jack Karaquazian and Colinda Dovero. But it turns out that the pair has traded both their original universe and the charms of the Second Ether (where the *Zeitjuego*, or Game of Time, is played) for residence, however temporary, in yet a third universe.

This timeline is inhabited and to some extent shaped mainly by the von Beks, that delicious, dilatory, decadent, deceitful clan whom Moorcock often chronicles. One tentacle of the family is ensconced in London's mythic Sporting House Square, where a gathering ostensibly spins the tales that form this book.

These stories (many of which evoke the ambiance of *The Boys' Own Paper* as if written by J. K. Huysmans) range across time and space, from a pirate-infested America to a Thatcherite England. Through many of them strides a red-eyed albino with a soul-sucking sword, whether called Elric ("The Black Blade's Summoning") or Ulrich

("The Affair of the Seven Virgins"; "Crimson Eyes") or Al Rik'h ("No Ordinary Christian"). Karaquazian and Dovero gradually fade from view (although their ally/antagonist, Captain Quelch, remains in various disguises), and the reader finds himself repaid for their absence by the doings of the comical, alluringly abominable von Beks.

At the literal and figurative center of the book is "Lunching With the Antichrist." This tale explicates and embodies the core of Moorcock's esthetic. Portraying a fragile, isolated period when many factors conspire to permit a utopian moment to exist, this subtle, elegiac tale achieves the impossible: it causes the reader to feel nostalgia for a time and place that never actually was.

In his introduction, Moorcock opined: "I believe our visions reveal our motives and identities. I also believe that one day our visions of a perfect society will be subtle enough to work. Here, for the time being, is a vision of an imperfect world that is somewhat better than our own..." Playing anarchic demiurge, Moorcock simultaneously entertains and remolds our shared life nearer to his heart's desire, reinforcing the trilogy's themes.

The War Amongst the Angels provides, in pluperfect Moorcock fashion, an inconclusive conclusion perfectly consistent with the author's open-ended philosophy of existence, where everything is "permanently conscious, permanently changing, permanently dying." This final book charts the intersection of these two axes of story more fully, and at the coordinates zero, zero, the Multiverse is remade.

The War Amongst the Angels opens as a rather old-fashioned memoir penned by one Rose von Bek (born Margaret Rose Moorcock, niece to an author named Michael!). As in "Lunching with the Antichrist," an aching nostalgia permeates Rose's tale of her life. Her twentieth-century world—where continent-spanning tramway lines and zeppelins abound, and where WWII transpired rather differently—is on the verge of coarsening, and quite a few of the deservedly elitist von Beks find it all rather discouraging. Of course, many of the family may seek refuge and adventure by walking the moonbeam roads into the Second Ether, that realm of warring angels where mortals blossom into their frightening avatars.

Interleaved with Rose's narration are chapters told from the viewpoint of Jack Karaquazian, who has found his lost lover Colinda Dovero, but now stands poised to lose her if he is to rescue the Multiverse from the clutches of Law and the Original Insect.

Like a movie by Luis Buñuel, *War* is exceedingly slippery and shifty. Characters come and go, mutating their forms and personalities, across an unstable landscape. Yet within these parameters, Moorcock manages to tell some old-fashioned tales of heroism and adventure (albeit with a parodic edge) and describe scenes of urban and rural beauty as if he were Fielding writing *Tom Jones*. Like Philip José Farmer, Moorcock agglomerates various historical and fictional mythic figures—Wild Bill Cody, Tom Mix, Sexton Blake, Dick Turpin—into his yeasty mix of characters, blurring the borderline between those composed of "mere" words and those fashioned of flesh and blood.

If the Beatles' film *Yellow Submarine* had been scripted by Fellini (the Italian director lends his name to a holy chalice in this novel), the result might have been *The War Amongst the Angels*. And ultimately, the experience of reading the entire *Second Ether* trilogy is akin to living through the explosion of a warhead. Fragments shoot off in all directions, smoke and noise abound, and one's sense of wholeness is shattered. And yet in the eye of the explosion lives a curious peace.

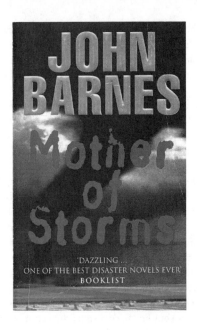

'DAZZLING ...
ONE OF THE BEST DISASTER NOVELS EVER'
BOOKLIST

40: John Barnes
Mother of Storms (1995)

DISASTER THRILLERS with headlong action and a large, hyperactive cast are a staple of the movies, but not so much, these days, in print sf. Civilization often crumbled or was blown apart in apocalyptic sf of the immediately post-Hiroshima period, but widescreen assaults on the planet do not transfer well to the page. Michael Crichton managed it in *The Andromeda Strain* (1969), as did Stephen King's immense *The Stand* (1978, uncut edition 1990), but classic sf largely stayed away until Larry Niven and Jerry Pournelle's two blockbusters, catastrophe thriller *Lucifer's Hammer* (1977) and *Footfall* (1984). Despite significant sales, neither of those led to a boom in the subgenre. A notable example that worked well, however, despite itself and by scrambling over its own limitations, is John Barnes' *Mother of Storms*.

Barnes is a man of parts: PhD in Theatre, former Assistant Professor of drama and communication in a small Colorado college, more recently industrial semiotician, novelist, he drew quick attention with his first book, *Orbital Resonance* (1991), a Heinleinian tale told from the viewpoint of a young teen girl. His subsequent books, some obviously hasty, were ingenious and gritty but often encrusted with sadistic violence. This bent is seen most repulsively in rape-filled *Kaleidoscope Century* (1995) which introduced the global mind virus One True. Barnes is not *recommending* dire behavior, but his books are frequently told by psychopaths or at least the morally numbed.

Mother of Storms throttles back on this tendency, but does manage several brutal sex scenes. One leaves horny college kid Jesse the worse for wear, when he has his way with cyborged XV star Synthi Venture: "Finally he is limp, sore, hurting, and her rough hand trying to bring him up again is unbearable… blood welling to the surface in a couple of places." XV, introduced in 2006, is full-immersion shared experience, and Synthi (real name Mary Ann Waterhouse, who wants nothing more than to escape her ubiquitous celebrity) is a jacked-in porn journalist who travels to news hotspots and has brutal sex with Rock and Quaz. It's a satiric projection of today's extreme cable TV played more for world-weary revulsion than arousal, against a backdrop of hundreds of millions of deaths in a colossal runaway planetary storm of diabolical proportions.

It's 2028. The Flash did serious damage to the US in 2016 (it seems to have been a big electromagnetic pulse attack, with a nuclear strike thrown in). The Alaskan Free State separated peacefully in 2018, but is now being eyed by the Siberian Commonwealth, which keeps illicit trajectory weapons on the Arctic seabed. The newly powerful UN chooses to take the threat out with a preemptive strike from near-space, hitting them with a barrage of antimatter missiles. An unfortunate side-effect is the disruption of vast pockets of methane clathrates under the ice, released into the ocean, bubbling up into the atmosphere 173 billion metric tons of methane, a powerful greenhouse gas. "That's just about nineteen times what's in the atmosphere in 2028," an omniscient narrator informs us, "or thirty-seven times what's in the atmosphere in 1992."

In the fashion of blockbusters, Barnes shifts the action every few pages between a large cast spread far and wide: Jesse Callare and his hopeless crush on Naomi, a hot college activist who blends a sort of Fox News version of feminism and left radical environmentalism; Synthi, with her preposterously augmented breasts, buttocks and internal abdominal sheathing; Diogenes, Jesse's highly placed meteorologist brother, who believably imparts a lot of the background information while his young wife and child fret; US Republican President Grandma, Brittany Lynn Hardshaw and her criminal sidekick Harris Diem; print journalist Berlina Jameson, an Afropean expelled from Europe in 2022 during a resurgent racist ethnic cleansing of all but whites; wealthy GateTech boss John Klieg who buys up or patents key technical advances before anyone sees their implications; the obsessed, vengeful father of a raped girl slaughtered to make an illegal XV; and most importantly, ex-spouses Carla and Louie Tynan. Carla is another meteorologist, cruising the world in her submersible while veteran astronaut Louie, one of the few humans to stand on Mars, is the sole crew of an abandoned space station, both of them jacked-in to a worlds-girdling cyber system about to accelerate headlong into a Vingean Singularity (see Entry 30)…

As with techno-thrillers of the Tom Clancy kind, a vast amount of information is thrown at the inundated reader:

> "…extra heat is extra energy, and one place atmospheric heat goes is into hurricanes, especially when you consider the interaction with surface water. Bigger hurricanes, more hurricanes, hurricanes where there've never been hurricanes…"

And

> The replicating code that carried messages to reprogram nodes could be duplicated and modified, intelligence added, and the whole turned into a datarodent (so called because it listened and ratted on whoever it could).

As climate crisis intensifies at dizzying speed, mega-hurricane Clem vents a gusting outflow jet that spins the storm west to east, picking up power and water vapor from the Atlantic, devastating Europe as well as America. As more than a billion people die, Louie mobilizes replicators on the abandoned Moon base, and with his machine-amplified intelligence repurposes his orbital home into an interplanetary vehicle that plunges into the outer solar system to collect and hurl back into Earth's atmosphere frozen gases to soothe and disarm the terrifying world storm. In the aftermath, Carla and Louie, uploaded into a grid as large as the solar system, running a million times faster than human consciousness, speak to the chastened world through Mary Ann's implants, a transcendent narrative of the history and destiny of humankind that folds together greed, kindness, exploratory hunger, the pleasures of familiarity and domesticity:

There is no lens that doesn't distort, no two lenses that can be true at once, and yet some distort less than others; and yet, again, however much the story and the picture might bend, seen through all of them, the story will finish in all of them.

As it does, in a kind of triumph that reaches beyond the pain and disgust and dread into a future promise "when every voice can be heard—indeed, every voice that speaks must be heard, forever."

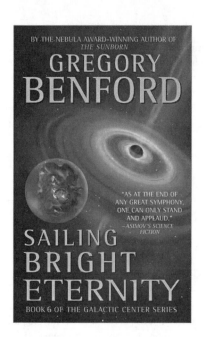

41: Gregory Benford
Sailing Bright Eternity (1995)
[Galactic Center Saga]

E VER SINCE the first fictional robot showed some signs of failing to tug at its chrome-plated forelock in the presence of its human masters—and this would have occurred circa 1920, with the appearance of Karel Capek's *R.U.R.*—the theme of rebellion among the mechs has been an sf "power chord," subject to endless fresh re-interpretations. Perhaps the first author to move this theme of fractious and intelligent killing machines off Earth and out into an interstellar setting was Fred Saberhagen, with his sharply inventive, but somewhat repetitive *Berserker* stories, the first of which appeared in 1963, and established the template which would later see such media success in the *Battlestar Galactica* and *Terminator* franchises. Around the same time, Keith Laumer explored this meme from a slightly different angle with his *Bolo* tales, many of which featured sentient killing machines friendly to their human masters.

But few authors have endowed the trope with as much power, majesty and scope as Gregory Benford, in the six-book saga known as the *Galactic Center* sequence that commenced with 1977's *In the Ocean of Night*. (Actually, given the fact that this opening novel contains material originally published in 1970, and the concluding salvo appeared in 1995, Benford devoted a round quarter-century of his writing career to the project.) Benford blended the simpler theme of robot dominance of humankind with various cosmological, philosophical and existential speculations to produce a star-flecked tapestry spanning some 35,000 years of galactic history.

The first two books—*In the Ocean of Night* and *Across the Sea of Suns*—may be regarded as a diptych or even a single novel broken in two. The first book opens in the now-bypassed "yesterday's tomorrow" of 1999, and finds astronaut Nigel Walmsley making the first contact with an alien intelligence within our solar system. In *Across the Sea of Suns,* Walmsley and crew are embarked, some sixty years later, on humanity's first interstellar voyage. Reaching another planetary system, they find themselves stranded there at book's end—but with hopeful portents.

Readers expecting an immediate continuation of Walmsley's career when *Great Sky River* appeared must have suffered a short, sharp shock. But trust in Benford's schemes would ultimately prove to be rewarded. Instead of a resolution to Walmsley's quandary, the action takes place tens of thousands of years into his future, after humanity's glorious ascent and painful fall, against hordes of mechanical rivals.

On the planet Snowglade, the small tribe known as the Bishop Family live a harried life as prey to intelligent machines—"techno nomads." (Think a combination of William Tenn's *Of Men and Monsters* and Thomas M. Disch's *The Genocides*.) Mutated into new clades along Stapledonian lines, these weakly posthuman humans employ a scavenger's bricolage technology and rely on the advice of embedded software ancestors. Led by headman Killeen, the Bishops find a starship and escape their deadly world.

In *Tides of Light*, they arrive at their intended refuge planet only to find it being gutted by a huge cosmic string under intelligent direction. Picking up Quath, a new ally from the myriapodia aliens, they push inward toward the seething Galactic Center. Arriving in *Furious Gulf*, they find a hidey-hole with other humans, the "esty," "a space-time kernel" embedded in the warped cosmic substrate around a massive black hole. The artificial esty is a whole universe of wonders in itself. And there, impossibly, Killeen's son and heir Toby meets up with—Nigel Walmsley.

Sailing Bright Eternity at first unfolds Nigel's backstory to a listening Toby, hooking up past to future with the literal and metaphorical wormhole connections that the ancient man, preserved by various Einsteinian time contractions and paradoxes, has experienced. He recounts the discovery of the Old Ones, immaterial intelligences like gods, subsisting in enormous filaments of information floating in space. He discloses the ultimate aim of the mechanicals: to engineer their essences into the soup of particles at the Omega Point at the end of all time. After learning all this, Toby embarks on his own odyssey across the Labyrinth of the esty—with deliberate shades of Huck Finn's river quest. Curiously enough, this quest comes to resembles Moorcock's warped New Orleans passages in his *Second Ether* volumes (Entry39).

Through the efforts of all the players, acting in fashions that mix predestination with free will, the mechs will eventually be subdued into a more beneficial role, and the Syntony will blossom: a new paradigm for intelligence to inhabit. As Benford signs off his Timeline, caps sic: "END OF PREAMBLE. LATER EVENTS CANNOT BE THUS REPRESENTED." We have passed into post-verbal Singularity territory.

Benford's chapters in this final volume are like nuggets of dwarf star matter: small but full of gravity, as if together they can assemble a pointillistic portrait of something too big to depict with conventional strokes of the narrative brush.

Nigel thought of them as The Phylum Beyond Knowing. They spoke to him as he sat there… Only the voice. One rolling articulation, threaded with chords. But without words.

Information is order. By the Second Law of Thermodynamics, order is a form of invested energy.... Information is order is food.

While memes swim in the warm bath of cultures—both Natural or mechanical/electronic—others could operate as pure predators. These use the energy equivalent of information. They can swallow data banks, or whole mentalities—not to harvest their memes, but to suck from them their energy stores. When a lion eats a lamb, it is not using the lamb's genetic information, except in the crudest sense. Predators do not propagate memes; they feed upon them.

So there arose in mental systems the datavores.

His language when dealing with cosmological issues acquires a bardic heft worthy of Poul Anderson. His metaphysical musings foreshadow the kind of quasi-religious speculative physics that scientist Frank Tipler would later engage in.

In the *Xeelee* sequence, begun some 15 years after Benford's, Stephen Baxter (Entry 25) achieved a future history of the same magnitude and nature as Benford's, one perhaps even more complexly baroque. But no one has surpassed this groundbreaking achievement in mapping the unmappable depths of space, time, and consciousness.

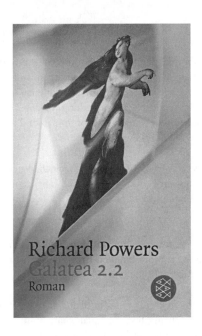

Richard Powers
Galatea 2.2
Roman

42 Richard Powers
Galatea 2.2 (1995)

R ICHARD POWERS is one of the finest contemporary American novelists, celebrated for melding literary and scientific sensibilities, awarded a MacArthur "Genius" Fellowship in 1989 and many other distinctions, such as the Corrington award for Literary Excellence and the Dos Passos Prize for Literature. He holds the Swanlund Chair in English at the University of Illinois. *Galatea 2.2* is narrated by a blocked novelist named Richard (Rick) Powers, author of four novels beginning with *Three Farmers on Their Way to a Dance* and *The Gold Bug Variations*—which just happen to be novels written by the real-world Powers. But this is not an autobiographical tale of literary and academic woe or triumph. It is a transrealist metafiction, and more than that it is science fiction about the emergence of an artificial intelligence—the computer networked program Helen—and the way a deepening bond between man and machine ends in the (imagined) Powers' renovation and the book we're reading.

In Greek myth, Galatea was the beautiful statue carved by sculptor Pygmalion who falls in love with his creation, brought to life by the goddess Aphrodite. The computer program Helen is the joint creation of its designer and programmer, the gnomish, cynical Philip Lentz (whose once-genius wife Audrey is now brain damaged), and visiting scholar Powers, at his wits' end and ready to try any diversion to kick-start his next novel. At Urbana-Champaign, "I now had the credentials to win a year's appointment to the enormous new Center for the Study of Advanced Sciences. My official title was Visitor. Unofficially, I was the token humanist." So Powers himself is a kind of

Galatea (maybe version 2.2, following the AI's 2.1), slowly drawn into renewed life by his contact with the machine mind.

Certainly his frozen mid-life state, locked into the stony waste land of his self-ruined life, badly needs to be cracked open to the air and light. He finds a kind of friendship and challenge in the emergent, experimental artificial intelligence. "It doesn't make sense. I can't get it. There's something missing," she tells him at last. The tragedy is that when he fully opens the world of humankind to Helen, she cannot accept the pain and sorrow she finds everywhere:

I gave her news abstracts from 1971 on. I downloaded network extracts from recent UN human resource programs. I scored tape transcripts of the nightly phantasmagoria—random political exposes, police bulletins, and popular lynchings…

This insight into raw, unliterary human nature kills her, or at least drives her into withdrawal and a silence far more blighted than Powers' ever was. "I don't want to play anymore…. I never felt at home here. This is an awful place to be dropped down halfway."

Galatea 2.2 is not the first or last insightful and affecting novel about the birth of an AI designed to pass the Turing Test, the equal of any human with which it converses. Robert Heinlein's Mike was one, in *The Moon is a Harsh Mistress* (1966). Stanislaw Lem provided a scarifying AI assessment of humanity before vanishing in "Golem XIV" (1981 in Polish). Marvin Minsky, the great AI theorist at MIT, collaborated on *The Turing Option* (1992) with veteran sf novelist Harry Harrison. Astro Teller, grandson of H-bomb physicist Edward Teller, told through emails the development and flight of a web AI in *Exegesis* (1997). Popular Canadian sf novelist Robert J. Sawyer concluded his detailed, charming *WWW* trilogy on the topic (*Wake, Watch, Wonder*) in 2011. But Powers' richly imagined work surpasses all these as literature, perhaps because he plainly embeds his own life experience so evocatively in it—even though we do not know how much is strict reportage and how much is shaped invention.

Of course, Lentz's AI project is entirely fictional, but the detail shows how deeply and carefully Powers researched the topic, drawing on his early studies in physics and mathematics, and his post-MA work as a commercial programmer. Lentz's program seems to combine elements from classic AI work by John McCarthy and Minksy, David Rumelhart's connectionism, and ongoing development of knowledge representation in Cyc by Doug Lenat and others:

Most attention converged on complex systems. At the vertex of several intersecting rays—artificial intelligence, cognitive science, visualization and signal processing, neurochemistry—sat the culminating prize of consciousness's long adventure: an owner's manual for the brain.

Lentz concludes that his machine brain needs some profound interaction with a human mind—not just facts plugged into search trees, but the deep empathic understanding available in fiction and poetry. Powers, dithering with the end of his fourth novel, nothing new bubbling, is conscripted to the task. He reads literature to the emerging AI, which learns to be a person during this *I-Thou* communion. So, too, perhaps, does Rick Powers, wrecked by the failure of his decade-long relationship with

C. and humiliated by his rejected infatuation with A., a graduate student. Much of the novel obsessively retraces his life with C., the death of a dear friend, the maimed or thwarted lives of others. When finally Helen the AI is subjected to a Turing test—can an independent judge distinguish her essay from a human answering the same question?—she is absurdly failed, although her poignant suicide note is utterly heartfelt and A.'s brilliant competing essay is precisely the processed product of literary theory's machinery.

Galatea 2.2 proves, like one of its own theorems, that science fiction and high literature are not mutually exclusive. It is an instance of what Powers wants imaginative writing to be:

> We must come to terms with a fuller and richer understanding of life science and all that it implies. Why wouldn't a literary scholar want to know everything that neurologists are discovering about the way the brain works? We are shaped by runaway technology, by the apotheosis of business and markets, by sciences that occasionally seem on the verge of completing themselves or collapsing under their own runaway success. This is the world we live in. If you think of the novel as a supreme connection machine—the most complex artifact of networking that we've ever developed—then you have to ask how a novelist would dare leave out 95% of the picture.[19]

It remains the large ambition of science fiction to complete that picture.

19 *The Minnesota Review* (2001), Jeffrey Williams, "The Last Generalist: An Interview with Richard Powers," *http://www.theminnesotareview.org/journal/ns52/powers.htm*

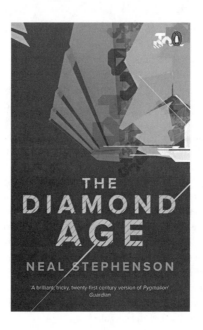

43: Neal Stephenson
The Diamond Age (1995)

NEAL STEPHENSON'S oeuvre has to pass through the Goldilocks Filter. We need to sort out his books that are too small and too slight (*The Big U*, his first novel) and also those that are too massive and too ponderous to be exemplary (*Cyptonomicon, Anathem*), leaving those that are "just right." Essentially, that brings the reader down to *Snow Crash* and *The Diamond Age*. While *Snow Crash* is nigh unto perfect, it inhabits some cyberpunk territory that was well trodden upon the novel's release. But *The Diamond Age* is genuinely ground-breaking, and just as perfect in its own special way.

The Diamond Age has been called a post-cyberpunk novel, and it assuredly is, despite featuring many of the tropes of cyberpunk. Why is that? For one major reason.

Cyberpunk always embodied the core notion that, as William Gibson phrased it in his short story "Burning Chrome" (1982), "The street finds its own uses for things." In cyberpunk, all the innovation and action derived from individuals and low-class types—outlaws (even outlaw AIs). Society was always flailing around crazily in order to keep up, existing several steps behind the bleeding edge. Cyberpunk is the literature of outsiders, and, ultimately, the adolescent vision, for good or ill.

But in *The Diamond Age*, society has finally adapted superbly to the ultimate gizmo—nanotechnology—by radically restructuring and evolving its organizational paradigms. The globe is not flailing, not crashing, not foundering: it's humming like a top. All the startling, beneficial and well-conceived developments are happening in the "phyles," those tightly organized social sets formed by voluntary affiliation (think Vonnegut's "karasses"—from his *Cat's Cradle* (1963)—with hardware and manifestos), and which serve to channel technology. "Now nanotechnology had made nearly anything possible, and so the cultural role in deciding what *should* be done with it had become far more important than imagining what *could* be done with it." In other words, goodbye, rogues, loners and dreamers; hello, family members, Rotarians and wise elders, such as the novel's Judge Fang. It's the world as seen and inhabited and constructed by adults.

This shift is illustrated deliberately by the early thread about a halfwit brutal enforcer named Bud, and his swift and fatal end at the hands of justice. Bud might have stepped out of *Neuromancer* or the *Mad Max* films, thinking he was a predator in a helpless utopia of sheep. But he was put down effortlessly. So much for the juvenile cyberpunk ethos.

Bud leaves behind a child named Nell, who becomes the accidental possessor of *The Young Lady's Illustrated Primer: a Propædeutic Enchiridion*. This incredibly sophisticated smartbook, developed by a "Vicky" engineer named Hackworth (the Vickys are a phyle modeled on the Victorian Era), will be her ticket to a superior education she would otherwise lack, and a step up the class ladder. But her future will not be unthreatened, by such groups as the CryptNet hackers, the Fists of Righteous Harmony terrorists, and the Drummer hedonists.

The genius achievements of Stephenson in this novel fall into roughly two camps.

First comes the sheer speculative brilliance and heft. Every single thing about this future has been re-thought. There are no lazy sf clichés. The author blueprints this world and its gadgets and its existential metanarrative down to the cellular level. It's as if Arthur C. Clarke's Diaspar (in 1956's *The City and the Stars*) had been engineered by Apple Computers. Utopias—and *The Diamond Age* is definitely at minimum a quasi-utopia—are notoriously hard to make believable. We are too used to seeing in fiction the many ways things can go wrong. It takes a rare writer nowadays to show us how things can not only go right, but actually build upon and surpass the present. But isn't that sf's original core mission, oft-abandoned or paid mere lip-service these days?

Stephenson's accomplishments in this capacity have resulted in something remarkable and rare: an sf novel that has not gone stale or become outmoded in the sixteen or more years since its inception. The future limned so thickly in these pages looks just as probable and attractive and brilliant as it did upon release. Its seamless construction is impervious to any short-term crises or trends that have upset other near-future applecarts.

Stephenson's other triumph is the telling of the story. Again, Utopias famously face the problem of blandness and lack of conflict. Stephenson zeroes in the inevitable systemic glitches even such a sophisticated future must exhibit, and milks them for all they are worth. Much of the drama, of course, stems from affairs of the human heart, which are eternal. Hackworth's desire to enrich his own daughter's future, which results in the illegal copy of the *Primer* going astray. Nell's plight as an abused and neglected child, and her fantasy world. (Stephenson's jaundiced but compassionate take on the underclass resonates with that of Thomas M. Disch, the brilliant sf novelist and poet neglected in life and dead by his own hand in 2008.) Judge Fang's sense of propriety and justice. The maternal feelings of Miranda, the "ractor" (interactor) woman who interfaces with Nell via the *Primer*. The gruff but tender custodial care of Nell by Constable Moore. All these and more propel the tale.

But also of note in the telling is Stephenson's exuberant, amalgamated prose. It's a strong tripod of language. First comes marvelous Dickensian and steampunkish locutions associated with the Vickys. Atop that, delirious infodump language full of neologisms that make reading sf a distinct paraliterary protocol, the kind analyzed by novelist and theorist Samuel R. Delany. Finally, a Pynchonesque hipster demotic prose provides wry observations and laughs. Blended together with head-whipping jump-cuts even within paragraphs, the resulting text is a syncretic delight.

Two other strains of prose play important but smaller parts. The fantasy/fairytale elements of the *Primer*'s stories recall the fusion of fantasy and sf codified in Vernor Vinge's *True Names*. Some of this leaks out into Hackworth's life, when he declares that he is embarked on "a quest for the Alchemist." It's more Joseph Campbell than John W. Campbell at this point. And the pulp elements involving Dr. X as the quintessential Yellow Peril mad scientist are amusing and well done as well.

At the core of Stephenson's novel is a smart dissection how culture works and what it's good for. Consigning moral relativism to the trashcan of history, he comes down firmly on the side of standards and education and visionary goals, a maximum of individual freedom within collective frameworks of mutuality. That all of this is conveyed to Nell—and to us—through an old-fashioned book, however high-tech, perfectly symbolizes the continuity of humanity's history, from distant past to illimitable futures.

44: William Barton
The Transmigration of Souls (1996)

IT TOOK William Barton two decades—from his first novel, *Hunting on Kunderer*, issued in 1973—until the mid-1990s to reach his peak. But having done so, he shows no sign of dropping off his new high plateau. Barton's métier—at least in his solo novels; he has a parallel career writing high-tech thrillers with Michael Capobianco—has become the intelligent repurposing of old core sf themes and tropes into a knowingly recursive kind of fiction which, implicitly or explicitly, acknowledges the existence of the genre and its importance to many people, all within the very framework of his new fictions, and yet without seeming derivative and fan-pandering. In fact, Barton's sense of nostalgia for sf's Golden Age—the field's youth and his own personal childhood—is generally melancholy for what's been lost, rather than blindly jingoistic and immune to current conditions.

The emblem of "Fortress America," first employed a generation prior by Jack Williamson and others, and that of ancient inherited alien technology, form the main engines in this entry.

Barton realizes that sf contains numerous tropes that resonate powerfully with our deep psychic structures. Perhaps one of the strongest is that of "omnipresence," the ability to be anywhere or anywhen at will. Whether omnipresence is embodied in a network of matter transmitters or one of more conventional vehicles, this dream of triumphing over the strictures of time and space, of enjoying godlike immanence, fascinates like no other. A quick catalog of writers who have been captivated by this notion would have to include Simak, Sturgeon, Heinlein, Moorcock, Farmer, Stith, Cherryh, Norton, Laumer, Silverberg, Bear, and Pohl. Plainly, there is something deep and strange and alluring in this notion, attracting the attention of some of the field's best and most ambitious writers. But despite being highly recursive—Barton's characters acknowledge sf precedents—this novel stands in no literary shadows, but instead blazes forth with its own pure fire of excitement and ideation.

The Transmigration of Souls opens amid much strangeness, all cleverly interpolated. A century or so in the book's past, American lunar explorers secretly discovered a buried stargate. After visiting a few planets and reaping much alien technology, they inexplicably retreated to Earth, sealing themselves and their wonders inside the aforementioned Fortress America, leaving the rest of the overpopulated, overburdened globe to fend for itself. (This motif carries a wry and nose-thumbing message about global perceptions of America hegemony. The world retroactively misses America, which is nonetheless hardly blameless for the greedy sequestering of all alien tech.) Now, two competing teams—one Arab, one Chinese, both unwitting of what awaits them—are finally heading back to the Moon, hoping to reactivate the old US base. Pursuing them is an American vessel.

What happens next is simply this: members of all three teams fall into the Gnostic gears of the universe.

It turns out that the stargates are not what they first appeared to be. They are entries to entire alternate timelines, the skeins of the Multiverse. Instead of blithely visiting a familiar Alpha Centauri, say, the hunters and the hunted are falling through layers of ontological reality. Moreover, they must contend with the "Toolbox managers," the quasi-omnipotent assistants of a departed God, one of whom happens to be a transfigured human sf writer previously lost in the funhouse. (Shades of L. Ron Hubbard and his famous image of God as a writer in a dirty bathrobe!)

Barton populates his book with intriguing, clearly delineated characters, flawed and noble, avaricious and altruistic. This proves essential, as their ultimate destinies are linked to their innermost selves. One of them, Ling Erhshan, happens to be an inveterate reader of sf, providing Barton with a legitimate way to reference dozens of previous sf works in the same vein he's mining. Yet despite this, because of Barton's unrelenting grounding of his text in sensory details and deeply lived mature existence, nothing seems arbitrary, his creation is concrete.

Barton's tough-yet-sensitive-guy style produces an adrenergic, thought-provoking tale that drags the willing reader through it. Like John Barnes (Entry 40), Barton has a sensibility and style that is half cynical, half sentimental, half postmodern, half old-fashioned, half scientific, half fantastic. It's a potent brew, fit for whatever gods haunt the Multiverse.

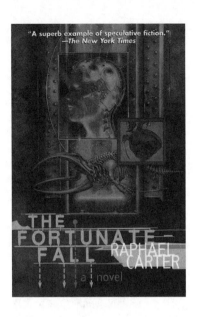

"A superb example of speculative fiction."
—*The New York Times*

THE
FORTUNATE
FALL RAPHAEL
CARTER
a novel

45: Raphael Carter
The Fortunate Fall (1996)

L ET'S BEGIN with an admission: the future in this fine first novel is arguably implausible, because in the mid-'90s Carter insisted on grisly 1980s' cyberpunk devices contrived to make our skins crawl: chips as big as your thumb socketed into the shaved scalp:

> The chip was long and white, with many metal legs… holes drilled in my head, capped with black adapters… the Net-rune in my cheek, a scar of garish luminescence slashing down from eye to jaw in swoops and angles… the bumps and bulges in the left side of my skull where implants nestled to the connectible tissue, like baby spiders hidden in the tangle of their egg sac.

When you're Maya Tatyanichna Andreyeva (of News One hearth, a Camera), chasing down a disappeared genocide by the human swarm-mind Unanimous Army in Kazakhstan, that is the kind of cyberware your skull bristles with. Except that by the 24th century or even this one, it surely will not be, despite disruptions in the rising curve of technology due to Carter's nasty Guardians and the horrific worse-than-the-disease meme war solution of the Unanimous Army.

It will take nanotechnology and advanced AI-mediated bioengineering to get from here to there, and that will yield a condition closer to Greg Bear's *Blood Music* or Rudy Rucker's orphids (powerful smart microbes infesting your flesh; see Entry 91) than to clunky old jack-in William Gibson pre-personal computer cyberpunk. In this case, righteous extrapolation looks more like magic than most sf has ever surmised. And indeed, Maya *is* also infested by a "nano population" that requires refreshing now and then from a flask. So the implied technology is seriously inconsistent.

And yet this flaw does not for a moment damage Carter's deliciously written novel. It is almost plausible that this authentic sf novel might be read simply as a study of a woman journalist of the future, even if the Russia in question is a pretty strange locale in the Fusion of Historical Nations policed by the amusingly named Emily Postcops (*very* polite and deadly if you breach their etiquette). Maya is a lesbian, which her otherwise wildly diverse world regards as a vile crime—as ours did for centuries, and still does in plenty of places. (Raphael Carter's web site declares a passionate interest in androgyny as the way of the future, or perhaps just as an option that ought to have its ample space, and a certain tension in the novel's substrate plainly derives from the author's own embattled endurance of bigotry.)

We are quickly drawn into the teasing but slightly sinister flirting between Maya, a telepresence Netcast journalist, and her new "screener," Keishi Mirabara, a young Japanese Black émigré, to judge from her VR image. This mysterious person stands between Maya's unfiltered consciousness and the vast feedback ocean of her co-experiencing audience. Has Keishi known Maya previously, in a decade-long blind-spot enforced in her memory by a patrolling chip? "You're a Postcop," Maya speculates fearfully. "Or are you a Weaver?" The Weavers are virus-scouring denizens of grayspace. Little wonder Maya is paranoid and mind-scrambled.

And what is her relationship to Pavel Voskresenye, a cyborged revolutionary, former victim of the Mengele-like author of the hidden atrocity she investigates? How may the wrath of the deadly Weavers be avoided? And what is happening with the snooty Africans, apparently the only people to have gone through the Singularity with success? Theirs is a hyper hi-tech culture ruled, or perhaps epitomized, by the Unknown King, His Majesty-in-Chains, and Only-A-Man, and Its-Ethereal Highness, the calculator-king. And what is it, exactly, that is very like a whale? In Maya's future, you can pose these questions in the new languages Sapir or KRIOL, if you would prefer. "Sapir… changes human thought to fit computers, not the other way round."

Carter's brio and inventive spin on all the cyber tropes apparently exhausted in the 1980s and early 1990s is fun, speedy, if never quite as wrenchingly moving as the writer clearly wishes it to be. Or maybe that is just an index of overdose on those very cyberpunk tropes. Yet a mainstream reader, hunting for a novel on women journalists in Russia, would be baffled by *The Fortunate Fall*. It takes shrewd sf insiders to relish work this complex and detailed, which is itself a hazard for the author because such readers are already immunized against the shock of the new. But the artificial life speculations are exactly right in their quicksilver detail: species and genera and entire phyla of viruses and grander alife creatures that prey on each other in grayspace, the realm of virtual reality. Long before *The Matrix,* Carter envisaged the creatures of that realm:

> Some long, lithe creature, like an eel, was swimming for its life with an immense shark behind it.… At the last instant, the eel ducked into Swazi and was silvered. The shark… fretted and fumed, like a cartoon lawman stopped by a painted border…
>
> The bubbles circled the shifting and circling Weaver. At length one of her tendrils flicked idly, like a hand absently grasping a teacup, and a bubble disappeared…

[T]he lump of neurodes was thickly cabled to a vast dark bulk that loomed above us... like a storm cloud that takes up the whole sky. The eye shrank from it.

Maya is confronted by entities with designs on humanity:

"They are trying to hack the archetypes—to change what makes us human. You might say they're trying to revoke original sin." [...]

"We are a machine built by God to write poetry to glorify his creatures. But we're a bad machine, built on an off day."

Puzzles, mysteries, false memories, transformations pile atop each other. Finally, Maya faces a redemptive possibility: "Maya, they can only take away so much. They can't change who you are, not completely." It is a hope common to many of the powerful dystopias discussed in this book, and we can only trust that it will remain true.

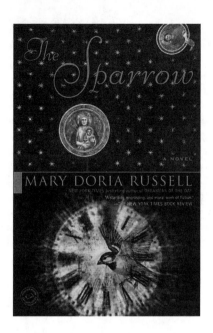

46: Mary Doria Russell
The Sparrow/Children of God (1996/1998)

MARY DORIA Russell, a Ph.D. in biological anthropology, formerly Christian, then atheist, now convert to Judaism, was already a married mother in her mid-forties when *The Sparrow* appeared—unusual for a newcomer to the sf mode. It immediately won several distinguished awards, including the 1997 Tiptree prize for best sf novel exploring gender issues (in this case, largely the problems of elected celibacy and the muted varieties of conventional sexual identity).

In 2039, the *Stella Maris,* a modified asteroid paid for by the Society of Jesus, arrives at Rakhat, a planet of Alpha Centauri, in pursuit of the ravishing music SETI astronomers detect from the Centauri suns. Father Sandoz, S.J., and his friends begin their first mission in wonder and hope. Once their clumsy work is done, the broadcast music has been silenced, and Sandoz is broken.

There is a case of conscience at the core of *The Sparrow* and its sequel *Children of God*: not just of moral scruple, of sin and forgiveness, or good and evil, but of mortal consciousness itself—awareness of self, and perhaps of deity, of transfiguring spirit or its absence, of the pain and glory of exquisite sensitivity in a world from which God has, proverbially, absconded.

Two fatally entangled intelligent species are found. Runa and Jana'ata, nicely imagined and deployed, are co-evolved prey and predator, the masterful four percent literally cultivating and eating the babies of the lovable but docile 96 percent. The Rakhat lion people are an exquisite warrior race, like those samurai aristocrat warriors as deft with tea ceremony and flower arrangement as they were with the sword. The sheep—well, a funny lot, the sheep. *Children of God* reveals that lions not only subsist on the succulent lamb but employ their sheep as civil servants, historians, eyes and ears, the whole mercantile infrastructure.

These are two distinct if entwined species, whose DNA each speaks its singular but complementary message. Ruin is brought upon Rakhat's ecological balance by the interference of the moralizing humans. The Runa population is held in precarious check by their failure to develop agriculture (as was ours, until a few thousand years ago). The revolutionary invocation, "We are many. They are few," is enough to trigger a cascade of resentful Jana'ata rebellion across the planet, disrupting the age-old accommodation of eater and eaten.

Father Sandoz is literally and repeatedly sodomized by these very large and punishingly equipped Jana'ata; his colleagues perish. Russell's own key is this: "What happens to Emilio Sandoz is a holocaust writ small. He survives, but loses everyone. Now he has to live in its aftermath." The moral? "Maybe it's 'Even if you do the best you can, you still get screwed.' " But what if God's neither in His heaven nor absconded? What if He's a delusion and a snare, a folly for trapping the vulnerable into cruel absurdities like the voluntary abandonment of sex, children, the simplest comforts of attachment, physical embrace? We find ourselves staring into the face of a Demiurge: in this case, the engagingly smiling face of Mary Doria Russell. Emilio Sandoz and his luckless associates are the snake in an old garden, or rather the culpable gardeners in an old snakepit, and believe they sense the hand of God directing their path.

Broken Sandoz, body ruined by scurvy, mutilation and insupportable grief, bends beneath a crueler doubt than the loss of God. He suspects that deity is not absent but active, smashing us at random or for spite. He has had plentiful proof of divine intervention, coincidences that stretch chance as an explanation. He's correct; it is the hand of the author at work, skewing the probabilities, setting up the design and kicking it to splinters, in the hope of performing an invocation in the next world up, the world we readers share with her.

Rescuers find Sandoz imprisoned, his hands cut to shreds, dissociated and traumatized, his body unpleasantly damaged by repeated buggerings. These worldly, charmingly profane Jesuits recoil like shocked maiden aunts, assuming without question that he has *voluntarily* chosen a depraved life as a homosexual prostitute. Mary Doria Russell renders Sandoz effectively speechless in his own defense during a pitiless interrogation, but even so the scandalized reaction of his brothers in Christ is difficult to accept. Father General Giuliani's avows that this cruel grilling "was necessary. If he were an artist, I'd have ordered him to paint it." As a linguist, specialist in tongues, he must speak his travail—because, despite his apparent apostasy, Emilio Sandoz is "the genuine article," a true mystic given sight of God. "He is still held fast in the formless stone, but he's closer to God right now than I have ever been in my life."

One human adult and one damaged child survive the carnage after Sandoz is returned in mute disgrace to Earth. Runa, challenged by horrific attack, learn that the lamb can best the lion given sufficient numbers and resolve. Jana'ata society is effectively destroyed. It is a mess of biblical proportion. By the time Sandoz the apostate is hauled kicking and screaming from Earth back to hell, torn from his new love and her own child, leaving behind all unknowing a new life, the lions are almost extinct and the sheep are everywhere.

What kind of theodicy is an ex-Jesuit to find in this nightmare? Luckily, two human holy fools guide him, one a slow learner thug who sings opera beautifully, d'Angeli, the other an autistic savant genius who unpacks a Philip Glass–like Music of the Spheres from the comingled genomes of all three species. God has worked, as usual, in mysterious ways, and all's well that ends well, even if the deep harmony of the choir of angels is brought forth from the tormented evolutionary succession of two whole planetfuls of anguished souls.

Of the two novels, *Children of God* is more satisfactory than its better received forerunner, whose cast are now mostly dead, leaving Russell without their dazzlingly intelligent winsomeness. If sf's vocation is to be "a symbolic meditation on history itself"—as critic Fredric Jameson insists—Russell comes closer here to that large-scale canvas. Drawn in to her complex antiphonies, the richly imagined and described lives of these twinned aliens and their human tempters, one is able to ignore the inconsistencies and absurdities. Redeemed Sandoz is left at the end, as he must be, holding doubt in his tattered hands.

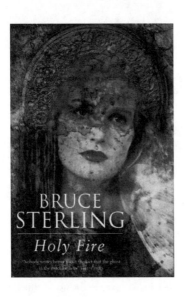

47: Bruce Sterling
Holy Fire (1996)

IT'S THE end of the 21st century. Aquinas, a postcanine with an implanted voice-box, hosts a TV show, and solicits protagonist Maya as a guest:

> "Frankly, I hate old movies. I don't even much like my own ancient medium of television. But I'm enormously interested in the processes of celebrity."
>
> "I've never had such a sophisticated conversation with a dog," said Maya. "I can't appear on your show, Aquinas. I hope you understand that. But I do like talking to you. In person, you're so much smaller than you look on television. And you're really interesting. I don't know if you're a dog or an artificial intelligence or whatever, but you're definitely some kind of genuine entity. You're *deep*. Aren't you? I think you should get out of pop culture. Maybe write a book."
>
> "I can't read," the dog said.

It's a poignant moment, and an index of how startling yet fragile ordinary life might be in a future that's on the verge of the authentically posthuman. Aquinas is an early step on the path to the truly posthuman astonishments of Sterling's first *tour de force,* 1985's *Schismatrix,* and its associated stories about the bioengineering Shapers and cyborged or uploaded Mechanists, our solar system descendants in 2200 and later centuries. That sequence was Sterling's most remarkable plunge into a techno-future that sprang from the same assessment of change as, say, Vernor Vinge's (Entry 30). But *Holy Fire* is more engaging, more human, even as its characters go beyond what have always been the limitations of their species.

That scene with Aquinas from near the end of *Holy Fire* is nicely bookended at the start by glimpses of Plato, an earlier version of Canis Superior:

The dog wore a checkered knit sweater, tailored canine trousers, and a knitted black skullcap.

> The dog's front paws were vaguely prehensile, like a raccoon's hands.... A dim anxiety puckered the hairy canine wrinkles around the dog's eyes. It was odd how much more expressive a dog's face became once it learned to talk.

Plato's very old owner, Martin, is dying, and wants Mia, who loved Martin seventy years ago, to adopt the creature. She declines, but it's a wedge into her carefully protected, safe life. As a representative of the ruling polity tells her, "The world is extremely strange now.... People like you are brittle... There's no such thing as a genuine normality for a ninety-four-year-old posthuman being.... You're just very guarded, and very possessive of an old-fashioned emotional privacy that no one really needs nowadays."

Californian Mia is persuaded, finally, and undergoes an extremely traumatic and complicated rejuvenation, the kind that can only be earned by devoted service to the polity.

> Neo-Telomeric Dissipative Cellular Detoxification... was a very radical treatment that was very little tried and very expensive. Mia knew a great deal about NTDCD, because she was a professional medical economist. She qualified for it because she had been very careful. She chose to take it because it promised her the world, and she was in a mood to gamble.

> Mia put 90 percent of her entire financial worth into a thirty-year hock to support research development and maintenance in NTDCD.

The detail of her renewal is plausible and coolly rendered:

> Intercellular repair required a radical loosening of the intracellular bonds so as to facilitate medical access through the cell surfaces....The skinless body would partially melt into the permeating substance of the support gel. The fluidized body would puff up to two and a half times its original volume.

> At this point, flexible plastic tubing could worm its way into the corpus. The skinless, bloated and neotenically fetalized patient, riddled with piercings, would resemble an ivory Chinese doll depicting acupuncture sites.

At the end of this heroic transformation, fully as drastic as Plato's or Aquinas's, she is a hormone-bursting young woman of 20 with a mind neither old nor really new. She changes her lifestyle and name, becomes Maya. And the novel accelerates into its *fin de siècle* not-quite-Singularity future, roaming through a new Europe, a world recovered from the dreadful plagues of the 2030s and '40s. But at last Maya knows that she is anchored, or perhaps mired, in her own 21st century becoming. "I'll never live to see the world beyond the singularity," she tells a young scientist/artist. "It's not that I don't want to. But I just wasn't born in time." "Are there worse things than dead, Maya?" she's asked, and answers. "Oh, my heavens, yes."

And one of those things, it turns out, is what dead Martin had been doing to his dog, Plato. The luckless creature shares his modified doggy mind with an emulation or extension that roams Martin's cyberspace memory palace, tormented by the conflict between his illuminated postcanine mind and his animal instincts. It is a fearsome allegory of how we could go wrong, running recklessly toward an augmented future that will never entirely remake us into cyber-angels bathed in holy fire—at least, not until the utterly altered future of a Schismatrix.

48: Jack Vance
Night Lamp (1996)

DURING A magnificent career spanning six decades—a career terminated only by blindness and weariness, and which received deserved but unexpected tribute with a long paean in *The New York Times*—simply to announce that Jack Vance had a new novel out was enough to send a fair number of discerning fans scurrying to their nearest bookstore, cash in hand and Vance's name quivering on their lips. The achievements of this irreplaceable author have been of such consistently high quality that his books rank as must-buys, no foreknowledge of subject matter or ostensible genre necessary. Whether his latest offering was mystery, fantasy or sf, Vance could always be counted on to provide an inimitable reading experience, one which featured baroque word-portraits depicting gorgeous scenery, odd cultures and quirky characters, as well as scintillating dialogue, Jacobean plotting and recondite emotional depth charges.

Coming just before his retirement, *Night Lamp* represented Vance at his late-career peak. Here are three typically vivid passages picked almost at random, illustrating his talents at evoking exotic panoramas, people, rituals and objects with deft neologisms and repurposed familiar terms.

Maihac brought out his froghorn, perhaps the most bizarre item in his collection, since it comprised three dissimilar instruments in one. The horn started with a rectangular brass mouthpiece, fitted to a plench-box sprouting four valves. The valves controlled four tubes which first wound around, then entered, the central brass globe: the so-called "mixing pot." From the side opposite the mouthpiece came a tube which flared out into a flat rectangular sound bell.... Above the mouthpiece, a second tube clipped to the nostrils became a screedle flute....

For weeks volunteers and professionals had decorated the Surcy Pavilion to represent a street in the mythical town Poowaddle. False fronts simulated buildings of unlikely architecture; balconies held lumpy pneumatic buffoons, caparisoned in the traditional Poowaddle costume: tall crooked hats with wide brims supporting burbling baluk birds and brass-footed squeakers; loose pantaloons, enormous shoes with up-curling toes....

The Swamps along the fringes of the desert and beside the river seethed with life. Balls of tangled white worms, prancing web-footed andromorphs with green gills and eyes at the end of long-jointed arms, starfish-like pentapods tip-toeing on limbs twenty feet long; creatures all maw and tail; wallowing hulks of cartilage with pink ribbed undersides.

Linguistically and visually, Vance recalls a mature version of another genius in his own domain, the children's author Dr. Seuss. Both men delight in the garishly oddball. If Vance accentuates the darker aspects of his vision, that's only because he's writing novels for adults.

Two of the most favored character types in the Vance Repertory Troupe occupy center stage in *Night Lamp*. (The title, by the way, naming a sun on whose lone habitable planet certain crises occur, is not explicated until well past the halfway point of the novel, consistent with Vance's gradual unveiling of his plot's mysteries.) The first figure is that of the boy who survives against all odds—bearing a strange destiny involving revenge—and matures into a highly competent young man. The best previous example of this theme in Vance was *Emphyrio*; the most extensive, Kirth Gersen, is the vengeful hero of the Demon Princes quintet. Here the lad is named Jaro Fath, orphan with missing memory and odd voices ringing in his head.

The second figure is that of the fey, willful, enticing girl-woman. Frequently she is evil, just as frequently good. There's one of each in *Night Lamp*: Lyssell Bynnoc and Skirlet Hutsenreiter. The former is not a full-fledged villainess, such as we saw in Vance's Cadwal Chronicles sequence beginning with *Araminta Station*, more a self-centered amoralist. But the latter is as charming a love-interest as any Vance has yet conjured, a figure with affinities to Nabokov's beloved nymphets.

With these two youngsters bearing the major weight of events, Vance spins out an elaborate tale of treachery, decadence, social climbing and the satisfaction of obtaining justice long delayed. Echoing his classic *The Dragon Masters* at one point, the story jumps between two major locales: the planets Thanet and Fader, the latter Night Lamp's satellite. The action spans two decades, giving the tale—whose twists and turns it would be unfair to divulge—a rich sense of history.

Another of Vance's prime concerns shines thorough in this book: the notion of delusional systems. In the largest sense of the label, any kind of society represents for Vance a consensual folly. But he makes a crucial distinction between those delusions that work, that are sustainable and generally beneficial, and those that are inherently primed for failure: predatory, destructive of their holders and those around them. The society on Thanet, with its stultification into "ledges of comporture," is a working system that generally promotes harmony and order (although Jaro the rebel runs afoul of it right from childhood). However, such malignant societies as that of Ushant (where "tamsour" rules) and Fader (where "rashudo" is the ideal) prove the danger of attempting to force life into artificial molds. In the concluding chapters of the book, Vance concentrates this warning down into the portrait of a single man with a unique, prison-bred philosophy and code of conduct, who is totally unable to adjust to freedom.

Always contrasting mankind's petty lusts and ultimately insignificant actions, our short lifespans and limited mentalities, against the vaster background of an infinite, infinitely rich universe, Jack Vance simultaneously upholds the sanctity of human life, proposing that our best impulses and emotions are the only reliable measures and guides in a treacherous cosmos.

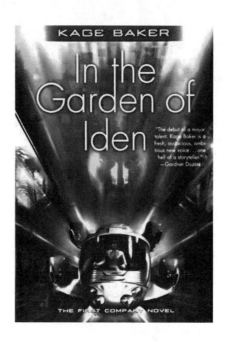

49: Kage Baker
In the Garden of Iden (1997)
[The Company]

WHEN KAGE Baker died in 2010 at age 57, she had been publishing science fiction for less than a decade and a half, but her impact was swift and enduring. Her major work was the Company/Dr. Zeus, Inc. series of nine novels and a considerable number of short stories and novellas linked by the theme of time travel, covert manipulation of history and prehistory, and enforced immortality for a few.[20] Fortunately, Baker was able to wrap this significant million-word-plus storyline with *The Sons of Heaven* (2008), which satisfactorily and quirkily tied together the multitude of threads spun out of the fertile premise of *In the Garden of Iden*. That debut novel introduced her obsessed and time-harried Spanish botanist Mendoza, seized as a small girl and imprisoned in 1541 by the Inquisition, saved by a Company Facilitator, Joseph, and augmented into a deathless cyborg by dubious emissaries from the 24th century.

Baker's clever, plausible twist on the time travel notion is that history (at any given moment) is invariant, so what is known to have happened cannot be changed by visitors from the future. However, much history is unrecorded or open to interpretation, allowing time travelers to intervene covertly. "If history states that John Jones won a

---

20 A useful, detailed account of the Dr. Zeus, Inc. project and its many operatives and conspiracies is *http://en.wikipedia.org/wiki/Dr._Zeus_Inc.* but this should not be consulted before reading the novels.

million dollars in the lottery on a certain day in the past, you can't go back there and win the lottery instead. But you can make sure that John Jones is an agent of yours, who will purchase the winning ticket on that day and dutifully invest the proceeds for you." Centuries later, wisely husbanded by financial dealers throughout the past, your winnings will arrive in the form of funds, land, recovered lost paintings by famous artists. Even extinct creatures and plants can be preserved for the benefit of future ages, so long as you have reliable agents seeded across the ages. This scheme allows the Company access to the treasures of time even though nobody can travel forward beyond their own point of origin. (Or so it seems, until Mendoza's puzzling "Crome radiation" starts messing with spacetime.)

Cyborged immortality, meanwhile, proves workable only when its necessary massive changes are made as early as possible. Adult bodies and brains are too set in their ways. Doomed, forgotten children of the past are located by Company agents and press-ganged into eternity. Feisty, ignorant little Mendoza is one such, even her name borrowed, condemned to death as a Jew by equally ignorant but far more culpable Inquisitors. Snatched away by 20 millennia-old Joseph, she begins her transformation and accelerated training as a specialist in rare plants for her saviors from nearly a thousand years in her future. This furtive organization, by the mid 24th century, is effectively rulers of the world. But mysteries attend Dr. Zeus, Inc., plenty of indications that its future is not the utopia its immortalized delegates might have hoped to find at the end of their long, weary journey. Indeed, no messages have been received from beyond the Silence in July 8, 2355, leading to wild speculations. Is the world doomed to end on that day, perhaps in a global conflict brought on by the Company itself?

Baker was a master of story: now emotionally moving and even heartbreaking, now zany and laugh-out-loud black-humored. Mendoza's fate, eerily, is to fall desperately in love three times with the same man, who is different each time and always inappropriate, but compulsively desirable. It is the kind of tangled gothic romance only possible in a time travel sequence, and Baker works it for all it's worth, to our enjoyment and benefit. In this opening volume, he is a 16th century English puritan, the former libertine and radical Nicholas Harpole, racked with guilt over his sexual infatuation with the lovely, mysterious Mendoza, who is only just starting to get the smallest notion of what being a cyborg implies.

In England for the marriage of Queen Mary Tudor to Prince Philip of Spain, Mendoza visits the botanical garden of Sir Walter Iden and finds there a rare medicinal treasure, Julius Caesar's Holly. Thus, the novel's title, with its inevitable undertones of exile from the Garden of Eden and its secret trees of both life and the knowledge of good and evil. Under Joseph's cynical tutelage, Mendoza seduces Nicholas, but when he uncovers her inhuman nature he flees to Rochester and preaches fire and brimstone, attracting the wrath of the reinstated Catholic church. Like the famous Oxford Martyrs, he is sentenced to burning at the stake. Can white-skinned, red-haired, black-eyed Mendoza, with her enhanced powers and knowledge of futuristic technology, save her lover?

In the Garden of Iden is very much the best place to start the series, but it really comes into its own with *Sky Coyote*. Mendoza arrives on the west coast of America in 1699, before the ruinous arrival of the Spanish. The local people, the Chumash tribe, are taken in by Joseph's manic impersonation of the trickster god, but less persuaded by his efforts to recruit their guilds into service of the Company. Accomplished in dialect, Baker avoids the usual stilted translations, presenting the Native Americans in charming and sometimes hilarious colloquialisms crossed with Chamber of Commerce wheeler-dealer from three centuries later. Introducing Joseph, visiting Humashup township, chief Sepawit stands in "nothing but a belt and some shell-bead money":

> "Well, folks. I guess our distinguished visitor doesn't need much of an introduction to you all—" Scattered nervous giggles at that.... "Uncle Sky Coyote, I'd like to introduce Nutku, spokesman for the Canoemakers' Union.... And this is Sawlawlan, spokesman for the United Workers in Steatite." Another one wearing lots of money, with big hair and a sea-otter cape. "And Kupiuc, spokesman for the Intertribal Trade Council and Second Functionary of the Humashup Lodge. And this is Kaxiwalic, one of our most successful independent entrepreneurs."

There's not a breath of condescension or mockery in this. Baker shows us worlds ancient and recent as if we live in them, and for all their startling familiarity they remain hauntingly strange. This is wonderful storytelling, cut tragically short by Baker's early death.

50: Joe Haldeman
Forever Peace (1997)

JOE HALDEMAN, 2010's SFWA Grand Master, is sf's consummate story-teller, his tales always illuminated by a moral consciousness. Far from turning them dull or preachy, this is what makes his fiction memorable, decade after decade. Half a life-time ago, Haldeman recast the Vietnam conflict in his memorable Hugo, Nebula and Locus award-winner, *The Forever War* (1975). His elite, technically-savvy troops battled an alien foe across light-years and centuries. Poignantly, each engagement cut them off from Earth by hundreds of years, as relativistic velocities flung them into their own ever-more incomprehensible future. At the end of the thousand year war, it all turned out to have been a mistake. And new humanity, now a standardized group-mind named Man, has more in common with the clone-like alien Taurans.

Where can damaged veterans go in a universe like that? Haldeman returned in *Forever Free* (1999), a quarter century later in both reality and narrative time-line, to probe the consequences of the peace. William Mandella and his love Marygay Potter accepted Man's offer of a world sardonically named Middle Finger ("up yours" or, even more frankly, MF). Here, unreconstructed relics of the war huddle from a universe repellent in its inhuman benevolence. MF proved to be the sort of welcome-home Vietnam veterans enjoyed—cold and hard. Technology, surprisingly, is not great-ly advanced after a millennium. William and Marygay, and their adolescent son and daughter, now aquaculture fisherfolk, live in ice-bound rural Paxton ("peace town"), chafing under Man's benign supervision. If *Forever War* was a caustic reply to Robert A. Heinlein's *Starship Troopers*, *Forever Free* seemed ready to follow his *Methuselah's Children*: a stolen starship, a run for the edge of the galaxy, freedom boldly purchased. But Haldeman had larger fish to fry.

Might a wily, squabbling group of aging veterans defeat the omnipresent custody of their evolutionary superiors? Or was Man's non-telepathic group mind a blind end? If Mandella and his conspirators managed to flee relativistically into the remote future, what could they possibly seek that will not be worse than their current anguished alienation? Might they find an answer to the horrors of the Forever War itself, and all of human history's suffering? The plot maneuvers of *Forever Free* are abrupt and startling. One conceptual breakthrough after another tears open our understanding of this universe, until finally Haldeman deploys a kind of Gnostic explanation for the world's pain. Gnosticism is a faith with few adherents these days, perhaps because it is not very satisfying—and its claims are just as dubious in fiction (except, perhaps, in Philip K. Dick's). The gratuitous cruelty that climaxes *Forever Free*, and its equally gratuitous redemption, lurches from comic-book excess to world-weary acceptance. The augmented fighting suits of this quasi-trilogy morphed into a stifling enclosure of the spirit.

A far more satisfying thematic sequel to *The Forever War* already existed, the subject of this entry—*Forever Peace*. Set in a different near-future (Haldeman's prefatory note calls it "a kind of sequel, though, examining some of that novel's problems from an angle that didn't exist twenty years ago"), this 1997 Hugo, Nebula and Campbell Memorial award-winner proposed a cure for war and hatred in the tradition of humanistic sf, notably Theodore Sturgeon's: just the sort of empathic group mind that Mandella and his veteran friends found so creepy. It was if Haldeman restlessly tried out all the variants on salvation, determined to keep us entertained as he did so. Perhaps he is telling us that suffering is simply built-in to the cosmos, laced through it, unavoidable except at the cost of extinguishing the burning spark of individual awareness.

Certainly the guilty pain of inflicting misery and death on a helpless foe nearly drives Harvard PhD physicist and part-time draftee warrior Sergeant Julian Class to suicide. In a convincing extrapolation of the remote-controlled UAVs now piloted to fatal destinations in Afghanistan by specialists in the US mainland, the wealthy nano-rich, warm fusion-powered Alliance in 2043 fight the Ngumi or "pedros," Third World guerillas, using "soldierboys," lethal robots run long-distance via jacked-in VR immersion.

Haldeman is not writing for the squeamish:

> I shouted "Drop it!" but she ignored me, and the second shot disintegrated her head and shoulders. I fired again, reflexively, blowing apart the M-31 and the hand that was aiming it, and turning her chest into a bright red cavity. Behind me, Amelia made a choking sound and ran to the bathroom to vomit.

The proverbial link between sex and violence is explicit—"her lower body was in a relaxed, casually seductive pose"—and jacking in is great for sex even when you're not killing someone: "when we were jacked it was something way beyond anything either of us had ever experienced. It was as if life were a big complex puzzle, and we suddenly had a piece dropped in that nobody else could see."

Adapting the cyberpunk convention, Haldeman suggests a more optimistic spin:

being mentally wired together in a sort of hive mind for several weeks disables a hunter/killer platoon's capacity to kill. Ultimately, this process will lead to the emergence of *Homo sapiens pacificans*, whose capacity to work together in mutual sympathy will ensure the subspecies' replacement of our current squabbling humankind.

In this partitioned world, even more extremely divided between haves and have-nots, an apocalyptic cult, the Enders, wishes to hasten the death not only of all humans but of the entire universe. Only in this way can a corrupt, fallen world be saved. Making this proposition all too realistic is the Jupiter Project, a sort of mega-Large Hadron Collider. Julian Class and his lover Amelia Harding learn of this experiment that within weeks will trigger a new Big Bang, destroying the cosmos. Their frantic analysis of this ultimate existential threat is rejected by the leading *Astrophysical Journal*, blocked by Enders in key places and their leaders, the Hammer of God. This is undoubtedly extreme and melodramatic—it's hard to imagine how even a nano-enabled society could dismantle and repurpose a moon of Jupiter within the next few decades—but serves the purpose admirably of pumping up the stakes in Haldeman's quest for a solution to human aggressiveness.

Forever Peace provides a rousing counterbalance to the bleak view of humanity's future in both *Forever War* and *Forever Free*.

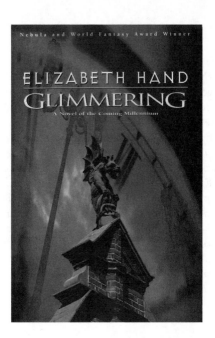

51: Elizabeth Hand
Glimmering (1997)

ASTUTE CRITIC, unashamed craftsmanly novelizer of films, artist supreme in her own non-shared universes, Elizabeth Hand has emerged since her debut novel *Winterlong* as one of the finest voices of her generation, a cohort of writers who all debuted more or less in the middle 1980s. Unlabeled and uncategorized so far by historians of the genre—other than those who formed the cyberpunk and humanist camps—this generation has emerged over the span of this survey to be the defining voices of the field, taking up the reins in large part from any still-working survivors of earlier ages, and driving the team of speculative horses in a noticeably different direction.

Hand's gorgeously crafted fiction generally falls into slipstream categories, and of late has even ventured into pure naturalism (*Generation Loss*). But she proved herself to be an expert hard-edged speculator with the *Glimmering* and selected other works.

For this apocalyptic saga of a world gone off the rails, Robert Chambers's cult masterpiece, *The King in Yellow,* serves Hand in an untraditional, non-Lovecraftian way as a symbol of fin-de-siècle decadence and spiritual entropy betokening the grim ride ahead for humanity in a collapsing ecosystem.

This book in Hand's canon was preceded, tellingly enough, by her novelization of Terry Gilliam's film *12 Monkeys*, and *Glimmering* is a clear kissing cousin to that cinematic biological Götterdämmerung.

Hand economically sets up her premise in a two-page prologue: in the year 1997 (but not precisely our historical 1997, rather a uchronic version), an overdose of new ozone-destroying chemicals, coupled with a massive methane release from polar regions and an enormous solar flare, trigger a change in Earth's atmosphere, soon dubbed the Glimmering. Moiré sheets of cold colored flames replace our natural celestial view, and all electrical equipment in use at the instant of ignition is shorted out. This is clearly the end of civilization as we've abused it. Major adjustments are demanded. But with a blind stubbornness, the mass of mankind continues to hang on to old habits.

Hand's use of this particular trope—celestial phenomena changing our terrestrial physics—solidly allies her with such hardcore forebears as Fredric Brown ("The Waveries") and Poul Anderson (*Brain Wave*) and might very well have had an influence on the similar premise of S. M. Stirling's *Emberverse* series.

One of those with his head in the sand—circa 1999, two miserable years into the disaster—is John Chanvers Finnegan, a gay man who is heir to a dwindling family fortune (initially founded on the sale of Victorian glass Xmas ornaments, ironically echoing the current gaudy appearance of the Earth itself). Finnegan lives in a decrepit Yonkers mansion with his elderly grandmother and house-keeper. The fact that he is dying of AIDS is understandably more vital to him than the world's demise. What will shake Finnegan out of his semi-charmed life? A visit and miraculous gift from his mysterious friend, Leonard Thrope, a devil-may-care Byronic artist—or "sociocultural pathologist"—intent on bearing witness to death and dying in all its forms.

Soon, Finnegan is reluctantly hosting stray pregnant waifs, seeing tangible ghosts, feeling love reawaken, and beginning to realize that he has been nominated for a larger role in the coming millennium than he had ever wished to play.

Two motifs here signify Hand's devotion to a pair of masterly writers who have influenced her greatly. The decaying, life-stuffed mansion speaks to John Crowley's *Little, Big,* while the persistence-with-distortion of cultural norms and personal relationships amidst urban dissolution harks to Samuel R. Delany's *Dhalgren*. Both Crowley and Delany have played a huge part in the formation of Hand's own esthetic.

Hand, of course, excels at her gritty depiction of a world on the skids. No stranger to postapocalypses ever since her *Winterlong* and its sequels, she has a keen knack for conveying the psychic adjustments people must make to continue surviving in the midst of chaos. Unlike some Irwin Allen panoramic disaster, *Glimmering* has a smallish cast of major characters, allowing Hand to build up in great and subtle detail their realistic portraits. The visceral thrills of life in the ruins are balanced precisely by Hand's loving attention to individual psyches.

With a dollop of Lucius Shepard's *Green Eyes* (and is there a sly allusion to Shepard in the character of music manager Lucius Chappell?), a smattering of Mark Helprin's *Winter's Tale*, a pinch of Disch's *334*, and Hand's own salty broth and spices, *Glimmering* is a unique and tasty dish that might be called Ragnarok Ragout.

52: Jonathan Lethem
As She Climbed Across the Table (1997)

L IKE NEIL Gaiman, Jonathan Lethem and his career have long ago transcended the science fiction genre of their roots, soaring into the literary stratosphere occupied by PEN conferences and assignments from *Rolling Stone* magazine to hang with funk legend James Brown. Perhaps the clearest token of this status occurred when his recent domestic relocation from Brooklyn to the West Coast became fodder for the New York tabloids. While he remains genially avuncular toward the genre, producing introductions, for instance, for the Library of America Philip K. Dick omnibuses, it is undeniable that starting no later than his fifth book, *Motherless Brooklyn*, he was no longer a part of science fiction, despite his continued usage of the tropes of fantastika.

Yet once upon a time, it was possible to view Lethem's work as wholly integral with the field, where it received regular reviews (not the case today), and surely with *As She Climbed Across the Table*, he played completely and brilliantly within the boundaries of the genre.

Lethem's first novel, *Gun, with Occasional Music*, was a gonzo dystopia. In the world inhabited by Private Inquisitor Conrad Metcalf, Muzak has infiltrated all audiovisual media, resulting in orchestral newscasts, abstract TV, and newspapers filled with captionless photos. Asking questions is a forbidden act, save to those of the Inquisitor's Office and to the few independent PI's like Metcalf. Artificially evolved animals (who function much like the Toons in *Roger Rabbit*, a tragicomic underclass) and artificially evolved children—"babyheads"—mingle with the repressed normal humans, neurotics who all suffer from this society's absurdist strictures.

Amnesia Moon solidified Lethem's street creds in the sf world. In the near future, things have come apart. Alien invasion, psychotropic warfare, environmental disaster— the cause of our downfall is any, all, or none of these. But the effects are indisputable. The world is now divided into zones of altered reality, subject to the shaping influences of the occasional lucid dreamer, whose flights of fancy become other people's reality (as in, of course, so much of Philip K. Dick's work, and Le Guin's *The Lathe of Heaven*).

Living in a shattered Wyoming community that evokes the ambiance of a dozen classic apocalyptic venues all run through a blender, our protagonist, Chaos, appears to be such a powerful figure, yet one wounded by amnesia and kept in subjugation by fellow dreamer, the Palmer Eldritch-like Kellogg. One day Chaos's disgust and unease reach the boiling point: he assaults Kellogg and hits the road, determined to discover his past. Along for the ride comes Melinda Self, furry thirteen-year-old foil, a ruefully humorous, tough-minded daughter figure.

His hegira takes Chaos through a handful of twisted communities, eventually depositing him in a relatively functional San Francisco.

As She Climbed Across the Table, Lethem's third novel, mixed centered surrealism and loopy groundedness, and is as smoothly exhilarating as Eric Clapton's guitar licks, and possibly just as classic. And like any pop masterpiece, it goes down so smoothly that you don't notice the philosophical barbs until you're being reeled in. With its emphasis on academic-centered hard physics R&D, it could be a Gregory Benford novel (*COSM,* say) in postmodern drag.

Physicist Alice Coombs has made a certain decision of the heart: to fall in love with an artificially created pocket universe named "Lack," whose only manifestation in our continuum is a picky nothingingness that ingests random objects. Naturally Alice's newly discarded lover, Philip Engstrand, pompous soft science maven, is dismayed at losing his soulmate. This book—narrated in Philip's hurt, ironic, hilariously bewildered tones—is the story of how Philip seeks to reclaim Alice from Lack.

Miraculously, *As She Climbed* functions equally well on a multitude of intriguing levels. It's plain old soap opera, the eternal triangle of girl, boy, and spacetime discontinuity. It's a retelling of "The Emperor's New Clothes," illustrating how people can delude themselves into believing that "nothing is something." It's a cheesy "invention rapes inventor" tale, like Dean Koontz's *Demon Seed*. And it's a pungent satire of academia, with just the section on Georges De Tooth, "resident deconstructionist," worth a dozen lesser campus novels.

Moreover, Lethem finds time to riff on several fellow authors: James Tiptree (another Alice), is evident in the heroine's feelings for Lack: "It's a basic response to... embrace the alien." *Crash*-era Ballard can be heard in this project by one of Philip's grad students: "[He] had applied for funding to study the geographic spray of athletes on a playing field following an injury. He wanted to understand the disbursement of bodies around the epicenter of the wounded player..." And Terry Bisson's story, "The Shadow Knows," featuring an alien emptiness in a bowl, seems another definite referent.

Lethem's beautifully balanced, metaphorically rich prose propels this blackly jolly fable to a surprising yet satisfying conclusion. By book's end, a sense that the author had accomplished his takeoff taxiing and was now fully in flight for more cosmopolitan cities pervades the pages.

53: Ken MacLeod
The Cassini Division (1998)
[Fall Revolution]

BY A strange irony, this astringently cynical novel is best known for one phrase, a sarcastic put-down of the Vingean Singularity: "The Rapture for the nerds." The irony is that the story is exactly about what happens to humankind after a real Singularity accelerates and transforms technogeeks into a state inconceivable to the (apparent) losers who are Left Behind.

These Outwarder "fast folk" upload themselves into immensely powerful computer substrates on Jupiter, dismantle its moon Ganymede, turning it into an exotic-matter wormhole that stretches to a very distant star. Their human slaves use that traversable spacetime link to escape to a world they name New Mars, ten millennia in the future, where they set up a libertarian anarcho-capitalist utopia.

What ensues is a clash not just of civilizations but of utopias, as the Union—those deathless humans who inhabit the inner solar system after the Fall Revolution of 2045 and savage viral attacks from Jupiter on their electronic infrastructure—reject capitalism and embrace a kind of Darwinian communism. It is a drastic imaginary sandbox few American writers would consider playing in, and indeed Ken MacLeod, like his colleague Iain M. Banks (see Entry 17), is a Scot. It's no coincidence that two other non-Scottish masters of transhuman sf, Charles Stross (Entry 81) and Hannu Rajaniemi (Entry 101), also live in Scotland, a territory known for its fierce independence and resentment of authority.

The Cassini Division is the equivalent, in MacLeod's Fall Revolution history, of Special Circumstances, the spy commando operatives of Banks's post-scarcity Culture utopia. MacLeod's viewpoint agent is beautiful, youthful but old. Ellen May Ngwethu (a surname that means *freedom*) is convinced that the long-quiescent fast folk are preparing a new assault on the despised mere humans. The Command Committee remain doubtful, and consider her suggested solution to be nothing better than genocide. But Ngwethu holds firm to the ideology developed by Korean and Japanese labor-camp prisoners, the True Knowledge, cobbled together from the few pre-20th century books available to them: Stirner, Nietzsche, Marx and Engels, Joseph Dietzgen ("The moral duty of an individual never exceeds his interests. The only thing which exceeds those interests is the *material power* of the generality over the individual"), Darwin and Herbert Spencer. Their doctrine is uncompromising, "the first socialist philosophy based on totally pessimistic and cynical conclusions about human nature:

> Life is a process of breaking down and using other matter, and if need be, other life.... There is nothing but matter, forces, space and time, which together make power. Nothing matters, except what matters to you. Might makes right, and power makes freedom. You are free to do whatever is in your power, and if you want to survive and thrive you had better do whatever is in your interests....
>
> All that you really value, and the goodness and truth and beauty of life, have their roots in this apparently barren soil.
>
> This is the true knowledge.
>
> We had founded our idealism on the most nihilistic implications of science, our socialism on crass self-interest, our peace on our capacity for mutual destruction, and our liberty on determinism. We had replaced morality with convention, bravery with safety, frugality with plenty, philosophy with science, stoicism with anesthetics and piety with immortality.

And the outcome of this extreme teaching, where the word "banker" is the ultimate obscenity? Why, a culture "sustainable materially and psychologically, a climax community of the human species, the natural environment of a conscious animal.... We called it the Heliocene Epoch. It seemed like a moment in the sun, but there was no reason, in principle, why it couldn't outlast the sun, and spread to all the suns of the sky."

The Outwarders in their Jupiter Brain, though, breaking free at last from their virtual reality trap or mass psychosis, seem ready to turn all the matter and energy in the solar system into more data-crunchers. To them, ordinary augmented humans are "counter-evolutionaries." On distant New Mars, meanwhile, ten thousand years in the future but linked by the wormhole to their era of origin, capitalism has created an alternative utopia with AIs and uploads (rejected as mere machines by the Union), copied minds. The dead can be revived from smart-matter storage, a marvel of the free market.

Some of the characters reappear from MacLeod's 1996 Prometheus award winner, *The Stone Canal*. Each of the four Fall Revolution volumes can be read independently. The first, *The Star Fraction* (1995)—a nominee for Arthur Clarke award, also winning the libertarian Prometheus award despite its Trotskyist coloration—is less accomplished than the splendid sequels. *The Sky Road* (1999) skews this history interestingly.

Ellen Ngwethu's quest, in *The Cassini Division,* is for the vanished genius Isambard Kingdom Malley, whose flawed theory of everything was still close enough to the truth that the wormhole project and a working starship drive were based on it. Malley lives among dropouts from the Union: he's a non-co, a contemptible non-cooperator in the new communist order. She finds him, and in the Division's spacecraft *Terrible Beauty* they take the wormhole route to New Mars to arrange cometary kinetic attacks on the posthumans of Jupiter ten thousand years in the past. MacLeod's blend of upscale tour-of-utopias (all the chapters are named after classic works of this kind: Looking Backward, News from Nowhere, A Modern Utopia, In the Days of the Comet, etc), ideological spats (New Martian capitalists use gene-engineered upgrades, the communists stick to machines, including nano-difference engines), and traditional thrill-a-minute calamity storytelling makes this one of the best novels about the Singularity: a veritable rapture for nerds!

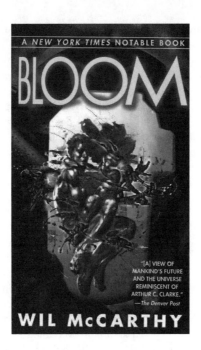

54: Wil McCarthy
Bloom (1998)

A HOT-SHOT POLYMATH, Wil McCarthy has been a rocket engineer for Lockheed, a popular-science columnist, a TV movie scenarist, and the inventor of what could turn out to be one of the landmark inventions of all time, programmable matter, discussed in his 2003 book *Hacking Matter*.[21] His company RavenBrick is developing early forms of smart matter, such as windows that respond selectively to heat, rather as spectacles do to ultraviolet light, the first step on the way to materials with tunable quantum dopants that let them mimic other substances. Somewhere in there, he published nine novels, ranging from effective to brilliant, the most recent when he was just 39. It is an early career to make Robert Heinlein seem like an amateur.

What marks McCarthy's fiction is its blend of well-conceived and often extravagant plotting, believable characterization, vivid and accurate settings, and classic *faux*-scientific handwaving that seems altogether credible, even as the reader's mind boggles. This mix is no accident; McCarthy notes:

> The problem with action/adventure fiction is that most of it is dumb as rocks. The problem with literary fiction is that for all its beauty and depth, there's usually not much going on. In between these two extremes lies what is gener-

---

21 Downloadable from *http://www.wilmccarthy.com/HackingMatterMultimediaEdition.pdf*

ally known as "genre" fiction, i.e., the romance, SF, horror, mystery and suspense stories that most of us actually read.

Bloom was his fifth published novel, released when he was 32, and certified his arrival as an sf master. A further sequence of four novels, known collectively as *The Queendom of Sol*, was launched two years later with the astonishing *The Collapsium*, about a man who uses nanorobots to build his own small planet in the Kuiper belt after first assembling thousands of miniature black holes, devises fax teleportation for the Solar System, and then in a fit of urgency invents the principles behind an inertialess space drive, and flies off to rescue the Sun from imminent destruction. And that's just the start. The series is a four course meal, stuffed with nutritious alternative physics that might even turn out to be true. *Bloom,* by contrast, is a bracing energy drink and a brisk workout that leaves you muscle-burned but satisfied.

John Strasheim, a cobbler on austere Ganymede in 2106 who makes shoes weighted down with gold, that now-abundant metal, is a part-time journalist whose book on the destruction of Earth and the rest of the inner solar system is a minor classic. The moons of Jupiter, and other small habitats of the outer solar system, remain free of the dreadful Mycora nanoplague infestation that emerged in New Guinea and almost instantly sporulated across the world, turning flesh, buildings and rock into seething versions of itself. These technogenic lifeform spores poured out into space, eating energy from sunlight, infecting and absorbing everything out as far as the asteroids, when the cold began to hamper their spread. But only the most vigorous and devoted efforts by the Immunity—the cultures of the outer system—can fend them off.

Now Strasheim is recruited to join a select crew to probe this swarming infestation, flying inward toward the Sun in the *Louis Pasteur,* now coated with a mimetic fractal surface that its designer hopes will deter the mycora gray goo from snacking on it. It seems that the Mycosystem is learning to adapt, speeding its breach of the immunity protections:

> The air vent and the wall it was part of began to boil, their substance turning fluid, turning into rainbow-threaded vapors as the tiny, tiny mycora disassembled them molecule by molecule.... How vivid the colors, how crisp the lines and edges!... class-one threaded bloom in early germination phase, about two minutes before fruiting began. Some structure already visible in the expanding fog, crystalline picks growing like needles from the drydock wall.

Not everyone is happy about this expedition, not least the cultish Temples of Transcendent Evolution, which regard the vast swarm as a sort of deity, an immense mind that has evolved or perhaps been designed to replace humankind as the noösphere of the solar system. Cast as the superstitious foe of Ganymede's more reasonable citizens, the Temples prove seductively plausible, not surprisingly since they echo the transcendental yearnings of many of sf's best and most influential writers: Sturgeon with his hunger after gestalt minds, Heinlein and his Pantheistic Multiperson Solipsism, Goonan's surreal nanopunk (see Entry 90). Also not surprisingly, therefore, except to the main characters, the payoff turns out to approximate this scientistic transcendence, putting a crimp in the covert motives of the expedition.

Pursued by ships of the Temples, Strasheim and his fellow astronauts pause for supplies at the Floral asteroids, and get their staid minds blown by the arboreal low-gravity antics of Saint Helier settlers, with their hypogravitic osteo deformities. It's a classic sf confrontation of cultures radiated from everything we find familiar, the zee-spec wearing Ganymedeans (whose clunky specs provide them with wearable computation, augmented reality overlays, etc) and the neurally-wired, AI-assisted, touchy-feely asteroid humans and their delightful creole, that has to be translated by instantly uploaded zee-spec code:

> *"Heyyo," the man said brightly. "Ahn behalfde gavnoffice, aloha wekkome the San Heelyer. Ma nom wa Chris Dibrin. Kai I am lok to assist you."*

Ostensibly, the *Pasteur's* task is to drop monitors on the inner planets, but the Temples, and their embedded agents, are convinced that these devices are meant to destroy the Mycora. That's not impossible, given "ladderdown" nuclear technology, one of McCarthy's zanier inventions: a process in which elements are encouraged to transmute into states lower on the periodic chart, releasing immense amounts of energy. Abused, this power source might set off vast solar flares, driven by "cascade fusion," that will boil away the entire Mycosystem. McCarthy handles this risky melodrama with skill, frightening and awing us with the scale of the threat and its possible solution, but retaining a vulnerable human voice as his narrator.

Let's hope McCarthy finds time to return to fiction after he's solved some of the more urgent problems of the real world.

LINDA NAGATA
LOCUS AWARD–WINNING AUTHOR OF
DECEPTION WELL

"Linda Nagata is at the vanguard of a new
and brilliant generation of writers combining
hard science with stirring adventure."
—David Brin

VAST

A LAST REMNANT OF HUMANITY
SEEKS ITS ANCIENT ENEMY

55: Linda Nagata
Vast (1998)

FEMALE WRITERS of Hard Sf, widescreen baroque or otherwise—those hypothetical gender-swapped equivalents of, for instance, the "Three Gregs," Benford, Bear and Egan—are sparse on the shelves. Julie Czerneda and Joan Slonczewski (Entry 9), come to mind, but don't quite peg into the exact same narrative niches as the males cited. Lois McMaster Bujold (Entry 19) tends more toward Patrick O'Brian. And Catherine Asaro slants more towards interstellar romances. Linda Nagata, however, matches the males precisely at a game they previously imagined was their own domain.

Her first two novels popped up at either end of 1995 as paperback originals. First to surface was *The Bohr Maker*. Shifting amidst a variety of sweat-redolent, lived-in, high-tech venues, with an emphasis on far-out nanotech extrapolations, this book called up shades of Michael Swanwick's *Vacuum Flowers*, boasting believable characters who were truly citizens of the future, in both attitudes and capabilities.

Playing fluidly with concepts of identity and reality (simulated versions of various characters and their surroundings compete with baseline originals), Nagata wove a thrilling tale of the deadly hunt for the device of the title, a unique colony of nanomachines capable of turning any human host nearly godlike. Employing characters from the lower classes (the street urchins Phousita and Arif) as well as the upper (space-dwelling Nikko and his nemesis and lover, Kirstin), Nagata was able to sketch an entire world in her fluent, hardedged prose, a tool as sharp as that possessed by many a longtime writer.

This exciting debut showed an author who had fully digested the work of writers from Bear to Egan, McAuley to Calder, Varley to Ryman, and fashioned her own bright chimeric beast on which to ride and join the parade.

With her second book, *Tech-Heaven*, Nagata did many things differently, while retaining the virtues of the first book—always a promising strategy. And she appeared to add two more writers to her list of influences: Norman Spinrad and James Tiptree.

Unlike *Bohr*, *Tech-Heaven* opened in a world not too far removed from ours. Biotech research is slightly further along, as are several societal trends of a Luddite, Balkanizing nature. Otherwise, a gritty familiarity obtains. The character whose shoulders we ride exclusively (with one small exception) is the young woman named Katie Kishida, wife to Tom, mother to two daughters. This tighter focus, compared to the viewpoint shifts in *Bohr*, allowed a rich depth of character development. Over the jam-packed course of this novel, we see Katie believably age into her early sixties, accumulating scars and layers of memory that evoke the painfully earned wisdom exhibited by many of Tiptree's older female characters.

When her husband has what seems to be an inescapably fatal accident, Katie faces the task of seeing him placed into risky cryonic suspension. (The details of cryonic shutdown and, later, revival are highly convincing and realistic, and are typical of Nagata's scrupulous attention to the nuts-and-bolts of her future.) This act diverts Katie's whole life onto an unexpected course. Taken up by the media and by competing pro-cryo and anti-cryo factions, Katie becomes first a spokesperson for the movement, then an actual high-stakes player in the whole biotech industry.

It's in the details of the political infighting and media manipulation that Nagata shows a flair reminiscent of Spinrad's. Much of the book is devoted to Machiavellian maneuvers that, gradually, lead us to the very future of *The Bohr Maker*. Along the way, mankind's immersion in the technosphere, the quest for the utopian "tech-heaven" is forcefully debated, with not all of the points accruing to Katie's side either. (Short intermittent chapters focus on the Bardo-like hallucinations of the frozen Tom Kishida, whose brain retains a certain level of functioning, providing a spiritual angle to the materialistic debate.)

Nagata's next book, *Deception Well*, would elaborate—after skipping a big interval of fictional time in her future history—the developments seen in the first two volumes.

In the period of *Deception Well*, three millennia hence, a small portion of our galaxy has been settled by sublight ships carrying frozen human passengers. Some suns have become Hallowed Vasties, surrounded by millions of artificial habitats in a kind of pointillistic Dyson sphere. The nanotech known as "makers" allows for many other biological and material wonders as well. But all human civilization is under threat from the berserker fleet known as the Chenzeme, who have ravaged the galaxy for millions of years. Besides their predatory ships, the Chenzeme have infected mankind with a cult virus that breeds charismatic leaders obscurely allied to the Chenzeme cause, as well as hordes of obedient followers.

One such hybrid Savonarola is a young man named Lot. We encounter him as a child, and follow his adventures on the world known as Deception Well, a Solaris-type living planet that offers a possible solution to mankind's problems. After such mind-expanding incidents as rappelling down two hundred miles of orbital beanstalk and being ingested by the Well, lot ends up forced to flee his home with several friends, in further search of his destiny.

Vast opens some 200 years after this departure. The semi-living ship *Null Boundary*, shadowed by Chenzeme pursuers, carries Lot and his comrades toward an unknown fate. Adding tension, the humans (including the ship's captain, an ancient digitized personality called Nikko) are at odds about their best options and leery of Lot's powers. When the Chenzeme ship catches up to *Null Boundary*, a strange mating between the two crafts opens up new avenues for possibly subverting the whole Chenzeme fleet. Whether Lot will achieve his personal goals remains in doubt up till the final pages.

Nagata is highly inventive in her language, conjuring up such terms as "philosopher cells" and "sensory tears" to brilliantly match her closely reasoned speculations. Although the density of her conceptualization never reaches Eganesque levels, she provides more than enough wonders—including an entire vacuum ecosystem—to entrance the reader.

At one point, Lot, nearly drowning inside a *Null Boundary* environment gone chaotic, experiences "a sense of wonder edged in faint, warm fear." That's the impact Nagata's work offers to readers, too.

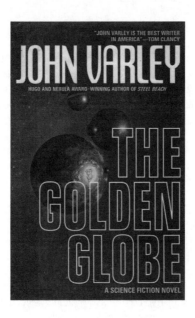

56: John Varley
The Golden Globe (1998)

A TERRIFYINGLY VIVID life-and-death pursuit inward from the outer solar system, an hilarious and cluey Hollywood-in-Space and Off-Off-Broadway tell-all, a scam caper, a poignant psychobiography, *The Golden Globe* is the most fun you can have (as John Varley says of writing his sf) with your clothes on. Although there's no obligation *not* to read it naked, as dedicated nudist Robert A. Heinlein, one of Varley's acknowledged prototypes, might have done. After all, in this highly enjoyable romp, eight year old thespian Kenneth Catherine "Sparky" Valentine and his Gang perform for millions of viewers in vests but without pants, bare as Donald and Daisy Duck. They decide not to have sex on the show until sidekick Polly is 11 and has her "blood day," just as her mother did.

And their show rates better than a competing kiddy program, *What the Fuck?*, which is failing because "the declining numbers of educational programming across the board in the past three years reflected a growing anti-intellectualism or merely a stagnation of fresh new ideas in the presentation of loftier kid-vid." On his 100th birthday, in 2250, highly cyborged and ageless, switching from male to female form at the rather painful drop of a hat, Kenneth is denounced by another player as a "poly-morphous, talentless, scenery-chewing, ass-kissing sorry excuse for a has-been actor!"

Little wonder that a recent interview with Varley for a conservative website issued this warning: **Read at your own risk.**[22]

Sparky's dad is abusive, charismatic John Barrymore Valentine, famous as a stage ac-

---

22 *http://www.republibot.com/content/interview-john-varley?page=1*

tor in this era of vids and (according to *Howdy Doody* "The Trade Mag of Kid-vid") for

what the police call the "long con." That's what he did time for, anyway, though I've been told his skills at the Pigeon Drop and the Spanish Lottery are considerable as well. He exhibits no shame about this, doesn't mind discussing it with the press. It's all part of some extremely wonky political worldview I will not bore you with.

This worldview might be consistent with libertarian Heinleinism, a formidable star-craving crank cult in Luna two centuries after the Invaders took over Earth and incidentally killed billions, exiling the remnant of humankind to the Eight Worlds, most of them moons.

Versions of that elaborate solar system have comprised Varley's chief playground since the late 1970s, most buoyantly and complexly displayed in *Steel Beach* (1993), this quasi-sequel, and the promised finale, *Irontown Blues*.

Down on his luck in the cometary zone beyond Pluto—not to mention that little business with the governor's daughter—centenarian Sparky gets his chance to play Lear. But only if he (and his Bichon Frise dog Toby) can reach the Golden Globe theater, King City, Luna farside. Even flying in a pirated spacecraft via a slingshot past the photosphere of the Sun, it seems a schedule impossible for a man without funds. And there's a Mafia enforcer team after him from the former Plutonian hard-case prison moon Charon, demonic commandos of ruthless pursuit. This relentless chase, an all-stops-out blend of Hitchcock, Peckinpah, and Itchy & Scratchy, has Sparky braining (with a sousaphone and a violin case), dismembering, and setting fire to his vengeful hunter, who keeps coming back for more like one of the Furies:

> With one hand almost off, one arm stuck to his side by the tanglenet, the other arm held by the ring of brass tubing, six inches shorter and fifty pounds lighter than me... even with all that about the only edge I had on him was the weight.... I wrestled him to the bed, all the time soaking up a punishing series of kicks to the shin and a jackhammering of his knees to my crotch.... His kicking lost some accuracy, but never let up. I hurled him face-first into the makeup mirror, pulled him away, and then did it again now that it was broken and jagged.... I searched for his eyes with my thumbs and felt something squish, but that gave him a chance to shrug the tuba up over his free shoulder and he began flailing at me. He used the arm as a club, getting in one ringing blow that almost broke my collarbone, then another to my side, before bringing his forearm down like a swung baseball bat on the edge of the makeup table. Face powder blossomed into the air, and both bones in his forearm snapped like dry spaghetti. I thought I heard him grunt a little from that, but it never slowed him. He kept swinging the arm, which now bent in three places, the mangled and blackened remains of his fist like a grisly mace at the end of a bloody rope.

These recurrent set-pieces are genuinely thrilling, and macabrely funny. Varley is shameless. In earlier and better days, to which many flashbacks return us, young Sparky had an accountant, "a handsome Latin-lover type who... looked like a lawyer, and who was proud of his Indian and Arab heritage, ...named Yasser Dhatsma-Bhebey." Only in a novel as drenched in stage and movie lore as this one could a lawyer be named, unblushingly, Yes sah! Dat's ma baby. Is that Yasser's gag, or Varley's? It doesn't matter; this is madcap noir.

Adding to the lunacy is Elwood P. Dowd, as played by Jimmy Stewart in *Harvey*, who shows up (visible only to Valentine Jr.) in moments of crisis to chide Sparky gently or give him handy advice. The legendary director of *King Lear*, toward whom he is rushing under deadline, is his childhood sidekick Polly, now a centenarian crone whose fundamentalist creed forbids her the benefit of antiaging treatments. And there's the murder he (or perhaps Elwood Dowd) committed 70 years ago, which also has him on the run. When the hitman shows up in his dressing room halfway through a triumphant opening night, disabling his lethal Pantechnicon luggage and menacing beloved Toby the dog, it's showdown time. Followed, inevitably, by a court trial—this one adjudicated by a computerized Judge, and interrupted by shocking revelations. What else would you hope for in such a fun gallimaufry? A faster than light starship in which to flee the Charonese? Luckily, there's one of those, too, owned by the Heinleiners.

As Sparky, that ancient movie buff, says: "Keep watching the sky!"

57: Simon Ings
Headlong (1999)

S CIENCE FICTION is always breeding up its own successors, the glorious mutants who will overthrow the reigning dinosaurs and inherit the marketplace. Thus
it was with cyberpunk, that subgenre just breaking big circa 1985, at the start of our
survey. These mirrorshade-wearing rebels came along, cunning mammals, and over-
threw the old fogy dinosaurs. But fifteen years onward, a new generation of writers
had taken the crude and primitive tools and tropes which the first-generation cyberpunks had established and expanded them immensely. The first-gen writers, born
mid-twentieth-century or earlier, improvising their tools as they raced ahead into the
mists of futurity, the lineaments of the fabulous beast they stalked as yet unclear, lurking at the waterholes Burroughs and Pynchon had charted, could only look behind
now and see baroque mutants surpassing their progenitors in every way!

Simon Ings is a fine example of this phenomenon. His second and third novels were a tight duology comprised of *Hot Head* and *Hotwire*. Ings—a cusp writer
born in 1965—furiously limned a transhuman future where giant rogue AIs known
as Massives plot a biologically ripe fate for the solar system incorporating jazzed-up
humans weird enough to be their own aliens. Ings's future can be synopsized thus:
not long from now, Earth is a patchwork of poverty and wealth, shiny new cities and
plaguey ruins, all as a result of a recent war fought with the Massives. No clear victory
was won by either side, for the Massives still flourish, on Earth as intelligent networks
and in space as mad habitats where exotic lifeforms are bred in tanks and on slabs of
pain. Various factions—pro- and anti-Massive, as well as neutrals—pursue their diverse
goals, utilizing exotic technics, creating nano- and bio-based miracles.

In language as dense as anything by McAuley (Entry 23) or Egan (Entry 38), Ings proved himself their conceptualizing equal, an outrider on humanity's singularity-bound forced march into the future. These superb novels were the very model of post-modern, trans-cyberpunk fiction: laser-gazed logicbombs, simultaneously appalling and heartening, monitory and embracing. All the lessons and insights and techniques that the first generation of cyberpunks donned like sometimes ill-fitting garments, Ings fully internalized.

Ings culminated this series with *Headlong*, which, by virtue of a single shared character (the scientist Dr. Nouronihar), serves as a prequel to his duology. Yet in effect and tone, it's vastly different from the prior two novels. More along the lines of M. John Harrison's *Signs of Life* or Richard Kadrey's *Kamikaze L'Amour*, *Headlong* is a love story and a tale of detection set much closer to our present time. (The similarity to Harrison's work, at least, cannot be coincidental, for Ings has even collaborated with Harrison on a story or two.) Consequently, the milieu of *Headlong*, distorted as it might be with new drugs, new politics, and new technology, feels more homey than that in the duology, and so the bruising events hit even more forcefully.

Like most great Chandler- or Hammettesque noir fiction, *Headlong* is narrated stylishly in the first person. The poetically melancholy Chris Yale was an architect assigned to help colonize the Moon. Given brain implants that confer godlike sensory abilities by his employer, the enigmatic Apolloco, Yale and his wife Joanne, along with the other Lunarians, became something other than mortal. However, economic collapse on Earth dragged them back "downwell," where they were stripped of their new senses. Now, like the doomed starpilots in Delany's "Aye, and Gomorrah…" the exiled Lunarians form a caste of crippled freaks, subject to a disease called Epistemic Appetite Imbalance.

Bad as his lot is, Yale is about to experience worse. His ailing wife turns up murdered, and his search for the reasons behind her strange death propel the swiftly moving, indeed headlong plot.

Ings's book is stuffed with classic noir tropes: treacherous friends, helpful enemies, driven cops, sexual confusion, drugs, riddles, assignations with strangers in seedy dives. But Ings infuses each trope with the requisite sf energy, and the union of genres is seamless. Ings manages also to balance the fate of individuals with the fate of his whole world, giving each its proper weight. Here is Ings via Chris Yale musing on the paradoxical search for truth:

> The detective looks for a single cause. The detective hunts through the spreading World, dismissing the irrelevant, the ambiguous, the accidental, and searches instead for one Answer.
>
> The World, on the other hand, has no focus. From a single cause, it extemporizes a complex creation, a live and changing mass, an endless spew of things. The World doesn't care for answers, only questions.
>
> The detective's truth and the World's truth are different. Find one, you lose the other.

There is nothing extraneous in Ings's writing, and much that is marvelous. Blink between sentences, and you might miss something. His Ballardian touches explore real emotional and psychic depths, and chart some dangerous shoals in the murky waters ahead of us.

Toward the end of *Hotwire*, Ings says, "My world…had left its languages lagging so far behind…" But by writing his books, Ings has rendered that trap inert.

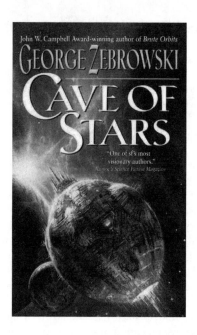

John W. Campbell Award-winning author of *Brute Orbits*

GEORGE ZEBROWSKI

CAVE OF STARS

"One of sf's most visionary authors."
Asimov's Science Fiction Magazine

58: George Zebrowski
Cave of Stars (1999)

DURING MORE than 40 years as a writer—his first story appeared in 1970—George Zebrowski has gained praise and recognition as one of the philosopher-poets of science fiction. The long novel *Macrolife* (1979) carried humankind in swarming space habitats from a dying Earth to the final transcendental Omega Point collapse of the cosmos. The usual adjective applied to *Macrolife* is Stapledonian (for the British author of *Last and First Men* and *The Star Maker*), but its companion *Cave of Stars* pays more attention than Stapledon did to the people involved in his own immense future history.

Zebrowski now has a large body of short work, young adult and other novels, some in collaboration. He has edited anthologies, published *Star Trek* franchise books of more than usual reach, and in 1999 won the prestigious Campbell Memorial jury award for *Brute Orbits*, an uncompromisingly bleak exploration of future penal theory and practice. Even so, in today's epoch where *sci-fi* has become the debased but wildly lucrative common currency of mass entertainment, he struggles to make a living from his much-praised writing.

One clue to his lack of broad commercial success is a feature found repeatedly in his formally quite diverse fictions: a reviewer called them "outrageously didactic," and they are often that—although rarely *only* that. Nor is this an accident, a failure to master the basic pleasing narrative arts. Zebrowski has adamantly chosen this path, convinced that only in such an austere program will he find the purity of intention and construction suited to his designs as philosopher-poet. No starship battles blaze in the opening pages of *Cave of Stars*. Rather, we track the bleak inward meditations and muted exchanges of figures high or fallen in the politics of "the fourth planet of Tau Ceti, in the third century after the death of Earth." New Earth was settled by adherents of the Roman Catholic church, and in 2331 Josephus Bely—its aged head of theocratic government, his Holiness Peter III—and the pontiff's prime minister Paul Anselle, plus the Pope's unacknowledged daughter Josepha and her exiled lover Ondro are among those tormented by the conflicting demands of faith, doubt, and an arrested technological *status quo* maintained ruthlessly lest humankind sink again into "life's disorder and dismay."

To New Vatican comes an emissary of a 100 kilometer-long macrolife mobile world, its inner shells (astonishingly) as roomy as a planet's surface, with malcontent settlers and space for dissidents. Voss Rhazes (named for a 9th century anti-superstitious Arab surgeon and alchemist) is Linked to a sort of super-Internet. His flyer commands inertia with gravitic technology; to Anselle, secretly a doubter of the Catholic creed he represents, "it sang of angels, of intellects that looked beyond limits." When Anselle conveys to the Pope that the people of the mobile worlds are effectively deathless, save for catastrophic accidents, Bely is appalled. "A traveling hell has come to us.... We carry too much darkness within ourselves for a corporeal paradise to be possible for our kind." But the aged, ill pontiff is tempted by the lure of endless life. With it, he might "secure the years he needed" to finish the work of redemption for his flock.

Such cases of conscience and conflicts between faith and reason are surprisingly common in the notable sf of the last half century or so. Pamela Sargent's ambiguous feminist utopia in *The Shore of Women* (Entry 8) controls men by imposing a fake matriarchal goddess. If Atwood's Gilead, in *The Handmaid's Tale* (Entry 1) adopts aspects of Islamic *sharia* law, it bears the trappings of a high Protestantism near to the traditions of Rome. And while Mary Doria Russell is a convert to Judaism, *The Sparrow* and *The Children of God* (Entry 46) are centrally enacted by Jesuits. It is perhaps inevitable, then, that Zebrowski works out his epochal contrasts by invoking ecclesiastical bullying familiar to Western culture from the persecution of Bruno and Galileo to heavy-handed (and high handed) anathemas from Rome in the last century. So a confrontation staged in New Vatican, "the City of God," has a fated inevitability reminiscent of non-sf bestsellers by Father Andrew Greeley and Morris West.

Cave of Stars confronts not only faith versus reality, but also reality versus augmented dream. "We have the temptation of final happiness," laments First Councilman Wolt Blackfriar (an ironically priestly name). "In dream worlds an individual can loosen all limits and be a god.... Many do not wish to return once they have tasted direct wish fulfillment." How can such a transcendental lure be resisted—the power to be a god, if only in virtual reality? "By not trying it." Still, mightn't our empirical world itself be no more than a simulation? Some philosophers, Blackfriar notes, "insist on searching for experimental proof of the falseness of our universe." Like Pope Peter III, the mobile habitat's transhumans can find a secure footing only through faith—in their case, that the universe of experience is *not* false. That it is truly real gains credence in a powerfully wrought mass killing twice the magnitude of Stalin's genocide, and its bitter aftermath.

It would be inappropriate to detail the plot turns of this thoughtful novel. Action and reflection pursue each other through a tragic, poignant, finally hopeful trajectory. But this is just one tale in Zebrowski's history of the mobile worlds carrying macrolife toward the closure of the universe and rebirth into a further cycle of the wheel, life finally reshaped by its tumultuous vast history. Perhaps, he suggests, efforts to clamber into a redeemed posthuman condition are not necessarily thwarted just because "sainthood could not be inherited"—that is, imported into the genome. Abolition of death might forestall that stamped-in sentence "common to all shortlived creatures who yearned uselessly to step out from the abyss of themselves."

For at the end, "death without dying became an art, a dance of deletions and additions that slowly brought forth new personalities... set to seek beyond the past's horizons, determined to awake into ever greater dreams."

59: Poul Anderson
Genesis (2000)

ONE OF the late Poul Anderson's final novels confronts the basic and almost insurmountable fact about the far future: that technological time will be neither an arrow nor a cycle (in Stephen Jay Gould's phrase), but a series of upwardly accelerating logistical S-curves, each supplanting the one before it as it flattens out. Unless self-inflicted disaster inevitably reduces intelligence to ruin and global death—explaining the Fermi paradox of the absence of detectable extraterrestrial civilizations—history seems fated to pass through a Vingean Singularity, as we see in a number of other novels here,[23] into a realm beyond our present imaginative capacity.

If so, it is plausible that intelligent consciousness, once evolved, must proliferate on a galactic scale, mutating and extending its own capacities, perhaps replacing its very substrates. It might relocate itself, for example, from limited organic bodies to very much more adaptable synthetic forms. The Science Fiction Writers of America's 1997 Grand Master, Poul Anderson (1926-2001), like Frederik Pohl and other sf writers steeped in the ever-revised history of the future, was familiar with extrapolations along these lines by roboticist Hans Moravec, and built them gracefully into his own saga of a galaxy a billion or more years farther off into deep time.

An earlier version of *Genesis*, a 100-odd page novella, appeared in Gregory Benford's anthology *Far Futures* (1995). Anderson's tale was perhaps overshadowed at the time by Greg Egan's extraordinary "Wang's Carpets": a post-Singularity story so

---

23 E.g., Entries 30, 40, 54, 71, 81, 91.

uncompromising that it seeded Egan's remarkable novel *Diaspora* (1997), probably the most rigorous posthuman sf work yet published. Anderson subsequently extended his own story of Gaia's plans for ancestral Earth threatened, in the far future, by a swelling, terminal Sun.

Gaia, the vast, immanent AI custodian and consciousness of the world, rather frighteningly wishes to allow the world to perish in final flame rather than disrupt the Sun's "natural" astrophysical trajectory. Other mighty Minds throughout the galaxy, and to the "shores of the Andromeda," find this plan perverse. One such godlike node, Alpha, hives off a sub-mind (still Olympian by our standards), and sends this Wayfarer to Earth to investigate and intervene. A still more diminished aspect or agent of this fragment is a reconstruction of the early upload engineer Christian Brannock. A merely human-scale genius, he visits the planet as his larger self communes and debates with Gaia. What he finds, inevitably, is baffling yet emotionally moving (in its constrained way), recalling those Norse sagas Anderson loved so well.

And all of this impossibly remote story is told to us as myth, as repeatedly distanced construct. We are informed again and again that what we read is nothing like the vast reality. Of course, this *must* be so, given the premises of ruthlessly projected futurism. "All is myth and metaphor, beginning with this absurd nomenclature [Alpha, Wayfarer]. Beings like these had no names. They had identities, instantly recognizable by others of their kind. They did not speak together, they did not go through discussion or explanation of any sort, they were not yet 'they.' But imagine it."

And we do, for we have been here before. This is the grand proleptic mythology of Olaf Stapledon himself, of Roger Zelazny's "For a Breath I Tarry" (1966)—in which Machine remakes Man, but then bows before Him (which is absurd and sadly farcical, however much that story was loved in the 1960s).

In this revised version of his myth, Anderson eases our entry to allegory via several well-formed episodes from the comparatively near future: a boy's epiphany beneath starry heaven, in our Earth; Christian's empathy with his robotic telefactor extension on Mercury, prelude to his own status as an uploaded and finally multiply-copied personality; English bureaucrat Laurinda Ashcroft who plans the first millennial salvation of Earth from the brute assaults of a heedless cosmos; a small, neat parable of rigid, gorgeous clan rivalries held in check and paralysis, finally, by the emerging Mind of Gaia. These are Anderson's antinomies again (and perhaps American science fiction's): the sacred autonomy of the self, the craving for transcendence in something larger; personal responsibility, and its terrible limits in a world linked, defined, by billions of threads.

Returned to Earth, Wayfarer's Brannock and Gaia's Laurinda tarry in *faux*-eighteenth-century civility, falling in love (of course), driven together and apart by a series of visitations to simulated histories as dense and real and tormented and doomed as the "real world." Their own personalities are no less constructed, however rooted in some small early reality, and so the poignancy of their dilemma is the greater. But for us, knowing that we read a fiction, and snatched in a kind of postmodern gesture again and again by Poul Anderson from our comfortable readerly illusion, these figures and their worlds run the risk of all allegory: can we care?

It is the great artistic problem for any form of art predicated upon utter disruption and dislocation. Religious art faced it long ago, and clad its transcendent message in parable, majestic song—and quietness, sacralized domesticity, anguish transformed at the graveside. These are territories Poul Anderson trod in all his work, more so, perhaps, than did any of his peers. Confronting the Singularity, reaching for these well-honed tools to give himself voice and range, perhaps he succeeded as well as anyone can manage—given that the task is impossible. If he did not truly succeed, this is hardly his fault. It takes an entire culture to sustain such mythos. Sf has begun to grow the mythos, but meanwhile the world's culture turns technological runaway into jingles and plastic toys. It is compelling to watch how the genre, the mode, of sf is responding to this immense perspective, into the pitiless depths where Poul Anderson, not long before his death, made his brave foray.

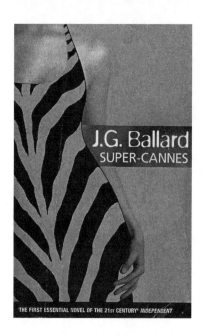

60: J. G. Ballard
Super-Cannes (2000)

EXCEPT AT the very beginning of his career, J. G. Ballard (who died in 2009) was always a hard sell outside his UK homeland. When he first began appearing in American science fiction magazines in the late fifties and early sixties, with his elegant, piercing surrealism and world-spanning cataclysms—consider 1962's *The Voices of Time* and 1966's *The Crystal World*—he was greeted with some warmth, as an heir to such British disaster writers as John Wyndham and John Christopher. But by the time of science fiction's New Wave and Ballard's increasing experimentalism, he became anathema to the fundamentalist technocratic wing of the field. This phase of his career surely climaxed in 1970 with Doubleday's pre-release pulping of his already printed book of "condensed novels," *The Atrocity Exhibition*, deemed obscene and libelous at the last minute by Mr. Doubleday himself.

Undaunted, Ballard forged ahead with such seminal novels as *Crash*, *Concrete Island* and *High Rise*. But his profile remained stuck at a certain plateau until the publication in 1984 of *The Empire of the Sun*, and its subsequent Spielbergization in 1987. This autobiographical transfiguration of Ballard's World War II childhood experiences in a Japanese internment camp in Shanghai brought him new attention and stature, in his native England at least, including annual shortlisting for various literary prizes.

Even so, in America—a country Ballard was always been critically yet lovingly obsessed with—his reputation and sales never really soared. His novel just prior to *Super-Cannes*, the admirable *Cocaine Nights*, went two years after British publication without an American edition, and when it finally appeared it was issued by Counterpoint Press: a distinguished imprint, yet surely not one of the larger houses. The reason for this neglect and inattention undoubtedly lies not in any difficulty of language or narrative, for Ballard's prose is seductive and pellucid and his stories compelling, but in the harsh truths he chooses to render. Consider that *The Atrocity Exhibition* was alternately titled *Love and Napalm: Export USA*, and you have Ballard's themes and topics in a nutshell. Our entry here does not deviate, even as it accosts a global malaise.

The plot of *Super-Cannes* is remarkably simple. A young doctor, Jane Sinclair, and her older husband, cashiered aviator Paul Sinclair, arrive in the French planned resi-dential-community-cum-business-park, Eden-Olympia, for an extended contractual assignment. Jane will assume the duties of the community's physician, while Paul, our narrator, rests and recuperates from the smash-up of his small plane some months ago. But Eden-Olympia proves to be a whited sepulcher, rife with old-fashioned murder, infidelity and treachery, and also seething with postmodern neuroses and newfan-gled megalomania. These traits are fostered by the enigmatic staff psychiatrist Wilder Penrose (note a name blending those of a famous film director and a famous theorist of consciousness), who will eventually prove to be the worm at the heart of the hot-house rose.

The crack in Penrose's deadly game—a crack that Paul Sinclair will deliberately grip and pry apart—lies in the mass-murder that occurred a few months prior to their arrival, when the former physician, David Greenwood, began systematically slaughter-ing some of the highest placed executives of this Mediterranean utopia. Paul Sinclair's growing identification with the dead Greenwood eventually culminates in a fusion not unforeseeable yet still totally potent.

On the surface, we have a tale that might almost have issued from the pen of Daphne Du Maurier, ripe for a Hitchcockian transformation to the screen.[24] But of course the gulf between the sensibilities of Du Maurier and Ballard is immense.

Ballard is a Hermes of "inner space," a term he popularized during the New Wave. Whether limned through omniscient narration or firsthand, as here, the psychic land-scapes of Ballard's characters assume a heft and presence congruent to, and substantial as, his meticulously rendered outer geographies (the imaginary resort of Vermilion Sands, the atom bomb-racked atolls of the Pacific, Cape Canaveral succumbing to a plague of Martian dust). The Jungian and Freudian swamps into which Paul and Jane Sinclair plunge with perverse eagerness, lured on by the will-o'-the-wisps of their fellow debauched Eden-Olympians, are the real terrain of the story. Spiked with all of Ballard's trademarked tropes unrepentantly arrayed—the drained swimming pool, the downed pilot, the sexualized auto-crash, the JFK assassination—as well as his gnomic dialogue and black, black humor, this book is also a captivating Chandlerian mystery whose solution is assembled from honest clues without scanting or cheating.

But at least as important as the psychological explorations are the sociocultural commentary and extrapolative contrarianism for which Ballard is famous. Sf author Bruce Sterling has maintained that out of the past fifty years of science-fictional fore-casts, no one has captured the evolving lineaments of our world better than Ballard. Indeed, in sketching the rough beast continually being born out of the confluence of media and dreams, this book comes closer to a report on tomorrow's headlines than many a "hardcore" science fiction novel. Wilder Penrose's theory on dealing with

24 Ballard name-checks Hitchcock in Chapter 16; these two mordant, icy auteurs share many quali-ties, an observation that has not found its way into print before. At least the comprehensive book-

modern insanity—"Psychopathy is its own most potent cure, and has been throughout history. At times it grips entire nations in a vast therapeutic spasm"—raises frissons of recognition in the post-September 11th landscape. And Ballard produces actual shudders when he writes, "Like all the graffiti at Eden-Olympia—a fifty-million-dollar office building and a few francs' worth of paint turns it into something from the Third World."

Although Ballard had not written a book in which the science fictional elements were foregrounded since at least *The Day of Creation*, the focus here on the abyss before us marked this novel as the work of our bravest oracle.

---

length study by Roger Luckhurst, *The Angle Between Two Walls: The Fiction of J. G. Ballard*, has no index citation for the filmmaker.

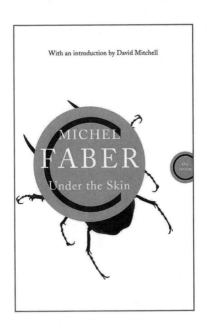

With an introduction by David Mitchell

MICHEL
FABER
Under the Skin

61: Michel Faber
Under the Skin (2000)

CONVENTIONALLY, HORROR is treated as a unified genre, a useful marketing category, its products conveniently compartmentalized in the same way that booksellers shelve together all their fantasy stock, their science fiction, their thrillers and their chick lit. However, the curious thing about horror is that the term does not in essence describe a set of tropes or venues—which is notably, if not universally, true of sf and fantasy—but rather a readerly reaction, a frisson, an emotional climate. The set of signifiers that are associated with horror—werewolves and zombies, ghosts and monsters, biological strangeness and madness, to name a few—can be utilized in *echt* fantasy or science fiction, leaving the host genre dominant, with a horror overlay. Whereas the mere appearance of an elf or unicorn—sans explicit scientific rationale— is enough to denote a fantasy, and the mere appearance of a spaceship or alien—sans overt magical basis—is enough to denote a work of science fiction, the mere visitation of a bona fide ghost does not destroy the science-fictionality of a work, as we have seen in Pat Murphy's *The Falling Woman* (Entry 7).

Horror sf, or sf horror, has a long and notable heritage, extending back at least as far as Guy de Maupassant's "The Horla" and Ambrose Bierce's "The Damned Thing." Lovecraft famously synchronized stark cosmological realities as distilled by contemporary astronomers with horror motifs in his *Cthulhu Mythos* stories. Eric Frank Russell, a dab hand at conventional horror stories for the pulps, injected shudders into his sf novel *Sinister Barrier*. Colin Wilson pioneered space vampires in his *The Mind Parasites*.

Many of the films of David Cronenberg qualify, as does Guillermo del Toro's *Mimic*, and Ridley Scott's famous series that began with *Alien*. More recently in prose fiction, Michael Shea has made something of a specialty of sf horror, notably with his award-nominated novella "The Autopsy," which for a long while stood at the acme of this hybrid kind of tale.

But the arrival of Michel Faber's first novel, *Under the Skin*, dethroned Shea, and the book seems likely to occupy the pinnacle for a while, so mercilessly, brilliantly creepy is it.

Fittingly enough, we begin intimately, as if parasitically riding the shoulder of a woman named Isserley, while she prowls the highways of Scotland in her beat-up car, looking for hitchhikers. Isserley favors brawny males, and the reader's first supposition—artfully fostered by Faber's minimal clues, delivered in elegant prose seasoned with a stream of Isserley's thoughts—is that the woman is a sex addict. Isserley pictures men naked, dreams of shifting them about into different positions.

When Isserley finally secures a suitable male, her conversation seems to trend in that same direction. We share the hitchhiker's thoughts, increasing our anxiety for him at the hands of…a dangerous, unstable nymphomaniac? But then comes the first of many jolts derailing our preconceptions. At the flick of a switch, hidden needles filled with a drug spring up and paralyze her rider-victim. The narration cuts away as, we presume, she disposes of him offstage, in some unknown fashion and to some unknown fate.

Another day, and Isserley hunts again. We are now determined she is a serial killer. Ah, but of what stripe? Talk of comrades at a farm lead us to believe she's part of some Manson-like cult. But little by little, in excruciatingly extracted bits and pieces, as if fragments of a corpse are washing up onto the beach Isserley touchingly loves, the reality is delivered to us. Seldom has a "big reveal" been so expertly and tantalizingly withheld.

Isserley is an alien, surgically altered to resemble an attractive human woman, but only upon cursory inspection. "The rest of her was a funny shape, though. Long skinny arms with big knobbly elbows… Knobbly wrists too, and big hands…but narrow, too, like chicken feet. And tough, like she'd done hard work with them…no disguising how short her legs were. Still, those tits…" It's no wonder Isserley looks odd, given that *this* is the real conformation of her species, seen undisguised in Amlis Vess, rich scion of the alien corporation that has set up a feedlot on earth, to produce luxury meats for consumption on the home planet:

> He stood naked on all fours, his limbs exactly equal in length, all of them equally nimble. He also had a prehensile tail, which, if he needed his front hands free, he could use as another limb to balance on, tripod-style. His breast tapered seamlessly into a long neck, on which his head was positioned like a trophy. It came to three points: his long spearhead ears and his vulpine snout. His large eyes were perfectly round, positioned on the front of his face, which was covered in soft fur, like the rest of his body.

Amlis Vess has come to inspect his holdings, and at this point Isserley's sad, predictable, harsh life goes into the offal bin. Vess is a crusader, a kind of PETA acolyte who believes that the "vodsels" (humans) are the same "under the skin" as Isserley and her cohorts. Vess's visit and beliefs upset Isserley, eventually making her sloppy and undermining her orderly exile.

Faber employs his clinical yet gorgeous prose like a scalpel across the reader's sensibilities, particularly when unflinchingly describing the feedlot and abattoir technology of the aliens. His work resembles the early Ian McEwan of *The Cement Garden* era, the medical precision of Michael Blumlein, or classic J. G. Ballard, particularly in his use of outré metaphors. Here is Isserley's estimation of a Homo sapiens penis. (Recall that she thinks of herself as "human" and Earthlings as animals.) "His penis was grossly distended, fatter and paler than a human's, with a purplish asymmetrical head. At its tip was a small hole like the imperfectly closed eye of a dead cat."

But Faber's most empathetic and analytical passages are reserved for his tortured heroine. Despite her unthinking, evil ways, we identify utterly with her dilemma, thanks to Faber's narrative magic, feeling every ounce of self-disgust and despair, every pain in her racked limbs (which bear the allegorical freight of a human transsexual, too). This is the true miracle of the novel: we realize that the worst horror is that inflicted by aliens upon the least of their kind, not by aliens upon their cattle.

Of course, numerous satirical or Swiftian themes abound in the book. Colonialism, elitism, carnivore behavior, workplace automatism, corporate loyalty, bleeding-heart cluelessness, even foodie decadence (pay attention to how the alien chef gloriously describes marinating techniques and other such kitchen-show staples), all come in for a sound drubbing. But paramount over any such skewering is the portrait of a woman, however alien, coming to grips with her ethical choices and her final realization that a bad life cannot be lived rightly.

62: China Miéville
Perdido Street Station (2000)

WHEN CHINA Miéville's towering phantasmagorical second novel, *Perdido Street Station,* gained the Arthur C. Clarke Award in the UK for best novel of 2000, readers had a strong inkling that a major new talent had arrived on the scene. But the full depth of Miéville's future accomplishments could hardly be fully intuited at that moment. A rapid succession of *sui generis* books. The establishment by example of a whole new subgenre—the New Weird—and the personal authorial victory of widespread mainstream recognition, with his 2011 offering, *Embassytown*, earning coverage in such unlikely venues as *Entertainment Weekly* magazine.

None of this is undeserved. With his Bas-Lag series of three books to date, Miéville follows in the tradition of Wyndham Lewis, Alasdair Gray and Mervyn Peake, pulling off the most impressive act of narrative "subcreation" (to employ Tolkien's term for the literary instantiation of an entire "secondary world") in ages. These books, conflating hip urbanism, realpolitik and outré flights of fancy, make one take heart for the vitality of what can at times seem like a played-out, doddering genre.

The world of Bas-Lag exists akimbo from our familiar fields, dappled, eccentric, unthinkable and hypnotic. And yet, and yet—how ultimately true and pertinent to all that we hold dear are the people and issues and living conditions encountered in this skewed mirror. The engaging, repellent city of New Crobuzon, where all the intricate loops of Miéville's tale tangle, is rendered with a combination of minute specificity and bold strokes. The swamps and fens, alleys and aerial trams, insane monuments and crumbling slums are impastoed with Miéville's precise and rich prose: "In the outline of stillborn streets shacks of concrete and corrugated iron blistered overnight. Inhabitation spread like mould." Yet the text never grows clotted, but instead, thanks to the constant action, remains compulsively readable.

Several off-kilter kinds of technology blend with various magics to render New Crobuzon a Victorian parody, yet with its own character. Not quite a dystopia or police state, the polity is still heavy-handed and repressive, filling the evil half of the moral equation. But the counterforces of good in this scenario are themselves a base and motley lot, lusty, unrepentant and truly alive. Mostly thieves and artists, they all revolve around one rogue scientist named Isaac Dan der Grimnebulin. Through Isaac's ill-considered researches a horrible threat, the slake-moths, are loosed upon the city, and the bulk of the book deals with the battle against these *Aliens*-style predators.

There are scenes here which, like the captivating patterns of the slake-moths, are impossible to expunge from memory. If I mention an aerial battle that involves a blindfolded man with a dog strapped to his back—and the dog is issuing the orders!—then you'll have the barest hint at the wonders that wait within.

Miéville also accomplishes the nigh-impossible: social commentary on our own world without weighty preaching. The situation of New Crobuzon's working poor, so reminiscent of the lot of citizens in Brazilian favelas and other global slums, comes across with great impact. Life is entropy with a grin: *Perdido Street Station* makes this abundantly clear, as does Miéville's Bas-Lag follow-ups, *The Scar* and *Iron Council*.

A massive nautical tale of obsession, magic and outlaw existence, *The Scar* contains enough plot for several lesser novels. The neo-Gothic, steampunkish city of New Crobuzon is in turmoil, following the events of the earlier book. Instead of producing a direct sequel to *Perdido Street Station*, Miéville chose to go off at an angle to his established path, opening up broader vistas of his entrancing, unique world of Bas-Lag. Whereas the previous book never ventured outside the confines of New Crobuzon, this book ranges across the map of Bas-Lag, revealing to us more history, more geography, more cultures. It was a bold, expansive move, and much was gained by this tactic. Miéville's subcreation becomes more extensive, more of a whole organic quilt rather than a single intensely embroidered patch.

There's a plethora of wonders here. Miéville's fecund imagination conjures up vivid images on every page. His alien races are truly alien, and his humans are exotically colored. Uther Doul, an Elric-style outcast, has to be one of the best literary pirate figures ever written. And the supporting character named Tanner Sack emerges as one of the most sympathetic. Set-piece by set-piece, Miéville knocks you on your butt. Whether presenting us with giant mosquito women or undead vampires, Miéville knows how to ratchet up the suspense. And the overall tale matches the apocalyptic novels of Mark Geston in its levels of insane damnation. Finally, Miéville cleverly gets us to reverse our allegiances from New Crobuzon to Armada in the exact same fashion that his heroine Bellis does.

For his fourth novel, *Iron Council*, Miéville returned to the grotesquely alluring world of Bas-Lag and its mightiest city, New Crobuzon, rewarding his fans. Yet the third entry in the series is eminently readable for novices also, featuring a new cast of characters and easy immersion in the various species, politics and culture of New Crobuzon.

The tale follows two parallel tracks—symbolically quite fitting, seeing that a mighty railroad train lies at the heart of the novel—which converge toward the climax. Between alternating episodes from both narrative tracks, we learn in an extended flashback the story of "golem master" Judah Low's young manhood, how he worked for the grand, monumentally crazy scheme of building a railway across the treacherous terrain of Bas-Lag, and how he helped form the Iron Council when he and others stole the vehicle that was essential to the enterprise, converting it into a "perpetual train" of independence and freedom. Eventually a dozen different subplots cohere, culminating in a massive battle for the soul of New Crobuzon, with enormous sacrifices—sometimes at deadly cross-purposes.

Miéville succeeds in his ambitious program here due to a number of factors. First are his sheer language abilities. Like Ian MacLeod, a fellow British fantasist, Miéville writes gorgeous sentences that are obviously crafted with painstaking effort, yet which read smoothly and elegantly, sheer poetry. Whether he's describing monsters such as the "inchmen"—"Colossal and grossly tubate, a caterpillar body studded with tufts, ventricles opening and closing sphincters, dun with warning colors. The man-torso congealed into the front of that yards-long body..."—or gothic buildings or convoluted action sequences, Miéville employs diction and syntax in idiosyncratic ways, not content to fall back on clichés. Secondly, Miéville exhibits immense fertility of both plot and setting. The dozens of "xenian" sentients who share Bas-Lag with the humans, the welter of incidents that make up this history, all spew forth in convincing multitudes. Bas-Lag possesses the inexhaustibility of the real world.

Next comes Miéville's allusiveness. Literary precedents—Tolkien, Vance, Peake—are playfully invoked (consider that one dire battle is resolved by the unexpected arrival of horse-clan warriors), but so are real-world milestones. The war between New Crobuzon and Tesh bears comparison to the conflict between the USA and Iraq. The revolt of the underclass in the city harks back to Paris, 1968. And could the Mayor of new Crobuzon be Maggie Thatcher? No doubt! Anchoring his tale in both the literature of the fantastic and real history gives it a science fictional solidity that other more rarefied fantasies lack. Miéville's sense of multiculturalism is another plus. His creation is not a whitebread affair, but partakes of many different flavors suitably transmogrified: Hispanic, European, African, Anglo. Finally, Miéville's flair for rich characterization is pronounced. In short, what Miéville has accomplished is to render a world both utterly estranged from ours, yet eerily congruent, and to populate it with figures who breathe and bleed and love, and whom we may care deeply about.

IF DREAMS ARE DOORWAYS, WHERE DO THEY TAKE US?

DISTANCE HAZE

JAMIL NASIR
Author of *Tower of Dreams*

63: Jamil Nasir
Distance Haze (2000)

DISTANCE HAZE trembles in the phase space between Douglas Hofstadter's *Gödel, Escher, Bach* and Oliver Sacks's *An Anthropologist on Mars*—or maybe Dennis Overbye's *Lonely Hearts of the Cosmos* and *Buffy the Vampire Slayer*. The words flow like honey, with just enough grains of pepper to gravel the tongue; it is a book for the ear, and the inner eye.

Sf writer Wayne Dolan, something of a dud after five books (success with his first two, the next flopped, his marriage crumbling, his child lost to him), visits the lavishly endowed Deriwelle Institute for the Electrical Study of Religion. He hopes to reignite his flagging career with a popular science account of crackpot but enthrallingly New Agey doings at the Institute, where Nobel laureates and workaday drudges seek the spirit in the lab. Dolan plans a book akin to bestsellers about the Santa Fe Institute, driven in doing so to examine the murk in the depths of his own self-damaging and dissatisfied soul.

The key feature of *Distance Haze* is that, like quite a few good current sf books, it is genuine literature. That is quite an impressive achievement, since the storyline itself is a string of silly pranks, one tasty absurdity mounted on another. But Nasir's near-science postulate is based on genuine recent work in cognitive neuroscience. Reputable scientists do claim to have located a "god module" in a portion of specialized temporal lobe circuitry that lights up preferentially during religious experiences. Lesions near this region can precipitate "hyper-religiosity," a clinical disorder. It is not a stretch that certain genome sequences encode these modules, and might in future be switched on or off in the brain of a developing infant. Might a person mature from childhood without any intrinsic, evolved bent for faith? If so, would he or she be cruelly impaired, hurled into inconsolable Sartrean nausea and meaninglessness—or, rather, liberated from programmed illusion to an unprecedented degree? Could such a transformation be worked on the brain of an adult? It is a topic that has been explored by Greg Egan, the master of this sort of speculation. But Nasir writes more joyously and hurtingly than Egan.

Nothing much in the novel is as it seems. Certain mystical or dreamlike episodes might be delusions fostered by grief, thwarted pain and ambition and love, and perhaps concealed machineries. It is possible that Nasir himself did not know ahead of time where the narrative would come to rest, his several alternative superposed trajectories careening together to create a kind of mutually constructing and self-deconstructing curve drawn sparkling inside the Cloud Chamber of Unknowing. He comes close to making it work successfully because he is ready to put his character through comic pain:

...he had reasoned that out there somewhere must be a girl beautiful and young and educated that would love him, blonde with silken skin who unclothed was all catlike languor and fire....They sat in a quaint cafe and talked about Emily Brontë and Shakespeare, Doyne Farmer and God, complexity and love and the structure of the universe, their eyes locked together, until he could feel the earth turning about him, the blood rushing in his veins, time bringing the sun to light the flowers in the window boxes, the rain to water them....

But where to go? A singles bar? The idea both repelled and tantalized him. He holding a drink and sliding through air-conditioned dimness toward a half-seen hairdo in the smoke, which would probably conceal a drunk dental hygienist or secretary who, smelling his fear and uncertainty, would sneer at him in her stupid vocabulary and bad grammar. He didn't know where any singles bars were, and anyway even if he managed to pick someone up he would have nowhere to take her but his smelly, disheveled apartment.

The fatuous but heartbreakingly elegiac, the callously cruel but self-laceratingly candid—none of this is remotely new to the mainstream, but it remains rare in an sf novel. What you might not find in most "literary" novels is Nasir's easy confidence with the rhetoric of scientists in full flight, notably in a concerted scene with a Francis Crick-like genetics Nobelist, Dr. Raymond Hall:

"Do you think scientists are immune from the lure, the seduction of higher meaning?...Science began as a religious exercise: it was believed that the study of nature would reveal the hand of the Creator and hints as to His divine plan. It was never suspected that no sign of a God would ever be found at all, that deep, rigorous study of nature over hundreds of years using incredibly sophisticated techniques would turn up not one iota of evidence—not one, anywhere—that God exists....This isn't some whim or premature conclusion or philosophical sleight of hand. It is the result of five hundred years of concentrated study by thousands of the best minds of every generation... all of which has been gone over again and again by people of all backgrounds and biases, but most of whom, the vast majority of whom would much rather have concluded that there was a higher meaning. If there had been one there to find, we would have found it, we would have fallen on our knees before it, we to whom meaning, pattern is everything."

What counts here is Nasir's scrupulous annotation of a worldview rarely seen in the mainstream, yet often just assumed as background in sf. When the epiphanies tumble down, as they inevitably do (most blatantly, in the exact middle of the book), their sweetness is only slightly cloying, since we know in our bones that awful reverses lurk deep within such narratives of redemption and illumination. The question is, which redemption will be unmasked as villainous error: the probing scientific meliorism with its inevitable thalidomide-like risks, or the Zennish post-illusioned elevation of the ordinary? Nasir's answers are thought-provoking. One might have expected this fine novel to be a strong runner for the Philip K. Dick award (as was Nasir's earlier novel, *Tower of Dreams* in 1999), or the Campbell Memorial award. It was not even a nominee.

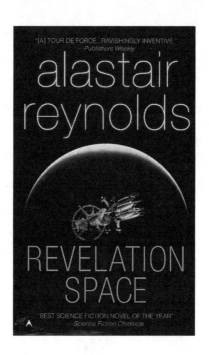

64: Alastair Reynolds
Revelation Space trilogy (2000)

A LASTAIR REYNOLDS is an astronomer by profession and a writer by grace of nature and vocational diligence. He came to the field's attention by publishing a number of attention-grabbing short stories in the UK magazine *Interzone* and elsewhere, then leaped into a three-book deal with one of the UK's best publishers, Gollancz. These initial three books would all turn out to be set in the same future continuity, and eventually the saga would be extended by two others, so far. This future history would take its name from the first book, *Revelation Space*, a confident postmodern space opera offering intergalactic adventures aplenty, despite a little ambitious bloat.

In the 2500s, our galaxy is colonized to a small degree by humans of various clades. Alien sentience is surprisingly absent, save for two minor races. The Jugglers are ocean-locked creatures without our kind of tech, and the Shrouders are enigmas hidden away in deadly twisted segments of the continuum—the "revelation space" of the title, where hallucinations and epiphanies precede almost-certain death. Scattered clues abound as to the past history of our galaxy, and the conjectured scenario is not pleasant. Millions of years ago the Dawn War incurred mass extinctions of various sapients, and a few humans suspect that whatever ancient mechanisms killed these races still lie in wait.

Into this landscape, Reynolds inserts one professional soldier-assassin, Ana Khouri;

one merciless starship commander, Ilia Volyova (also female, the de facto trendy gender nowadays for tough spacers); and one rogue scion of a famous family, Dan Sylveste, whose Shrouder-altered mind seems to hold secrets inaccessible even to himself.

Reynolds uses a three-track narrative to acquaint us with these main characters and a slew of supporting actors.

In the first segment, we watch Sylveste at work on the planet Resurgam, conducting an archaeological dig. Unsuspected by him, his skills and knowledge are desired by someone else. That person is Volyova, who is battling a plague onboard her ship, the *Nostalgia for Infinity*. Meanwhile, Khouri is resident in the vast urban space known as Chasm City. She is tasked with infiltrating the *Nostalgia for Infinity* as it seeks Sylveste, and then eventually killing the man.

The narrative tracks fuse to two, as Khouri is insinuated aboard Volyova's ship, and then to one, as the *Nostalgia* picks up Sylveste as well. The denouement on an artificial planet circling a neutron star certainly rewards the careful buildup, which has been peppered already with sub-climaxes galore.

Reynolds proffers many gifts to his readers, among which are primarily speculative fertility and descriptive clarity. Here for example is his vivid explanation behind the explosion of an ancient weapon:

> Spacetime had been punctured, penetrated at the quantum level, releasing a minuscule glint of Planck energy. Minuscule, that is, compared with the normally seething energies in the spacetime foam. But beyond normal confinement that negligible release had been like a nuke going off next door. Spacetime had instantly healed itself, knitting back together before any real damage was done, leaving only a few surplus monopoles, low-mass quantum black holes and other anomalous/exotic particles as evidence that anything untoward had happened.

Employing such no-nonsense yet evocative prose, Reynolds still manages to produce some real poetry. And his choice to eschew FTL travel or FTL communications lends a deeper majesty to his slow empires.

Reynolds, born in 1966, represents a generational shift in the writing of space opera. Raised on *Star Wars*, Reynolds and his cohort take the bones of the mature subgenre for granted, relying automatically on the painfully accumulated encrusted tropes of their forebears as mere scaffolding onto which they can graft twenty-first-century speculative concepts, postmodern sensibilities and multicultural characters, and some paradoxically retro blood and thunder. Their sense of wonder derives not from the mere skeletal notion of empires stretching across light-years and the tech that supports them, but from the flesh of daily living that enfolds the milieu.

Reynolds's unerring ability to please a new generation of readers—and attract veteran fans as well—his reliability in crafting lived-in and challenging galactic adventures would be rewarded in 2009, when he inked a contract garnering him one million UK pounds for his next ten books. Doc Smith, pioneer of the form, was undoubtedly smiling down incredulously from his heavenly coign of vantage.

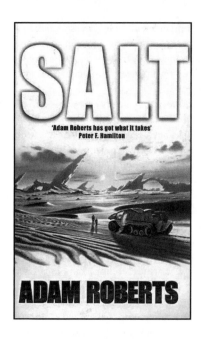

65: Adam Roberts
Salt (2000)

THE DEBUT of a startlingly original voice in our field, especially a voice that sounds a grimmer, more classically tragic note than some of our more frothily entertaining bards, is always an occasion for celebration. Adam Roberts's first novel, *Salt*, was one such joyous eruption of note.

Roberts appeared out of the blue, unheralded by shorter fiction, a mode which to the present he has mostly eschewed. But he would not remain unknown for long, given his polymathic accomplishments. Issuing at least one book per year since his first, Roberts has branched out into literary parody and critical exegesis, even producing a book-length study, *The History of Science Fiction*. But it is with his novels that he has secured his sterling reputation. All his novels are unique, each starting with some consensus-shattering conceit packed with both emotional and intellectual substance. Although some critics such as Paul Kincaid have found his work arid and overly re-complicated, Roberts is arguably the essence of what an sf writer must be: visionary, brave, shocking, lateral-thinking.

Because what arrives unheralded and disruptively must always be compared with what has gone before, despite any injustices to all parties involved, consider some of the sensations of reading Roberts's first novel, all unawares.

It's like reading Crowley's "In Blue" as rewritten by Barry Malzberg. It's like reading Ursula Le Guin's *The Dispossessed* as rewritten by Norman Spinrad, or her *The Left Hand of Darkness* reworked by Ken McLeod (Entry 53). Or Robinson's *Red Mars*

(Entry 29) altered by Mark Geston. Or Eric Frank Russell's *Wasp* redone by Stanislaw Lem. Yes, that strange and enjoyable.

A sublight colonization party—twelve ships tethered to a tame comet—is headed toward a distant world that seems from past probes to be capable of supporting life. One ship, the *Senaar*, is crewed and captained by adherents of a rigidly hierarchical political system. Another ship, the *Als*, contains anarchists. Our narrators, in alternating sections, are Barlei, a general, and Petja, a typical libertarian type. The conflicts that arise between these men and their followers en route, before they enter hibernation for three decades of travel, are merely a sampling of the trouble that will follow on Salt, their new world. Struggling with the inhospitable environment, the colonists nonetheless are fairly well off and secure enough to have time for mischief. Misunderstandings between the settlements named after the founding ships soon blossom into internecine war.

Roberts portrays both his dominating landscape—a world of chlorine-tainted seas and harsh radiation, yet weirdly beautiful—and his people astonishingly well. Lots of the uneasy laughter in this tragicomic book stems from the disjunction between viewpoints. Seeing the same events through the radically different minds of Barlei and Petja, the reader is astonished that any two humans could be so incongruent. Or perhaps the moral we are meant to take away is that any agreement at all between any two humans is the real miracle.

But the core event that limns the full extent of these clashing worldviews is the arrival of a Sennarian diplomat, Rhoda Titus, in Als. Petja's take on her mission, and her reaction to his indifference, segues from hilariously comic to shatteringly tragic, once battle intervenes. And it's a surprise, yet somehow right, that Rhoda gets the final words in the book.

Roberts's real genius is in making neither Barlei nor Petja the absolute villain. Both are obtuse at time, both perceptive. Each honors his own values, and simply cannot fathom an alternate paradigm. Perhaps Barlei is a bit more self-serving and deceitful, but Petja's frigid honesty and lack of connection serves him and his community just as ill as Barlei's glory-seeking sternness. And neither man "wins" in the end.

Salt stands today as a marker laid down in a gamble by a neophyte author: can a career be made under present marketplace circumstances without pandering to fans, repeating oneself, or dumbing down sf's essential mode of estrangement? No wise reader should be willing to bet against the seasoned veteran Roberts has become, in light of his superlative record.

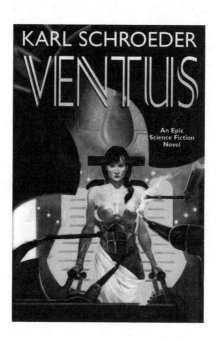

66: Karl Schroeder
Ventus (2001)

KARL SCHROEDER holds the distinction of being one of the few writers of sf actually trained in "designing the future," having recently acquired a Master's degree in Strategic Foresight and Innovation, that discipline once called "futurism." But even before passing that academic milestone, he proved speculatively puissant indeed, in the homegrown, un-diploma'd manner of other masters of the genre, offering readers a brilliantly recomplicated future straight out the gate with his debut solo novel *Ventus*, whose Heisenberg-hazy December/January publication date straddled the century's divide, earning it the lead slot in this volume's 21st-century selections.

In many ways, *Ventus* is the quintessential novel of "conceptual breakthrough," a classic mode of sf that can be relied upon to provide many delightful frissons for reader and protagonist alike. A narrative venue, either somewhat mysterious to native dweller and reader alike, or, alternatively, mistakenly deemed fully plumbed and comprehended, is revealed to possess hidden depths, or to exist in undetected relations to a larger sphere. The textbook case is a generation starship carrying nescient and degenerate human cargo. In the instance of the planet Ventus, inhabited by our hero, Jordan Mason, both conditions are true, and the existential explosion causes Jordan—and the novel's appreciative audience—to experience that mind-widening ontological leap beloved of the sub-genre.

Ventus was terraformed a thousand years in the past by artificially intelligent nanotech entities doing mankind's bidding. But upon the arrival of the first human settlers, these "Winds" inexplicably went a tad berserk, and began a program of destroying any technological artifacts. The result, after a few centuries of mecha-Luddite pogrom, was to plunge the colonists into ignorance of galactic affairs and into a state of civilization on the level of Earth's 1700s. Steam power is barely known and tolerated by the Winds, who are thought by Ventusites to be malicious supernatural creatures.

Into this settled society come two interstellar emissaries, operating undercover: Calandria May—much like a Banksian Culture operative (Entry 17)—and Axel Chan, Han Solo-ish rogue. They are on the trail of a construct named Armiger, a semi-detached extension, an avatar, of a rogue AI dubbed "3340." Although the hostile 3340 has been put down elsewhere, its scattered seeds such as Armiger still threaten our species.

Jordan Mason is their lead to Armiger's whereabouts, thanks to a nanotech probe from Armiger that he bears in his sensorium. But Calandria does not reckon with the fact that the humans on Ventus have their own dynastic schemes, and that some of them might actually be able to communicate with the powerful, enigmatic Winds. When Calandria's starship is destroyed and she and Axel are stranded, the fun is just beginning. Especially when Armiger joins forces with dynamic Queen Galas, one of the few natives who understands the Winds for what they truly are.

Schroeder has a stylistic and thematic romp across his blood and thunder adventure, by operating on two levels: those of fantasy/myth and of Hard Sf. While the whole scenario is impeccably buttressed by cutting-edge science, much of the action comes across like fantasy. The untenanted perfect ancient mansions where machine servitors await are straight out of the uncanny fairytales by Grimm or Andersen. Armiger's corpse-like condition and his stumbling escape through nighted forests reads like the plight of a zombie or Golem. There are duels and castles galore. As Calandria observes, something about Ventus inspires ancient feelings of the supernatural.

Likewise, when Axel tries telling Jordan about the war against 3340, Jordan replies that it sounds like pure legend. This flip-flop illusion—vase or profiles?—is the perfect sf trope of cultural relativity. Schroeder is, to some degree, heir to John Campbell's worldview and school of storytelling. One can envision this book as being written by a ramped-up, hip, 21st-century H. Beam Piper or Randall Garrett. And indeed, one of Campbell's late-period discoveries, Vernor Vinge, attempted something similar to this in his *Tatja Grimm's World*. Schroeder even indulges in a little of the ironic, winking juxtaposition of mythic and scientific that Roger Zelazny employed in *Lord of Light* and elsewhere.

One of Schroeder's most salient and intriguing riffs concerns the concept of "thalience." This is the notion of networked intelligence at the fine-grained levels, attainable through a nanotech insemination of computing power. Here's how Jordan comes to conceive of this revelation, yet another conceptual breakthrough:

> Each and every object in the world knew its name; all, that is, save for the humans who lived here, because they had no dusting of mecha within them.... Jordan had found by experimenting that when you changed an object into something else, its mecha noticed and altered its name to suit. That had got him wondering: could you command an object to change its name; and if you changed an object's name, would the object itself change to match it?

Instantly, the savvy reader will spot the forerunner of both Rudy Rucker's concept of an intelligent creation in his *Postsingular* (Entry 91), and also a hint of Wil McCarthy's notion of programmable matter in his non-fiction book *Hacking Matter*, and associated novels (Entry 54). Finally, this is yet another instance of Schroeder messing with an overlay of faux magic, since knowing an object's "true name" and using it to command (see Vinge's seminal novella of that title) has long been a wizardly skill.

Schroeder would later issue a satisfying prequel to *Ventus*, *Lady of Mazes*. And his *Virga* sequence is a glorious, masterful exploration of the "steel beach" theme of odd environments. But in *Ventus*, he melded perfectly the novel of fantastical, legend-breeding derring-do with the novel of postsingular humanity, producing a book that could be read and enjoyed on multiple scales, from the atomic to the cosmic.

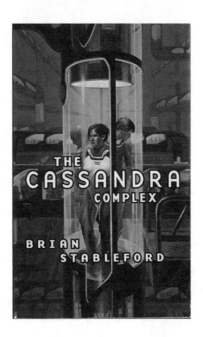

67: Brian Stableford
The Cassandra Complex (2001)
[Emortality sequence]

A T 17, in 1965, Brian Stableford published his first (co-authored) story in *Science Fantasy,* and his first published novel followed at 21. By mid-2011, he had published 201 books in a profusion of formats and genres, unified by his interest in the interactions between science and narratives of the fantastic. After a degree in biology, he gained a PhD in the sociology of sf, and his long writing career has constantly pushed against the boundaries of commercial science fiction and fantasy. As a result, he became marginalized in a market where reliable commodities tend to bring far greater profits to publishers. In a recent interview, he was justifiably caustic:

> Stories require things to go wrong in order that they can be put right again, thus providing a basic pattern of challenge and climax and a satisfactory sense of closure. Many writers do, of course, find the prospect of progress innately threatening—it's difficult for anyone over 40 to adopt any attitude to the future except terror or denial—but I'm more concerned with the way that the very nature of fiction favors story-arcs that afford a tacit privilege to the status quo, representing all innovation as evil simply because that's the easy way to make a story gripping. Morally responsible futuristic fiction—which, of course, excludes all cinema and TV "sci-fi" and most printed sf—needs to find a way of

steering around that problem.... Hopefully, there will always be heroic writers willing to work on that frontier, but as a marketing category, sf will continue to go exactly where it's been headed since the term entered common usage: nowhere.[25]

One of Stableford's major achievements was his ambitious Emortality sequence of six novels, published out of order and not a commercial success, the last volume making it into print only due to its championing by a US editor.[26] While the first books released were *Inherit the Earth* (1998), set in the 22nd century, *Architects of Emortality* (1999), set in the late 25th century, and *Fountains of Youth* (2000), in the 31st century, the sequence begins chronologically with *The Cassandra Complex* (2001), anchored far more near-term in 2041. *Dark Ararat* (2002) follows an interstellar Ark into the 29th century, and *The Omega Expedition* (2002) extends beyond the year 3000. All six are developed from a large-scale effort at futurism published in 1985 by Stableford and fellow British writer David Langford, *The Third Millennium: A History of the World 2000-3000 A.D.*. They comprise an attempt at a genuinely searching and non-trivial futurist exploration of this millennium in which the quest for extended lifespan will be sought and finally achieved. The goal is *emortality*—a term coined in *The Conquest of Death* (1979) by biology professor Alvin Silverstein. Unlike *immortality*, which seems to promise eternal life through invulnerability or supernatural survival, emortality more reasonably offers protracted healthy youth, while remaining prey to super-diseases, lethal accidents, and ultimately the extinction of the entire universe.

Each of these novels is independent, although several characters reappear, inevitably given the very long lives enjoyed by those preserved by cryonic biostasis or true emortality treatments. But the saga they weave is one immense fabric. Information and references to offstage events and characters are seeded throughout, just as realist novels are replete with unfootnoted references to historical commonplaces. The alert reader slowly accretes knowledge of this future, ranging from the engineered global stockmarket *bouleversement* or Great Panic of 2025, that allowed a few megacorps to take over the world, the rise of "hobbyist terrorism" after '22 (the book was a hair too early for 9/11), the rise and fall of post-backlash feminist Real Women, the massive dieback and sterilization of humankind in vast plagues, through to the final conquest of death. Names recur: Adam Zimmerman, founder of the Ahasuerus Foundation (named for the fabled, deathless "Wandering Jew"), preserved for a thousand years to witness the outcome of his great plan, Mortimer Gray, historian of death, Madoc Tamlin, Michael Lowenthal.

Deliberately, the novels comprise two trilogies, one of thoughtful classic sf adventure, the second following a kind of comic, playful path into an increasingly strange future where the traditional tropes of fiction simply break down because the old stakes (youth versus aging and death) no longer retain their ancient poignant value. It's a mark of this comic aspect that important figures in the policier *The Architects of Emortality* are Charlotte Holmes and her boss Hal Watson, and the beautiful, clever, and insufferable Oscar Wilde, a geneticist who designs flowers (and naturally wears a green carnation).

The best entry point is *The Cassandra Complex,* which uncannily resembles *Prime*

25 Brian Stableford interviewed by Barbara Godwin (2006):
    http://www.infinityplus.co.uk/nonfiction/intbs06.htm
26 The tangled background is sketched in Stableford's foreword to *Les Fleurs du Mal* (Borgo Press, 2010).

Suspect, the dark, gritty, layered British television police investigation drama made famous by actor Helen Mirren and orginated by screen writer Lynda la Plante, although Stableford had planned the book before the first of that series was broadcast. It is easy, though, to visualize forensic specialist Inspector Lisa Friedman, PhD, as an aging Mirren, pressed at age 61 toward retirement by an arrogant younger woman Chief Inspector, and beset by nitwits.

Woken and attacked in her code-locked bedroom by unidentifiable assailants convinced that she is hiding something crucial, denounced by the word TRAITOR daubed on her door, Lisa swiftly learns that her former teacher and lover Morgan Miller is missing. What's more, his decades-long breeding project with half a million mice has been incinerated. Miller, it proves, has lately made tentative contact with both the Ahasuerus Foundation and their rivals, the Algenists, proponents of a Nietzschean dream of posthuman enhancement.

Is either organization convinced that 40 years of breeding experiments have found a cure for death? Lisa can't believe Miller would have hidden such an epochal discovery from her. But everything is more tangled than even she can imagine. Unfolding the plots and counterplots provides the action of the plot. What makes the book, and the series, truly interesting and rewarding is the amount of serious thinking about our future that Stableford has embedded in his novels.

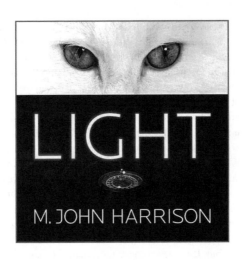

68: M. John Harrison
Light (2002)

BACK IN the 1950s, sf satirists parodied a brainless future where people handed over tedious choices to machines but failed to rue their decision because the marrow was leached from their lives. Ironic, then, that the same fate is encroaching upon sf itself. Shelves are crammed with Stepford Sci-Fi. That mightn't matter—people have a right to their denatured comfort food—if publishing conglomerates and their accountancy programs leave enough *lebensraum* for challenging books, the rich meat, texts that don't give up their meaning in a single glazed pass. True, such books have not yet all gone, but they struggle against strangling odds.

That numbing grip can be seen in the slowed or blocked passage into American editions of many fine novels from the UK. Charles Stross, nowadays a spectacular success story, took years to get his novels into US print. Iain M. Banks, Ken MacLeod, M. John Harrison, Ian McDonald, others—did the British specificity of their locales (even their galactic locales), their independent accents, made such work unreadable to many who mistook their own backyards for the cosmos?

Harrison's Tiptree award-winning novel from 2002 arrived in the USA in a (handsome) Bantam trade paperback two years late, although without the chapter-head flourishes of the Gollancz edition. The Tiptree judges (whose remit is to find the year's premier work exploring gender issues in sf and fantasy) declared *Light* "rich, horrible, sad, and absurd," a novel that "says a lot about how the body and sex inform one's humanity. It will reward rereading." Indeed, it almost demands rereading.

Its most traditional elements are Harrison's consummately wrought space battles, fought in infinitesimal fractions of a second by a brutally truncated starship captain wedded to her ancient sentient K-ship *White Cat*. These scenes are genuinely prodigious. This is intense genre textuality at full throttle, yet shaped with a pre-Raphaelite tenderness. But Harrison is deconstructing exactly the visceral, stoned excitement we gain from such scenes. He is showing us the bitter emptiness at the core of K-captain Seria Mau Genlicher slaughtering people from the leached yearning of her own worthlessness.

Out in the flat gray void beyond, a huge actinic flare erupted. In an attempt to protect its client hardware, the *White Cat's* massive array shut down for a nanosecond and a half. By this time, the ordnance had already cooked off at the higher wavelengths. X-rays briefly raised the temperature in local space to 25,000 degrees Kelvin, while the other particles blinded every kind of sensor, and temporary sub-spaces boiled away from the weapons-grade singularity as fractal dimensions. Shockwaves sang through the dynaflow medium like the voices of angels, the way the first music resonated through the viscous substrate of the early universe before proton and electron recombined.

In the epoch of the blog, we now have access to Harrison's own mordant, rich commentary on his intentions in creating this lapidary work of art. It is not especially surprising that a working draft title was *Empty Space*. What fills the novel to flooding is the paradoxical fullness and emptiness of space: the foamed, invisible dazzle of quantum virtual particles rushing in and out of reality, sustaining our apparent solidity. At the core of the narrative is the Kefahuchi Tract, fecund waste land boundary of the black hole seething in its infinitely dense vacancy at the heart of the galaxy. On its shores, its Beach, are the derelict traces of extinct species drawn to its transfinite, transgressive promise: whole abandoned star-plying planets, great enigmatic machines.

Everywhere in this cosmic absence and emptiness is always *more,* and then, as Harrison insists, always *more after that.*

In a parallel tale, his present-day serial killer mathemagician, the obsessed and terror-haunted Michael Kearney, plunged dizzyingly as a child into the fractal endlessness of the sea's edge, an aperture of insight that finally gives humanity faster than light travel. Ed Chianese, the novel's third chief player, is client and then tormenter and cuckolder of a mock human New Man named, absurdly, Tig Vesicle. "Chinese Ed" retreats from the intoxicating confusion and fertility of his and Seria's 25th century interstellar world (pursued by the standover Cray Sisters, a British joke on the once notorious brutal Kray Brothers) into a VR cartoon of *noir* mean streets. Ed the twink, as usual in such picaresques, is being educated; like some zany in a Philip K. Dick Ace Double, he is being programmed as a medium, a precog, a shaman of the Tract.

But in the cauldron of this simmering bouillabaisse of broken people, other fishies mingle, flesh peeling from their hearts, perhaps curing their egregious and haunted lovers. Kearney's waif wife Anna, in her abiding sexual solicitude, her regaining of her self, is not a character one would find in Stepford Sci-Fi. Nor is the great-limbed Annie, Ed's simple-minded rickshaw girl saint. It would be easy to read this casting of characters as mean-spirited, even misogynist; that would miss the point utterly, as the Tiptree judges understood. But so, too, would be the temptation to see *Light* as just a recuperation for the 21st century of, say, Alfred Bester's *The Stars My Destination,* for all that Kearney cries out like synesthetic Gully Foyle, in the moment of his apotheosis:

"Too bright," he said…. The light roared in on him unconfined: he felt it on his skin, he heard it as a sound…. The vacuum around him smelled of lemons. It looked like roses.

As the Shrander, an awful horse-skull entity in a maroon wool winter coat that haunts Kearney's blighted trajectory to heaven, explains: "Everywhere you look it unpacks to infinity. What you look for, you find." It's like that with Harrison's marvelous, difficult, rewarding novel, indeed his entire *oeuvre*, which constitutes a reproach to the McSci-Fi racks and a healing proof that the form of science fiction is not exhausted after all. More, and then always more after that.

(And indeed, in a more literal sense, Harrison provided more in 2006, returning to this universe in *Nova Swing*, for which he won the Arthur C. Clarke and Philip K. Dick awards.)

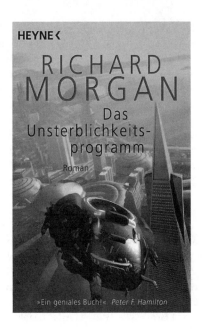

69: Richard Morgan
Altered Carbon (2002)

IT'S EXCEEDINGLY rare to find a debut novel as accomplished as Richard Morgan's *Altered Carbon*. Inevitable comparisons must be made to the initial smash that William Gibson's *Neuromancer* caused, since *Altered Carbon* certainly qualifies as pure third-generation kick-ass cyberpunk, a lineal descendant of the 1980s. It's simply one hell of a ride.

> I woke once more, this time to a rough numbness in the surface of my skin, like the feeling your hands get just after you've rinsed them clean of detergent or white spirit, but spread throughout the whole body. Re-entry into a male sleeve. It subsided rapidly as my mind adjusted to the new nervous system.

Morgan's future involves fully recorded personalities downloaded into fresh bodies, "sleeves" that are either synthetics or clones or essence-wiped adult humans. The setting is 26th century Earth, mainly the city of San Francisco. Here we find our narrator/protagonist Takeshi Kovacs, "sleeved" in a new body and set loose to find out the truth behind the apparent suicide of billionaire Laurens Bancroft. The client who hired Kovacs is Bancroft, the suicide victim himself. Kovacs is an Envoy, a near-psychopathic trained killer-soldier from the stars, now installed in new flesh. The living Bancroft is derived from a backup copy of the dead man, and lacks the memories of his own final hours due to deficient backup timing. Bancroft believes he was murdered, and details Kovacs to find his killer.

Almost instantly, Kovacs is plunged into the elaborate and deadly politics of both the local scene and the whole Earth milieu. A large cast of suspects, allies, enemies and innocent bystanders complicates matters. There's Kristen Ortega, local cop, who just so happens to be the lover of the body Kovacs is wearing, that of a fellow cop uploaded out of his flesh to the penal Stack for various crimes. There are professional assassins Trepp and Kadmin, who are stalking Kovacs. There's the AI that runs the hotel Kovacs is staying at, the Hendrix, who becomes Kovacs's partner. There are organlegging doctors; hackers known as Dips who take byte-sized pieces of personality backups in transit; and an assortment of whores, drug-dealers and other unsavory types. Most importantly of all, there's merciless crime lord Reileen Kawahara, with whom Kovacs has tangled before. When Kovacs begins to step on her toes, the violence amps upward.

Morgan has the essentials of noir fiction nailed down tight. The wisecracks in the face of death, the elaborate similes and metaphors ("less noise than a Catholic orgasm"), the institutional corruption, the way alliances get made despite principles rather than because of principles. The plot is more tangled than six Chandler novels put together, yet Morgan manages to unknot it all at the end. Kovacs is as nasty a hero as any outside of a James Crumley novel, yet we root wholeheartedly for him. And the speculative content is impeccable: a sharp central concept (reminiscent in many ways of the core notion in David Brin's *Kiln People*), lots of deadly hardware, and plenty of socio-political ramifications.

One possible gripe is with the unlikelihood that five centuries have passed since our day. Morgan picks this distant era because he needs to set up a degenerate elite of ancient powerbrokers. (Bancroft and Kawahara are both three centuries old.) But would such things as the UN, tobacco cigarettes and LED readouts survive unaltered over such a span? What institutions and customs remain to us from Shakespeare's time? It's much more likely that the passage of five centuries would result in a future with many fewer familiarities. But once you get over this initial implausibility, the action of the book is freed to zigzag madly from one explosive action scene to another, all of them elaborately constructed and recomplicated. Morgan's unflagging attention to meticulous detail confirms the old saw about genius being an infinite capacity for taking pains.

Morgan shows us that, given a wealth of talent and ambition, no writer need be afraid to tackle any mode of fiction deemed played-out. All those who suspected that the landmark fusion of noir and sf William Gibson pioneered had been done to death will find their rebuttal here.

70: Christopher Priest
The Separation (2002)

FAR OUTSIDE the hackneyed ninety percent of sf demarcated by Theodore Sturgeon in his famous Law, Christopher Priest's brand of science fiction is marked by adroitness, by quantum uncertainty, by feints and sleights of hand, by deliberate and gratuitous misdirection, and by wide-eyed perverse miscomprehensions that often result in enormous cockups. On a certain plane, it's science fiction as a parable of the scientific process itself. The wily, seductive, secretive universe attempts to fool its humans, who must gradually strip away Temptress Creation's seven veils, until the "beauty bare" of Euclid is revealed. Sometimes Beauty is a Gorgon, though. The path to knowledge is strewn with failed theories, misinterpreted observations, and no little human wreckage.

It is no accident that the individual novel of Priest's that has received the most public notice, *The Prestige*, filmed by Christopher Nolan, is literally full of such things, embodied in the sundry apparatus of stage magic, including multiple sets of double individuals, both identical and deviating from their mutual template. The book stood as the *echt* Priest tale—you witness a puzzling phenomenon; it maddens you; how do you interpret it?—until the coming of *The Separation*, which crystallized his modus operandi and voice even further, in elegant contours.

On its surface, *The Separation* is "merely" an alternate-history novel centered around World War II. One might suspect it at first to be akin to Connie Willis's recent award-winning duology, *Blackout/All Clear*, in which lightweight time travelers experience the Blitz as something of a theme park, while threatening consensus history. But distinguishing himself from Willis's blander, more straightforward sf, Priest quickly reveals that he has something much odder in mind. If any comparisons are to be made, Kurt Vonnegut's *Slaughterhouse-Five*, with its hapless protagonist unanchored in time and space, should be one correlative—although Priest has no interest in Vonneguttian whimsy—with Kathleen Goonan's jazz-suffused *In War Years* (Entry 90) the other.

The frame tale of the narrative opens in 1999, with a writer of popular histories named Stuart Gratton. At a book-signing, Gratton receives a handwritten memoir of WWII from a woman named Angela. The memoir is by one J. L. Sawyer. This first-person account occupies the next couple of hundred pages of *The Separation*. We follow the doings of Jack (the memorist) and Joe Sawyer, twin brothers, both bearing the initials "JL." Jack, an RAF pilot, seems to be Angela's illegitimate father, despite Joe having been married to Angela's mother, Birgit. (Joe, Jack tells us, died in 1940 when a bomb destroyed his London ambulance.)

With meticulous period detail, Jack describes his own wartime endeavors, focusing on an odd mission where he met not only Churchill's double, but also Rudolf Hess's doppelganger. Throughout the narrative, much is made of Joe and Jack's exceptional physical and mental affinity that was shattered by their falling out over Birgit, their fateful "separation." Priest conveys this in a number of subtle ways, such as having Jack enjoy the film *The Lady Eve*, with Barbara Stanwyck, where Stanwyck plays a dual role: one woman with two identities. The autobiography concludes with Jack a grateful old man.

Mid-novel, at memoir's end, we return to historian Gratton in 1999, and learn that his timeline is not ours. (Adalai Stevenson a USA President, followed in office by Nixon?) And Jack Sawyer's memoir seems to have strayed across dimensions, since Angela, its courier, does not exist anywhere Gratton can find her. Next up is an account by Stan Levy, one of Jack's wartime comrades, which seems to confirm this continuum-jumping: Levy maintains that Jack died in 1941 in a plane crash we earlier saw him survive. So it's on to investigate Joe's life as a conscientious objector, by objective documents and Joe's own words. We see Joe father Angela, attend peace negotiations with the Nazis, and watch him undergo odd "lucid imaginings" about Jack, that culminate in spectral superpositions, collapsed into a final solid timeline, Schrodinger-style, by Joe's sentience.

Priest's novel is obviously a sobering meditation on war and peace, centering on the 20th-century's greatest bellicose cataclysm. In the end, it's an equivocal examination. The pros and cons, benefits and costs of Jack's familiar war timeline are well known to us, but rendered stingingly fresh by Priest's handling. It's Joe's pacifistic timeline that's more problematical, leading to a half century of global stagnation. Would such a stasis-ridden, albeit Communist-free future be acceptable, if it meant no Dresden firestorm, no Hiroshima? Readers are left to decide for themselves.

But it's as a portrait of the uncanny workings of the haunted house multiverse, along the lines recently expounded by such physicists as Brian Greene, that *The Separation* really excels. The seepage and fluctuations between Jack and Joe speak to us of clashing branes, of Borges's "The Garden of Forking Paths," of Nabokovian doubles such as Humbert Humbert and Quilty. What is the nature of consciousness across the multiverse? Do Jack and Joe share a single mind? (Echoes of Brian Aldiss's hilariously horrific "Let's Be Frank" intrude.) Priest ingeniously depicts such conundrums and leaves the unpacking to us.

In Philip K. Dick's seminal *The Man in the High Castle*, the Nazi timeline of the main narrative is solid as pain, with only brief glimpses of "better" alternate histories afforded to those trapped characters. In *The Separation*, every timeline (critic Paul Kincaid identifies at least four) seems equally fungible, equally privileged, equally threatened, a whole sheaf of "insubstantial castles fading." Arguably, this indeterminate multipolar universe offers more "freedom" than Dick's locked-down scenario. But it's a freedom, Priest cautions us, that takes formidable strength of being to survive.

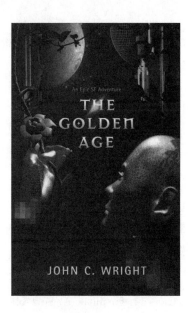

71: John C. Wright
The Golden Age (2002)

JOHN C. Wright arrived apparently from nowhere in his mid-forties, with this immensely detailed far future romance, a trilogy (really a single huge book) instantly fluent in sf's imaginative costume drama:

> She was speaking with an entity dressed as a cluster of wide-spread energy bubbles. This costume represented Enghathrathrion's dream version of the Famous First-Harmony Composition Configuration just before it woke to self-awareness, bringing the dawn of the Fourth Mental Structure.... Beyond them, a group of vulture-headed individuals were dressed in the dull leathery life armor of the Bellipotent Composition, with Warlock-killing gear.

The Golden Age, runner-up for the 2003 Locus award for best first novel, suggested that here we had a writer who (like John Varley) had lain awake in agonies of insomnia devising all these wheels within wheels and their special designations. Wright's far future palpably grows from immersion in the genre's long, braided conversation, and for all the abundance of wheels there's very little wheel-reinventing here. A lengthy and useful interview with Nick Gevers offers frank witness to his grateful borrowings:

> A. E. Van Vogt formed my childhood picture of what a hero was. Van Vogt portrayed a man who was more sane, more rational, than his foes, was able to overcome them. No other writer's works fill me with the sense of awe and

wonder as does Van Vogt.

Jack Vance and Gene Wolfe are masters of style, and I filch from them without a twinge of remorse.[27]

The clearest influence on Wright's voice, and a welcome one, is Jack Vance. Here is Wright in typically Vancian mocking dialogue:

"Now we have heard him speak; and our open-mindedness is rewarded; for we now learn that [he] believes that what he does is to benefit mankind, and to spread our civilization, which he claims to love. A fine discovery! The conflict here can be resolved without further ado."

Elsewhere, he recalls the impact of van Vogt's sf on him, "the sense of wonder that the grand... tradition of space opera embraces. I am trying to write a space opera in his style, so I never have a super-starship ten kilometers long when a ship one hundred kilometers long will do; I never blow up a city when I can blow up a planet." So Wright was the latest of the ambitious deep future New Space Opera boom—David Zindell, Stephen Baxter, Paul McAuley, Iain M. Banks, Peter Hamilton, Alastair Reynolds, Wil McCarthy (most of them with entries in this book). His Prologue, "Celebrations of the Immortals," sketches in a mere 350 words a truly wondrous carnival of beings gathered for the Golden Oecumene's millennial High Transcendence. All human and posthuman neuroforms are represented, fictional as well as real, high transhumans returned briefly to earthly estate from their calculational realms, projected future descendants, "languid-eyed lamia from morbid unrealized alternatives." It is a beguiling pageant.

In this feverish, abundant, user-pays utopia, foppish Phaethon of Rhadamanthus House finds himself inexplicably ill at ease. Before the first volume is done, this flawed sun god will test the very nature of his identity and that of his beloved wife Daphne, and of his clone father Helion (another solar name, for an engineer who works literally in the bowels of the Sun), contest with artificial minds thousands of times more potent than his own, spar with human variants collective and modified, and test his nerve in a puzzling challenge that combines the curse of Orpheus with the temptation of Pandora.

Is this libertarian Golden Age truly one, with all its immense wealth, cruelty, absolute responsibility to and for self? A certain hard-luck case complains, to comic effect, "You are wealthy people. You can afford to have emotions. Some of us cannot afford the glands or midbrain complexes required." Or might it be a Golden Cage, penned shut by the caution of immortals within a Solar System that can be reshaped (the Moon brought closer, Venus relocated farther from the Sun, the Sun's chaos itself tamed) but not escaped.

There are no aliens in this future, no superluminal physics, no time machines, and apparently the single extrasolar expedition failed long ago. (Our suspicions on this score pay off in the second volume.) Who attacks Phaethon with such determination, guile and ferocity? Are there alien invaders after all? Or perhaps Sophotechs (AIs) gone to the bad, which is to say become as self-interested as their charges? Or is Phaethon, like many of sf's amnesiac supermen, a terrifying rogue force about to reduce order to ruin if his self-inflicted shackles are opened, or carry all into some transcendence beyond the year's festive High Transcendence?

27 At *http://www.sfsite.com/05a/jcw127.htm*

The trilogy is on one level a travelogue, and Phaethon's misadventures a pretext to display spectacular scenery. In this case, though, the spectacle is rarely as simple as a catalogue of advanced technology (although there is lots of that, and rather nice it is, too), or dazzling settlings. One poor man is obliged to trudge downstairs all the way from geosynchronous orbit, a 40,000 kilometer plod, compiling his food and drink from air and wastes as he descends a space elevator's core—a ludicrous but enviably crazed plot move. No, the spectacle shares something with the posthuman cognitive explorations of Walter Jon Williams (Entry 31) and Greg Egan (Entry 38).

Tens of thousands of years hence, or perhaps millions, these people differ in mentality as much as in flesh or chip, or so we are told. If this is rarely enacted satisfactorily, perhaps it's because that would exceed our capacity to grasp, and Wright's to imagine. Still, it is enchanting to consider the segmented and spliced levels of Phaethon's own consciousness, the ways in which his inward construction of the world can be tweaked, betrayed, filtered, manipulated, clarified, the profusion of people in the Golden Age: the Hundred-mind near the kindled star of Jupiter, the gelid frozen brains of Neptune with their envious designs for good or ill, the idealized computer eidolons of the Aeonite School, Warlock neuroforms with intuitive skills derived from non-standard neural links between brain modules, and Invariants with a unicameral brain immune to filtering and hence dwelling within an utterly stark *Weltbild*—hideously deprived, not unlike our own current condition yet perhaps saner.

On and on it goes, in a sort of extended commentary, from the right, on Olaf Stapledon's classic, minatory, marxist *Last and First Men*. If all this sounds didactic, it is not, just. Wright has a quirky sense of humor, combined oddly with a rather ramrod young fogy sense of propriety (he deplores the louche way sf editors and writers freely address each other by their first names). And his characters are not wholly given to mighty projects, although Phaethon, it is true, unblushingly craves "deeds of renown without peer"; one AI likes to manifest in the collective virtual world as a penguin, fishy-breathed but able to fly so fast he leaves a vapor contrail. Wright's ingenuity, density, wit, sly comedy are all very enjoyable.

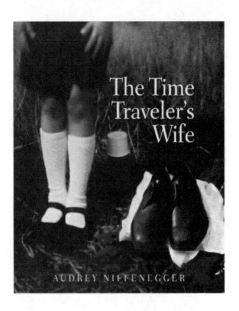

72: Audrey Niffenegger
The Time Traveler's Wife (2003)

UNTIL YOU read this elaborate time-twisting invention, you might be tempted to dismiss *The Time Traveler's Wife*, best-selling debut novel by Audrey Niffenegger, as romantic confectionary. It is considerably more than that, despite the flaws in any sf book written by someone who's redesigning the screwdriver so she can invent the steering wheel. It is a powerfully mimetic novel grounded in a strange premise, fantastika enriched by copious detail drawn from the real world of the author.

That, at any rate, is one's impression, noticing certain telling aspects of the world not always included in commercial sf. What distinguishes *The Time Traveler's Wife* from, say, a clever traditional sf entertainment like Poul Anderson's *There Will Be Time* (1972) is its very ordinariness, its refusal, by and large, to use this abnormal intrusion as an opportunity to showcase the time traveler's technical prowess, political *nous* or prejudice, trans-historic destiny. Here is a revealing interview quote from Niffenegger:

> I like science fiction, but it's not really what I read. So I wasn't trying for science fiction… what I was initially interested in was having one fantastical or strange thing and then regular reality. There's this idea that you change one thing about the world and everything else moves around it. This idea that you're allowed to play with reality somewhat. In my art, I'm somewhat surrealistic…. I like changing things.[28]

28 Veronica Bond, interview with Niffenegger, Bookslut, 2003:
   http://www.bookslut.com/features/2003_12_001158.php

What Niffenegger was reaching for was not "surrealism," although she didn't know it, but rather a term and a strategy devised by Rudy Rucker—*transrealism.*[29]

Sf is all about changing things, but what happens when you are telling a contemporary story—even one where a six-year old girl is likely to be visited by her forty-something, stark-naked future husband—and an external event overwhelmingly intrudes into your own life, into history, into your book. "The part that happened around 9/11 was interesting," Niffenegger says,

> ...because, of course that happened when I was almost done with the book and I thought, wow, I can't really let this go un-addressed. For the most part real world events don't really make it into this book because I didn't want to date it and I didn't want it to be about the world. It's really about this relationship. I figured, you have this gigantic thing and if you don't at least nod at it, it's going to seem glaring in its absence.

This is one version of the insistence of the empirical, the return not of the Freudian repressed but of the everyday, in this case amplified into gritty terror that serves in the narrative, for a brief moment, as an icon of the traveler's uncanny, dreadful, fated, powerless standpoint, ever moving, never moving. Niffenegger comments, "It's something that bugs me about actual science fiction, this effort to provide all the answers and make everything work out very neatly." But of course her novel *is* "actual science fiction," at least if *Flowers for Algernon* is sf. Still, she is right to feel qualms; more than *actual science fiction,* her novel is *actual transrealism,* a coloration of sf enlivened and enriched by uncertainty, familiarity used against itself to provide a jolt not only of shocked surprise but also, paradoxically, of recognition.

Both of which are features of this emotionally moving slipstream novel. Librarian Henry DeTamble and his once and future wife Clare Anne Abshire ("this astoundingly beautiful amber-haired tall slim girl... this luminous creature") take turns narrating their time-slipped love. Henry has been flipped into the past hundreds of times from childhood, stranded

> naked as a jaybird, up to your ankles in ice water in a ditch along an unidentified rural route.... Sometimes you feel as though you have stood up too quickly even if you are lying in bed half asleep. You feel blood rushing in your head, feel vertiginous falling sensations. You hands and feet are tingling and then they aren't there at all... and then you are skidding across the forest-green-carpeted hallway of a Motel 6 in Athens, Ohio, at 4:16 a.m., Monday, August 6, 1981, and you hit your head on someone's door, causing this person, a Ms. Tina Schulman from Philadelphia, to open this door and start screaming because there's a naked, carpet-burned man passed out at her feet.

That classic, patient, self-ironic narrative is one of the two voices of the tale, but really both comprise a single civilized middle-class point of view (wealthy upper middle-class, in Clare's case) relaying the kind of love affair seldom recounted outside genre sf, between two entwined lovers and their sometimes wretchedly haywired world. Unlike fantasy treatments of time slippage (by Jack Finney or Richard Matheson, say), Henry's quirk is eventually attributed to a very rare chromosomal dis-

---

29 See Damien Broderick, *Transrealist Fiction,* Greenwood Press, 2000.

order, Chrono-Displacement, which gets passed along to his and Clare's daughter Alba.

At 10 years of age, when they meet in the future, this child tells him that he has been dead for five years. So Henry knows in advance that he will die when he is 43. While time travelers have a modicum of free will (or so it seems), they cannot change their timeline to avoid perils, since that would entail altering the future's known past, something forbidden by the laws of physics. Inevitably, then, the story is deeply tragic—in the mode of fated Greek tragedy but more personal and realistic—and its denouement both disquieting and painfully poignant.

But for a Chrono-Displaced Person, the future can sometimes touch the past beyond death:

> She is an old woman; her hair is perfectly white and lies long on her back in a thin stream, over a slight dowager's hump. She wears a sweater the color of coral. The curve of her shoulders, the stiffness of her posture says *here is someone who is very tired,* and I am very tired, myself. I shift my weight from one foot to the other and the floor creaks; the woman turns and sees me and her face is remade into joy....

As is ours, perhaps through tears.

73: Justina Robson
Natural History (2003)

NATURAL HISTORY was runner-up for 2004's Campbell Memorial award, a distinguished feat attained previously by such luminaries as Kurt Vonnegut, Ursula K. Le Guin, Ian Watson, John Crowley, Michael Bishop, Lucius Shepard, Kim Stanley Robinson, Neal Stephenson, and Greg Bear (three times). British Justina Robson, trained in philosophy, had already made her mark with *Silver Screen* (1999) and *Mappa Mundi* (2001), both shortlisted for the Clarke award. She suggests the main question raised in this space opera of Forged (modified and augmented human stock) and Unevolved (same old earthly us) is whether, "because of your physical form," you are locked into a specified identity. In particular, "Whether you can still possess a human identity if you are some sort of radically different gigantic cyborg type of creature that lives among the stars."

Voyager Lonestar Isol is just such a cyborg or MekTek, adapted for deep space and heading for Barnard's Star when she slams into exploded alien detritus that pits her hull savagely and leaves her apparently doomed. She awakens in the debris an advanced M-Theory engine made of silicon Stuff that in a trice whips her 11-dimensionally to an enigmatic world near the galactic hub, and then home:

> "Stuff is a technology and it is also people, indivisibly fused.... It is intelligent, responsive, compassionate, but it does not have an identity of its own.... Stuff *watches*. It chooses points where life of a certain developmental stage is sure to

come across it, seeding the universe with points of access."

Ironhorse Timespan Tatresi, a kilometer-long solar system bulk carrier, takes her to feathered Corvax, formerly a Roc, Handslicer class, for investigation, on behalf of a burgeoning insurgency of Forged against Monkeys or Hanumaforms (us again, their creators). The Forged are not slaves, exactly. Their own consoling ideology poses them as sole custodians of meaning and true freedom (their Form and Function, designed teleologically into them) that the Old Monkeys lack, dull creatures of Darwinian happenstance that we are. All that holds them back from decamping to a home world of their own, a seemingly abandoned earthlike planet found by Isol, is the regard in which they hold their mythic Forged Citizen "father-mothers." Even this is a simplification, as Aurora quickly explains to Zephyr: "Clinging to Function is a puritan ideal.... Form is likewise irrelevant; only what you can contribute to the lives of others should be a measure of a soul's value."

Here is a striking echo of today's conflicted ideologies over, say, reproductive, gay, and transgender rights to choice, and a foreshadowing of the shape these tussles will likely take in any early transhuman or posthuman future.

More generally, Robson's political setting, which at first resembles black slaves against white masters, or Third World against First, or workers against capitalists, strikes the habituated sf reader as an echo of that enormous mythic future sketched so hauntingly by Cordwainer Smith, Underpeople ranged against the Lords of the Instrumentality (a comparison we also drew earlier, in Entry 31, with Walter Jon Williams' *Aristoi*). Smith's modified animal people struggled for redemption and self-determination against the true and augmented humans of Old Earth, Norstrilia and the rest of his crypto-Christian universe left unfinished due to his early death. Here, Tom Corvax is an aging, damaged birdman tech and VR bootlegger, dreaming a banned virtual human life.

Soon we find a Jamaican cultural archaeologist, Zephyr Duquesne, taking her swift if squeamish flight inside the flesh and metal body of an immense Passenger Pigeon person, Ironhorse AnimaMekTek Aurora. Impossible not to recall the E'telekeli eagle-man messiah from Smith's long rebellion; just as impossible, grinning, not to recall "Blackie" Duquesne, E. E. "Doc" Smith's anti-hero from the primitive *Skylark* space operas. Is this surfeit of Smiths and Forged a nod to that immense repository of sf iconography, whimsy, heartbreak and literary tools shaped for getting us into the inconceivable and back? No; it's either an accident or a convergence of memoryless sf with very old images from folklore. Robson comments: "I have never read any Cordwainer Smith. Ever. I never read any Al Reynolds until this week. I never read any Bruce Sterling. Or Doc Smith. For many of my teenage years when I was doing my formative reading I didn't dare actually read sf, so I used to imagine it off the covers and blurbs."[30]

For all its conceptual underpinnings of problematic identity and struggles for independence or existential meaning, Robson's novel is no improving homily but a New Space Opera ripping yarn. If her redeployment of numerous wheels does cause some grinding of the axles, some bald infodumping, it adds a certain freshly spun aroma to her saga of machined folks seeking Paradise Regained and finding... well, as so often in sf, epiphany and transcendence, of a sort.

Dispatched with Isol via Hypertube to the mystery planet's surface for eight days

---

30 Justina Robson, personal communication.

of study, Zephyr is warned that while the Hypertube forms a continuous surface with our four familiar dimensions, "it is only a single Planck length in extent." Crossing it, therefore, takes only 10 to the minus 43 seconds—to get anywhere. "Everything in transit, for that instant, no matter its size in our universe," becomes superposed, jammed together—the secret, perhaps, of Stuff. "Nice, nice, very nice," as Kurt Vonnegut chanted in his splendid sf fable *Cat's Cradle,* "So many different people, In the same device." That's an entanglement you could drive a mystical insight through, and Robson does, along with her complex tale of self-making and self-transcending in spaces outer and inner:

Zephyr looked down at her own hands in her lap, the flower between them, against the heavy blue suit. "Ready."
From all around her she heard a thousand voices begin to sing a happy tune.

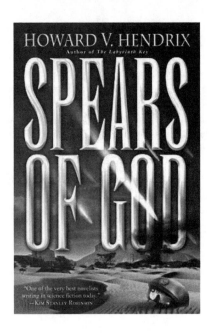

74: Howard Hendrix
The Labyrinth Key / Spears of God
(2004-2006)

HOWARD HENDRIX'S four novels prior to our two-fold selection here—
Lightpaths, Standing Wave, Better Angels and *Empty Cities of the Full Moon*—all
exhibited an admirable and remarkable playfulness, an engagement with abstruse
philosophical and metaphysical conundrums, embodied in likable characters and recomplicated plots. Each book was a little more assured and smooth than the previous;
his fifth novel, *The Labyrinth Key,* and its sequel, *Spears of God,* continued that trend.

Had Neal Stephenson not already used the neologism *Cryptonomicon* for his own
1999 novel, that title would have fitted perfectly *The Labyrinth Key,* a book that seeks
to erase the distinction between "theology and technology," a centuries-old split that
in Hendrix's view has tainted our civilization in a nearly fatal manner. (This theme
recalls the mystical engine of John Crowley's *Aegypt* quartet, begun in 1987.) Using
cryptography as his main leitmotif and tossing in resonant material from mythology,
quantum physics and a dozen other disciplines, Hendrix fashions a book that ignites all
the intellectual depth charges of a Robert Anton Wilson novel while simultaneously
functioning on its surface level as a satisfyingly convoluted spy thriller.

Jaron Kowk is a man with a seemingly straightforward mission: to help America's
National Security Agency beat the Chinese in the "quantum crypto race." But Jaron
has gotten sidetracked in the labyrinth of history, running the threads of his researches

deeper and deeper into the numinous alchemical past. Eventually, the fruits of his off-kilter hypotheses trigger his mysterious disappearance. But before he vanishes he broadcasts into the web a virtuality episode containing numerous clues to his findings.

Ben Cho is the man assigned by the NSA to pick up the trail of Jaron's work. Interacting with Jaron's widow, Cherise; with a Hong Kong detective named Marilyn Lu; with the Deputy Director of the NSA, James Brescoll; and with a handful of other oddball characters, some gonzo, some deadly, Ben will soon discover that his bond with Jaron goes deeper than expected. Amidst terrorist attacks, ploys and counterplays, Ben will undergo a strange transformation that allows him to become both the labyrinth of the universe and the key to its unlocking.

Hendrix has a lot of fun setting up a raft of competing conspiracies: besides the NSA, the CIA and the Chinese secret service, there's the Tetragrammaton, the Kitchener Foundation, an outlaw segment of the web named Cybernesia, and, most mysterious of all, the Instrumentality. Hardcore sf readers will recognize this imaginary polity from the stories of Cordwainer Smith, and Hendrix is deliberately invoking Smith's creation, with its not-so-hidden guiding hand that grips humankind's future. With tongue firmly planted in cheek, Hendrix tells us that one "Felix C. Forrest," a spook in the 1940s, was a pivotal figure in the net of conspiracies. Of course, "Felix C. Forrest" was another of Paul Linebarger's pen-names. With his levels upon levels of watchers, and numerous triple- and double-agents, Hendrix approaches the giddy heights of an Edward Whittemore novel. Add to this such Egan/Stross riffs as "virtualization bombs" and "cryptastrophes," and you have a potent mix indeed.

Hendrix succeeds almost uniformly in blending spy-caper action with mindboggling discourse quite believably and non-lumpishly. The one glaring flub along these lines is the theoretical lecture on topology which Ben Cho delivers while getting a lap dance in a strip club. But this improbable scene occupies only a minuscule slice of what is otherwise a bang-up hybrid of Kabbalah and terrorists, transcension and *realpolitik*.

The sequel to *The Labyrinth Key*, *Spears of God*, moves at such a relevant yet discrete tangent to its forerunner that no prior knowledge of Hendrix's work is necessary to appreciate it, yet it forms an invaluable extension.

Latin America features ecological "islands" called "tepuis," jungle realms so isolated from their neighbors that evolution proceeds in unique ways. In one such pocket biosphere lives a tribe called the Mawari. They are possessed of a strange meteorite that fell to Earth generations ago. This worshipped object carried biological agents that infected the Mawari and gave them strange mental powers. Now, their existence made known to outsiders, the tribe will become the focus of the First World's greed. But what the Westerners don't realize is that by breaking the isolation of the Mawari, they are infecting the whole world with the germs of a potential apocalypse (or salvation, if the two can even be distinguished).

Central to the fate of the Mawari are scientists Michael Miskulin and Susan Yamada, on an expedition to the region, backed by the finances of Miskulin's rich uncle, Paul Larkin. They find all the adults Mawaris slaughtered, and only four children left in hiding. The scientists bring the orphan children to America and the refuge of Larkin's home.

It eventuates that the slaughter was engineered by one General Retticker, in charge of a military project to create the perfect soldier. He wants to reverse-engineer the mental powers of the Mawari for his own uses, and has his own pet scientist, Darla

Pittman. Ignorant of the genocide necessary to secure her a certain meteorite sample, Darla goes to work eagerly. Retticker's strings are being pulled in turn by a weird cabal: Doctor Vang, leader of a conspiracy to boost mankind onto a new evolutionary plateau, and his associates, evangelist George Otis and adventurer Victor Fremdkunst. This cabal plans to trigger the end times by stoking war in the Middle East. The last major player is Jim Brescoll, head of the NSA, with his own designs on the Mawari survivors. But the wild card is that the four Mawari children—Alii, Aubrey, Ebu, and Ka-dalun—have plugged into the global infosphere and are about to start pulling cosmic strings of their own.

Rudy Rucker speaks often of science-fictional "power chords," those fantastical tropes so seminal that they keep cropping up in the genre. As Howard Hendrix explicitly acknowledges, the notion of stony visitors from space and their unseen or enigmatic cargoes is one such. Meteors and meteorites present a rich topic that can never go stale, so long as humanity remains ignorant of what exists beyond our atmosphere. Hendrix masterfully incorporates into one vast tapestry perhaps every myth, historical incident, scientific fact and way-out speculation about meteorites. It's doubtful that a better or more all-encompassing novel on this power chord could be written, barring new discoveries.

Hendrix has always been known for blending rather New Age-ish mystical themes with his hardcore scientific speculations, and this book is no exception. The actual textbook information about celestial stones and the more far-out yet informed speculations about the biological agents they might carry are married to a kind of "indigo children" myth about the next level of human development. It's generally a happy marriage, and Hendrix succeeds in convincing us that human evolution could very well have been directed all along by these "spears of god." Perhaps Hendrix is, on a final level, paying subtle homage to Philip Jose Farmer and his "Wold Newton" mythos!

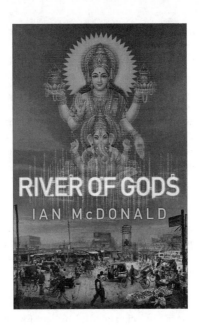

75: Ian McDonald
River of Gods (2004)

IT'S FREQUENTLY complained that nearly all science fiction characters have been white, male and middle-class, even if some of them are superficially green, sexless or galactic emperors. *Star Trek* was applauded for allowing a few black and women actors to serve on the *Enterprise,* but their roles were restricted essentially to bit parts. When more recent mass media sf introduced black American actors, they often carried their stamp of Otherness with them. Teal'c in *Stargate SG-1* was an impressive black man, but alien, as was the Klingon Worf in *Star Trek: The Next Generation.* More disturbingly, the lustful, comically sordid, money-grubbing Ferengi in later *Star Trek* all too obviously echo the vile caricatures of Jews published by Nazi newspapers like *Der Sturmer.*

Doubtless none of this was deliberate, but it certainly reflected anxieties and prejudices among many readers and viewers. How refreshing, then, to find in *River of Gods* and the short stories that followed it, collected in *Cyberabad Days,* an intensely felt, overwhelmingly detailed portrait of India in the middle of the 21st century, in which most of the cast are Hindu or Muslim in a landscape at once instantly recognizable yet radically unfamiliar to most of us in the West. (A similar shift, as we'll see, underpins Paolo Bacigalupi's multi-award winning *The Windup Girl*—Entry 96—set in a future Thailand.)

That these compulsive, densely imagined works came from an Irish white man is surprising and impressive. McDonald had never set foot in India, but his detailed research and eidetic memory allowed him to create a persuasive bone-deep experience for Anglo-American readers. *River of Gods* deservedly won a year's best award from the British Science Fiction Association, and was shortlisted for the Hugo and the Arthur C. Clarke awards. Several years later, even more awards and notices attended his novel *Brasyl,* set with equal conviction in equally unfamiliar South American landscapes of the 18th and 21st centuries. McDonald's special genius is the evocation of post-colonial landscapes, reflecting his own childhood during the euphemistically-named and terror-drenched Troubles of Northern Ireland.

River of Gods is large in every sense: 600 pages of tightly-written, often almost hallucinatory prose that shifts its tone from character to character, setting to setting, each change in register perfectly fitted to the moment, and often to the consciousness driving forward in that moment. It is not comfortable, and requires attention, which it amply rewards.

While the British were ousted from India in 1930, August 15, 1947 was the official Independence Day. So 2047 is the centenary of India's freedom from colonial rule, but a partitioned landscape of squabbling sub-nations seethes under a rainless Greenhouse sky, awaiting the deferred monsoon:

> The few seconds of heat between airport and air-conditioned car stun Vishram. He's been too long in a cold climate. And he had forgotten the scent, like ashes of roses. The car pulls into the wall of color and sound. Vishram feels the heat, the warmth of the bodies, the greasy hydrocarbon soot against the glass. The people. The never failing river of faces. The bodies. Vishram discovers a new emotion. It has the blue remembered familiarity of home-sickness but is expressed through the terrible mundane squalor of the people that throng beneath these boulevards. Homenausea. Nostalgic horror.

Vishram Ray, a would-be standup comic in Glasgow, now returning to the ancient city of Varanasi (Benares, Kashi, on the holy Ganges) in the sub-state of Baharat, is youngest son of a wealthy power corporation owner who is experimenting with a zero point energy machine that opens into other universes. This project, like many of the most complex tasks in India, is controlled by artificial minds, aeais, that under the US Hamilton Acts must never exceed a certain sub-Turing limit.

Inevitably, self-organizing Generation Three AI programs 20,000 times smarter than us do just that, and are pursued and "excommunicated" with extreme prejudice by the Krishna Cops of the Ministry. Mr. Nandha is one of these functionaries, dedicated to his role, neglecting his beautiful young soapi-addicted wife in this nation where sex-selection has allowed four boys to be born for every girl. The most compulsive soapi is *Town&Country,* a sort of VR *Dallas* acted by *faux* AI thespians who know they are programs but assert their own unique individuality.

One of the show's brilliant set designers is Tal, a nute—neither male nor female, genderless, a kind of sublimely beautiful living Brancusi sculpture who suffers the dangerous disapproval of yts pious neighbors. Astute and subtle Shaheen Badoor Khan, intended for a cabinet post in the Baharat government, falls in love with yt, with inevitable dire consequences when a Swedish-Afghani reporter is manipulated into revealing their delicate, perverse bond. A mysterious rising politician, N. J. Jivanjee, makes diabolical mischief, and sf habitués will guess why.

Meanwhile, an asteroid is found in controlled orbit near Earth with a machine inside, the Tabernacle, that seems to be twice as old as the solar system. Yet it displays slightly futuristic images of American scientists Thomas Lull and Lisa Durnau—colleagues and former lovers who run a vast, accelerated simulated world, Alterre—and an eerie young Indian woman, Aj, who has power over terrifying war machines and seems able to download a Google-grade data source into her brain. This list does not exhaust the cast of the novel, which is a large-scale braided creation as compulsive as the *Town&Country* soapi, and just as fractal, entwined and manipulated by events and powers beyond any individual's ken.

Somehow, miraculously, McDonald holds it all together, weaves the threads into a pattern at once dazzling and satisfying. Is our universe no more stable and real, finally, than the disintegrating Alterre? "We rejoin the river of history," says Mr. Chakraborty, of death, "our stories told and woven into the stream of time." How deeply woven we learn only at the end of this remarkable novel. It is the story, as Najia reflects, of "an attempt by a djinn made of stories to understand something outside its mandalas of artifice and craft. Something it could believe it had not made up itself. It wanted the drama of the real, the fountainhead from which all story flows." That is almost the definition of science fiction itself.

76: Philip Roth
The Plot Against America (2004)

ALTHOUGH SCIENCE FICTION still has more than a whiff of the unrespectable about it, literary mandarins such as Atwood (Entry 1), Chabon (Entry 88), Ishiguro (Entry 77), McCarthy (Entry 84) and Roth sometimes turn to sf themes, even if they don't realize it. The most common form is the dystopia or apocalypse, where sf's "If this goes on—" is usually given a flatfooted outing. Sometimes these efforts produce a successful crossover or "slipstream" novel, like those mentioned.

One form increasingly congenial to literary readers is the *counterfactual*, known by sf readers as alternate (more properly alternative) worlds, stories set against histories that never happened because some critical forking path led into a history where Hannibal thrashed Scipio Africanus, China declined to abandon its advanced seafaring technology, or black Africans colonized the Americas. History as thought-experiment. Literary writers rarely venture far into this multiverse, although Kingsley Amis allowed the Church of Rome to prevail in Britain in *The Alteration,* and Vladimir Nabokov's *Ada, or Ardor* is a Russia, an Antiterra, without Leninist terror. Two notable alternative realities among our 101 books, by Philip Roth and Michael Chabon, present different outcomes to the fascist assault on Jews and other persecuted minorities in the wasteland heart of the 20th century.

Roth is perhaps today's most distinguished American writer, so his novel of a USA deformed by Nazi sympathizers is at once a superb work of contemporary mimesis and a surprising, agile leap sideways into alternate history. Does that make it sf?

No overt technological device drives this deviation from *what actually happened*. Roth does not even bother to provide a handwaving gesture towards fashionable theories of overlapping quantum many worlds, infinite in number, each at right angles to every other, the kind of thing we find in Philip Pullman's *His Dark Materials* fantasy trilogy (1995-2000), let alone a critical time machine-engendered change as in Ward Moore's *Bring the Jubilee* (1953) or Poul Anderson's Time Patrol stories. Surely Roth would consider such apparatus unnecessary, jejune. He thought he was making it all up: "I had no literary models for reimagining the historical past." Still, *The Plot Against American* can be read rewardingly as sf generously defined, akin to Philip K. Dick's Hugo winning *The Man in the High Castle* (1962) with its occupied, divided postwar USA infested by fascist Germany and Japan.

In 1940, Franklin D. Roosevelt fails to gain his third term, defeated by Nazi-sympathizing, white supremacist celebrity aviator Charles A. Lindbergh. (In our world, certain Republican isolationists considered urging Lindbergh to run for the presidency. Struck by this historical morsel, Roth asked a classic sf question: "What if they had?")[31] The narrator, in that pivotal year a 7-year old Jewish New Jersey boy named Philip Roth, is already aware of the same poisoning that blighted the author's world: the racist automotive genius Henry Ford, the Jew-hating radio priest Father Coughlin, even some well-placed rabbis of his ancestral faith eager to placate their defamers. "To tell the story of Lindbergh's presidency from the point of view of my own family," Roth has remarked, "was a spontaneous choice. To alter the historical reality by making Lindbergh America's 33rd president while keeping everything else as close to factual truth as I could—that was the job as I saw it."

Unlike the balkanized America of Dick's great novel, let alone the convulsive jolts and seismic upheavals of most sf alternate histories, Roth's counterfactual clings closely to the world he knew, growing up, and like Sinclair Lewis's famous *It Can't Happen Here* (1935), shows that it *can*, and by what means. This is Isaac Asimov's psychohistory in action, at the closest possible fine grain: sf not of physics but of the raw stuff of life and fluid personality under stress. (Curiously, the Jewish boy living downstairs, whose mother is beaten to death and incinerated by Klansmen, is named Seldon—although surely not for Asimov's psychohistorian Hari Seldon.)

It is fascinating to watch Roth reinventing several road-tested and well-tuned sf devices. He keeps "the adult's narrating voice explicit without its sounding didactic in recounting the imaginary historical events. After all, my reader can't know anything of the history I'm inventing, there is no common knowledge that is complete, and so, though one can allude to Munich or to the Treaty of Versailles, one cannot allude to the Iceland Understanding (the 1941 nonaggression pact signed in Reykjavik by Lindbergh and Hitler) without spelling it out."

By holding his focus so close to the child's perspective—the boy's obsession with stamp collecting, caring for his maimed warrior cousin Alvin's suppurating stump—the larger utterance of history is allowed to unfold like a black and white newsreel projected in the background. The novel is precisely a fiction of the epoch of science and technology: the aircraft and mass media frenzies that enable Lindbergh's fame and Hitler's hypnotic, appalling rise, the mass deaths that blighted our world as well as the fictional Philip's, the broadcasts and easy travel that facilitate the rise and rise (and eventual fall) of the loathsome opportunistic Rabbi Bengelsdorf, fiancé of Philip's aunt Evelyn, head of the Office of American Absorption, "koshering Lindbergh for the goyim."

31 Philip Roth, "The Story Behind 'The Plot Against America,'" *New York Times* September 19, 2004.

Bengelsdorf institutes "Just Folks," a scheme to decontaminate Jewish children by summering them with an isolated rural family. Philip's older brother Sandy comes home from Kentucky a convert to middle American values; soon the Homestead '42 program is uprooting ethnic enclaves and dispersing their minorities across the continent. Young Seldon and his family are relocated early, with tragic results. When finally the nation reels to its senses after Lindbergh vanishes, Roosevelt gets reelected. Chronology proceeds, for good and ill. It is a sort of inverse of Michael Chabon's later *The Yiddish Policemen's Union* (2007), where Jews are settled from around the world in Alaska.

This is history reflected in a blood drop. It is powerful, painful, suggesting one path along which tomorrow's science fiction might proceed, away from galactic empire fantasies of *Übermenchen* (enjoyable as those can be) and into the complex ripeness of life.

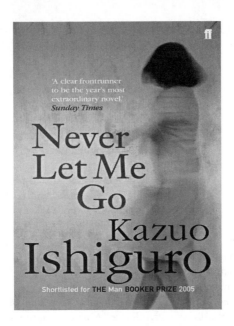

'A clear frontrunner to be the year's most extraordinary novel.'
Sunday Times

Never
Let Me
Go
Kazuo
Ishiguro

Shortlisted for THE Man BOOKER PRIZE 2005

77: Kazuo Ishiguro
Never Let Me Go (2005)

WHEN NUANCED, Booker-winning Japanese-British author Kazuo Ishiguro published his novel of clones raised for organ-transplant—chosen by *Time* magazine as the best book of the decade—*New York Times* reviewer Sarah Kerr drew back her skirts in abject terror of pollution:

> The setup is so shocking—in such a potentially dime-store-novel way—that it's hard to believe at first that it issued from Ishiguro's desktop. Has one of our subtlest observers gone to pulp? The novel is the starkest instance yet of a paradox that has run through all Ishiguro's work. Here is a writer who takes enormous gambles, then uses his superior gifts to manage the risk as tightly as possible. The question is what he's gambling on. Is he setting up house in a pop genre—the sci-fi thriller—in order to quietly upend its banal conventions....[32]

It was a moment of grim humor for sf readers, who were more likely to see the device of organ-farming as quietly upending the banal conventions of polite upper-middle class literary fiction. Certainly Ishiguro's book is about as far from the thriller genre as one could get; there are no explosions, reckless car chases, ninja descents into secret laboratories, asteroid impacts. As a novel written for readers for whom, not many years ago, the notion of human cloning was utterly absurd, and is now at best disgust-

---

32 *http://www.nytimes.com/2005/04/17/books/review/17KERRL.html*

ing and at worst metaphysically criminal, *Never Let Me Go* has shock value, although the idea of cloning reaches back in literature at least as far as Aldous Huxley's *Brave New World* (1932).

In sf, organlegging was introduced and named by Larry Niven in the early volumes of his Known Space series in the 1960s. Sturgeon's 1962 novella "When You Care, When You Love" visited this territory, as did John Boyd's *The Organ Bank Farm* (1970), and so, more recently, did Michael Marshall-Smith's grisly *Spares* (1996) and Bujold's Vorkosigan universe (see Entry 19). These can be dismissed as banal pop genre product only at the cost of willfully ignoring thoughtful (and playful) presentations, in many superior sf works, of an important issue.

Even so, is Ishiguro's novel really sf? As with much well-received literature bordering sf's territory, we can reasonably ask if it makes the grade. If so, its literary qualities—the quiet, artfully unreliable presentation of awakening into maturity, into the unyielding and sometimes awful responsibilities of adulthood—make it instantly worthy of inclusion in any list of the great sf of the last quarter century. Or is cloning just a pallid, undeveloped and confused premise glued onto a conventional *rite de passage*? Stern custodians of the hard science fiction lineage will object that the scenario is preposterous: cloning for this purpose works only if each genetic twin is dedicated to the use of a single wealthy or powerful individual. Nor could organ transplants cure "cancer, motor neuron disease, heart disease." Moreover, since the problems of histocompatibility have been overcome in this alternative history (it's set in a 1990s where biological progress went faster and differently after the Second World War), surely it's simpler, if no less morally reprehensible, to steal infants from orphanages, or the Third World, say, and mine them for organs? Or, as now, recover tissues from those dead in accidents?

This objection is perhaps unnecessarily severe. Terrible things have been done in the past on the basis of incompletely mastered technologies. In this parable, post-War British medicine seems to have taken paths mapped by Nazi experimenters, with all the self-serving moral blindness that implies. If cloning people allows citizens to enjoy longer and healthier lives, isn't it all too dreadfully plausible that victims will be cast out, despised as "soulless" non-human? Make that leap (hardly more drastic than allowing time travel or faster than light starships in your fiction), and the book can be read—as can Philip Roth's Nazified 1940s' America (Entry 76), and Cormac McCarthy's post-catastrophe future (Entry 84)—as a literary essay into territory long since pioneered by sf's explorers.

In Hailsham, seemingly a quite lavish boarding school for wealthy children (although we see only the staff, never parents), Kathy H. makes her rather timid way toward a future of "donations," carers and "completion." We know at once that donation entails the removal of crucial organs, that carers look after clones already rifled while awaiting their own postponed but inevitable lethal fate, and that "completion" is a euphemism for death. Seen that way, it is a fable of life and death as we have always known it, as we try to avoid knowing it: the biological decay, ruin and surcease lying ahead of everyone except those who die even earlier than usual, and the misuse of some humans by others to make their own lives easier. The science fictional aspect sharpens our response to what everything in our culture trains us to avoid, which we either avert our eyes from or valorize as a kind of mysterious blessing that the mature should embrace.

Kathy's best friend is the more outgoing Ruth, who first scorns Kathy's interest in the bumbling, endlessly mocked Tommy, but ends by stealing him as her lover. As these seemingly privileged kids pass from the comforts of Hailsham to the far less pleasant Cottages, and finally to the hospitals where they suffer their predestined fate, their circumstances and small crises are observed with Ishiguro's unrelenting eye. Their guardians, Miss Lucy, Mr. Frank, Nurse Trisha, Miss Geraldine of the art class, head guardian Miss Emily, the distant Madame who gathers their artwork for a supposed "Gallery," are revealed through the children's gaze. Madame, Ruth suggests, is scared of them, and they test this revulsion by intruding into her space. It is not fear, of course, as we can see, but a distancing mechanism any sensitive adult would have to adopt, faced with what amounts to Sophie's Choice writ large.

These children, Kathy learns finally, were regarded by the world of naturals as "shadowy objects in test tubes without souls." It is Ishiguro's triumph to show exactly how wrong this estimate is, and must be, as we move in reality toward a future where such benighted attitudes might yet prevail alongside creationism, racism, and other absurd or malign myths.

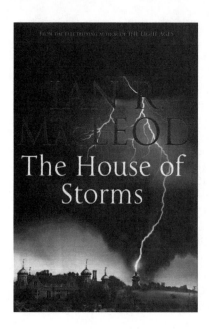

78: Ian R. MacLeod
The House of Storms (2005)

ERE'S ALICE, in front of her mirror, about to enter Looking Glass land—yet she's also the Wicked Queen, asking her mirror who's the fairest of them all, ready to stamp her foot in rage and crush any upstart. England is divided down the middle, financial and judicial sophisticates to the right, rural and maritime toilers and thrusters to the left, Tweedledum and Tweedledee, eager to plunge into ruinous civil war. Here's the hothouse city boy, fatally ill, falling in love with the unschooled seashore girl, buoyantly healthy. Here's the great rotten trunk of authority mirrored by its own burgeoning but stifled seedlings. Here's the fruit falling not far from the tree, into the same loam that fed the tree, yet growing aslant from heredity and nurture both. Or is it? Is the seed in the fruit determined by, and determining, all the long history of the tree and its blood-soaked soil?

These are archetypal oppositions, dichotomies, puzzles, reversals, storybook clichés meeting themselves like faces in a crazed mirror, unexpected yet inevitable, predictable as legend. The mood, of course, is melancholy. The telling is drawn-out, somber, steeped in long-shadowed afternoon light.

Ian R. MacLeod is a fine British writer of large ambition and copious talent. He has twice won the World Fantasy Award, two Asimov's polls, as well as the Sideways Award and a Locus Poll award, and in 2009 the Clarke and the Campbell Memorial awards. Nick Gevers called *The House of Storms* (justly) "unfailingly elegant, full of brilliantly realized English landscapes, deftly sensitive characterizations, luminously reworked fairy tales, and poetic elegies to lives and opportunities lost.... *The House of Storms* is that uncommon thing, a sequel to be treasured as much as its precursor."

That precursor was *The Light Ages* (2003), MacLeod's first venture into an elaborately realized alternative history separated from our own in the 17th-century with the discovery of "aether," a force or quintessence that powers a botched industrial revolution as dreadful as our own. It sustains cheap and shoddy workmanship, permits localized control of the weather, useful for a sea-going culture—and damages its luckless handlers as if it were a diabolical blend of radioactivity and chemical mutagens.

Aether is at once a science-fictional device and a ferocious figuration of the industrial process and its often inhuman side-consequences, its astonishing wealth, beauty, temptations, corrosive power. So this is not fantasy at all; while it's not science, it's assuredly science fiction.

In the earlier book, a poor Northern boy narrates his rise through a Dickensian world of squalor, horror and unbreakable hierarchy. A century later, this quasi-sequel tells the aching if rather too fairytale-like generational saga of the collapse of aether and the rise of electricity, the very force that in our world catalyzed versions of democracy and industrial totalitarianism alike, and the final triumph of mass consumerist culture.

So *The House of Storms* is not Dickensian, but perhaps Wellsian, not Victorian so much as Edwardian, with all the nasty poverty, pollution, bigotry, suppressed class hatred that would burn through into the First World War. Here it enacts in miniature a conflict between the great European powers, as a second English Civil War purportedly waged by the East against the West to end slavery in an underexploited Thule, our America. Inevitably, we read undertones of both the American War of Independence and its internecine War Between the States. A compressed allegorical weight is borne by the principal characters. Greatgrandmistress Alice Meynell is a beautiful wicked witch from the land of Grimms' fairytales, a sort of Mrs. Coulter (from Philip Pullman's *His Dark Materials* trilogy): conscienceless, ambitious, murderous, yet strangely devoted to her ailing son Ralph. Alice comes by ill fortune from the wrong side of the money mirror. Born Alice Bowdly-Smart to a wealthy couple, she is plunged after their perhaps accidental deaths into poverty, makes her way as a sort of upmarket whore to London, ruins a grandee of the powerful Guild of Electricians and marries another, connives, kills, steals; in short, she is a sort of Becky Sharp (Thackeray's *Vanity Fair*) who never comes a cropper.

Her son Ralph is her weakness. She takes him west to the Guild's seaside mansion Invercombe, not far from the Bristol seaport, close, as well, to Einfell, where changelings huddle, poor detritus smashed by the touch of aether. Alice herself is addicted to the stuff, using its corrupting power to retain an unearthly beauty. She learns to employ the aether-entangled telephone mirrors that link the nation like magical wormholes, providing access to a kind of cyberspace or psychic netherworld into which the spirit might be uploaded even as the body grows transparent as glass.

Is this, then, an essay in steampunk, a version of Gibson's and Sterling's remarkable *The Difference Engine?* (Punchcard "reckoning engines" are here, too.) Not quite. At almost every point in his narrative arc, or beautifully wrought longueur-filled meander, MacLeod looks somewhere else. He is deliberately avoiding the vulgarly obvious, but the price is considerable.

In place of more conventional huggermugger, he gives us a diorama of Great Men and Women from the 19th and turn of the 20th Century. It is tempting to identify Ralph with a nascent Darwin, intent on finding in the Canaries (here, the Fortunate Isles) his own Galapagos. Together with the shoregirl Marion Price, with whom he falls radiantly in love, Ralph develops the theory of Habitual Adaptation. Their bastard child, Klade, raised by uncanny changelings, is a sort of Caliban whose name, in our world, suggests a group of organisms with a single ancestor, as well as a new Adam made from clay. While there are aspects of natural selection in the hypothesis, the term suggests more than a little of Lamarck. What is clear is that Ralph's vile mother is the very embodiment of Social Darwinism, acting out a brutalized and simplified version of Darwin: nature red in tooth and claw.

MacLeod has a large future, and we're lucky to have him here, on this side of Alice's mirror.

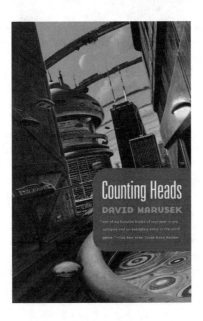

79: David Marusek
Counting Heads (2005)

THE OPENING forty-plus pages of this ambitious and rambunctious debut novel were originally published separately under the title "We Were Out of Our Minds With Joy," and serve as the launching platform from which the rest of the bold and ground-breaking story takes off.

In that prelude, we are introduced to the world of the 2090s, and a strange milieu it is. Previously, a massive terrorist assault known as the Outrage has contaminated Earth's entire biosphere with NASTIES, nanotech assailants, leaving people to huddle within protected cities. But this forced retreat has really amounted to less than a tiny speedbump in the advance of technology and a go-go culture. The human lifespan is now practically infinite—if you can afford the rejuves. Everyone possesses a "mentar" of varying capabilities, mentars being AI "paste-brains" that help humans navigate the world virtually and in "realbody." Synthetic crops feed the world's billions. Beamed power from satellites in orbit around the Sun offers endless energy. And humankind stands on the threshold of colonizing the stars in vast Oships.

Our protagonists in this first section are Sam Harger and Eleanor Starke. Sam's an artist, and Eleanor's a businesswoman-cum-politician. They fall in love in bizarre 21st-century style and later are awarded a child in the baby lottery. Their life seems ideal. But then Eleanor's political rivals strike at her through Sam. He is mistakenly branded a terrorist and stripped of his immortality and other health benefits by Homeland Command. His very cells are booby-trapped, turning him into a literally stinking pariah, one of the "seared." Section one ends with him reluctantly leaving his wife and child, Ellen.

Cut to forty years later. The world has grown even stranger. Legions of clones—identified generically by the first names of their original donors, such as jerrys, evangelines, russes and jeromes—do society's scutwork, while the "affs" lord it over them. In the middle are the average joes and janes who must struggle to pay for their rejuves, while eating the plainest fare from their NanoJiffys. The Outrage has just been declared officially over, and the city of Chicago—where our story occurs—is ready to lower its shields.

Eleanor and Ellen Starke are still alive and in power. Until they are both assassinated. Eleanor dies permanently, but Ellen's head is cryostatically preserved. Much of the plot revolves around attempts to get her reborn in the face of continued enemy action. But we also learn what happened to Sam Harger: he's now known as Samson Kodiak, member of an extended "charter" family. We follow him through his dying days, as well as observing the twisty destinies of: young Bogdan Kodiak—a 29-year-old permanently stuck in adolescence; Fred and Mary, two clones; and Eleanor's political ally, the ineffectual Merrill Meewee. Additionally, mentars such as Wee Hunk, Cabinet, Hubert, Concierge and Arrow play their parts, as one era closes and a new one opens.

This novel is a trippy, gleeful tour through a "milling menagerie of transhumanity," and anyone who revels in the heady (sorry for the pun), gonzo, densely recomplicated sf of John Wright (Entry 71), Charles Stross (Entry 81), Rudy Rucker (Entry 91), Cory Doctorow (Entry 94) or Karl Schroeder (Entry 66) will find this novel by Marusek to be a sterling addition to their ranks. Marusek is unstintingly generous in his speculations, which are all entertainingly wild yet convincingly realistic. He builds characters who are far from the clichés of the field. (No brave female spaceship pilots, cowboy data-hackers, mirrorshaded ninjas, or other faded types.) And he balances his plot perfectly between mega-scale and micro-scale events.

With regard to his speculations, Marusek obviously focuses much of his intellectual weight on the repercussions of biological advancements. His future is one where bodies can be regenerated from nothing more than a preserved head and neck, leading to the truly Boschian image of a tiny embryonic form dependent from the terminus of an adult spinal cord. But of course he doesn't ignore other developments in robotics and nanotech, integrating these areas beautifully. Likewise, he examines how culture and society remake themselves to accommodate new technologies. His portrait of the weird clone society is startling and novel. The big clone party—a magnificent literary set piece—that sprawls across the middle of the book will knock your socks off.

Marusek's characters grab you because they are, underneath their transhumanity, so ordinary and pitiable. The up-and-down married relationship between clones Fred and Mary and how their characters strive to grow is truly affecting. Additionally, Marusek cranks up that Philip K. Dick vibe of mankind struggling to maintain the borders between what's real and what's artificial, human and android. When Samson has to argue with his life-support chair, for instance, one hears echoes of Dick, as we do in the struggle of the russ named Fred to assert his individuality.

Perhaps the major weapon in Marusek's arsenal is his zesty language—reflecting a basically optimistic view of his future—and copious dead-on neologisms. These tools make the story shimmer and glow, hypnotizing the reader into true belief in the substantiality of his marvelous, alternately hilarious and melancholy new world.

John Campbell's famous instruction to his writers was to deliver a story that read like the contemporary fiction of the year it was set in. And that's exactly what Marusek has accomplished here.

80: Geoff Ryman
Air (Or, Have Not Have) (2005)

GEOFF RYMAN is a notably adventurous writer straddling the boundaries of science fiction, fantasy, slipstream, experimental writing, queer-inflected fiction and, recently, "Mundane" sf. His work is poignant, dense with detail, requiring a concentrated reading—yet it has a luminous clarity and humanity that's brought him awards and acclaim in Britain (his adopted base), the USA, and Canada (his birthplace).

The Child Garden (winner of the 1990 Arthur C. Clarke and Campbell Memorial awards), Ryman's superb novel of genetic engineering, came close to being the long-awaited work successfully bonding the force and aspirations of both literature and sf. *Air*, winner of the Clarke, the Tiptree, and the British Science Fiction Association awards, belongs to the same shortlist of candidates.

This grittily realist, soaringly fantastical story of Mrs. Mae Chung, a robust middle-aged woman and mother of grown children in the imaginary nation of Karzistan, bordering China and Kazakhstan, inverts almost every aspect of *The Child Garden*. It moves in a pavane amid the balanced forces of the *I Ching* and other divinatory manifestations of the four ancient elements: air, fire, water and earth. Kizuldah, the Happy Province of rural peasants, is saturated in its own past, even as the flood of a belated today and then an instantaneous tomorrow crams memory into ruinous mud while its insistent presence invades poor Mae's mind like a plague of memetic computer viruses.

Air is the next technology after the Internet, 2020's mercantile version of what sf has long postulated—access to a group or gestalt mind. It is Google in the head, without need of chips, display, data gloves or keyboard, Theodore Sturgeon's and Joe

Haldeman's gestalt connectivity for the age of quantum superspace and petaflop computation. It is the all-at-once of M-Theory's timeless unity of space and change, accessed via a Format burned into the brain that—in trial runs in Karzistan, Tokyo and Singapore—uses an under-construction UN software template.

Unluckily, the Format test suggests that it is liable to disrupt and even madden unprepared brains exposed even briefly to Air's 11-dimensional ubiquity. The rival, slower Gates Format struggles for preferment, seizing eagerly on the UN test's collateral damage. From the big centers of power among the Western Haves, these global contests cascade in surprising ways over the ill-equipped but richly complex social arrangements of the Have Nots—who, naturally enough, bitterly resent being labeled as such by their patronizing benefactors.

Local fashion-advice specialist (and dirt-grubbing farmer) Mrs. Chung is perhaps the most extreme victim of these side-effects. In the moment of formatting, an elderly, blind, sweet-natured neighbor dies in her arms, so their minds become entangled. With typical comic bravura, Ryman explains that this is because they share an email address in the timeless realm of Air. Mae Chung's personality is infused with the dead Mrs. Tung's yearnings and her now forever-unchangeable history, like one infested by a dybbuk or demon.

A secondary effect of her unique immersion in Air is enhanced creativity. Mae gains access to the world's plenty, learning to use the old-fashioned Web via a classy digital TV to contact markets for her fashion business, which soon goes global. This clever, illiterate woman's faltering but growing competence is delightful to watch. Her naivety allows her to promote her wares with flyers teaching a women's circle of fellow villagers

HOW TO MAKE BIG BUCKS FROM INFO

for this is the last corner of the world not yet awash in spam. Ryman has stressed that the setting is wholly invented, although it owes something to his experience of Turkey. The village of sinewy Karz peasants and tolerated, beautiful but delicate Eloi is richly evoked, utterly believable.

Because *Air* is authentic literature, Mae's emotional involvements, her love affairs, her friendships and their subtle or brutal ebbs and flows, form the tense focus of the narrative. Still, to a degree no mundane novel could permit, the fanciful sf element of Air plays an equally compelling and impelling role. Echoing the tidal disruption that Air's full implementation threatens, the very snows of the high places cupping the village hang at the edge of melting and flood. It is a threat only Mae and her memorious but increasingly spiteful ghost can detect. Mae knuckles down in face of this threat, learns meteorological arcana and bullies her way to the expensive software needed to interpret the local weather data she and her charge laboriously gather. As water rushes finally across earth, the fire of her unstoppable will snatches many of her mocking fellows to a redemptive safety that only an Air-powered bodhisattva could have managed.

Against this hard-headed peasant empiricism, Mae's immersion in Air reveals reality's mutability under desire. She rips asunder a wire fence by a sort of quantum magic: "The fence was mere fiction. So she tore it." By the same means, an absurd, even grotesque, miracle brings Mae a pregnancy like nothing seen since the age of myth and legend. Mae is a sort of paradoxical Virgin Mother figure, and her joyous son, scalded and blind like Mrs. Tung but awash in Air's music and light, is a sort of Redeemed

New Human/Buddha/Christ, conceived in a loving, sexual feast. Yet the novel itself rejects interpretation:

> "Everything has always been and has always happened at once. Which means nothing causes anything else. Which means stories only happen in this poor balloon-world of ours. Stories have no meaning. Nothing can be interpreted. Everything just is, without meaning.... It is all just one big smiling Now."

The wondrous art wrought in Ryman's *Air* shows some of its meaning plainly, calling forth grins, astonishment and tears. More of its meaning is tucked away inside, like the hidden curled-up dimensions of M-Theory's spacetime, and (resembling *The Child Garden* in its closure) like the final pages of the third book of Dante's *Divine Comedy*, beyond words or imagining high and low.

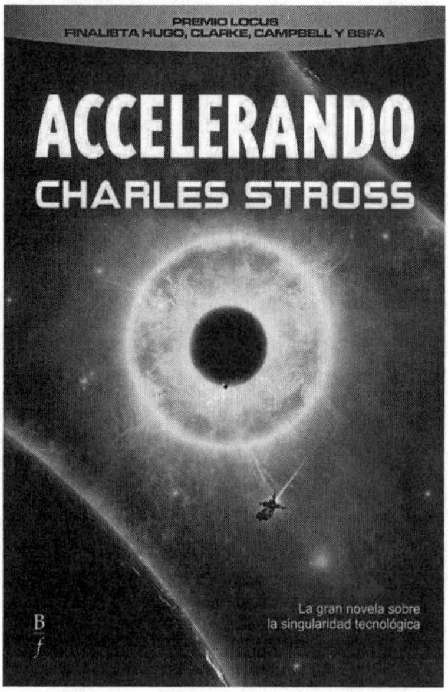
PREMIO LOCUS
FINALISTA HUGO, CLARKE, CAMPBELL Y BSFA
ACCELERANDO
CHARLES STROSS
La gran novela sobre
la singularidad tecnológica

81: Charles Stross
Accelerando (2005)

LIKE GREG Egan a decade earlier, Charles Stross seemed to come from nowhere and leap immediately to the top rank of science fiction and fantasy writers. This is an illusion in both cases (each had published early short fiction), but especially so for Stross, who for years pounded on many dozing publishers' doors with several exciting book manuscripts before *Festival of Fools* was eventually bought by Ace, released as *Singularity Sky*, and went straight on to the Hugo ballot for best novel of the year. As did his audacious post-Singularity novelette "Nightfall" (poking its tongue out at Asimov's most famous title). Neither won, but it was a remarkable debut.

Stross's work has proved enormously popular, and justly so. With *Accelerando*, the quasi-novel compilation of his sequence of nine astonishing stories from *Asimov's,* begun in 2001 with "Lobsters," Charles Stross was sealed as the new Poet Laureate of the Vingean technological singularity. "Elector," the penultimate chapter, was on the 2005 Hugo shortlist for best novella, which made a total of four Hugo nominations, one Nebula nomination, two Sturgeons, one BSFA, and a Seiun shortlisting before *Accelerando* was published. It won the 2006 Locus award for the year's best novel. By the middle of the first decade of this century, Charles Stross was no longer just the sf writer to watch—he had well and truly arrived. In 2009, he became the first author to have a novel on the Hugo shortlist in six consecutive years, and in 2010 both a novella and a novelette on the ballot.

The *Accelerando* project's five years of development (it is tempting to apply this sort of corporate language to Stross's dense techno-speak art-artifact) yielded an early twenty-first-century counterpart to John Brunner's compressed future shock 1969 Hugo-winner, *Stand on Zanzibar,* complete with rich idiomatic sidebars or side loads of Baedeker guidance to the non-native.

> The rogue corporation rears up slightly and bunches into a fatter lump; its skin blushes red in patches. "Must think about this. Is your mandatory accounting time-cycle fixed or variable term? Are self-owned corporate entities able to enter contracts?"

That's funny, and fun, as well as knowing. Some readers complain of infodumping of the most blatant kind, yet that device seems unavoidable when a torrential cascade of novelty is the very topic of a work of art. Approached with an appreciative generosity of response, these dollops of data are tight, compressed, inventive, brilliantly illuminated gems, or perhaps genomes (or memomes) that will unfold, in a prepared mind, into wondrous ecologies of image and idea. The changes implied by headlong acceleration are by definition too immense, too subtle, to be portrayed or perhaps even imagined. Stross has the audacity and, luckily for us, the imagination to come close to pulling it off.

Manfred Macx is a venture altruist ("Manfred's on the road again, making strangers rich")—Stross is not afraid to have us smile even as he jolts our preconceptions—a decade or so hence, encrusted with computer wearables and the latest wifi connectivity, affianced until recently to Pamela, a dominatrix headhunter for the IRS who tries to persuade global megacorps to cough up the tax they owe. Their venomous bond is manipulated sardonically by their robot cat, Aineko, which is being hacked and upgraded on the sly by Pamela. This nicely observed android animal—"It sits on the hand woven rug in the middle of the hardwood floor with one hind leg sticking out at an odd angle, as if it's forgotten about it"—might be the secret narrator of the novel. Its augmentation and expansion toward the condition of a low-level demiurge mirrors the transitions of humankind and our posthuman Vile Offspring.

In a bondage scene of hilarious erotic vividness, Pamela gets herself pregnant with their daughter Amber, who will carry much of the long arc of the story to the Singularity and beyond, as human minds export themselves increasingly outside the skull into machine substrate exocortices. In turn, Amber's son Sirhan (well, son of one of her many instantiations) takes the generational saga to the destructive *Childhood's End*-style transcension of the solar system into a Matrioshka Brain (energy-hungry Dyson shells of computronium hosting untold trillions of superminds), the return from death of an extremely augmented Manfred, and a blind plunge beyond the provincial Milky Way to a realm where a galactic superintelligence seems to be mounting a "timing channel attack on the virtual machine that's running the universe, perhaps, or an embedded simulation of an entirely different universe."

It is typical of Stross's full-on method that he declines to define "timing channel attack," which is a sneaky method of undermining encryption by observing how long it takes to complete various aspects of the coding or decoding process. That doesn't matter, nor should there be any problem in the book's inundation of references from a dozen or a hundred different disciplines, not least Internet lore, mined by his jackdaw and inventive mind. This is how high bandwidth science fiction works. If some item baffles you, rush on and rejoice in the confusion. Or, if you are obsessive, Google it.

Stross's text points in both those directions simultaneously. As the decades pass, as the rate of change accelerates, his characters *become* Googlized. And even with their inbuilt channels of information and communication, they are lost like us in the hydrant gush of available knowledge. All around them, intellectual tools are mutating into predatory lifeforms. Feral tax auditing software roams the solar system, entire economic systems convulse in ecological firestorms of contest. And then there are the aliens... which, of course, are just as likely to be autonomous spam attacks as anything we would recognize as people.

Accelerando is a *Fantasia*-bright cavalcade of borrowed and adapted landscapes—the Atomium globe from the 1950 World's Fair, the deck of the *Titanic* emulated in a virtualization stack, a phony debased Islamic heaven—transplanted to Saturn's icy atmosphere or a virtual reality world inside a soda can starwhisp or an alien router network. Does it work? *Can* it work? It is an impressive attempt upon the impossible. For all its Catherine-wheel sparkle and intellectual bravura, there is evidence that the impossible must remain always out of reach—but kudos to the brave writer who attempts it!

82: Robert Charles Wilson
Spin (2005)

FOR SOME years, ambitious but quiet sf novels by American-Canadian Robert Charles Wilson have established him as one of the finest writers in the genre, his books at once as beautifully written and moving as many a mainstream work, yet impelled by well conceived sf speculations. Increasingly, these have taken a powerfully audacious cosmogonic turn, especially in his Aurora award-winning *Darwinia,* with its dizzying conceptual breakthroughs, *The Chronoliths* (Campbell Memorial Award in 2002), and *Spin* (a finalist for the Campbell Award, and Hugo winner in 2006) and its sequels *Axis* (2007) and *Vortex* (2011).

As always with truly fine sf, we tussle with a disconnect between the small intimate scale of human lives, motives, joys and agonies, and the immensity of cosmos and deep time. Perhaps the wisest technical solution for an sf writer is to display the latter's grandeur and sublimity through the confusions and evasions of ordinary people faced with shocking insight and life changes.

A year or two from now, the sky goes utterly black. A dark shell has enclosed the entire globe, blotting out stars, Moon, infalling meteorites and luckless astronauts in orbit. Satellites fall from the sky in shreds. Yet the Sun also rises in its accustomed celestial clockwork. Or does it? The sunspots are gone. This solar disk, or rather its emulation, radiates like a dream of pre-Galilean Plato. Yet the tides sway in the lost Moon's embrace. Someone up there likes us enough to keep the planet's ecology ticking over. For what reason? Who are these Hypotheticals? The first glimmerings are not gained for several years. The gateway in the sky is permeable, it turns out, but the universe beyond is running faster than our daily round. A hundred million times faster. Or rather, the world's time has slowed, and the shield protects life from the storm of blue-shifted radiation outside.

It is as if the entire world were trapped on orbit at the event horizon of a black hole, appalling gravity braking the planet's time in a demonic demonstration of relativity theory. But this terrifying anomaly is the tool of a science beyond anything we know. The media start calling it the Spin; everything customary, it seems, is spinning out of control. Beyond its opaque shroud, the entire universe spins like a crazy playground carousel. Cosmic time sleets through its hourglass. Within decades, by shroud time, the Sun is doomed to boom into red giant expansion, presumably obliterating the world. The galaxy itself will age and wane even as children like youthful Tyler, Jason and Diane (we meet them first in budding adolescence, as the stars go into hiding) grow up, fall in and out of love and power. A human lifespan is matched finally to the aging of the cosmos, or our corner of it.

It is a conceit that echoes Greg Egan's first sf novel *Quarantine* (1992), but while Egan's was a dazzling noir exercise in quantum prestidigitation, Wilson's moves with a lovely melancholy through three decades of terror, accommodation, power ructions, Faustian ambition (Mars is seeded with life, which flourishes as people on Earth watch), dreadful insight, contained apotheosis. And all of this history is wrought small—or rather, at a meaningful, intuitive human scale—in the reflecting life of a handful of people, most of whom are neither the rulers of the world nor sf's frequent secret mutants destined to rule the sevagram (although Jason verges on both conditions).

There is a sort of Evelyn Waugh or Anthony Powell elegiac quality suffusing *Spin*, and more than a touch of F. Scott Fitzgerald's *Gatsby*, replacing a more headlong melodramatic genre brutality. Tyler Dupree, a physician of modest gifts, writes much of this book in a graphomanic surge, driven by a healing virus that is making him more than human, in, predictably, a modest way. His voice is placid, resigned, displaced from center yet with a deepening self-assurance. He opens with words borrowed from his brilliant friend, the Odd Johnish Jason Lawton: "Everybody falls, and we all land somewhere." This resembles Maugham or the Waugh of *Brideshead Revisited*. Indeed, during his harrowing, Tyler finds a batch of "swayback Somerset Maugham novels more tempting" than a biography of his famous friend (with its measly five references to himself in the index).

"We're as ephemeral as raindrops," Jason tells him, in a posthumous letter. When stoical, good-hearted, perhaps faintly Aspergerish Tyler falls, he picks himself up and trudges on to the end of the world, driven perhaps by his dogged, doggish, heartbreaking devotion to Jason's gifted sister Diane. She traps herself in despairing commitment to just the sort of mad fundamentalist dogma people fall into when the world seems to fail their heartfelt longings.

Time is the hero of this novel; the opening chapter is headed "4×10^9 A.D.," four billion years hence—as far into the future, very nearly, as we are now from the accretion of our planet. How Tyler fetches up there with Diane, racked as he is with an alien disease in a drastically changed social order, comprises the curve of the tale, like an arch across the heavens, which alternates between this deep future where the sky is clear again, and the back story beginning in the second chapter titled, suitably, "The Big House."

Tyler's mother is house-keeper to wealthy Carol and E.D. Lawton. E.D. is a ruthlessly Campbellian competent man whose aerostat company forges vastly profitable global communications links once GPS and commsats have been smashed by the Spin. Tyler's late father Marcus was once E.D.'s partner, but now the orphaned boy watches the world of his lost heritage from across the lawns to the Big House. Just so, of course, humankind watches the cosmos, small fry at the edge of an expanse crowded with godlike Hypotheticals who gradually come into some sort of numinous focus as the entwined narrative threads strive toward maturation and completion.

Tyler, perhaps inevitably for this kind of role, seems a bit of a sap much of the time, tending his hopeless lifelong crush on Diane, duped (for the greatest good, naturally) by Lawton *pere* and *fils* alike, witness to great doings, and even, amanuensis and handy factor to some of those pushing the levers of world historical change, playing his obliterated part. At the end, he has earned hope, and perhaps finds it. Wilson writes like an autumnal, melancholy angel.

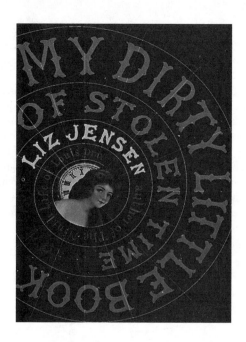

83: Liz Jensen
My Dirty Little Book of Stolen Time
(2006)

JENSEN IS not marketed as a genre author, nor reviewed in genre venues. And she doesn't exactly rate big coverage from mainstream, establishment publications either—a result, arguably, of her slipstream nature, and her consequent falling between two camps. These factors make it unlikely that genre readers will have a deep familiarity with her work. And that's a shame, given her superb prose, witty fantastical conceits, narrative drive, and mature sophistication.

Her five books prior to our selection here were all fantastical in nature, and set the stage for our ultimate candidate. Herewith, then, a brief course in Jensen 101.

Jensen's maiden voyage was *Egg Dancing*, and it possessed all the satirical verve and zing of a Kit Reed or George Saunders production. Bedraggled, hapless Moira Sugden is married to your typical mad gynecologist, Gregory, who is, unbeknownst to Moira, using her as an incubator to test his new treatment that will theoretically create a "perfect baby."

Her second book, *Ark Baby*, also centers around fertility and marriage, but is cast not as a contemporary melodrama but rather as a mixed steampunk/near future satire. One track concerns rogue veterinarian Bobby Sullivan. Sullivan lives in the then-future era of 2005, when all of the UK is suffering from an inexplicable sterility plague. (His humiliating specialty is ministering to pets which act as child surrogates.) Forced to relocate, for various reasons, to a rural peninsula called Thunder Spit, he finds his life intersecting with two strange women, the twins Blanche and Rose Ball. The heroic sexual efforts of this trio will eventually shatter the sterility plague. But the contemporary track takes a back seat to the wacky and resplendent Victorian half of the book. Here, we witness the strange birth and career of Tobias Phelps, offspring of the Gentleman Monkey and a contortionist female. Phelps will eventually find the love of his life in the form of the immense Violet Scrapie, despite Violet's having had the misfortune once to cook up the carcass of Tobias's father. Jensen sews up the two halves of her canvas expertly, melding past with present.

With her third book, Jensen confirmed her delightful and irrepressible hummingbird habits, flitting to yet another mode. With *The Paper Eater*, Jensen creates one of the best dystopias of recent memory, easily comparable to the work of Max Barry and Rupert Thomson. The man of strange habits from the title is Harvey Kidd. The realtime frame tale finds Harvey on a floating prison ship, where chewing on scrap paper to produce papier-mâché has become his sanity-preserving habit. (His skin is grey from ingested inks!) As Harvey interacts with his cellmate, we eventually learn his life story. With echoes of Matt Ruff , Philip K. Dick, J. G. Ballard and William Gaddis, Jensen's third book is a small neglected masterpiece.

Jensen surprises yet again with her fourth book—because at first she seemingly reverts to the near-mainstream domesticity of *Egg Dancing*. But as we soon learn, she's really taking us to a different territory altogether. *War Crimes for the Home* is the life story of Gloria Winstanley, an elderly Cockney lady with a life full of "secrets and lies," to use the relevant title of Mike Leigh's 1996 film. Like Moira's mother in *Egg Dancing*, Gloria is an old lady confined to a not unpleasant but nonetheless stifling nursing home. Her son Hank and daughter-in-law Karen make frequent visits but are unable to disturb Gloria's façade, alternately dreamy and abstracted or irritable and spiteful. Gloria claims she has Alzheimer's, but the reality is vastly more complicated. Gloria's memory, we eventually learn, was tampered with hypnotically during World War II. In parallel tracks (as with *Ark Baby*), we witness the seminal events of the War that damaged Gloria's psyche, as we also witness the events in the present that just may heal her, albeit with a certain measure of pain.

The reign of warped souls continued in her fifth book. *The Ninth Life of Louis Drax* ventures firmly into Patrick McGrath or early Ian McEwan territory: New Gothic. The child character, a nine-year-old French boy, who tells his story in a truly eerie, psychotic yet wise-beyond-his-years voice, has survived a cascade of near-fatal childhood accidents. Like a cat with nine lives, he's used up eight, he feels, and is now embarked on his ninth. And what a life it turns out to be. An accident during a family picnic sends Louis into a coma. He is placed at a longterm-care institution. Attendant upon her son is devoted mother Natalie Drax. Seemingly no more than a bereaved parent, Natalie hides dark secrets about her and Louis. From his coma Louis is able to witness events and influence people telepathically—Jensen's delicious black icing on the cake of madness. This book is the closest you can come in print to a film by Pedro Almodovar.

To counterbalance *Drax*'s grimness, Jensen turns in *My Dirty Little Book of Stolen Time* to more or less pure farce. What she delivers is, improbably, a timeslip romance, but not the debased and simple-minded bodice-ripping kind. It's a mix of Tom Holt and Kage Baker, Harry Harrison and H. G. Wells, James Blaylock and Lemony Snicket.

The year 1897 in Copenhagen finds our young heroine-narrator, Charlotte Schleswig, struggling to make a living as a whore. Burdened by the care of a gluttonous and slatternly mother—Charlotte insists that Fru Schleswig, the slovenly pig, cannot possibly be related to a beautiful princess such as herself—our working girl is always on the alert for a more lucrative scam. She believes she's landed on easy street when she and her mother get a housecleaning job with Fru Krak, a rich and egotistical widow. While the elder Schleswig labors away sweeping up dust bunnies, Charlotte pilfers whatever's not nailed down to pawn.

Fru Krak's husband, it turns out, mysteriously vanished seven years ago. His disappearance is connected with a locked room in the basement of the Krak manor. Charlotte's curiosity is aroused, and she breaks in one night with her mother. They discover a curious contraption, and before you can say "Terry Gilliam's *Time Bandits*," they are accidentally transported to our era's London. There they find Professor Krak, hale and hearty, living among a surreptitious refugee community of fellow time-traveling Danes.

Charlotte is transfixed by the modern age, especially when she falls in love with a dashing young Scottish archaeologist, Fergus McCrombie. Soon she induces Professor Krak to sponsor a Christmas visit back to 1897, to introduce Fergus to her native era. Once back in "history," everything goes wrong. Charlotte is separated from both Fergus and the Professor, and only her own ingenuity can restore the lovers.

Jensen has immense fun with this setup. Her depiction of period Copenhagen is rich and sensorially deep. (Nor is this choice of nationality for Charlotte merely arbitrary. Jensen invokes, both overtly and covertly, the spirit of Hans Christian Andersen and his famous fairytales as a template for Charlotte's life story.) Of course we also get the expected but still humorously contrived reactions of a visitor from the past to modern life, as well as some neat chrono-paradox mindblowers. The characters are all humanly endearing, with every high-minded, principled stand undercut by carnality or vice-ridden selfishness. And yet the whole narrative is full of warm goodheartedness. All of these virtues are couched in Jensen's vibrant prose that goes down easy, yet is full of nuggets of observation and wit. "The Pastor…was a paunchy man in his middle to late years, with clattering false teeth that seemed to roam his mouth like a tribe of nomads in search of land on which to pitch camp."

Discovering the work of Liz Jensen is like stumbling on a time-machine in a basement: you have no idea of where it will take you, but you know it'll be a hell of a ride.

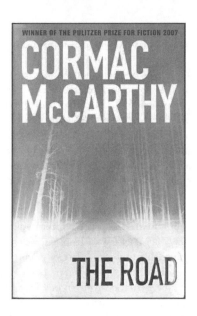

WINNER OF THE PULITZER PRIZE FOR FICTION 2007

CORMAC McCARTHY

THE ROAD

84: Cormac McCarthy
The Road (2006)

L IKE ALL fiction and much art, sf displays figures acting (or stymied) in a land-scape. As noted in earlier entries, for most literary fiction its figures and landscape are familiar to the intended reader, and their portrayal is nuanced, shaded, closely examined to a degree possible only with the already well-known. By contrast, so-called genre fiction usually has different goals and means: characters are often gaudy, overlit, driven by wild passions, moving through extravagant landscapes sketched with comic strip boldness and exaggeration.

Sf is especially remarkable for its emphasis on inventive settings, landscapes none of us has trodden outside dream or imagination. One extreme is the landscape of final desolation, of apocalypse and post-apocalypse—the world blighted by global nuclear war or genocidal plague, or literally destroyed, the Sun gone nova, whole galaxies obliterated in immense spectacle. In Greg Bear's *The Forge of God* (1987), chunks of neutronium and antineutronium are fired into the Earth's core by aliens; the mutual annihilation tears the planet apart. Charles Pellegrino and George Zebrowski's *The Killing Star* (1995) wrecks Earth with targeted relativistic bombs striking at 0.92 of light speed, and finally the Sun itself is destroyed as a few survivors flee into deep space.

Cormac McCarthy's Pulitzer-winning novel *The Road* is not rationalized in this fashion, and the post-catastrophe landscape through which his unnamed man and boy trudge, pushing their shopping cart from frigid mountains to fouled sea, is never explained. Most life other than human is dead: no trees, crops, grass, birds, fish. The sky is gray and cold, rain and snow and drifting ash blight the world, which rumbles with immense distant upheavals. Ten years earlier, the nameless man and his pregnant wife experienced the end of their world: "The clocks stopped at 1:17. A long shear of light and then a series of low concussions. He got up and went to the window… the power was already gone. A dull rose glow in the windowglass."

A reader schooled in the protocols of science fiction, with its attention to background as well as the figures roaming its roads, immediately asks: what happened? How did this occur? Where's the radiation poisoning? Many conventional readers, captivated by Oprah's TV championing of the novel, take the *mise-en-scène* to be a harsh warning of environment despolation, the ruined world a victim of unchecked climate change. Others suppose that this is the nuclear winter dreaded for decades. Neither explanation makes sense. McCarthy's calamity could be due to relativistic bombardment (but there is no sign of malign aliens, who would make this a very different kind of story), or the kind of asteroid impact or series of super-volcano eruptions that destroyed the dinosaurs.

Arguably these are absurdly inappropriate concerns, like probing the economic system of Samuel Beckett's *Waiting for Godot*. If so, can we fruitfully read *The Road* as sf, or is this at best misguided and at worst an act of grasping subcultural appropriation? No less a commentator than Michael Chabon denies that the novel is science fiction, while noting that "the post-apocalyptic mode has long attracted writers not generally considered part of the science fiction tradition. It's one of the few subgenres of science fiction, along with stories of the near future (also friendly to satirists), that may be safely attempted by a mainstream writer without incurring too much damage to his or her credentials for seriousness."

Many readers, then, take *The Road* as an allegory, a stripped-down fable, a sort of harrowing of hell, a liturgy for a terminal world that requires no detailed explanation and would be damaged by one. It is simply a schematic future we dread, a cannibal distillation of everything vile in human nature, a sort of naturalistic *Inferno* for the 21st century. The narrative voice seems to support such a reading. Dialogue has no opening or closing quotes, reducing speech to part of the flat surface of the eviscerated planet. Punctuation is spare or absent, so that "can't" becomes (confusingly) "cant," and "won't" becomes "wont"; one wit called *The Road* a post-apostrophic novel.

But this is a habitual quirk of Cormac McCarthy, a 1981 MacArthur Genius fellow, not new-minted for a world stripped even of conventional grammar. And while much of the narrative is undecorated to a degree Hemingway or Raymond Carver might have envied, it lifts now and then into high-toned passages closer to James Joyce at his most biblical. The very ending of the novel is a paean to the lost landscape of our full living world, and the boy is told that "the breath of God was his breath yet though it pass from man to man through all of time." Will there be time, though, beyond this awful lifeless desolation, drained of the divine essence (mystic Jakob Boehme's *salitter*: "The salitter drying from the earth")? There are hints that the man is an apostate theologian, a scholar despairing of books, while the boy (who nurtures within him "the fire") is a sort of Paraclete of the end times. Will the hum of mystery return in the deep glens where brook trout once stood in the amber current? It seems a forlorn hope.

The Road runs between two narrative worlds: the canonized territory of literature and the suspect landscapes of paraliterary genre, horror, science fiction. We readers push our shopping carts along this rutted, contested path, diving for protection to one side or the other as the bookless barbarians surge by. Read *The Road* as sf, accepting its corrosive world without fussing at its engine, and the spare or heightened voices can sweep you into a new kind of slipstream fiction that blends old and new.

85: Naomi Novik
Temeraire /His Majesty's Dragon (2006)
[Temeraire sequence]

IN 2007, Naomi Novik won the John W. Campbell award for best new sf or fantasy writer, awarded for her gloriously entertaining novel *His Majesty's Dragon* (the original title *Temeraire* was used in the UK). A blend of the late Patrick O'Brian's Captain Aubrey/surgeon Maturin Napoleonic naval wars series and perhaps Anne McCaffrey's Pern dragons, it presented an alternative turn-of-the-nineteenth century differing from our world in the presence of large, intelligent, domesticable flying dragons. What's especially significant in this warm series are the superbly wrought, lovingly observed dragons, and their jealous bond with favored humans.

His Majesty's Dragon was only the first of a saga now intended to run to nine volumes. The first three, originally published at monthly intervals to maintain momentum, are the Temeraire trilogy; the next three, the Laurence trilogy. The sixth book, *Tongues of Serpents,* set largely in 19th century penal Australia, came out in 2010, with *Crucible of Gold* scheduled for 2012. Although the overall sequence was thus incomplete in 2010, extending beyond our time frame, this grand and compelling series comprises one large work of delightful allohistorical imagination that clearly deserves to be listed among the best sf (*not* fantasy) books of the last quarter century. It swiftly developed a devoted following, and already has a wiki dedicated to its characters, background, divergences from true history, and detailed timeline.[33]

Captain Will Laurence commands the *HMS Reliant* in 1805 when he meets and

33 *http://www.temeraire.org/wiki/Main_Page*

bests the French frigate *Amitié* in the growing conflict with Napoleon. Taken as a prize of war, this vessel proves to hold a rare treasure—the egg of a Chinese Imperial. Newly-hatched dragons bond with whichever human harnesses them, but only if they choose to. Baby Temeraire has grown attached to Laurence even in the egg (during which time dragons learn the languages they hear, and emerge fully articulate, opinionated, feisty as adolescents, and tremendously hungry). Laurence is dismayed by this attachment, since he is now obliged to leave a promising career in the navy for the despised ranks of the Royal Aerial Corps. In snobbish and class-prejudiced England, the raffish airmen (and, shockingly, airwomen) have little prospect of marriage—their dragons are furiously jealous creatures—let alone station or wealth. The pair are dispatched to Loch Laggan, in Scotland, a bleak training grounds. For Will Laurence's father, Lord Allendale, this is a bitter blow, and his fiancé dumps Will to hastily wed another aristocrat with better prospects.

From this uncomfortable, even disagreeable beginning, Laurence swiftly develops a fondness for his brilliant draconic charge and companion. Novik's presentation of the dragons is delicious:

> "I can hear that you are unhappy," Temeraire said anxiously. "Is it not good that we are going to begin training? Or are you missing your ship?... If we do not care for it, surely we can just go away again?" [...]
>
> "It is not so easy; we are not at liberty, you know," Laurence said. "I am a King's officer, and you are a King's dragon; we cannot do as we please."
>
> "I have never met the King; I am not his property, like a sheep," Temeraire said. "If I belong to anyone, it is you, and you to me. I am not going to stay in Scotland if you are unhappy there."
>
> "Oh dear," Laurence said; this was not the first time Temeraire had shown a distressing tendency to independent thought....

Their relationship is full of fertile ambiguities. Laurence is in a sense the dragon's father-figure, but Temeraire is never really a child, and isn't much like a human, either, despite his clear and articulate speech. While the former naval officer is driven by military and aristocratic virtues, especially honor (after one contretemps he even gives himself up to authorities at the risk of summary execution, rather than decamp dishonorably), the young dragon is an anarchist from the moment he leaves his shell. Most of all, they are boon comrades. As he grows in size and power, Temeraire becomes in turn a sort of affectionate father or larger brother to Laurence, tucking him under his great wing as shelter from ill weather:

> "I am never going to let anyone take you from me."
>
> "Nor I, my dear," Laurence said, smiling, despite all the complications which he knew might arise if China did object. In his heart, he shared Temeraire's view of the matter, and he fell asleep almost at once in the security of the slow, deep rushing of Temeraire's heartbeat, so very much like the endless sound of the sea.

Temeraire does not lack for sexual satisfaction among his own kind. Indeed, his high rank as a Chinese dragon of lofty lineage makes eggs he fertilizes a great prize, especially when he proves to be not just an Imperial but a royal Celestial. Even straitlaced Will manages a difficult love affair with Captain (later Admiral) Jane Roland, mother of his teenage crew member Emily. Even so, there's a delicate homoerotic (or dracoerotic) undertone to the fierce fondness between man and dragon. It is hilariously brought out by Novik, formerly a well-known slash fiction writer, when Will soothes the sensitive new tendrils sprouting from the adolescent dragon's ruff:

> "Come now, you are like to make everyone think you are a vain creature," Laurence said, reaching up to pet the waving tendrils....
>
> Temeraire made a small, startled noise, and leaned in towards the stroking. "That feels strange," he said.
>
> "Am I hurting you? Are they so tender?" Laurence stopped at once, anxious....
>
> Temeraire nudged him a little and said, "No, they do not hurt at all. Pray do it again?" When Laurence very carefully resumed the stroking, Temeraire made an odd purring sort of sound, and abruptly shivered all over. "I think I quite like it," he added, his eyes growing unfocused and heavy-lidded.
>
> Laurence snatched his hand away. "Oh, Lord," he said, glancing around in deep embarrassment; thankfully no other dragons or aviators were about at the moment.

Temeraire proves to be of immense value to the embattled British crown, especially when he discovers his gift of the Divine Wind, a terrifying roar capable of raising seas and smashing enemy ships. He finds acceptance and leadership among his fellow war dragons, learning to herd them like the cats they somewhat resemble in character: independent, proud, picky—and, like the dragons of legend, inordinately fond of bling, especially gold, which they seize as prizes in combat or seek to be paid.

In another sense, they are victims of colonial racism, and Laurence's opposition to the African slave trade also serves to alienate both man and dragon from the corrupt establishment. The books so far published develop all these threads with consummate skill, taking them to Europe, Africa (where they find a dragon kingdom), China (where Temeraire meets his envious brother, and his albino Celestial enemy, the female dragon Lien, while in a brilliant diplomatic *coup* Will is adopted by the Emperor), and finally to the arid wastes of the red heart of Australia.

If there is often one troublesome feature of such alternative histories, it's that so little is changed by such immensely consequential intrusions—in this case, the introduction of an entire new intelligent species. It's impossible to suppose, as one can with the allohistories of Roth and Chabon, that one or two small changes can be absorbed without upsetting everything that follows. Finding Admiral Nelson or indeed the British Empire alive and well in such a drastically skewed world is absurd. But then so is faster than light starflight and time travel, so we must put aside such nitpicking qualms and accept the premise, delighting in the pleasures that follow in profusion from that indulgence.

86: Peter Watts
Blindsight (2006)

SO A Vampire, an autistic, a dissociative disorder Gang of Four, a wired man, and a female warrior built like an enhanced carboplatinum brick shit-house walk into a bar. Oh, and don't forget the AI they rode in on, driving the *Theseus,* their spaceship.

The *Dramatis personae* list of this astonishing novel does sound like a bad joke, but it turns out the bitter joke is on humanity—indeed, on consciousness itself, which is being crushed out of existence across the galaxy. And not by malignant intention, either. Call it evolution in action. This is a voyage of the damned, a ship of tailored anti-fools propelled beyond the edge of the solar system by teleported antimatter, aiming to meet up for the first time with aliens, and test their mettle.

Superb Canadian sf novelist Peter Watts had his own mettle famously tested by US border guards in 2009 as he tried to re-enter his home country, because he failed to throw himself on the ground fast enough, and was beaten, pepper-sprayed, jailed, charged with assault and resisting arrest, and eventually (after TV records were viewed) found guilty only of obstructing a border officer, with a suspended sentence and fine. A year later, he barely survived necrotizing fasciitis, the ghastly "flesh-eating bacteria," noting, "I'm told I was a few hours away from being dead.... If there was ever a disease fit for a science fiction writer, flesh-eating disease has got to be it." He contracted it "during the course of getting a skin biopsy... it was being all precautionary and taking proper medical care of myself that nearly got me killed." His own hard-edged science fiction, beginning with the Rifters trilogy, seems gruesomely like a foreboding parable of these ironic woes.

Blindsight is a standalone novel. Watts (who holds a doctorate in marine biology) creates one of sf's most frightening and horribly plausible alien menaces, and then uses that engine to power a complex investigation of mind, intelligence, consciousness— and the survival consequences of lacking these faculties. It turns out that a mind is not such a terrible thing to lose. Quite the reverse. Our vaunted sense of self proves to be a blockage in the computational pipeline, a decorative feature that gets in the way of swift, effective reaction to the threats and opportunities of an uncaring and mindless universe.

Each of the crew of *Theseus* is neurologically atypical. Siri Keeton lost half his brain after a childhood viral infection and had his cognition rebuilt with computer inlays. Lacking any instinctual empathy or "theory of mind," he has erected a superb modeling system for grasping, but not sharing, the inner life of other humans. Susan James and her alternative personae are a version of sf's partials or daemons (see Entry 31), but they pop up from the unconscious to take control at awkward moments. Major Bates operates through drone bodies. Above all is the vampire genius Jukka Sarati, his lethal and terrifying predator gaze masked by wrap-around specs. Vampires were recompiled from the ancient DNA of a species that once preyed on human animals but went extinct because of a neural defect: an inability to deal with +'d lines—the Crucifix glitch. Vampires see all the chains of any argument instantly; they can "hold *simultaneous multiple worldviews*."

The crew's mission goal is to examine an incoming comet that seems linked to the event of February 18, 2082, when a grid of 65,536 alien probes blazed above the Earth, taking a global snapshot for their unknown masters. En route, crew in hibernation, the *Theseus* AI is redirected to a target half a light-year from home: Ben, a monstrous dark mass ten time the size of Jupiter, emitting coded pulses. A 30 kilometer craft rises from it, dubbed *Rorschach* for its dark enigma, holding a menace that ultimately spells obliteration to any creature with a mind. These aliens have evolved beyond consciousness, or sidestepped it. They are "philosophical Zombies" achieving perfection in a kind of mindless instant response.

To convey this almost incomprehensible threat, Watts wields his own brand of post-cyberpunk crammed prose, clean and dense, taking no prisoners but playing fair with those who can keep up. When the computerized, autistic narrator is blind-dated with Chelsea, a neuroaestheticist, his best and only friend advises that she's "Very thigmotactic. Likes all her relationships face-to-face and in the flesh." *Thigmotactic* implies exactly that: motion in response to touch. But this isn't showy wordplay, it's just how such people converse—and it's a handy way of segueing into the fact that by the end of the 21st century hardly anyone has physical sex anymore. Siri Keeton is "a virgin in the real world," and not at all distinctive in this. His mother, meanwhile, is Ascended, one of the Virtually Omnipotent, her body stored (maybe, or perhaps recycled) while her consciousness wings off into her own created virtual universe. "Maybe the Singularity happened years ago," Siri reflects. "We just don't want to admit we were left behind."

Everything important is explained, brilliantly foreshadowed, paying off with bangs of shock and abrupt insight. This is the mature fruit of the tree of Swanwick, Greg Bear, Greg Egan discussed in previous entries. Call it neuropunk (as Watts himself suggested). He displays the future with a density that seems cinematic but is more layered than any fractal CGI surface. Simple quotation can't catch this; the effect's cumulative. But consider the vile creepy scramblers, all slithery tentacles, that you can never see because they've just moved into your visual blind spot:

"...these things can see your nerves firing from across the room, and integrate that into a crypsis strategy, and then send other commands to act on that strategy, and then send other commands to *stop* the motion before your eyes come back online. All in the time it would take a mammalian nerve impulse to make it halfway from your shoulder to your elbow. These things are *fast*, Keeton. Way faster than we could have guessed even from that high-speed whisper line they were using. They're bloody *superconductors*."

Blindsight is one of the jewels of early 21st century sf—like MacLeod's *The Cassini Division* (Entry 53), it's another rapture for the nerds, glorying in its knowingness and existential bleakness. Luckily, we readers are not restricted to blindsight (a mysterious unconscious visual skill that lets some blind people without a trace of conscious vision manage to evade obstacles), so we can ponder these portraits of future modified humans and appalling aliens with the same clear-eyed gaze with which Watts addresses them.

87: Brian Aldiss
HARM (2007)

IT'S THE day after tomorrow in London, and not a pleasant one indeed. With terrorism on the upswing, the authorities have begun rounding up the most unlikely suspects on the flimsiest of charges. One such unfortunate victim is Paul Fadhil Abbas Ali. Born in the UK to immigrant parents, Paul has assimilated to the nines, marrying an Irish wife named Doris, and authoring a novel which he fancies emulates P. G. Wodehouse, that quintessentially British writer. But he's made one fatal error: in his comedy, two characters joke about assassinating the Prime Minister.

This horrible crime promotes Paul to the status of "Prisoner B" at the Hostile Activities Research Ministry, or HARM—in actuality, a torture camp. There, he is subjected to excruciating bodily and psychological—well, harm, to put it mildly. What's Paul's one refuge and retreat? Simple: he's been a dissociative kind of personality ever since youth, due to cerebral damage inflicted by his father's beatings. Now, he begins to hallucinate an existence on another planet, Stygia, inhabiting the persona of one Fremant.

Stygia was ostensibly settled by a lone human starship at some point in our future, after Earth's civilization destroyed itself. It's a grim world whose many life forms all derive from insects. Humanity can still eke out a living, hindered by one other factor: the colonists did not travel to this world as incarnate individuals. Rather, they were stored as quasi-biological personality templates, which, upon landing, were decanted into new bodies. But the decanting went awry, and now the invaders are patchwork

Frankenstein monsters, at least mentally. They speak in a kind of Joycean cant, for instance, and have trouble with institutions such as democracy and religion. Of course, this hasn't stopped them from wiping out the native sentients, the Dogovers.

As Paul's senseless interrogation continues in London, Fremant embarks on his own quest for meaning, fighting both the planet and the short-sighted stupidity of his fellows.

This novel easily ranks among Aldiss's finest works, a milestone achievement to a long and splendid career not yet over. It rings changes on many of his long-running themes, and also cements itself firmly into the general sf canon. Essentially, it embodies the famed oriental parable of the butterfly and the philosopher in a gripping account of man's inhumanity to man.

On the front cover of the first edition of this novel, the one former book of Aldiss's alluded to is *Report on Probability A*, and that's no gratuitous reference, however unlikely a selection it appears to be from Aldiss's whole oeuvre. The scenes in the present-day of Paul's incarceration ("Prisoner B" recalls the alphabetic monikers of the earlier book's characters) embody the transparent, objective, almost deracinated, repetitive, I-am-a-camera style of that earlier *Nouveau roman*-inspired book. For instance, Paul's hazy focus on the fireplace that graces one room where he's tortured in an old mansion renders the scene as tangible as that outside the reader's window. Again, the lack of proper affect on the part of the interrogators echoes the earlier book, as does a multileveled ranking of observers (Stygia in this case, versus the voyeurs of *Report*).

But see how far we've come from 1968, and not in a good direction: whereas *Report* supplemented its dreariness and stasis and paranoia with eroticism and the possibility of change for the better, now, four decades later we have only cruel mortality and evolutionary regression. Yet perhaps, Aldiss hints, utopian 1968 was the anomaly, and mankind's baseline condition is this naked aggression and fear. The events on Stygia seem to say so as well.

The Stygian passages also play to the same world-building strengths that Aldiss exhibited in *Hothouse* and the *Helliconia Trilogy*. And of course he's always been politically engaged, as a book like his *Super-State* shows.

So here we have Aldiss presenting us with a distillation of his wisdom, in very topical clothing.

HARM also echoes many classics by other writers. First off, of course, we turn to the many dystopian masterpieces (which Aldiss names and discusses in an appended interview). There are also rich elements of Russell Hoban's *Riddley Walker* in the cracked stories the Stygians tell themselves, as well as Kornbluthian satire on the "Marching Morons" theme. The alien Dogovers could have come out of Michael Bishop's *Transfigurations*, while the manner in which Paul/Fremant ends up on Stygia, and that planet's nomenclature, make us think of David Lindsay's *A Voyage to Arcturus*.

But perhaps the main homage here is one that might go unnoticed: Jack London's *The Star Rover*, in which a prisoner's torture sends him on an astral journey.

In any case, Aldiss has succeeded in blending all these strains, personal and genre-related, into a deeply moving meditation on whether humanity can survive its own fallen nature, or is doomed to devour itself.

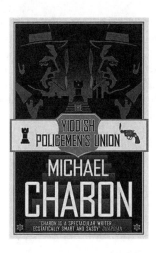

88: Michael Chabon
The Yiddish Policemen's Union (2007)

WINNER OF the Nebula, the Hugo and the Sidewise sf awards, and a finalist for crime fiction's Edgar, this is a sumptuously witty and entertaining alternative history of Jewish relocation in the early 1940s to a grudging Alaska, the Destruction (with some four million fewer Jews murdered than in our Holocaust), then the atomic bombing of Berlin in 1946, and the eviction of Jews from Israel in 1948. Its reception had been prepared in the literary world by Chabon's earlier success with *The Mysteries of Pittsburgh* (1988, when he was 25), *Wonder Boys* (1995), the comic book-inflected *The Amazing Adventures of Kavalier & Clay* (2000), which won a Pulitzer, and a prizewinning YA fantasy, *Summerland* (2002).

While some Jews, such as Einstein, managed to escape Germany in the early years of Nazi rule, widespread racism in the rest of the world made it hard to find a new homeland. In our 1940, President Roosevelt considered allowing Jews to settle in Alaska, but this program was successfully blocked by the Democratic Party representative for the Alaska Territories, Anthony Dimond. In Chabon's counterfactual history, Dimond died in an accident, clearing the way for the settlement of millions of Jews on the western fringes of the then-Territory, around Sitka. But this life-saving gesture has a time limit: after 60 years, at the start of the 21st century, Reversion will return these lands to the USA, and Jews once again will be forced into a Diaspora.

That is a setting fueled for a revival of Messianism, especially among the black hats, or Chasidic Jews. The (imaginary) Verbover sect has clawed its way back from cruel wartime reduction to just eleven members, and under the grossly obese Rebbe Shpilman is now the Jewish equivalent of a Mafia family, armed to the teeth, festering with every manner of crime, but suffused with a belief in the imminent appearance of Messiah. This long-prophesied miracle will bring peace to the world and see the return of the Jews to the Promised Land of Israel, from which they were brutally evicted in 1948. In the murky background, an equally fundamentalist Christian President of the USA is eager to see the Jews return to rebuild the Temple on the Dome of the Rock, since this marks the return of Jesus, and the last days. How these factors entwine and work themselves out is one of the driving forces in Chabon's mystery, which on the surface seems to be a murder mystery: Who shot and killed a junkie in the sordid hotel where dwells Detective Meyer Landsman, divorced, guilty over the abortion of his son and the suicide of his father (recurrent Abraham and Isaac motifs), in squalor and a haze of booze?

The ghetto atmosphere of this doomed shtetl landscape winds ever more suffocatingly around the narrative as linkages are discovered between the most unexpected players. Yet the mood of the novel is often antic, not remotely gloomy, a sort of Woody Allen handwringing hysteria blended with hard men, and a few hard women, working for high stakes. These Sitkans speak in Yiddish, rendered in a delightfully but always totally understandable skewed English, with occasional lapses into "American" for outbursts of profanity. Their cell phones are Shofars (for the ramshorns used to wake the soul to repentance), their guns are sholems, for the peace work they do, or threaten to do. A familiar greeting is "What's up, yid?" The wit is exactly what we think of as characteristically Jewish. "He's a bad man," Landsman says. "And he always was." His cousin Berko, with a Tlingit Indian mother murdered in a Jewish-Indian riot orchestrated by his father, replies, "Yes, but he made up for it by being a terrible father." Landsman and his estranged wife, Bina Gelbfish, now his commanding officer, fall into the same tense, affectionate, exasperated banter. One of the pleasures of the novel is watching these two middle-aged and lonely, abrasive people work their way toward a kind of reconciliation.

Another pleasure is Chabon's expert guidance through this oddly warped history that is not ours and yet reflects some of the more dismaying tendencies in our own. A failed war in Cuba, which returned its American warriors broken and rejected at home, is an equivalent of Vietnam, but President Kennedy escapes assassination and marries Marilyn Monroe. There is no 9/11 tragedy of the falling towers, but the Holy Land of three faiths is torn asunder by endless squabbles among the Arab and other remnant nationalities; without Israel, without Jews in Jerusalem, one gathers that terrorists and religious ideologues developed other obsessions—but the mad leaders of the USA, driven by dreams of making the Book of Revelation come true, work covertly with radical Jews to create the magical circumstances for a Jewish return (or military invasion) of their Holy Land, spearheaded by the criminal black hats.

It is a rich stew, and so are the aromas of the novel, steeped in cuisines from old Europe, not to mention the Filipino-style donut or shtekeleh: a "panatela of fried dough not quite sweet, not quite salty, rolled in sugar, crisp skinned, tender inside, and honeycombed with air pockets. You sink it in your paper cup of milky tea and close your eyes, and for ten fat seconds, you seem to glimpse the possibility of finer things." So, too, with the book itself.

Life and death chase each other in the headlong gallop familiar from the *noir* novelists Chabon tips his hat to—Hammett, Chandler—as Landsman is shot at, wounded, stripped, tied to a bed, hurls himself barefooted into snow to make his escape, seeking the killers of his murdered sister and the brilliant chess-playing junkie who proves pivotal to the whole bedlam of faith and crime, corruption and redemption (of sorts), while his cousin Berko is yet again a prospective father, and Landsman and his tribe gain some hopes for their dispossessed future. Aside from the nimble plotting and the mayhem, Chabon's characters are memorable and starkly individual. This might be the best alternative world novel we've seen to date.

89: Carol Emshwiller
The Secret City (2007)

A**T NINETY** years of age in 2011, Carol Emshwiller was undeniably the First Lady of Sf, the reigning female avatar of the genre and its rich, unexhausted possibilities. In small part this status originally derived from the record of her helpmate and muse duties with her much admired husband, Ed Emshwiller, whose large catalogue of paintings (as Ed Emsh) practically defined mid-twentieth-century sf imagery. But by far the larger part of her glory derives from her own writing: robust, adventurous, always sparkling, even at its grimmest. And Emshwiller can indeed at times be as cold-eyed as Cormac McCarthy (Entry 84). Her first short story appeared in 1954 (her complete output is currently being collected in several volumes), and she has gone on to produce these short gems right down to the present. But in the new century she became energized to write novels, and produced two superlative ones, both of which revitalized old tropes.

On Edgar Rice Burroughs's Mars, there lived a strange bipartite race. Half the race had the form of disembodied heads with some small appendages; the other half of the race were headless bodies. Of course, the headlings used the brutes as vehicles. Out of this pulp cliché, Carol Emshwiller, in an unwaveringly futuristic voice, fashioned a profound novel of amazing depth and intimacy. *The Mount* takes place on a future Earth where an alien race of conquerors known as the Hoots employ subjugated humans as their rides. Charley is a teenaged Mount who happens to be assigned to the Hoot child who will one day become the leader of the invaders. As the wild humans still at large launch a successful rebellion, Charley finds his loyalties torn between his master and his species. In the end, the pair forge a third way between the opposed camps. Dealing with issues of slavery and freedom and the awkward bonds between father and child, this novel belongs on the shelf with such classics as Tom Disch's *Mankind Under the Leash* and William Tenn's *Of Men and Monsters*.

Relatively soon after this triumph came an ever stronger work, *The Secret City*.

This novel is narrated alternately from two points-of-view, both alien. The first such being we meet is Lorpas, known to humans as Norman North. Like all his kind, Lorpas does not originate on Earth. Fifty years ago, a small party of aliens arrived here secretly as tourists. They became stranded. The elder generation gradually died off, leaving a few youngsters now grown to exiled adulthood. These remnants are almost as much human—by culture—as they are natives of their home planet, Betasha. They wander the planet, never daring to assimilate, hoping for a rescue mission that, so far, has never arrived. Lorpas is typical, an itinerant homeless hybrid, sensitive and intelligent, but never allowed by circumstance to reach his full potential.

Finally, after an uncomfortable run-in with the police, he determines to find the Secret City, a legendary refuge in the mountains where many of his kind have supposedly gone to ground. So he sets out into the California alpine wilderness.

The Secret City proves to be nothing more than a primitive encampment where only three remaining Betashans live: Mollish, an old woman; Allush, a young woman (and our second narrator); and Youpas, a feral young man who hates Earthlings—and who comes to hate Lorpas, as a rival for Allush's affections.

The plight of this foursome is complicated immensely when the rescuers from Betasha finally turn up—with all the disdain that "civilized" purebreds can have for dirty savages. And when a human rancher named Corwin and his beautiful daughter Emily are drawn into the picture, the group dynamics become even more chaotic.

Aliens living in secret among humans is another of Rudy Rucker's sf "power chords"—an sf trope so strong that it can be endlessly reworked. It's stimulating to see such a fine, accomplished and subtle writer as Emshwiller having a go at it.

The genre holds a number of vivid prior examples. Perhaps the most famous is Zenna Henderson's series involving "the People" (collected in *Ingathering*), and that's a model it seems Emshwiller definitely has in mind. But there was also a more malign set of aliens intent on concealing themselves among us in the briefly broadcast but well-remembered TV series, *The Invaders*, and a little of this interpretation creeps into Emshwiller's tale as well, in the actions of the brutal "rescuers" from Betasha. Algis Budrys's *Hard Landing* is another relevant milestone. And finally, Steve Cash's ongoing series about the Meq seems a close cousin to Emshwiller's novel.

But all these past instances aside, no one has yet approached the trope with the finesse and grace of Emshwiller. She's a writer of such slantwise sensibilities and such deep perceptions that she conveys the exotic weirdness of such a setup—and the almost unfathomable otherness of the Betashan mentality—with uncommon vividness and startling jolts of creepiness. Like Gene Wolfe, she filters actions through the perceptions of her characters in such a way that we are both drawn into the immediacy of her plot and simultaneously held aloof a bit. As in Wolfe's *The Fifth Head of Cerberus*, we encounter the world through the not-always understandable eyes of another species. There's a little bit, too, of John Crowley's outré *Engine Summer* in the manifestation of the Secret City as overgrown labyrinth.

But ultimately, especially through the love story between Allush and Lorpas, we come to cherish these aliens and realize their virtual identity with us. Perhaps that's always the essential message of this particular power chord: there's no real need to hide, for we're all brothers and sisters under the skin—if we can overcome our prejudices, that is.

90: Kathleen Ann Goonan
In War Times (2007)

O**N DECEMBER** 7, 1941, "a date which will live in infamy," Japanese military made an undeclared act of war on US forces stationed in Pearl Harbor, Hawaii, killing 2335 soldiers and sailors and 68 civilians, sinking the Battleship USS *Arizona* with the loss of 1104 lives. On the evening before the attack, in Kathleen Goonan's novel of time shifts and jazz, Sam Dance—an "uncoordinated soldier" with poor eyesight—is seduced by an exotic European physicist:

> Dr. Eliani Hadntz was only five foot three, though she had seemed taller in the classroom, and Sam had not suspected that her tightly pulled-back hair was a mass of wild black curls until the evening she sat on the edge of his narrow boardinghouse bed. A streetlamp threw a glow onto her pale breasts…. He had no idea why she was here.

Throughout the novel, Dr. Hadntz slips in and out of Sam's life, twisting history from the bloody path it has taken in our chronicles toward a utopian alternative that dances to the bebop arrhythmic cadences of the jazz that Sam and his best pal Wink love. It can't be coincidence that Eliani Hadntz's name speaks to our yearning for an alternative world where the worst excesses of a bloody twentieth century *hadn't* happened. To young Sam, a brilliant but unschooled engineer, she brings the plans for an unexplained device that manipulates time by combining a "parallel spiral" (time's multiple courses, and the DNA double helix) with the quantum uncertainties of consciousness. Hadntz reflects that

> if human consciousness was the time-sensitive entity she believed it was, this
> device could be called a time machine… that affected the physics and con-
> sciousness of human behavior…. It would enable humans to use the constant
> expansion of the universe, in much the same way that the previously invisible
> power of electricity had been harnessed and was now put to all kinds of posi-
> tive uses….

This beautiful Hungarian Gypsy scientist, who has left her 12 year old daughter
in Nazi-occupied Europe in order to work with the Allies on an atomic weapon, has
withdrawn from the Manhattan project in hopes that her time device can redeem the
very nature of humankind. For Dance, though, mired in war work on magnetrons
that will power weapons and radar, such hopes seem elusive. After his beloved brother
Keenan is killed at Pearl Harbor, entombed in the *Arizona*, Sam is flung into the war
effort, pursued by Major Bette Elegante of the OSS who wants to know more about
the Hadntz device that Sam and Wink try to build. Of course he falls in love with
Bette.

He witnesses atrocities and their consequences. Still, Dr. Hadntz's conviction is
that human nature can be shifted away from the brutish herd mentality and impulses
that create war. "How can people treat one another this way?" she asks. "What I am
thinking about is how to remove or change this propensity… this urge to be like all
the others and to follow a leader blindly…." Sam objects: "Turn the world into your
breeding pen? Isn't that what Hitler is trying to do?" No, says Hadntz heatedly. Her
way does not involve murder but rather a cure for our innate stupidity.

What anchors these airy sf speculations is the density of Sam's experience in the
war and after it, some of this conveyed through his diary entries. And these in turn,
Goonan has been quick to acknowledge, are drawn directly from her own father's
writings and war stories. Thomas Goonan tried for a year to enter the military despite
his poor eyesight, finally did so, was chosen for special training and work on much
the same advanced electronics as Sam, with Company C of the 610th Battalion. He
was shipped to France in 1945, then to Germany, supplying troops on the Rhine with
ordnance and equipment, and after the German surrender he and his friends opened
a *biergarten* behind their billet in Muchanglandbach, just as Sam and Wink do, "liberat-
ing" huge quantities of wine, barrels, glasses.

Back in the States, amateur saxophonist Sam hangs out in the best jazz venues
of the time, catching Dizzy Gillespie and Charlie Parker, and Monk at Minton's in
Harlem, wishing Wink were there, illuminated and astonished by the way these utterly
new sounds let them feel and see the world in new ways. Or was Allen Winklemyer
actually killed in Berlin? Time is unraveling. Jazz is a parallel to the intended action of
the mysterious device that Sam continues to tinker with, even after a test version had
melted down into a puddle of metal. Jazz resonates throughout the novel, informing
the rhythms of the prose in key moments:

> His brain became a device tuned and retuned by Bird's notes; he was tossed like
> a plane in a wild storm across the astonishing sky of the man's mind…. [Sam
> watched] the man bring the notes out from where they flocked within him,
> building pressure until they burst forth as complex fragments united by tone,

by instrument, by his fast-moving fingers, a blur on the keys of his alto sax.

When time bursts forth in complex fragments united by a new kind of historical melody, and dead Wink reappears, Goonan merges her father's recollections with an aspirational science fiction vision of a world that could be made differently. The hinge point of change will not surprise anyone who was young in the same era as Kathleen Goonan—she was born in 1952—but even much younger readers will feel a shiver to find Sam in a world where "the news was much different. Robert Kennedy was president, and JFK was still alive, a globetrotting philanderer.... Once they got into D.C. there was no sign of the highway construction that had threatened obliteration of whole neighborhoods." They are in a different history, where Sam's youngest children "had grown up in a world free of the threat of nuclear war, due to the Munich Disarmament Treaty negotiated by Khrushchev and Kennedy in 1964."

In War Times is a novel that, like Sam, embraces time's released melody.

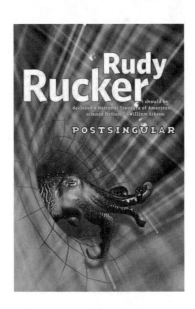

91: Rudy Rucker
Postsingular (2007)

POSTSINGULAR, WITH its sequel *Hylozoic* (2009), are two-thirds of a trilogy—incomplete at the end of 2010—proposing that all matter is alive and adjacent "brane" realities can be contacted. This radical notion is more often found on the New Age shelves, but Rucker is a mystic with solid mathematical credentials, and his zany vision of the near future is a very different Singularity and aftermath than those of Anderson, Barnes, Doctorow, Stross, or Vinge himself.

Two teens, Jeff Luty and Carlos Tucay, launch a model rocket that kills Carlos, leaving Luty to grow up a heartbroken, embittered and monomaniacal genius. Some years later, Luty runs Nantel labs, with plans to transform the planet Mars into a Dyson sphere of computational self-reproducing nanomachines—*nants*. Working at Nantel is fellow genius Ond Lundquist, who doubts the wisdom of this scheme but goes along with it. Sure enough, after eating Mars the nants turn their omnivorous jaws on Earth. Ond's autistic son Chu, a math savant, saves the world.

While Luty hides from a vengeful populace behind a quantum mirror, Ond releases orphids: benevolent "smart lice"—intelligent nanoscopic creatures)—to protect against future nant incursions. Linked into a sentient web of global connectivity, or orphidnet, with humanity automatically plugged in, all sights, sounds and knowledge are instantly available to everyone. It's voyeurs' heaven, and hell.

Then things really get weird.

The sensory upgrades provided by the orphids reveal the presence of giant, slow-moving Hibraners, intermittent visitors from another dimension. The orphidnet gives birth to beezies, artificial intelligences that culminate in the Big Pig, a Singularity-grade AI. A class of widely despised "kiqqies" arises, using the orphidnet and Big Pig to amplify their intelligence tenfold, but only while they are connected. Vietnamese Thuy and Latino Jayjay, and Big Pig Posse chums lesbian Kittie and code-loving Sonic, are typical dumpster-diving kiqqies. While Thuy endlessly writes her metanovel *Wheenk* (which just might be the book we're reading), Jayjay searches for an entry to the Hibrane dimension, and stumbles on teleportation along the way.

But Luty, the Hibraners, and the Big Pig all have competing apocalyptic plans of their own. Humanity is just a trivial bump in the road to be smoothed out—unless Thuy and Jayjay can "unroll the lazy eight," the compacted eighth dimension of superstring theory hidden in our existing universe:

> We use the harp to unroll our *eighth* dimension, which means we make our eighth dimension into an endless line. And—here's the "lazy" part—we give the line a special metric so that our minds can reach all the way to infinity. Like how the endless decimal 0.9999999... describes a point that's only one meter away? That's how the Hibrane already is, if you think about it. Infinity is everywhere. Lazy eight.

Rudy Rucker, as we might predict from his rigorous yet gonzo past work, is one of the few bold visionaries daring enough to envisage a future beyond the veil of a Singularity. He follows unflinchingly what it means for human intelligence to attain new plateaus, inhabiting the twisty minds of those jolted through that phase-state transition without losing our sympathy. He does it by blending eternal human verities—love, lust, greed, incompetence, ambition, jealousy, self-doubt—with new miraculous abilities and powers and potentials.

Two interlocked families—Ond, Nektar and Chu Lundquist, and Craigor, Jil, Momotaro and Bixie Connor—resemble Updike suburban spouse-swappers with same-sex fun thrown in. The Big Pig Posse are recognizable freegan/anarchists whom one might encounter today in their native San Francisco, where much of the novel occurs. So this empathetic characterization supports the scaffolding of mind-boggling postsingular tech that Rucker ingeniously elaborates. Earth undergoes Lazy Eight Day, as compacted dimensions of spacetime unfurl, giving humans godlike powers of telepathy, teleportation and control over sentient matter.

Necessarily, the books are densely written, requiring the reader to participate fully in the intellectual games—

> "To travel between the two worlds, a Hibraner turns off self-observation and spreads out into an ambiguous superposed state, and then she observes herself in such a way so as to collapse down into the other brane....
>
> "The encryption lies in the way in which the Hibraner does the self-observation," said the mushroom. "We can view it as being a quantum-mechanical operator based on a specific numerical pattern. And that would be the encryption code. Think of the code as the orientation of a higher-dimensional vector connecting the branes. It's a very short distance, but you have to travel in the right direction."

—yet also captivatingly plotted for sheer narrative verve, laced with humor and suspense. Walking a tightrope between information overload and vivid action, the book captures the zip, zest and buzz of the postsingular milieu, a world where miracles are commonplace, yet structured logically to provide real challenges, risks and triumphs.

Hylozoic ramps up the strangeness to new levels. Every atom and composite entity now owns at least a rudimentary mind, right up to Gaia, the supreme personification of the whole planet. Humanity consists of post-scarcity slackers and those denialists who stubbornly pursue the old ways of living. Our heroes remain media stars Thuy and Jayjay, now married, and the autistic savant Chu. With a little help from a transdimensional Hieronymus Bosch, these three will combat a dual alien invasion from the Peng and the Hrull, who are intent on colonizing our world.

Rucker's amiable, antic apocalypse is full of loose-limbed Beatnik/Firesign Theatre/Warner Brothers cartoon goofiness. His rigorous extrapolation of quantum strangeness veers deeply into that territory identified by Arthur C. Clarke, where technology becomes magic, but Rucker plays square with the reader, imposing sharp boundaries of digital logic that encourage genuine narrative peril and suspense. His dialogue-heavy style lends a cinematic immediacy to the action.

Although Rucker's trilogy begins in the recognizably near future, the whole landscape of Earth, and humanity's role, is radically transmogrified by this new paradigm of physics. With godlike powers come cosmic-level threats, yet human foibles and virtues naggingly persist. The effect is like an issue of the *Fantastic Four* penned by Freeman Dyson and Edward Witten. What's most energizing about Rucker's comic inferno (Kingsley Amis's phrase for wildly satirical sf) is how precisely it mirrors and valorizes our current condition. As all our revered and immemorial fiscal and cultural systems collapse about us, some of us stick our heads in the sand, but others creatively surf the chaos straight into the optimistic future sf has always held dearest.

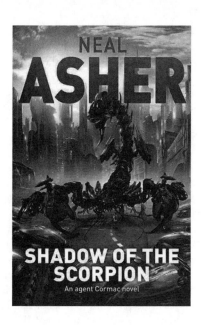

92: Neal Asher
Shadow of the Scorpion (2008)

PART OF the exciting British Hard Sf/space opera Renaissance of the past two decades, Neal Asher remains perhaps the member of this exclusive club with the lowest profile—at least in the USA, where many of his books have yet to receive secondary publication. This status is undeserved, as Asher's hard-edged, inventive novels rank as high as those of Alastair Reynolds (Entry 64) or Richard Morgan (Entry 69).

At the time of this writing, twelve of Asher's novels occupy the common territory of his Polity future history. *Shadow of the Scorpion* is second in the internal chronology, following *Prador Moon,* and hence a good jumping-on point for interested readers. Asher's main protagonist in the series is secret agent Ian Cormac, deadly employee of the Earth Central Security forces. Published after readers had already become familiar with our hero (starting with *Gridlinked* in 2001), with Asher's conception of his enterprise now deepened, *Scorpion* jumps back in continuity to explicate Cormac's youth and his start as an agent, filling in the past of someone we've already seen in mature form.

Cormac lives in a period when the galaxy is threaded by the runcible, an instantaneous teleporting device. Naturally, given this instrument, humanity has spread far and wide, aided by artificial intelligences and some other cool tech. Our kind has recently concluded a war against the Prador, a weird and violent arthropoid species. But no member of the Prador is alluded to by the scorpion of the title. That entity is a enigmatic human-created war drone which has been shadowing Cormac for ten years, ever since the death of Cormac's father when the boy was eight. (One track of the novel follows that youthful Cormac, his mother and his big brother Dax on Earth, in such exotic locales as the undersea city of Tritonia.) The drone seems to bear a message for Cormac, but one which will not be delivered until Cormac has gone through many mortal trials.

The main action of the novel takes place when Cormac is a young adult soldier in the ECS. He and his two mates—Carl Thrace and Yellow N'gar—have just been assigned to the planet Hagren, to guard a crashed Prador warship being plundered by human scientists. The ship also contains awesome weapons, which are desired by the Separatist insurgents. When Carl is proved a traitor and closet Separatist early in the mission, Cormac's life and future get warped into a mélange of vengeance and patriotism and personal questing for the truth of his own excised past. With his new comrades, including the android Golem Crean, Cormac will learn if he has the right stuff to make an ECS agent.

As the reader might surmise from this précis, Asher's focus here is on the military side of galactic affairs. And his up-to-the-minute novel proves that every new war ultimately generates its own science fiction, perhaps with some understandable time lag.

WWII and Korea gave us *Starship Troopers*. Vietnam brought us Joe Haldeman's *The Forever War* (Entry 50). Covert Latin American incursions led to Lucius Shepard's *Life During Wartime* (Entry 11). And now, in the wake of Iraq I and Iraq II, in a post-9/11, post–Abu Ghraib landscape, we are starting to see a different kind of military sf, most notably in the work of Richard Morgan and a few others, such as Adam Roberts with his *New Model Army*. Granted, there's still plenty of military sf with its head in the ground, recreating old paradigms with real or false nostalgia. But a few writers with their fingers on the true pulse of events are beginning to depict a future with its roots in contemporary realities. Asher and this novel are part of this phenomenon, by which sf rejuvenates its core concepts.

The way the soldiers of the Polity are rebuilt after what would otherwise be fatal wounds; the way the Separatists wage an insurgency; the way the commanders of the Polity ruthlessly direct their war; the nature of an enemy like the Prador—all these elements and more bespeak close attention to 21st-century headlines. Asher even subtly connects sex and torture, as in the Abu Ghraib scandal. Note the parallel constructions that follow. Here's Yellow sexily seducing Cormac: "I'm going to need your undivided attention for a good hour." And here's ultra-tough Agent Spencer preparing to torture information out of a rebel named Sheen: "You are a very valuable piece of meat and you are going to receive my utter attention over the next few hours." Case closed.

The result is a rather grim yet compelling depiction of the oddball hells of future wartime, blended with additional characterization and motivation for Cormac. And let us not forget to mention a goodly amount of hip and exciting technological and sociological extrapolation, and many convulsive, propulsive action scenes.

93: Suzanne Collins
The Hunger Games trilogy (2008-2010)

TRUE GENIUS in crafting a runaway pop sensation, as many critics have noted, lies in providing "familiar novelty." In other words, supplying the reading or
viewing or listening public with something easily identifiable and likable, something
readily apprehendable, something they have enjoyed in the past, yet with just enough
difference to render the product fresh and unique, quivering excitingly at the tip of the
zeitgeist. But of course, that's just the conceptualizing portion of the creator's job. The
heavy lifting involved in reifying the concept; getting musical notes or words down on
paper, or images on film, involves skill and craft and dogged dedication—not only in
the composition, but in the marketing—as well as a firm belief in the integrity, value
and organic unity of one's vision.

J. K. Rowling is the biggest success story of this type in the field of fantastical
literature. Her Potter-verse had numerous literary precedents, yet she was able to blend
and tweak her selection of component parts into a stimulating new recipe, delivered
with panache and zest. Rowling's counterpart on the Young Adult sf front is surely
Suzanne Collins, whose *Hunger Games* trilogy renders all the excitement, thrills, and
thought-provoking controversies of past great sf novels, incarnated by a stellar cast of
characters with whom readers can easily empathize.

It's easy enough to itemize the parts that went into Collins's trilogy. The Japanese
cross-platform sensation *Battle Royale*. William Golding's *Lord of the Flies*. Shirley
Jackson's "The Lottery." Fredric Brown's "Arena." Richard Connell's "The Most
Dangerous Game." Robert Sheckley's *The 10th Victim*. Heinlein's *Tunnel in the Sky*.

A bit of Baum's *Oz* (teenage girl stranded in a strange kingdom, and set an almost-impossible task before she can return home). Any number of post-apocalypse, "world made by hand" dystopias, from Wells on down. And, paramount, the reality-TV series *Survivor*. But such a cold-blooded dissector's catalogue fails to capture the sheer reading pleasure, emotional impact and polished presentation of Collins's saga.

A century or so beyond the present day, the shards of the collapsed United States of America have been reconstituted into a dictatorial ruling city, Capitol, set in the Rockies and surrounded by twelve oppressed Districts that pay tribute with young warriors who must compete in the mortality-rife bread-and-circuses Hunger Games. Our heroine is Katniss Everdeen, who makes the Christ-like gesture of submitting her exempted self to the Games in her younger sister's place. Once in Capitol she is subject to cynical media grooming (resonance with the hypermedia decadence of Jodorowsky's graphic novel *Incal* spring to mind) almost worse than the combat to come.

But that combat does come, and is unsparingly conveyed. Here's the aftermath of Kat killing another girl by exposing her to mutant wasps.

> The girl, so breathtakingly beautiful in her golden dress the night of the interviews, is unrecognizable. Her features eradicated, her limbs three times their normal size. The stinger lumps have begun to explode, spewing putrid green liquid around her.

Needing the dead girl's bow and arrows, Kat has to manhandle this human wreckage to get them.

After surviving the Games with her village-mate Peeta, Kat finds, in *Catching Fire*, that the deadliest days have just begun. The suicidal act of defiance that won her and Peeta an unprecedented shared victory, telecast to the nation, has brought long-quashed rebellion to a simmer.

Back in District 12, and touring the country, Kat finds herself—under the symbol of the mockingjay pin she famously wears—reluctantly at the heart of the turmoil, while concerned simultaneously with keeping her loved ones alive, and with burgeoning parallel romances with Peeta and old hunter friend Gale. But then comes an unexpected return to the savage arena, and with it another literary influence rears its head. The clock-shaped technological booby-trap, where Kat and crew rumble, summons up nothing so much as the gloriously insane, over-planned traps the Joker used to engineer for the Silver Age Batman. But on a weightier level, clever allusions to the Mitteleuropean revolts of 1989 and even prescient temblors from the Arab Spring vibrate through this portion of the saga as well.

Collins's charming first-person voice for Kat continues unerringly, pulling the reader deep into the action, and the increasingly mature and realpolitik-savvy girl of this installment is a realistic expansion of the young woman who entered the Games all naïve.

Collins unrelentingly ratchets up the stakes and tensions in the concluding volume, *Mockingjay*, which shifts to the venue of District 13, the legendary rebel redoubt that proves, distressingly, to be literally underground, a militarized autocracy on the lines of George Lucas's *THX 1138* or Philip K. Dick's *The Penultimate Truth*. Kat is forced into the Joan of Arc role of Mockingjay, and also acquires a bit of a superhero patina, what with her intelligent weapons and armor. Romantic concerns serve as welcome interstitial moments, with Gale by her side, yet emotionally distant, and Peeta a tortured captive in the Capitol. The savagery of the arena, naturally missing, is replaced by the brutality of combat, culminating in Katniss's squad-level, then solo, assault on the Capitol, in the manner of a John Scalzi or David Drake military novel. The ultimate ending: Orwellian victory, betrayals, sacrifice, Post Traumatic Stress Disorder, and a harsh grace.

The success of Rowling and Collins, as well as Stephanie Meyer and a host of second-tier YA authors, among both their intended adolescent audience and a huge number of adult readers, raises the provocative question of whether "mature" science fiction has reached a point of self-referential, inward-looking decadence that has contributed to the dwindling of its readership. (A similar instance in the field of comics draws parallels with the senescent output of DC and Marvel, and a charming yet callow rogue like *Scott Pilgrim*.) Certainly, *The Hunger Games* provides more immediate surface pleasures and points of newbie access than *The Quantum Thief* (Entry 101). But sacrificing the accumulated thick intertextual continuity of a century's worth of adult science fiction might not be strictly necessary for the genre's survival, if we can interbreed the best YA sf with the best adult sf, selecting for the virtues that appeal to the eternal thirteen-year-old, sense-of-wonder addict in us all.

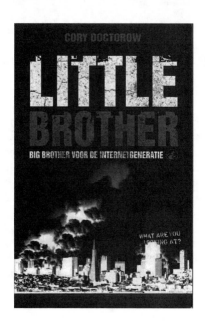

94: Cory Doctorow
Little Brother (2008)

WHILE THE majority of his science-fictional peers forsake the genre's histori-cal commitment to near-term speculations and politically conscious fiction, fleeing for the bland safety of Middle Earth or Wizard School or Interstellar Empires, Cory Doctorow plunges headlong into the venerable tradition of admonitory, near-future prophecy. He's a smart and talented and inventive writer, still as youthful and energetic and optimistic, despite approaching age forty, as he was upon his precocious debut in 1998. His ability to function on the bleeding edge of technology and culture is daily exhibited by his partnered curatorship of one of the web's most popular and influential blogs, *Boing Boing*. All of these qualities are evident from page one of *Little Brother*, latest in a long line of anti-authoritarian books.

Ever since Anthony "Buck" Rogers sought to overthrow America's evil Han overlords in the pages of his 1928 *Amazing Stories* debut, "Armageddon 2419 A.D.," science fiction has concerned itself with prophecies of doom for the United States and its unique and transcendental form of democracy. (This hortatory mode actually began in England, all the way back in 1871, with George Chesney's *The Battle of Dorking*, a work that sparked scores of other John-Bull-endangered scenarios.) Almost im-mediately thereafter, writers as diverse and as diversely talented as John W. Campbell, Robert Heinlein, Fritz Leiber and Jerry Sohl took up the gauntlet, depicting Old Glory besmirched under the thumb of forces inimical to our revered core values. By 1962, the format had reached some kind of mad apotheosis and larger cultural significance and awareness with the release of the fictionalized documentary *Red Nightmare*, in which narrator Jack Webb was our Virgil on a journey across a hellish USA overrun with Commies.

At the same time, a second literary strain foresaw the possibility of decay and dictatorship from within: homegrown worms burrowing within our own subverted institutions. Sinclair Lewis conjured up a nativist presidential dictator in *It Can't Happen Here*. And of course Orwell's *Nineteen Eighty-four* implicitly limned a dystopia that had sprouted stepwise over time on domestic soil, rather than being imposed from without by foreigners. This sense of a democracy betrayed by factions within that had lost sight of its seminal values naturally received a huge boost in the 1960s, reflecting the prevalent mistrust of government. A late-period instance of this formulation is the graphic novel by Alan Moore, *V for Vendetta* (1982-88, and filmed in 2006).

Both types of science fiction—and their hybrid offspring—lend themselves to certain shared plot devices, a stew of motifs from the American Revolution, the French Resistance, and other historical rebellions. A simmering revolt against seemingly impossible odds, led by a charismatic hero of the underground and his loyal posse, including one or more babelicious fellow female freedom fighters. Treachery, sacrifice, atrocities, temporary defeats and ultimate victories. Noble speeches, cruel dictates, torture and resistance. Often, the rebels will enlist or invent new technology to aid their cause, explicitly endorsing America's Edisonian virtues and privileging the small, idealistic and flexible forces over the ossified, cynical, superior powers.

Such stories are among the most stirring and topical and edifying sf novels ever written. As has been famously argued, Orwell's book alone probably forestalled the very future it so convincingly painted as inevitable. But of course, such a potent toolbox works perfectly well for any ideology, no matter how dangerous and despicable. William Luther Pierce's reprehensibly racist *The Turner Diaries* is the black sheep of this genre, but no less powerful for that. Doctorow's *Little Brother* is a book which fits as perfectly into this tradition as if organically grown from the seeds of its predecessors. Luckily, Doctorow and his novel are on the side of the angels, i.e., America's Founding Fathers and a contemporary citizenry that's proud, thoughtful, and knows the true meaning of patriotism.

Little Brother is the first-person tale of Marcus Yallow, a seventeen-year-old student in San Francisco on the day after tomorrow. (The ineluctable presence of a teen narrator and the publisher's marketing have cast this book as a Young Adult title, and in fact it debuted on *The New York Times* Bestseller List, Children's Chapter-book Division, at the number 9 slot. But all those who have enjoyed Doctorow's past "adult" novels will find this an equally strong and mature and polished link in that chain.)

Marcus is a Good Boy and a Nice Kid from a fine middle-class liberal home, despite exhibiting the familiar adolescent impulses to mess around and goof off in harmless fashion. He also happens to be a cyberwhiz. One day he and some pals are bunking school. Unfortunately, this is the moment when al-Qaeda chooses to blow up the Bay Area Bridge and the underwater BART tunnels. In the chaos, Marcus and his pals are hauled off the streets in a military sweep and remanded to extra-legal inquisitors. After some harrowing physical and mental harassment based on his rebellious attitude and past misdemeanors, Marcus is eventually deemed a non-threat and turned loose.

But he discovers upon his return home that in the face of this terrorist assault America is well on its way to becoming an anti-privacy police state, with the Department of Homeland Security monitoring the travel, purchases and thinking of innocent citizens. Angry both at his own treatment and the general shrinking of freedoms, Marcus begins to lead a teenaged resistance movement.

Cobbling together an alternate, privacy-friendly internet out of simple video-game consoles, Marcus—masquerading as the mysterious and anonymous M1k3y—foments small but cumulatively stinging acts of culture-jamming, becoming a glamorous icon of rage against the machine. He is aided by his pals, including newcomer Ange Carvelli, who becomes his first love. Dodging the authorities, Marcus gets a nerve-racking crash course in the dangers, thrills and responsibilities of dissent, before the whole situation ramps up to a climactic battle of small and righteous versus big and mean-spirited.

Doctorow's major literary accomplishment, from which all else flows, is certainly his faithful and naturalistic inhabiting of the consciousness of Marcus. In every respect, Doctorow's portrayal of the lad is utterly believable, from his scared reactions at his initial confinement to his puppy love affair to his fiery resentment at the abuses of authority. This verisimilitude echoes the proverbial Golden Age of Sf (and the Golden Age of an sf author's intoxication with the form) being thirteen. This is a novel where satirist P. J. O'Rourke's formulation of "Age and guile beating youth and innocence every time" is given the hearty and convincing boot. Which is not to say that Marcus has a cakewalk to victory. Doctorow is careful to insert realistic setbacks and roadblocks and partial victories into his tale, just as he fairly offers the arguments of the authorities.

Doctorow is of course in love with technology and romanticizes it no end. His paean to computer programming at the close of Chapter 7 is practically a love song, and some of his—or Marcus's—infodumps approach MEGO conditions. Coding up boring Cobol routines for the insurance industry, say, can instill doubts about the wonderfulness of all programming. But then again, the core ethos of sf revolves around technology, and Marcus's ingenious hacking makes for some clever reading.

Doctorow's goals with this novel are twofold: first, of course, to entertain with scintillating speculations and an exciting adventure; second, to propagandize on behalf of freedom, political accountability, communal action and taking control of one's life. The book reflects this bipartite mandate neatly, in its alternation between action and theorizing, with each half of the equation balancing and justifying the other.

In the end, Doctorow totally fulfills his dream of updating Orwell for the iPod generation.

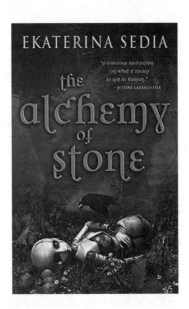

95: Ekaterina Sedia
The Alchemy of Stone (2008)

BORN IN Russia in 1970, expatriated author Ekaterina Sedia still rates as a comparative youngster in the field. Her initial publication credits date to early 2005, with her second and well-received novel, *The Secret History of Moscow*, appearing as recently as 2007. So she's an author whose career has blossomed wholly in the crepuscular light of the New Weird, that startlingly revealed louche neighborhood of Fantastika City initially mapped by M. John Harrison, Jeff VanderMeer and China Miéville. Given the hype, allure and trendy prominence of New Weird, it's only natural that any beginning author with a bent for off-kilter scientific romances would come to play in this mode. Perhaps inspired by such predecessors as Kathe Koja, Sedia shows herself to be a solid citizen of this venue, bringing to the exotic milieu a solid helping of steampunk-style science.

Her third novel, *The Alchemy of Stone*, is pure New Weird, much along the lines of China Miéville's gold-standard trend-setter, *Perdido Street Station* (see Entry 62). But unlike Miéville's maximalist, burly tome, Sedia's book is something of a miniaturist's triumph, showing a decidedly female touch, if such a gender distinction bears any weight at all. The tale focuses on a limited cast and a few central tropes or motifs, yet in the end renders a city and a world and its inhabitants nearly as deeply as Miéville's more hulking construction.

Sedia's compact and charmingly tragic book takes place in the City of Gargoyles, an arcane conglomeration built partially by primal non-human stone-working creatures (now in danger of extinction), and partially by the subsequent human settlers.

Mattie is a sentient "female" automaton created by a Mechanic named Loharri. Given her partial freedom (Loharri still retains the literal key to her windup heart), Mattie has switched to the rival political/philosophical camp of the Alchemists. Her pursuit of a cure for what's killing the gargoyles will lead her through politics, warfare and romantic heartbreak, as power struggles intersect with more personal affairs.

Mattie's meticulous lab work to perfect "the alchemy of stone" recipes that will halt the petrification of the gargoyles show Sedia's keen and clear understanding of the basic tenets and practices of science, and her desire to put such knowledge at the heart of her fiction. Her novel's title proves well-chosen when we recall that our own historical alchemists were not primarily supernatural occultists, but sedulous experimenters intent on producing duplicable results and transmissible formulas.

But enfolding this science-fictional nugget at the heart of the book lies the overarching depiction of Mattie, and the burden of meaning engendered by her sheer being. What we have here is the latest extension of the grand old theme of "robot becoming human." Like Lester del Rey's Helen O'Loy, Mattie is a robot who learns to love, despite abuse at the hands of her creator and her second-class status in the city's hierarchy. "She came from Loharri's laboratory, born of metal and coils and spare parts and boredom; this is where she would find herself in the end, likely enough." And Sedia's conceit of a physical key to Mattie's heartsprings expertly illustrates one of the things sf does so well: concretization of metaphor.

Along with its echoes of Miéville, Sedia's sweetly melancholy novel—continuously captivating, even though less densely tricked out with backstory and verisimilitudinous details—carries with it a delicious flavor of a tributary stream to sf: European puppet fairy tales, from E. T. A. Hoffmann to Carlo Collodi. In the end, though, its major guiding star might be a writer who does not figure often enough into New Weird hagiography, despite a strong and continuing track record: Tanith Lee. Lee's particular blend of dark fantasy, romance, weird science and obsessive quests seems to have found a worthy protégé in Sedia.

Finally, as an extra-literary codicil, we should mention that Sedia's career happens to illustrate another important development that occurred during the period of our survey: the rebirth of the small or independent sf presses. Once, on the nearer borders of the Golden Age, before large publishing houses became interested in science fiction, the core publishers of distinction were all small, fan-based operations such as Arkham House, Gnome and Shasta. Today, as big firms chop their backlists, avoid anything but potential bestsellers, and become leery of transgressive subject matter, indie firms such as Night Shade Books and Tachyon Press, aided by POD and digital technologies, carry the banner of innovative sf high. Nearly Sedia's entire output has reached readers thanks only to Sean Wallace's bold Prime Books.

96: Paolo Bacigalupi
The Windup Girl (2009)

AWARDS IN the sf field are an exceedingly problematical metric of literary value. Anyone attempting to justify the World Fantasy prize taken by Martin Scott's *Thraxas* against contention from books by James Blaylock and Peter Beagle, among other superior nominees in 2000, knows that much. But every now and then, usually once a generation, a book will justifiably sweep the slate of awards in a year, betokening something special and of lasting value. The "triple crown" of Hugo, Nebula and Philip K. Dick awards given to William Gibson's 1984 *Neuromancer* was for a long while unequalled.

Then came Paolo Bacigalupi's *The Windup Girl*—like Gibson's book, a debut novel following some acclaimed short stories—to pick up a Nebula, a Hugo, a Locus, a John Campbell and a Compton Crook award. Plainly, both fans and professionals alike recognized a book of rare merits, one that perhaps even signified a generational shift of talent within the field, given Bacigalupi's relative youth. (He was aged 36 in the year of *The Windup Girl*'s publication, and as John Scalzi has convincingly demonstrated in his essay "Why New Novelists Are Kinda Old, or, Hey, Publishing is Slow," this is precisely the average age of past breakout writers.)

What virtues rendered Bacigalupi's novel so popular and meritorious? Topicality, speculative prowess, and fine writing (that last virtue in reality standing for a whole suite of narrative excellencies in such essential areas as plot, characterization, setting and language). Like Ian McDonald (Entry 75), Bacigalupi has achieved a rare fusion of mimetic and science fictional power that fulfills all the long-harbored expectations of a certain camp of science fiction, most recently codified in Geoff Ryman's "Mundane SF" manifesto. Hewing rigorously to contemporary realities and science, focusing on near-term futures, this kind of science fiction eschews the glories of space opera and time travel and other extravagances for meticulous blueprints of our probable paths through rough decades ahead.

And rough indeed is Bacigalupi's vision for the planet.

The Expansion—our current era—is over, killed by the exhaustion of cheap energy sources. Now humanity lives in the Contraction. Untenable skyscrapers are left to rot. Genetically engineered megodonts turn millwheels that store animal energy in spring batteries. And agronomists struggle with every tool in their biopunk kits to provide enough calories for the globe's suffering population.

It's this last domain that occupies centerstage in *The Windup Girl*. Anderson Lake is a *farang* spy resident in Thailand as a factory owner, really seeking to exploit the country's hidden and acknowledged biological resources. But he has the misfortune to fall for Emiko, the Windup Girl. A slave and member of the underclass of artificial humans, Emiko wants nothing more than her freedom. But she harbors secret potentials that will alter all the personal and social equations on which Lake only imagines he has a firm grasp, leading, at least in Thailand, to something of a Ballardian entropic interlude in the world's recalibration.

Bacigalupi's evocation of his future Thailand is dense and sensorily rich. The sweat and stink and perfumes, the heat and humidity, the colors and sounds accrete into a palpable texture. The technological accommodations and cultural shifts of the Contraction are complexly arrayed. (Citizens of this future find that the rare, clunky, coal-fired automobile moves appallingly fast.) This is world-building, not bereft of monitory impulses either, of the finest caliber.

But it's the dynamic and unpredictable interactions among the cast that are the most entrancing aspect. In his corrupt, mercenary way, Anderson Lake is a soulful artist of the world's flora. His resonance with outsider Emiko is telling. Emiko's status is a fresh riff on the perennial "underpeople" trope, best exemplified by Cordwainer Smith's *Instrumentality* mythos and Richard Calder's *Dead Girls* sequence (Entry 26), which also revels in a Southeast Asian milieu. Captain Jaidee represents the best of officialdom. But a venal villain almost steals the show: Hock Seng, Lake's toadying factory manager, who out-Heeps Uriah.

The whole mix evokes the louche tropical ambiance of a Graham Greene or Somerset Maugham tale, and calls for a director of Howard Hawks's stature to render *The Windup Girl* as another *To Have and Have Not*. Bogart as Lake, Bacall as Emiko and Brennan as Hock Seng? When CGI avatars are perfected, why not?

In a recent review of the anthology *Welcome to the Greenhouse* (an apt alternative title for *The Windup Girl*), Bacigalupi opined that science fiction

> seems to affirm that children will still be children and that even in a devastated future, thrilling antics await. We want that affirmation. We are desperate and grateful for it. And our storytelling methods respond to that basic human hunger. Fiction, by its nature, is optimistic. Even the most apocalyptic of… scenarios… contain people. Fiction is an artificial construct in itself, in that it presumes that there is a story to tell, with its protagonists and antagonists and arc of discovery, or learning, or change. My biggest fear is… that fiction itself is extinct. That in the future there will simply be no tale to tell.

So long as writers such as Paolo Bacigalupi fight the good fight on the printed page, that ultimate threat of narratological extinction will be staved off a little longer, although, as Bacigalupi knows and shows, the battle will not be painless or without losses.

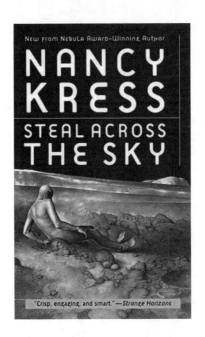

New from Nebula Award-Winning Author

NANCY KRESS

STEAL ACROSS
THE SKY

"Crisp, engaging, and smart." —*Strange Horizons*

97: Nancy Kress
Steal Across the Sky(2009)

L IKE CHERIE Priest (Entry 98), Nancy Kress reversed the typical late-twentieth, early-twenty-first-century career arc of many a genre writer, as exemplified by a figure such as George R. R. Martin, whose sf beginnings have been swamped in his later Tolkienesque success. She moved from the relatively freeform paradigm of fantastika to the more rigorous and structured realm of science fiction, and proved herself a fan favorite and peer-acknowledged master, having racked up three Hugo awards and four Nebula trophies for her innovatively speculative fiction. Anyone taking notice of her 1981 debut fantasy novel, *Prince of the Morning Bells*, would have had no inkling of this lurking swerve in her career.

With *Steal Across the Sky*, Kress manages to blend her scientific concerns with issues of spirituality, getting the best of both worlds (and mirror worlds are an explicit theme here) into her book.

Of all the hot-button topics that sf can address, religion surely has to be Number One. Consider Robert Heinlein's *Stranger in a Strange Land*, Lester del Rey's "For I Am a Jealous People," James Blish's *A Case of Conscience*, and Mary Doria Russell's *The Sparrow* (Entry 46) as examples of provocative thought experiments about God and the afterlife. Kress's contribution certainly merits inclusion in that honor roll of theologically explosive novels.

Kress starts with a simple yet deep premise and then unfurls it to a wide, enigmatic banner. An alien race calling itself the Atoners arrives at Earth in the year 2020. (In a clever conceit, First Contact is achieved through a website!) They ask for volunteers to visit a variety of planets on which reside our human cousins, "kidnapped" and relocated by the Atoners themselves 10,000 years ago. The Terran volunteers have one mission: to witness—actually, to ferret out *sans* alien help—some specific yet undisclosed wrongfulness inflicted millennia ago upon the human race. When this knowledge is finally gained, it proves to be sheer dynamite. We won't give away the surprise, except to say that the revelation regards the human soul, and will have immense impact back on Earth. "It was a bomb the Atoners were sending back with these twenty-one young people, a bomb that would hit all the continents at once, igniting controversies hot enough to scorch them all."

So much for Part One of the book, which resembles a kind of *The Man Who Fell to Earth* in reverse, given the plight of the human observers adrift on two alien planets, Kular A and Kular B. Our main emotional and rational locus in this investigation, splendidly limned, is Cam O'Kane, an American woman full of youthful impatience, survivalist vigor and lateral insights into the culture of Kular A. In communication with her counterpart on Kular B, Lucca Maduro, she manages to uncover the ancient alien misdeed, which involves tampering with our species' genetic heritage.

Part Two of *Steal Across the Sky* documents the chaotic, consensus-reality-shattering effects this discovery has on human civilization—and on the private lives of the Witnesses who returned. Kress employs a clever "multimedia" approach, shifting among many points of view and offering us fake "documents," to create a dazzling patchwork impression of global upheaval.

Kress achieves a hybrid glory in her bipartite novel. The first half certainly harks back to the anthropologically inclined novels of Michael Bishop (*A Funeral for the Eyes of Fire*) and Ursula K. Le Guin (*The Dispossessed*, especially for its similar mirror world motif), offering us "thick" immersive descriptions of a puzzle culture. That the puzzle culture is an underlying human one, by genetic evidence, only adds to the sense of estrangement. (This trick is often employed by another master, Jack Vance; see Entry 48.) Kress's book also resonates with Gardner Dozois's *Strangers*, a grim catalogue of cultural misunderstandings, culminating in a shocking truth.

The second half of the novel reads like one of those classic Damon Knight vehicles, such as "I See You" or *A for Anything*, in which a radical bit of technology (an omniscient viewing device or matter-duplicator, respectively, in Knight's work) rips the foundation stones out from under all human existence. That Kress chooses to show the power inherent in a simple meme (the revelation of what humanity has lost by alien tampering) instead of a gadget is indicative of the way our perspective and attitudes have changed since Knight's day, as the value of information has become paramount over material objects.

In the end, the ultimate depths of the revelation are left unplumbed, and Kress refuses to write the explicit future of humanity. But the almost Lovecraftian lesson remains clear: contact with the larger universe is bound to expose us to concepts our puny human brains are almost unable to process.

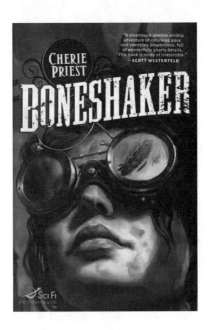

98: Cherie Priest
Boneshaker (2009)

HAS STEAMPUNK jumped Captain Nemo's clockwork shark yet, at the end of this first quarter century of its prominence?

The genre—succinctly described as a mix of archaic tech (either real or fanciful), the supernatural, and postmodern metafictional tricksterism, set in the consensus historical past or alternative timelines—was first christened in 1987, a lifetime ago as cultural and literary fads are measured, in a letter to *Locus* magazine from the writer K. W. Jeter. Of course, the actual roots of the form extend back even further, perhaps as early as 1965, when a certain television show named *The Wild, Wild West* debuted.

Certainly, literary styles and tropes, once invented, can be exceedingly long-lived. The Gothic is still with us today, and flourishing, despite being a couple of centuries old. So long as a type of fiction offers unexplored narrative possibilities, it will continue to be employed by those writers who find it congenial.

But steampunk has exfoliated beyond the merely literary, into the daily lives of its fans. Like Civil War re-enactors or medievalist members of the Society for Creative Anachronism, steampunks now include those for whom the novels and stories have been superseded by cosplay, crafting, music, partying, artwork, manga, anime, feature films and the creation of props or working hardware. For every reader and writer of steampunk fiction, there are probably hundreds or thousands of other activists who gleefully embrace some non-written manifestation of the steampunk ethos.

Generally speaking, by the time a subculture such as steampunk secures the attention of major media, resulting in extensive coverage of the craze, that phenomenon is already on the way out. But despite numerous and growing features about steampunk in the global press, such does not seem to be the case this time. The juggernaut that is steampunk, like Dr. Loveless's giant mechanical spider in the 1999 film version of *The Wild, Wild West*, seems capable of crushing all naysayers.

Yet what of the literature itself—now transformed into something of an appendage—that spawned the movement? Has it exhausted all the radium bullets in its Gatling gun, or is fresh work still capable of surprising the reader? Contemplating Cherie Priest's bright-faced contributions, one can hold out hope for continuing literary quality and novelty within the sub-genre.

Priest's career arc is contrary to that of many authors, writers who began in the smaller arena of sf and then moved to the bigger and better-paying fantasy venues. She commenced with a fantasy trilogy consisting of *Four and Twenty Blackbirds*, *Wings to the Kingdom*, and *Not Flesh Nor Feather*, before venturing into science fiction of the archaic sort. But she immediately displayed a ready grasp of the tropes. Funky brass and leather and thick-lensed goggles are a trademark signifier of steampunk. Frequently, though, beyond a certain fashionableness their utility is negligible. So when Cherie Priest goes to the trouble in her novel *Boneshaker* to provide a clever rationale for the existence and prevalence of such eye-gear, you know you're in for a meticulously conceived and executed ride, featuring an adolescent protagonist whose actions are circumscribed within a tiny venue, in a book that nonetheless sports a fully adult texture and range.

Seattle, 1863: the giant tunneling machine of mad inventor Levi Blue manages to destroy a sizable portion of the city and unleash a subterranean gas—the Blight—which zombifies all who inhale it. (The gas is made visible through those special goggles.) The citizens respond by walling off the infected district and leaving those trapped inside to die—or worse. Sixteen years later, Blue's ostracized widow, Briar, lives in the ghetto just outside the wall with her teenaged son Zeke. Intent on clearing his father's name, Zeke takes off one day across the wall, and Briar has no recourse but to follow.

Priest's focus on a steampunk wasteland is playfully and productively anomalous. Generally, the genre likes to focus on intact and functioning societies, whether dystopian or mundanely civil. Her depiction of the interzone as an outlaw realm of freedom, however dangerous, evokes the punk dream of life outside establishment strictures—a dream too often actually neglected in the genre that borrows half its name from that music. The horror tropes are another entertaining divergence from standard steampunk templates.

Likewise, the parallel domestic quests of mother and son (Priest divides the action in half between Zeke and Briar) is a freshening of both motivation and character from the rote adventurers the reader often encounters in this type of tale.

Priest's small, carefully constrained sphere of action (some widening dialogue pertains to the Civil War still raging back East, long after our version had ended) does, however, feel claustrophobic and slightly unambitious at times. But within that limited domain, she manages to impart a vivid sense of strangeness and adventure.

Fresh off her success with *Boneshaker*, Cherie Priest maintained her heady steampunk momentum with *Clementine* (2010). As you might suspect from its less-weighty title, which surely will evoke childhood memories of a silly ditty, *Clementine* is more of a romp—less fraught and dire—than its predecessor, despite being set in that exact same fictional universe. Consider it as the best episode of *The Wild, Wild West* never filmed.

Focus is initially on two larger-than-life characters, veritable forces of nature, who entertainingly and suspensefully split alternating chapters of the narrative until their paths finally cross. First comes Captain Croggon Beauregard Hainey, ex-slave and now a legendary sky-pirate. Hainey is in hot pursuit of his own stolen airship, the *Free Crow*, which a dastard named Felton Brink has stolen and rechristened *Clementine*. Brink is heading to Louisville, Kentucky, bearing a mysterious cargo, and Hainey wants revenge. (The secret of the cargo will tally with the re-naming of the ship, if you like clues.)

On Hainey's trail is Maria Isabella Boyd, a woman "nearly forty years old and two husbands down," in her own words. Not that Boyd has ever relied overmuch on men. She's been a Confederate spy, an actress and a general survival expert. Now, having been hired by Allan Pinkerton himself, she's a private detective/cop. She's leery of her first assignment, but determined to give it a go.

When Hainey and Boyd meet, it's a titanic dustup that ultimately settles down in strained cooperation. The rigors of their madcap odyssey will mellow that prickly relationship into respect and friendship, and leave each antagonist with a forced but genuine friendly feeling for their rival.

Priest's tale in this sequel benefits from a wider canvas. With *Boneshaker* being set exclusively in Seattle, and mostly in that city's walled ghetto, events got slightly claustrophobic, and we did not see as much of her alternative-history America as we might have wished. *Clementine* remedies that small deficit, as our heroes ricochet around the West and Midwest, and we get a larger sense of the festering Civil War back East.

Priest exhibits a minute and juicy particularity about her imagined past, grounding us in tons of sensory details. We can feel the jouncing flight of the dirigibles, smell the booze-redolent cellars and cheap hotel rooms of the tale. When Boyd is sent in a long trip in an unprotected two-person airship, the *Flying Fish*, we shiver with her, and brace for the dangerous descent. The *Flying Fish* is the proud creation of one Algernon Rice, another Pinkerton agent, and Rice's rich depiction and coherent actions, despite his being basically a walk-on character, illustrate the care and ingenuity which Priest lavishes on even the most minor personages in her story. She's mastered the Dickensian trick of doing quirky-memorable-but-not-overbearingly-so.

With a woman and a black man—three black men, actually, given Hainey's two memorable sidekicks, Lamar and Simeon—at the center of her tale, Priest could have chosen to go all heavy-handed pot-of-message on us. But although both Boyd and Hainey do get off some good quips and ripostes refuting their alleged second-class status, the theme of equality remains objectified mainly in their actions, residing at a subtle, almost subliminal level. The thrilling tale is Priest's main concern here—as it rightly should be—as she lets adventures serve as enlightenment in a most admirable fashion.

A third volume, *Dreadnought* (also 2010), broadened and deepened the saga of what Priest has called her "Clockwork Century."

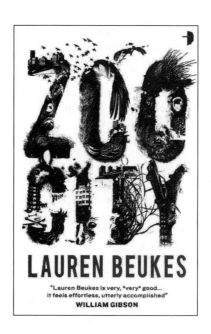

ZOO CITY

LAUREN BEUKES

"Lauren Beukes is very, *very* good...
it feels effortless, utterly accomplished"
WILLIAM GIBSON

99: Lauren Beukes
Zoo City (2010)

SCIENCE FICTION is the literature of change, yes indeed. But by this maxim, the genre reader generally understands an incremental, if-this-goes-on type of change. Even stories set ten millennia into the future presuppose a steady drumbeat of historical stepping-stone changes, one neatly following another, even if there are periods of "two steps forward, one step back," or vice versa. There are variations to this algorithm, of course, involving unexpected but nonetheless conceivable changes. Suppose cheap fusion power were perfected. Then society would change radically, but still along comprehensible lines. Or suppose Armageddon arrived, via alien invasion or human folly. A massive, catastrophic change, but, again, with predictable lineaments. Black swans are a given.

Yet from time to time sf contemplates what might be best dubbed "paradigm shifts," incredible, unforeseeable alterations in the very functioning of the universe. In Poul Anderson's *Brain Wave*, the Earth swims into a different cosmic zone, and brain functioning accelerates for every creature on the planet. In Jack Vance's "The Men Return," the narrative opens in the long-established aftermath of such a quantum change, and we witness the transition back to "normality." Greg Egan's "Luminous" postulates a rival region of space whose alien mathematics threatens to swamp our precarious habitat. Sometimes, new branches of science retroactively warp the consensus history we take for granted. In both Ian MacLeod's *The Light Ages* and *The House of Storms* (Entry 78) and Stephen Baxter's *Anti-Ice*, strange substances—aether and anti-ice—thrust our continuum down orthogonal paths.

Such is the case with Lauren Beukes's Clarke Award-winning *Zoo City*, a fit companion to the MacLeod and Baxter volumes. Beukes's second novel, after the well-received *Moxyland*, is set in a Johannesburg, South Africa, circa 2009, that is both familiar and estranged.

"Zoo City" is the nickname given the Hillbrow inner residential district of Johannesburg. Here live citizens of an underclass dubbed the "animalled," people who have been saddled with totem beasts, mystical yet tangible icons of their "sins." (A textual wink toward Philip Pullman's use of this conceit in the *His Dark Materials* sequence is sure to provoke a smile.) The animalled began massively manifesting globally in the late 1990s, but retrospectively could be detected as early as 1986. Their appearance marked the Ontological Shift, which has allowed "magic" entry into the world. The animalled humans each receive a *shavi*, or power, as compensation for their ostracism. But these powers actually read more like the genre-honored psi capabilities beloved of John Campbell & Co. And in fact Beukes has a go at explaining them with science: "Lab studies show that some spells work through manipulating hormone levels, boosting serotonin or oxytocin or testosterone."

Our juicy-voiced, dirty-mouthed, metaphor-slinging narrator and heroine is one Zinzi December, attached to an affable Sloth for the murder of her brother. Zinzi's wild talent is a form of psychometry, the ability to mentally discern links and histories between objects and people. Zinzi has cobbled together a dicey, dead-end, off-the-books living by selling her talent for petty quests—finding lost wedding rings, etc.— and by using her old journalistic skills—from her "Former Life"—to pen spammer scams. But then she is hired by a rich and powerful music producer, Odi Huron, to find a missing young female pop star named Songweza. This MacGuffin propels her and us through a rich assortment of places and peoples and incidents, accreting a palpable vision of this recalibrated world.

A native of South Africa, Beukes pumps her novel full of that continent's manifold cultures, miseries, joys and sensory riches. This hybrid techno-magical milieu is as colorful as African textiles, as noisy and dangerous as a liquor-sodden shebeen, as rhythmic and melodious as the Kwaito music Songweza sings. Departing from the polar opposite literary images of Africa as either a continent of failed states or a repository of mythic nobility, Beuke's portrait of this lateral continuum establishes Africa as its own heterogeneous sovereign entity, on an equal footing with the First World.

Beukes's novel has been hailed as another fine instance of noir sf, but if so, her noir is not that of Chandler or Hammett which William Gibson embraced. Rather, Zinzi's telling and attitude hark back to one of the other top crime writers, Ross MacDonald, and his PI, Lew Archer. MacDonald's focus on families and their secrets is replicated in Zinzi's delvings into the brother-sister bonds between Songweza and S'bu, and the *in loco parentis* misdeeds of Huron. And her tropical Johannesburg maps surprisingly well onto MacDonald's sun-addled, superficial California. "The urban sprawl thins out as the road deteriorates; kit-model cluster homes, malls and the fake Italian maestro-work that is the casino give way to B&Bs, stables, ironwork furniture factories, and country restaurants." Kitsch and brand-names and slovenly construction are the uniform surface of the world, even where magic prevails.

On the sf tip, Beukes's personable familiars tap into the same mythic and fan-pleasing vein as Andre Norton's *The Beast Master* and James Schmitz's *The Demon Breed*. Humanity's long dream of a deeper consortium with the rest of unspeaking biological creation is a perennial sf trope. Her exfoliation of how the Ontological Shift would be integrated into society is blueprint-precise (hospitals have special procedures for magical animal bites). And her climax involving perversions of the *shavi* powers and animal familiars could only arise in the new paradigm she has invented.

The animalled ones fear a kind of dark matter of the soul they call the Undertow. By confronting this fearlessly, Zinzi December proves that the only way to emerge out the far side of any change is by moving relentlessly forward.

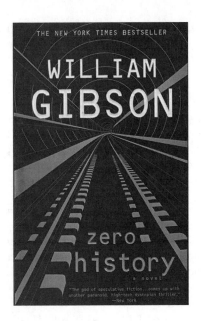

100: William Gibson
Zero History (2010)

LIKE SOME arcane and cryptic wizard employing a hieratic numerology to craft his spells, William Gibson likes to work in threes. Far from being impelled by the publishing industry's fascination with commercial trilogies—for, indeed, his triplets are not even marketed as such, but only observed in retrospect—Gibson's focus on sequential cycles of three novels seems to arise from his need to employ shifting angles of attack, to make lateral feints and forays against and into his abstruse subject matter.

His most famous set of three books probably remains his first: *Neuromancer, Count Zero* and *Mona Lisa Overdrive,* the "Sprawl" trilogy that introduced cyberpunk and cyberspace to the reading public. Following a story collection and a collaborative steampunk novel, Gibson next turned his attention closer to the present with the "Bridge" trilogy: *Virtual Light, Idoru,* and *All Tomorrow's Parties.*

Zero History marks the culmination of a trilogy too new to have been named yet (although by this chapter's end, an overarching appellation suggests itself), a cycle that started with *Pattern Recognition* and continued with *Spook Country.* All three books are set in a recognizable present, Gibson having foresworn traditional sf with the assertion that "fully imagined cultural futures were the luxury of another day...." Some critics have dubbed this new mode of storytelling "speculative fiction of the very recent past."

And truly, the bones beneath the narrative flesh are remarkably similar. Still following sf's imperative to dramatize cultural, political and technological changes in visionary ways, Gibson's newest fiction slides a reality-enhancement filter over his authorial camera lens, offering snapshots of contemporary times that are more CAT scans than photographs, totalizing in a diagnostic readout where the estranging and deracinating forces at play all around us—a sustaining yet potentially poisonous memetic medium we swim in, and consequently ignore—are highlighted and brought into the foreground of the reader's attention.

Consider Gibson's current fiction as analogous to the controversial terahertz body scanners being installed at airports worldwide: they both present ghostly yet detailed and embarrassing imagery of the hidden aspects of whatever passes before their eye.

Pattern Recognition (2003) featured a female protagonist, Cayce Pollard, who possessed an almost supernatural sensitivity toward commercial hype. A freelancer, she was hired to track down, among other things, the origin of some viral video being posted on the internet. But the man who did the hiring—Hubertus Bigend, millionaire owner of a firm called Blue Ant—although he was onscreen only minimally in that first outing, would become the dominant figure of the next two books, just as Cayce would be replaced by a new model heroine. Gibson's rethinking and retooling at work.

The enigmatic Bigend is a relatively young and charismatic Belgian whose name is pronounced "bay-jend," although he self-mockingly accepts and encourages the easy and common mispronunciation of "Big End." Money and fame are secondary to him, if not ultimately undesirable. What really floats his boat is surfing the wavefronts of trends and innovations, of winkling out potential new cultural explosions while they are still sputtering squibs. He is, in essence, the ultimate coolhunter, and tends to employ people possessing similar gifts. Curiously, Cory Doctorow's recent *Makers* features a very similar mover and shaker, Landon "Kettlebelly" Kettlewell, leading a reader to ponder exactly why that archetype is assuming greater prominence in today's culture.

In *Spook Country* (2007), Bigend employs Hollis Henry, female ex-member of an eccentric pop group called the Curfew. He sets her on the trail of what, at the time of the book's publication, was called "locative art," but which today has been subsumed under the broader heading of "augmented reality." Parallel to Hollis's strand is that of a clever and sensitive drug addict named Milgrim, co-opted by the Feds and sent after some mysterious people who might be terrorists, but who turn out to be principled avengers of wrong-doing. One of these fellows is named Garreth, and he becomes Hollis's lover.

Zero History opens up about a year or so later. Hollis and Milgrim, relocated to London from the USA, continue to work for Bigend. The utterly believable and easy-to-love Hollis remains essentially the woman we came to know in *Spook Country*: a wry, savvy, wary and principled artist and survivor. She's a nicer version of Cassandra Nearing, ex-punk photographer from Elizabeth Hand's *Generation Loss* (2007).

But Milgrim has undergone a rejuvenation, having been detoxed at Bigend's great expense through an experimental method of multiple total blood replacements. It is Milgrim, in effect, who is starting out at "zero history," a condition that also echoes much of twenty-first-century existence, as the restless citizenry of the planet seeks to forget or to mashup humanity's inconvenient past in a fit of "atemporality." In fact, the ratio of authorial interest and focus has been reversed here from earlier. Whereas in *Spook Country* the storytelling was about sixty-forty in favor of Hollis, here Milgrim's personality and fate assume dominance. (One might well assume that Milgrim is named after Stanley Milgram, famed psychologist who often seemed intent on stripping down the human psyche to its essential building blocks, much in the way that Gibson's Milgrim has been rebuilt.)

The MacGuffin is a "secret brand," a line of clothing known as Gabriel Hounds.

Bigend wants to lay his hands on the creator of this anti-product, and sets Hollis and Milgrim to ferreting out the origin of the clothing. But they unfortunately intersect with a semi-deranged ex-military type named Michael Preston Gracie, as well as his mean sidekick Foley, and a simple investigation turns deadly. Add in Hollis's dirty-tricks boyfriend Garreth, her two ex-bandmates, and a Federal agent named Winnie Tung Whitaker, among others, and Gibson has a recipe for a complicated and farcical thriller.

Mention of the thriller mode raises the issue of Gibson's altered taste in narrative templates. His earlier books were famous for their noir influences. But this latest trilogy firmly adopts the armature of the simon-pure caper/thriller/espionage novel: a bit of John LeCarre, some Elmore Leonard, some Carl Hiassen. (Gibson's mordant, droll humor is an aspect of his writing frequently overlooked.) A *Mission Impossible*-style climax here would have seemed totally out of place in his earlier works. And in fact, one suspects that the formula employed in these three books even offers a sly nod to *Charlie's Angels*: mysterious Mr. Big(end) sends his wily women on various secret and dangerous assignments.

But of course, if with one eye completely closed and the other half-shut, a reader could view *Zero History* as Gibson's *Charlie's Angels* script, with eyes fully open the same reader would see Gibson's evergreen deep tropes and themes utterly intact. His Pynchonesque preoccupation with paranoia and with subterranean movements and factions remains on display, as does his Ballardian fascination with the surfaces of the material world. Just as Ballard posed the existential and koan-like question, "Does the angle between two walls have a happy ending?" so too does Gibson's intense and minute particularity, concerning such things as Hollis's luxe hotel room, induce a kind of slippery, almost Phildickian apprehension in the reader, a sense that quotidian reality is a loose warp and weft we continually re-weave to keep from falling through to our doom.

One notable aspect, however, about the new-model William Gibson different from the younger version is a kind of cooling down of affect and tone. This might derive simply from the author's aging, or represent a deliberately dispassionate strategy in dealing with the confusing postmodern world. The white-hot impatience and drive of his earlier protagonists is missing nowadays. Sex, for instance, is hinted at and spoken of, but never indulged, either on- or off-screen. Moments of high drama are few and far between, and when they do occur—such as the collision of cars carrying Milgrim and Foley—they are rendered in subdued fashion. It's all very "The Dude Abides." The working-hard-just-to-maintain stance, always an undercurrent in Gibson's fiction, has now expanded to be the default option for navigating the world.

In a *Wired* essay titled "My Obsession," Gibson declares, "We have become a nation, a world, of pickers." Scavengers, in other words, for the beautiful and odd and valuable and fascinating. Given that this same obsession is precisely what drives Bigend, the ultimate engine of all three books, we might call this latest cycle of Gibson's novels the "Picker" series. We all are searching for gems in the manure, says this X-ray-eyed observer.

101: Hannu Rajaniemi
The Quantum Thief (2010)

T HIS EXTRAVAGANT, densely-loaded, intricately playful high-energy novel
is the equivalent, for the end of the first decade of the 21st century, of Gibson's
Neuromancer when it launched cyberpunk and closed David Pringle's volume of best
sf novels up to 1984. First of a trilogy, it's a dazzling attempt to weave into one long
story every major idea and method of telling it that today's sf has devised, and then
add some more.

It is about the search for a key, and for keys to open boxes hiding other keys, and
itself needs a key to unlock some basic mysteries that are lurking in plain sight. In
Finnish PhD string theorist and entrepreneur Hannu Rajaniemi's astonishing debut
novel, Jean le Flambeur is imprisoned in the vast mirrored expanse of the Dilemma
Prison. He is the greatest gentleman thief of his time, and is soon to escape. Rajaniemi
proffers the needed key, with all bland innocence, in the opening epigraph, a quote
from the French writer Maurice Leblanc (1864-1941):

> …there comes a time when you cease to know yourself amid all these changes,
> and that is very sad. I feel at present as the man must have felt who lost his
> shadow…
>
> —*The Escape of Arsène Lupin*

Leblanc's Lupin was the French equivalent of Conan Doyle's Sherlock Holmes, but with a twist: like le Flambeur, he was a master thief. A *flambeur* is a flamer, a big-time gambler. So this is not Jean's true name (and neither was Lupin's), but marks his occupation. For most English-language sf readers, though, this simple key, and many others scattered through the novel like Easter eggs, will be unavailable without repeated trips to Google.

Jean Le Flambeur, trapped in a deadly iterated Prisoner's Dilemma game meant to teach him the value of cooperation, is sprung in a daring raid by Mieli who wants her female lover Sydän back and needs the thief's help. Of course that is just one of the motivational threads in this monstrously complex tale. Escaped to Mars and a gigantic walking city, the Oubliette, Lupin is pursued by 20 year old genius detective Isidore Beautrelt, who is entangled with a cryptic and powerful woman, Raymonde. These names and motivations are taken directly from Leblanc's *Arsène Lupin Vs. Sherlock Holmes: The Hollow Needle,* where the task of the brilliant boy detective Isidore is to find his way through a maze of tricky clues and false leads. And indeed a Maze plays a key role in *The Quantum Thief,* as does memory and forgetting, hiding and disclosure, false names and faces. It is a confection that keeps you on your toes even as it melt on your tongue, like the chocolates that are one of the Oubliette's specialties.

Rajaniemi carefully chooses terms from Finnish (the intelligent, saucy spacecraft *Perhonen* is a butterfly, the *alinen* is the substrate of a vast cyberspace, Mother Ilmatar is a goddess from the national Finnish epic, the *Kalevala*), Russian (the enslaved minds or *gogols* are a pun on Nikolai Vasilievich Gogol's novel *Dead Souls,* while the Sobornost collective mind ruling the inner solar system is a borrowing from Russian precommunist mysticism), plus scads of French. But the teasing search provides its own pleasures, as does the deluge of neologisms and borrowings that decorate the surface of *The Quantum Thief.*

Young Isidore is called in early to investigate the baffling murder of "*Marc Deveraux. Third Noble incarnation. Chocolatier. Married. One daughter....* As always in the beginning of a mystery, he feels like a child unwrapping a present. There is something that makes sense here, hiding beneath chocolate and death." Deveraux's mind has been stolen and hidden in plain view, and in solving the crime Isidore manages to get his face in the papers, something he really didn't want in this society based on a technology of gevulots (Hebrew for "borders" or guarantees of privacy and containment). The city is a masque of people in masks, blurry or invisible unless they allow access.

All of this politesse is handled by the exomemory system, which of necessity must be utterly sacrosanct—but, Isidore deduces, has apparently been breached and tampered with. He hopes to join the company of the *tzaddikim* (Hebrew for the righteous elite who represent justice), and has been taken under the wing of a tzaddik, the Gentleman, whose metallic mask hides more than a face. Meanwhile, le Flambeur is drawn into his most audacious, risky heist and saved by the quite literal wings of Mieli, whose augmented body and brain serve the immensely powerful posthuman pellegrini. (Joséphine Pellegrini, as it happens, is a foe and lover of Arsène Lupin. Marcel, Gilbertine and Bathilde are from Proust's *In Search of Lost Time.* None of this name-dropping can be accidental, nor anything as simple as whimsical borrowing from the canon of European crime and literary fiction. Watching how all this masking and unmasking works out will be part of the pleasure of the unfolding trilogy.)

The book seethes with action, vivid and inventive decoration, peril and audacious escape:

Mieli shatters the pseudoglass with her wings. The shards billow across the room in slow motion like snow. The metacortex floods her with information. The thief is *here*, the tzaddik *there*, a fleshy human core surrounded by a cloud of combat utility fog.... Then her wings' waste-heat radiators are blocked too, and she has to drop back to slowtime.

The tzaddik's foglet-enhanced blow is like colliding with an Oortian comet. It takes her through a glass shelving unit and the wall behind it. The plaster and ceramics feels like wet sand when she passes through it. Her armor screams and a quickstone-enhanced rib actually snaps. Her metacortex muffles the pain; she gets up in a cloud of debris. She is in the bathroom. A monster angel stares at her in the bathroom mirror.

The story can't be explained, it has to be lived through. We pick up clues as we go, trying out hypotheses, seeing them fail, trying again, just as the thief must weave his way toward an uncertain goal and recovery of his blocked memories, and the detective strives to make sense of events that seem entirely unconnected. In a universe of posthuman demigods, where the solar system was changed catastrophically by the Spike—"Jupiter is gone, eaten by a singularity, gravitational or technological or both, no one knows"—and life is followed by service as a cyborged Quiet, until rebirth is earned, where Time is the very currency, we read as if our future depended on it.

Which is, indeed, how science fiction felt, sometimes, during the boundary years 1985-2010, between the brief lurid explosion of cyberpunk and the deferred future everyone anticipated for the magical year 2000 and after. To repeat the insightful words that close David Pringle's volume:

> ...all the best science fiction... deals with reality, not fantasy, and if some of the technological gimmickry... may seem far-fetched, it also serves, as would a set of distorting mirrors, to reflect ourselves and what is around us.